Medieval Woman

Village Life in the Middle Ages

Ann Baer

MICHAEL O'MARA BOOKS LIMITED

When icicles hang by the wall,
And Dick the shepherd blows his nail,
And Tom bears logs into the hall,
And milk comes frozen home in pail,
When blood is nipped, and ways be foul,
Then nightly sings the staring owl,
                    Tu-who;
Tu-whit, tu-who: a merry note,
While greasy Joan doth keel the pot.

When all aloud the wind doth blow,
And coughing drowns the parson's saw,
And birds sit brooding in the snow,
And Marian's nose looks red and raw,
When roasted crabs hiss in the bowl,
Then nightly sings the staring owl,
                    Tu-whit;
Tu-who: a merry note,
While greasy Joan doth keel the pot.

Love's Labour's Lost, Shakespeare

Published in Great Britain in 1996 by
Michael O'Mara Books Limited
9 Lion Yard
Tremadoc Road
London SW4 7NQ

The verses quoted at the beginning of each
chapter are taken from John Clare's *The Shepherd's Calendar*.

A CIP catalogue record for this book is available from the British Library.

ISBN 1-85479-656-9
1 3 5 7 9 10 8 6 4 2

Typeset by Bibliocraft, Dundee
Printed in England by Clays Ltd, St Ives plc

CONTENTS

THE CHARACTERS

Marion, a medieval woman
Peter Carpenter, her husband
Peterkin, their son
Alice, their daughter

Sir Hugh, the Feudal Lord
Dame Margaret, 'M'Dame', his wife
Magda, their daughter
Rollo, Sir Hugh's brother

Tom
Ed-me-boy, his son
Joan, bastard half-sister of
Sir Hugh
Milly
Old Mavis, Joan's mother
Loppy Lambert

Father John, the priest
Old Sarah, his housekeeper

Simon Miller, Marion's
older brother
Betsy, his wife
Lisa, Roger, Gib, Ellen, Kate,
their children

Matt, ploughman at the Hall
Nell, his wife
Rob, their son

Dick Shepherd
Hilda, his wife
Meg, Mary, their daughters

Molly
Old Agnes, Molly's mother
Old Marge, Agnes's sister

Jack Plowright
Small Sarah, his wife
Unnumbered small children

Hodge, a labourer
Cecily, his wife
Jo, Harry, Edwin, Hoddy,
their sons
Hodge's Old Mother, sister of
Old Sarah

Hal, a widower, father of Hilda

Old Fletcher

Old Mam Fletcher, his wife,
and village midwife
Andrew Fletcher, their son, a
labourer
Polly, his second wife
Ned, Andrew's son
Sal, Andy, Izzy – their other
children

Simkin, a labourer
Joyce, his wife

Nick, a labourer
Martha, his wife
Steve, Kit, their sons
Several other small children

Paul Hunter, a freeman
Margery, his wife
Steve, Midge, Paulo, their
children

Widow Annie
Wilfred, her son
Dobbin, Annie's younger son
Jill, Dobbin's wife
One-eyed Wat, Dobbin's son

Wat the Tall Rockwell
Nancy, his wife, daughter of

Old Agnes
Martin, their son, married to
Lisa Miller
Joyce, their daughter, married
to Simkin
Stephen, vaguely engaged to
Ellen Miller
Several other teenage children
Edward Rockwell, Wat the
Tall's brother
Red Mary, his wife, Dick
Shepherd's sister
Tim, their son
Several other small children
Old Lambert Rockwell, uncle
of Wat and Edward and father
of Loppy

Chris Foxcap, a tinker

Animals
Tibtab, Marion's cat
Jix, Sir Hugh's terrier
Trover, Magda's dog
Unnamed bitch of M'Dame's
Janty, True, sheepdogs
Caesar, Chris Foxcap's donkey
Heart-of-Oak, Sir Hugh's horse

Down the Common

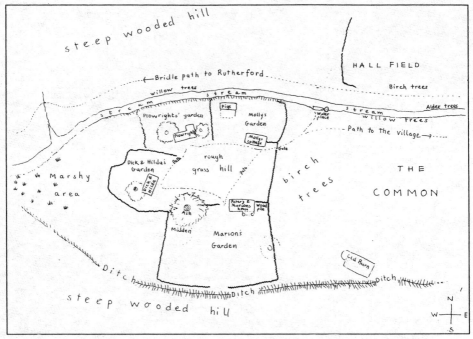

The Village

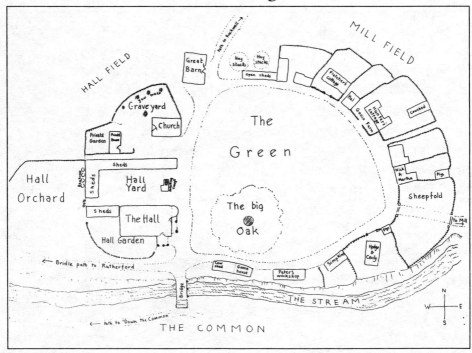

MARCH

Yet winter seems half weary of its toil
And round the ploughman on the elting soil
Will thread a minutes sunshine wild and warm
Thro raggd places of the swimming storm
And oft the shepherd in his path will spye
The little daisey in the wet grass lye

Marion rolled over on to her back to ease the ache in her hip. She moved slowly so as not to wake the others, but Peter, her husband, did not stir and his slow groaning breathing did not alter. She stretched out her feet, which touched the back of eight-year-old Peterkin, curled up at the end of the bed, deeply asleep. She put out her right hand, feeling for the cradle, and her fingers touched Alice's tiny hand, soft and cold as a little frog. She pushed it under the sheepskin cover.

It was intensely dark, but a mother's sleep is never deep when her infants are near. The raw night air, that penetrated the bedding, and a hot uneasiness in her stomach both combined to prevent Marion sleeping deeply. A sudden whimper from Alice awoke her. She stretched out an arm, felt the edge of the cradle and slid her hand over the cover to feel that Alice's face was not covered. She had not forgotten the horror, some years ago, of seeing the cat heaving itself up in the cradle, stretching out tense limbs and then jumping down, leaving the already cold corpse of the baby which had earlier made it such a warm bed. But Alice's face was clear, her nose a button of ice. She slept on.

It was still pitch-dark in the cottage. There was no pale line of dawn or moonlight above the door. Marion pulled the cover, damp with her breathing, up to her face. Her nose was as cold as Alice's. Into the silence dropped a tiny clink of bark falling from a burnt log, indicating that the fire was not out. Peterkin, still curled up at her feet, breathed more heavily. Peter, a lump rolled in blanket at her side, moved slightly, altered the tone of his breathing for a moment, then subsided into silence again. There was a faint rustle of straw and a thump from the goat, the other side of the partition. Silence again, and perhaps Marion dozed until another whimper from Alice, almost a wail, woke her. But Alice quietened at the touch of her mother's hand. A dream, perhaps a nightmare, had frightened her, and Marion lay wondering what forms fear and horror might take in the mind of a two-year-old child.

The unease in Marion's stomach continued and she wondered whether she should attempt to relieve herself. The thought of rising into the chilly air, of going out into the icy dark was very unpleasant. They had always been against adults defecating in the cottage. Perhaps she should wait for the dawn, but no bird in the forest had tried his voice and the cock on the other side of the partition had not even croaked, so dawn could not be imminent. Drowsy but undecided she lay still.

Suddenly Alice gave a yelping cry, a choking cough, and a loud wail. Marion slid out her hand again and encountered warm slimy vomit, which seemed everywhere round the child's face. Instantly alert to the danger of a baby choking to death, she sat up, pulled away the feather quilt, which seemed sodden, and picked up the wailing child. The cheesy smell of the vomit was increasing her own queasiness. She felt Peter heave and turn over.

'Alice has been sick,' she muttered.

He grunted and lay still. Alice continued to cry as much as before. After a while Marion sat on the edge of the bed holding Alice on her lap and wiping at her with a handful of straw from the floor. Peter heaved again.

'Put her back in the cradle, she'll soon go off to sleep,' he said.

'The quilt and the straw are probably covered in sick – the quilt certainly is. She'd freeze.'

Peter could not sleep with the wailing child, so he sat up. He pulled their blanket over Marion's shoulders.

'She'll quieten down soon,' she told him, trying to reassure herself.

'Get back into bed with her,' Peter said. 'You're getting too cold yourself.' Marion continued sitting and nursing the smelly bundle. 'Come,' Peter urged, 'roll her up in the blanket and keep her on your side of the bed. She'll go to sleep again. You can clean the cradle in the morning.'

In their fourteen years of marriage they had had many babies, who had often been sick in the night. He was used to it.

Alice's cries became more intense, as though they were being squeezed out of her twisting body, and then there was more choking and Marion felt the warm wet of another flood of vomit down her front.

The blanket dragged on her shoulders as Peter heaved himself up and edged past her on the bed. 'Want a light?' was all he said, and then she heard his feet in the straw and his fumbling under the shelf for the bellows. Tibtab, who usually slept on the shelf, was wakened, and fled with a tiny mew. Peter began to explore with puffs from the bellows some places on the logs which might be brought to incandescent red.

The vomit seemed everywhere. Marion, wiping in the dark with little bits of straw, tried to hush Alice's cries. She wondered how the little body on her lap could have contained so much. The bellows puffed, Alice moaned, Peterkin lay still, determined not to wake.

In time Peter's bellows blew an area of glowing red on a log. He reached out in the dark and found a branch with dead leaves on it which he kept for tinder, stuck into the cottage wall above the shelf. Propping this twig up in the ashes with a leaf against the red glow and continuing to bellow, he got the dried leaves alight. They flared up, lighting the whole inside of the cottage for a moment. Peter grabbed at the little rush candle that he kept in a block of hollowed out wood on the shelf. But the flaming leaf had died down and he had to blow again and press more leaves against the glowing scrap of wood before he finally managed to light the candle.

It made a tiny area of faint light but it was enough for Marion to see Alice's white glistening face surrounded by mess. Alice's cries had lessened and the flame took her attention. She drew in each breath tremblingly and then Marion saw her lower lip quivering, so adult a show of grief, so unlike the outward rolling of the lip of a crying angry infant, that Marion was filled with compassion for her child. With Peter holding the light, she laid Alice across her knees and pulled her hooded robe over her head. The folds of the hood were filled with vomit and she dropped it on the ground. Alice's body was wrapped round with a broad strip of woollen cloth, its upper part smeared with vomit, its lower part sodden and stinking.

'I'll sit by the fire with her for a bit,' said Marion. 'She's shivering. Put the blanket round me, then you get back to bed and get warm again.'

An ancient crescent-shaped log, half circling the hearth, was their usual seat, and Marion moved to it and sat down close to the remains of the fire, leaning back against the log. She undid the front of her robe, itself wet and slimy, and pushed cold Alice in. Peter put the blanket over her shoulders, this action blowing out the candle's flame. In darkness she heard the bed boards creak and the straw rustle as he got back in. Except for the red glimmer from the fire, they were in darkness again.

Marion crouched there holding shaking Alice against her breasts and shivering so violently that every shiver made her arms squeeze and shake Alice. Though her bare feet were on the hearthstone, she felt no warmth from the pile of ashes. Alice's breathing slowly quietened and Marion, guessing she slept, did not dare move for fear of waking her. Though she was sitting on a little straw, her bottom ached with the cold and the hard ground. Marion endured. Her head felt heavy and the hot boiling in her stomach increased. Once or twice she feared she would be sick herself, for the smell was nauseating. There was still no pale line above the door. How endless the winter nights were. She would have liked to rest her head somewhere, but the log was too low, only high enough to rest her ribs against. Peter was silent; she did not know if he slept or not. Alice, she guessed, did sleep. Her thoughts turned from Alice, this wretched little life, lying against her body, to all her children – how a mother gave and gave and gave to each child, its being, its birth, its food, its shelter; how all her days and nights were spent in giving to her children; how the children took and took, and how, even so, she could not give enough and so many babies had died. Alice, fortunately, had been a hearty baby and was growing into a strong child. 'My poor little girl,' Marion whispered, putting her head down to where Alice's was under her dress, 'my poor little girl.'

Her thoughts drifted to her most recently dead child, Margery, who had died two months ago. She had been twelve years old, an age by which, having passed through the dangers of childhood, children could be expected to survive. Margery's face came sharply to mind, thin and narrow, hung around with lank dark hair, her anxious dark eyes, her half-open mouth too full of teeth for her lips to meet easily, her lower lip scaly and cracked, her breathing guttural. She had always been a skinny silent child, undersized, with little strength and no vitality. Marion had often compared her with her brother, Simon's, two girls, Ellen and Kate, one four and the other two years older than Margery. So different were they, bouncing busy young women, both advanced in their adolescence while Margery still had the slight body of a child.

Since the previous summer Marion had watched her daughter with some anxiety. She had been quiet and still, she had not perceptibly grown, though she had accepted all the duties that Marion had given her. She had weeded for long hours in the garden, carried and fetched corn and flour, minded Alice, ground beans in the quern, and sorted and spun wool. But Marion had observed the increasing slowness in her movements, longer and longer moments of idleness and, as autumn came on, a more frequent cough, plaintive and purposeless. In spite of her lackadaisical idleness, her complexion seemed improved and a pretty pinkness showed through the dirt on her thin cheeks, but as autumn turned to winter her eyes became duller, the cough more persistent and no exhortation from her mother could rouse her. By Christmas she could do nothing but crouch on the log by the fire, minding Alice and now and then spinning a few yards of wool, but winding what she had spun on to the spool seemed to use all her reserves of energy. She had begged Marion to let her stay in the cottage with Alice and not go to the Christmas feast in the Hall, and Marion had agreed. It had been snowing and a raw wet wind, smelling of melting snow, was rattling the ivy on the ash tree above the cottage. It was better to stay at home. Between Christmas and the new month, Margery became indifferent to food. She soon became incapable of rising and lay curled in her blanket at the foot of the bed. The weather turned very cold. A hard frost crisped the remains of the snow. The bushes on the Common were a mass of twigs in a network of ice.

On the morning of the second such day, Marion pushed open the top half of the door and let into the cottage the pink light of a frosty sunrise. Margery did not move. From her pinched nose and colourless face Marion knew she had died.

It half horrified Marion to realize now how little she missed Margery, how little she grieved for this child who had been with her for twelve years. It was almost as though she had always expected her to die. What a wasted little life, she thought, and suddenly realized that Margery had probably never had a moment's happiness, not one day, not one easy summer afternoon. It had all seemed like suffering. Marion recalled so sharply the red-rimmed anxious eyes, fearful, uncomplaining, unquestioning, and now closed for ever.

Alice heaved and sighed, twisting her head to and fro against Marion's breast, and drew Marion's thoughts from her dead daughter to her living one. There was no doubt that Alice was a very different child, lively and sturdy. It would be very cruel if fate killed such a promising baby, but Marion knew only too well how quickly even a strong child could sicken and die. Nolly, her second child, never quite absent from her thoughts, sprang to life in her memory, her dear round Nolly, plump and quick-eyed like a robin, strong and lively as a puppy, and then dead in a week, before he was three. He died, as so many babies did, with a sudden diarrhoea, screaming with pain, unable to take any food which did not at once pass through him. His chubby body dwindled, his strong rounded arms became limp like scythed weeds in the sun, his head rolled on her arm and his whole body hung limp across her knees. She held him for three days and nights while he gradually cried less and less until she felt he had no more strength to cry. It was early April and very cold. She recalled how Peter had urged her to put Nolly in the cradle and come to bed herself. 'He's quiet now, he'll sleep – you are worn out, come to bed,' he had urged. She, racked with grief and exhaustion, had finally agreed, had laid Nolly in the cradle and lay down on the bed beside him. She had slept and in the morning Nolly was dead and the sodden cloths wrapping his body were frozen to the straw in the cradle.

For Marion, grief was interwoven with anger against Peter for telling her to leave Nolly in the cradle, and guilt that she had succumbed to his command. She had never expressed to Peter her anger at his suggestion, but she could never quite forget it. *If* she had sat up with Nolly, *if* she had kept him warm, he *might* not have died. Might – it was all might. She might have saved him that night, he might have died later. She could not say to Peter, 'If you had not told me to put him in the cradle he might be alive now,' though these 'mights' were threaded forever in and out of her grieving thoughts. 'My poor Nolly,' she sighed as she held Alice closely, 'My poor Nolly.' How was it that three years of Nolly – ten years ago – should still be more precious than twelve years of poor Margery, poor hare-faced, suffering Margery?

Marion's bottom was numb. Waking Alice or not, she must move. She hitched herself down so she could rest her head against the log, and she scooped up a bit more straw under her buttocks as padding. The deadly stillness returned, the silence pervaded. Her thoughts returned to Margery but became less coherent. Alice's heavy body on her stomach was warming. Marion dozed.

The aching stiffness in her neck awoke her. Alice lay still in her lap, heavy and damp. The air was filled with the shrill singing of birds. Marion dozed, listening. The song of one bird, a thrush, probably in the ash tree above the roof, dominated the mingled clamour of a thousand other songs. Marion imagined the wooded hillside that rose steeply at the end of her garden. It was thickly covered in a mesh of brown twigs, motionless in the grey dawn, and scattered all through, like brown fruit on branches, were these little feathery ovals, so light, so weak, yet each filling the vaults of space with its piercing song. She wondered *how* they did it. She knew how tiny they were, once the feathers were off there was only a little dangling lump, smaller than Alice's fist, one mouthful to crunch and not really worth catching and plucking. Pigeons were fine, even rooks were worth the bother – but these little ones . . . Her thoughts strayed back to the thousands of voices singing away up the hill. She wondered *why* they did so, like this, all together, so vehemently, of a spring morning. She imagined the hills beyond her own familiar hill, where in other trees in the never-ending forest, millions of tiny birds were at this moment singing away, unheard, unremarked.

Marion was recalled to full consciousness by a renewed boiling in her stomach and a griping pain accompanied by a feeling of fluid weakness in the bowels. Catching her breath against the pain, she pushed Alice off her lap into the straw, felt around hastily to make sure the child was not touching the hearthstone, rose as quickly as her stiffness permitted and took two steps to the door. She pushed back the wooden latch of the lower half, bent down and crept out. No one in the cottage stirred. A grim grey light showed her the frosty grass at her feet, the plaited wattle of the garden fence, and the lumpy midden. The birds still sang wildly. She had no time to go further and squatted down at the edge of the midden and with tufts of frozen grass tickling her buttocks, she relieved herself of much poisonous liquid. Though her head felt faint and time seemed suspended, the icy cold in her bare feet kept her conscious and she raised herself. She pulled a handful of frozen grass, managed to get enough to wipe herself with, threw it on the midden and crept back to the cottage.

As she closed the half-door behind her, Peter whispered, 'What is it, Marry?' The diminutive conveyed concern. She explained. The straw rustled and he was close to her.

'You're shivering. Here, wrap this round you, get well into the straw. I'll take Alice into my blanket.'

Marion wrapped herself in Peter's warmed blanket and rolled herself into his warmed straw nest. It seemed heavenly. She heard him feeling around the floor for Alice, Alice's little whimper, his shushing murmur and then the rustle and thud as he lay down beside her with Alice, asleep, in his arms. Marion stretched out her numb feet, hard with the cold, and touched Peterkin through his blanket. He slept on obstinately. She lay, trying to control her shivers. Peter was warm against her back; he seemed to sleep again very soon.

Marion wondered what it was that she and Alice had eaten that had made them so sick. Perhaps it was the scrapings of the bean pottage that she had eaten at noon the day before, of which Alice had had some too. The beans had been cooked with the end of a bit of bacon, mostly rind, to which she had added more beans several times in the last few days. It was all finished now – just as well. They had all had a bit of bread and cow's milk for their supper last night, given them by a neighbour whose cow was still in milk, but it could not have been the milk that caused the sickness, for Peter and Peterkin were unaffected.

Her thoughts became less coherent as she dozed again. She felt what a kind husband she had, how unusually lucky she had been to have such a gentle, unfussing man – no, not quite: he fussed about the quality of wood and about meticulous craftsmanship, and how his tools were kept. But he was always good to her, not fussy about what he ate, kind to his children – no, not quite: kind to the girls when they were little, critical of the boys at any age – a strange, mixed man, but she had never much wished she had married anyone else. She had always known, in spite of loving him, that she could never have married Dick Shepherd. Her Peter was a very able carpenter. Although he had rights to strips of land in the fields, as almost all the other cottagers had, he spent all his time in the carpenter's shed in the village and one of the Hall's servants ploughed his strips for him. Long before Marion had married him it was realized that Peter was too short-sighted to plough.

'Put his hand to the plough and he can't see the ox's tail!' said one scornful man. 'His furrows are like the paths of a hare – he wouldn't even notice if he'd ploughed his neighbour's land instead of his own!' Yes, short-sighted, but everything within his arms' range was very clear to him, even to the finest markings on his measuring stick. So others ploughed his land and he made the ploughs. Marion sometimes thought he was the happier man for it, for he saw the work of his hands in enriching use whereas many of the villagers saw the work of their hands beaten down by wind and rain or wilting under unknown pests and curses.

Kind Peter, thought Marion, and warm feelings of gratitude filled her dazed mind, and with gratitude came sleep at last.

Marion heaved herself up on to an elbow. Both halves of the door were open and it was broad daylight. Peter and Peterkin were gone. She peeped into the cradle. Alice was still asleep. The fire had been rebuilt with three logs and was smoking, the trap door in the roof was propped half open.

I must have slept hours, she thought. She felt very feeble but clear-headed now. Her feet were still stiff with cold. With the blanket still round her, she stepped to the big log and sat down with her feet on the hearthstone. The sour pungency from her dress rose to her nostrils in the warmer air. She sat, breathing heavily, enduring. The birds had quietened. Only a constant cheeping of sparrows on the roof and occasionally a distant squawking of hens down the garden (Peter must have let them out) reached her ears.

Soon she caught the sounds of Peter's voice and of a spade being struck into the ground, and then Peterkin's more plaintive child's voice, 'But I can't carry it when it's any fuller,' and more distant grumbling from Peter. Clearing out the goat shed, she thought, taking the muck to the midden – hope he doesn't disturb the sitting hens – making Peterkin carry the buckets of muck.

The blessings of warmth gradually penetrated her feet. She pulled up her dress and let the warmth spread to her shins and fill the cave created by her thighs and skirt. She glanced at the shelf. The fat earthenware pot, which, standing inverted over bread, protected it from mice, was on its side, and the bread, a pile of flat scones, had been reduced, telling Marion that they had breakfasted. She wondered how far advanced the day was. The cottage dimmed as Peterkin appeared at the door, even his small body taking the light.

'Mam – are you awake? Father said I was to look in and not wake you if you wasn't.'

'Yes, I'm awake. Did you have some bread?'

'Yes, and Hilda Shepherd gave me some milk. Her bucket's just outside, and father got a bucket of water up. You did sleep, Mam.'

'How's Nanny?'

'She hasn't had her kid yet. Father gave her more water.' He turned and called out, 'Mam's awake.'

Peter appeared at the door, dimming the cottage. He bowed his head and came in, spade in hand, and asked how she was.

'I'm all right,' she said, tradition forbidding complaints, specially from women. 'I slept.'

'You did indeed,' said Peter. 'So did the little one. She woke up soon after light and I gave her a bit of bread sloppy in water and she slept again. She's in a real stinking state.'

'I'll wash her stuff,' said Marion, wondering how she would find strength to do so, and even if she had the strength, would the stream at the water-place be frozen over, and how would she get Alice's clothes dry?

'Will you come to Mass?' Peter asked.

'Is it noon already?'

'Can't be far off. I told you, you *slept.*'

Marion stretched out a hand to the boot-drying rack under the shelf and pulled her sheepskin boots to her. Once they had been a treasure; now they were mostly worn clear of wool inside and had a large split by the toes on the left boot. She pushed her superficially warmed feet into them, rose, threw back the blanket on to the bed, picked up a small roll of woollen material from the supports under the shelf and lifted Alice from the cradle.

Alice woke and objected but Marion proceeded to unroll her from the stinking blanket that wrapped her. She pulled off the woollen tunic, also stiff with drying vomit, wiped Alice's body with parts of the blanket which seemed driest and then rolled her up again in the new blanket. Alice protested. Marion tried to appease her with a little bread but Alice turned her face away. Marion sympathized with her; all food seemed nauseous.

A distant *tanger-tanger-tanger* sounded. Along in the village the 'bell' hanging from an extended roof beam in the church was being swung by one of Father John's boys. It was not a real bell, just an old round iron cooking pot with an unmendable hole in the bottom which had been plugged by a knot of wood from which it was hanging, upside down, with part of its old handle attached as a clanger.

'Mass already?' asked Marion again, longing to sit still by the fire, but Peter grunted and rearranged the fire logs for greater safety and put a bit of blanket round her shoulders. She stood up, trembling, and pushed her loose hair up under her cap, picked up grumbling Alice, and they set off for the church with Peter's arm half round her and with Peterkin limping and hopping behind.

Marion and Peter's cottage stood, with three others near, on a bit of rising ground at the end of the Common. They walked down the little path, passing the old sisters' cottage on their left. The sisters, Old Agnes and Old Marge, would still be indoors, but Agnes's daughter, Molly, could be seen on the path ahead, dragging her way towards the village. Of the other neighbours, Dick Shepherd and Hilda and their little girls were probably already at the church – but the Plowright family, surly Jack and slatternly Small Sarah and their brood of ill-cared for children, were probably still huddled round a fire, long since gone out, cold, hungry and dirty, and never willing visitors to the church.

The walk to the main village was some quarter of a mile along the path on the Common that ran next to the stream. They came to the plank bridge which they crossed, holding the rail and going gingerly on the sparkly icy surface. Then passing the Hall and its yard on their left and the Big Oak and the Green on their right, the path took them up to the church. Little groups of their neighbours, hooded and wrapped round in any fabric they had, with shivering children about them, were trudging across the Green to the church.

Everyone in the village was proud of their church. Though it had been completed before anyone, even Marion's father, could remember, it still appeared new and clean. It had been built, so the story went, with the assistance of some men from Rutherford, from the creamy pink sandstone cut from a curious cliff-like quarry a mile or two away up in the forest. The huge bits of stone had been eased down a path on log rollers (tree trunks placed on the ground in front of a stone as it rolled down and then the freed roller taken out at the back and put down in front again), and then dragged by ox sledges across the Common to where the stream oozed from the edge of the marsh. Here the stones had been cut and trimmed, then hauled across the stream and up the bank the other side, then dragged on the sledges up the slope to the site of the church. The men from Rutherford had brought with them sacks of a white powdery earth which they described as burnt chalk. This they mixed first with the dust from the cutting of the stone and then with water, and to general amazement this sloppy mess had hardened when they stuck the stones together with it, and so the walls of the little church had a solidity that no other buildings could match. And here, to prove it, so many lives later, still stood the church. Though outside the stone had weathered into an uneven grey, the mortar was as hard as ever. The place by the edge of the stream where the stones had been cut was still strewn with the chips, now grey and greened over by exposure to the water, and these, part blocking the stream, had spread it out so there was now a wide shallow stony area where women went to tread clothes or sheep-shearings in the slow-flowing water for washing.

Cleanliness was not a state that Marion was much aware of, and barely recognized it as the special quality that always impressed her as she entered the church. The pale stone walls with seams of white mortar, the split beech-trunk beams which formed the roof, the wooden shutters hooked back from the windows each side and over the altar, gave the place a light, clean look that no other interior had. It was, of course, the only building, except sheds, that never had any fire to darken the walls or soot the beams.

Though the Manor Hall was far larger and higher, it was dark and gloomy and never impressed Marion as did the airy lightness of the church, which became in her mind an attribute of religion.

Father John was fussing around the altar, trying to light two thin tallow candles from a bit of smoking twig, muttering to his boy assistant, Tim Rockwell, and making these mutterings inaudible by the frequent wiping of his nose on the back of his hand. Tim's red bony hands seemed to project even further from his sleeves than they had last week, and the oozy chilblains were more numerous. By capping his hands round the candles and blowing gently on the smoking twig, he managed more successfully than Father John in lighting one and then the other. Their tiny flames could add nothing to the sharp winter sun shining in through the open windows and door. Father John still trotted to and fro, often tripping over his belt which had become untied and dangled before his feet.

The altar was a small wooden table, solidly made, and covered with a thin whitish blanket. On it stood the two wooden candlesticks holding the thin tallow candles with their wavering flames, the earthenware dish holding the bread to be consecrated, and the communion chalice. This was a small horn vessel, conical in shape, its rim bound by a strip of metal which shone with a faint gleam, and which Marion believed, on no evidence, to be gold. It was possibly the only bit of bronze in the village. Sometimes this gold gleam was dulled to a greenish tinge when the acid of the 'wine' corroded the copper in the metal. There was also a small granite cross, grey with a hint of sparkle about it. It was carved on its upright part with an intertwining pattern. Its real origin had long since been forgotten, but it was generally believed to have been brought to the village by St Paul to whom the church was dedicated. Beside it on the altar lay what Father John called his 'missal'. Marion knew it was in some way holy and confused it in her mind with the strange green white-berried plant which sometimes hung in lumps in the apple trees in the Hall's orchard, and which was also, but vaguely, considered to have mysterious, perhaps holy, powers. Father John's 'missal' was a board with a handle like a butter-making hand, on which had been stuck a sheet of vellum, over which a brown gummy varnish had been spread. It was very old. Just discernible on the vellum were a large red A and some lines of black writing. The whole object was blackened and shiny with age.

It was uncertain whether Father John could ever read. He often told stories of his going to a great church, called Rochester, by a river wider than the whole village. He was a boy then, and there were many other boys too, being taught to be priests. The great books of vellum sheets covered with black marks and sometimes tiny jewel-coloured pictures, were often before his eyes and the repeated intonings of the priests in his ears. He learnt everything by ear, and, like a child, knew when to turn over the large vellum pages as he repeated the strange words. Perhaps he had been able to recognize a few words, none, of course, in his native language, but it was doubtful if he ever understood any of the Latin words he learnt to repeat. In any case all this was many years ago and since leaving the great church at Rochester he had never had any opportunity to practise this strange reading. Understanding the words was of no importance; the correct performance of the rituals was all.

The vellum sheet with *Ave Maria* written on it had been given to the church long before his time, and he venerated it as a holy object and could not say Mass without it. It was an object of great familiarity to everyone in the village, who saw it in the priest's hands every week of their lives. It, if not an idol, was certainly part of their religion.

In many aspects of life, Marion did not believe in Cause and Effect, but she believed firmly in *tendencies*. She thought that with foreknowledge and skill one could influence these tendencies. In her mind the world was full of powers which worked either for or against her will. She would have called them, following the priest's muddled teaching, the powers of Good and Evil, two words which with only tiny alterations were God and Devil, but it was more than morality that these powers influenced, it was the daily material of life as well. The powers of health battled with those of disease, and though she believed that the herb potions made in the village, and drunk with the ritual sing-song words, strengthened the powers of health and weakened those of disease, she did not believe in any cure, nor any physical change that the potion might exert on the diseased body. She only imagined influences of a spiritual nature *might* lessen the powers of disease. There was therefore no searching for proof and no drawing of conclusions from evidence, it was just *prudent* to drink the right potion, to recite the correct incantation, often with Father John's blessing and prayer – for that was all that could be done to influence those powers in *her* favour.

When a cow or goat miscarried, it was only prudent to bury the foetus under the stable threshold, not because that would *prevent* a future miscarriage but because it was believed it would lessen the likelihood. It was known that for a menstruating woman to cure bacon did not *always* turn the bacon reasty, but it was believed that it was likely to have this effect, and therefore it was only *sensible* for a woman to avoid making bacon at these times.

The Mass, as performed by Father John, fitted into this general attitude very well. He produced, or rather Old Sarah who looked after him did, the special bread for consecration. From the hedgerow sloes and his own not-to-be-enquired-into process he made a sour red liquid which was called wine. When he was a boy in Rochester a sour red liquid was always available in barrels, and some of it was duly consecrated for Mass. He had assumed that any red-stained water was wine, so what should he do in the village but find berries which coloured water a dark crimson. Elderberries he used as well as sloes and they produced a good colour which looked like the stuff in little glasses on the table of the Last Supper, a huge picture which he dimly remembered on the refectory walls at Rochester. With the ritual of the Mass and with the mysterious meaningless words which he intoned, he gave out bits of bread to all present except babies in arms, and drank a gulp of the acid 'wine' himself. Everyone in the church believed that this action would influence God in their favour, and that not to attend Mass would be not so much imprudent, but downright asking for trouble.

For Marion and for most of the others in the village, their religion was no more than a part of the constant struggle for the influence of good in their lives. 'Good' meant big harvests, fine weather, health, babies (preferably other people's) and death to rats and crows. It was a kind of insurance against disaster. She was aware that in return for this unreliable protection she would have to behave in certain ways, but she had no particular sense of guilt or sin, nor did she feel any need to examine her mind or repent anything before going to Mass. Nor did she feel it behoved her to behave any differently after the sacrament. It did not put her into any awareness of God. As long as she attended Mass it was up to God to look after her and her family in a benevolent way.

There were Commandments and everyone knew there were ten of them, but they were not enumerated, and when asked for details Father John was as vague about them as anyone else. Some confusion prevailed. Marion understood that she must not swear, but she did not distinguish swearing from common speech. She knew one must honour one's parents, but of course one looked after the old things. One must not kill people – well, of course not, everyone knew that. One must not lie with others outside marriage – it was difficult to do so in the village anyway except that everyone wondered what went on in the Hall in the long dark nights and the servants of both sexes in the straw under the tables. One must not accuse people falsely – Marion would never do so. One must not steal, but stealing was not an easy thing to get away with in the close village life, and one must not work on Sundays. This Commandment did not affect Marion for no one ever considered that this prohibition concerned women's work. In fact women did not have 'work', they had 'duties' and it was their nature to fulfil them.

Marion would not have doubted that she was a virtuous woman, although she rarely considered the matter. She sometimes fed a couple of eggs to her children from the dozen that she knew should, by tradition, be given to the Hall, and she told Rollo in the Hall that the hens were not laying as they should, but she never felt any guilt at the lie, nor did she think she might be 'stealing' her own eggs from the Hall. On a more positive side, she knew she helped old people in the village, not only her own father at the Mill. She had done her share in caring for orphans when they occurred, too – she had breast-fed one of the Fletcher babies for two months after Fletcher's first wife had died. She had always worked hard to feed her family, and had had many babies, and it was hardly her own fault that so few had survived. She was faithful to Peter, in fact she loved him, she had been a dutiful daughter, but mostly she had been too busy for introspection.

As they found their places near the back of the church, Peter took heavily sleeping Alice from Marion's arms, so that she could lean against one of the thick wooden posts which were built into the stone walls. The rough earth floor hurt her feet through the old boots. She looked at the lumpy backs of her neighbours, broad, bowed shoulders heavy in grey cloaks, the men's hoods pushed back revealing scraggy necks through straggly hair, women's caps covered again with extra cloaks which sheltered babies in arms while longer cloaks hanging to their ankles sheltered little children whose dirty red feet stuck out below the shelter like chicken's claws below the mothering feathers. The damp cloaks steamed slightly and the air smelt of damp wool, long unwashed bodies and the tallow candles.

Sir Hugh and his family, standing on the chancel platform at the east
end of the church – a structure recently built by Peter after Sir Hugh had
seen a similar one in the church at Rutherford down the valley – could
be seen above the villagers' shoulders. Sir Hugh, so tall, so thin, his black
hood hanging down his back and the sharp light shining on his pale bald
head, his pale thin nose and his pale long beard. How sad his face is, Marion
thought, how weary, how without any hope.

Beside him stood Dame Margaret, always called M'Dame, a small woman
wearing her tall white fur Sunday cap, coming up only to Sir Hugh's
shoulder. Her sharp profile was intent on Father John at the altar. With
tense eyes and tightly pressed lips, hers was a face of long endurance. Her
body was wrapped round in a dull green cloak which almost covered her
dark brown dress. Her bare hands, with a chilblain on every finger, were
pressed together in prayer.

In front of her stood Magda, their eldest and only surviving child, an
undergrown twelve-year-old, whose thick brown hair poured out round
her face from under a small white cap, too small, but as like her mother's
as she could make. Marion could see Magda was not attending. Her eyes
strayed round the villagers, the building, the wall paintings round the
window over the altar, and her hands twisted and untwisted the leather belt
with red stitches that held her cloak around her. However much her eyes
wandered, her lips joined in all the responses with her parents.

Behind them was Rollo, Sir Hugh's brother, a man disliked and feared in
the village as an efficient steward of the Manor's affairs, a tireless rememberer
of who owed what, and when, a persistent nagger of defaulters, fair, accurate,
merciless, humourless – everyone knew that Sir Hugh, had he *really* been
in charge would have been easier to handle, easier to persuade, easier to
deceive. Rollo stood, hood off, his brown cloak reaching his boots, his nose
sharp and thin like Sir Hugh's, but the rest of his face lost in his hair, which
hung over his bushy eyebrows, and in his great beard which concealed all
expression in his face. 'You can't ever tell what he's thinking,' Marion had
complained once to Peter, who had answered, 'You wouldn't like it at all
if you could.'

Rollo lived at the Hall, sleeping on a straw bed on the dais between Sir
Hugh's and Magda's leather-curtained beds, though it was said, mostly by
Milly, that Rollo spent many nights at the priest's house. Old Sarah, who
was always in and out of the priest's house, looking after him, so she said,

informed villagers that Rollo and Father John often sat together in his house speaking of God and the Virgin and holy things and Rollo tried to teach Father John to sing – 'And sometimes I join in too,' Old Sarah added with a smirk, and she denied there was any other association between the two men, but among the villagers other rumours were muttered. Old Sarah, they said, didn't understand a thing. She was senile wasn't she? Hadn't she told several people she was an angel and flew to heaven every night? But on the other hand, Milly, with her poison-loving mind, would invent any evil story and spread it around if she could.

Father John was proceeding with Mass. He had used for some mysterious purpose the board with the large red A on it and had laid it carefully on the altar again with more mysterious words intoned in a sort of monotonous sing-song – which usually made Rollo twist his face in his beard. The sacred bread was broken up smaller and Tim Rockwell and another, smaller boy – one of the Hunter boys from Goose Farm, Marion thought – were taking it round in flat baskets to all the congregation. There was a scuffle somewhere, and hoarse boyish whispers of 'Your fault', 'Wasn't, you knocked me,' and Rollo's sudden severe shout, 'Silence, boys!'

Meanwhile Father John, having faced his audience and intoned some more strange words with both his hands raised, turned back to the altar and started pouring his 'wine' from a narrow-necked jug, a very dear possession, into the little horn vessel that was the communion cup. He always held the jug high so that all could see the crimson liquid falling (and today the sunlight caught the colour in ruby sparkles), and so know that proper wine was being used in this vital ceremony. His hands were cold and there were numerous splashes on the altar cloth.

As she watched the ceremony, Marion's thoughts went back to Margery's recent death and burial. 'She has gone to be an angel,' Father John had told her, a thing he said to all parents of dead children. She had been uneasy at this remark at the time and her uneasiness increased as she looked up to the two angels painted in brown lines on the wall above the altar. They were at the top left side of a large picture of the end of the world, where half the people were falling headfirst and naked into Hell, and the other half were going up top left, all in white shifts with their arms up. The painter, whoever he had been, had not done the details well, and a bump on the wall had spoilt his drawing of one of the angel's faces, giving it a nasty sneer, and some damp had come through the other angel's face so that half of it had fallen away in a powdery smear. Father John sometimes said he must get a ladder and put it right, but he did not know how to. No one realised that Gib, the miller's son, could have repainted it, least of all Gib himself. Marion had not been comforted by the idea that Margery could now be an angel.

Mass over, the villagers shuffled aside to leave a way for Sir Hugh and his family to pass to the church door and out into the sunshine. Many muttered greetings, 'Morning, sir,' and 'Morning, M'Dame,' as they passed, but no greetings were given to Magda, who followed her parents, nor to Rollo or Father John. Outside the church door the two Rockwell families, some fifteen people mostly in good pigskin boots and the big black-and-white-striped cloaks they made, called out, 'Good day, sir. Good day to you, M'Dame,' before they turned left in an orderly fashion and started their long walk up through the fields to their settlement at Rockwell. Sir Hugh and his family, Father John with the rest of the congregation following, turned right and walked down the path along the edge of the graveyard, past the entrance to the Hall's yard with all its sheds and outhouses, past the end of the Hall with its stone bread oven and open sheds and there at the door of the Hall stood Tom, who only sometimes went to Mass, smiling and welcoming. It was part of the weekly ceremony.

'Morning, sir. Morning, M'Dame,' he said, though he had seen them all before that morning, ruffling his curly hair in a gesture of deference. 'Morning, Miss Magda. Morning, sir,' to Rollo, 'Morning, Father.' They proceeded into the Hall and up to the table on the dais at the far end, with all the villagers jostling for early entry behind them. In the gloom of the Hall four big logs were blazing and a large iron pot stood on the central stone of the fireplace and round it on the other flat stones were numbers of flat round loaves. This welcome bright sight, this welcome warm smell brought gasps of 'Ah!' The Sunday ceremony of Mass followed by free food in the Hall was welcomed by all. Any ceremony was comforting, but this one most of all.

Tom, the Hall's chief servant, was in charge, and no one resented it for Tom was everybody's friend. He was fussing around – 'Close the door, boy – no, wait, Ed-me-boy's fetching the ale. Did you boys *shut* the church door? Sure? Ah, Ed-me-boy, put the bucket down there – no, I've already put a flagon on the dais table. Joan, mind your skirt by the fire – loaves all round to everyone. Don't splash the soup, Milly. *Careful*, Magda – miss – keep that dog of yours by you, please. How's the ale today, sir? Joan's brew.

Not *that* ladle, that's the soup ladle, ask Ed-me-boy – he's got the ale ladle,'
and so on and on. He had got the Family seated at their table on the dais
and most of the adult villagers seated on benches along the walls and the
children on the ground at their feet. Milly and Joan had handed out the
hard round loaves to the women and wooden bowls full of bacon and bean
soup to each family, while three tall green-glazed jugs were passed round,
from which each took as long a drink as he dared, and which Ed-me-boy
filled up with a big wooden ladle from the bucket by the door.

As everyone ate and drank, Tom's monologue ceased, for there was
nothing left to say. Families crowded round each other, feeling for the
wooden spoons most of them had tied to their belts. Peterkin had recently
been given a spoon, carved by his father, and was proud to use it. They bent
over their family bowls, spooning up the soup before it got cold, glad, *so* glad
of the hot air and the comforting food. The soup finished, the groups fell
apart and each person ate his hard bread and awaited his turn for a swig from
the ale jug. There were grunts and sighs but little talk. Marion's brother,
Simon, from the Mill, and his bouncing family were there, seated opposite.
They waved to each other and continued eating. Marion had Alice on her
knee and tried her with a spoonful of soup but Alice turned her head away.
Marion put the spoon to her own mouth and swallowed the warm, gritty,
bacon-flavoured liquid with distaste. She could not endure the valuable fat
which floated on the surface. She could not attempt another spoonful. Peter
and Peterkin finished the bowl between them. She leant her head against
Peter's shoulder and closed her eyes, and many others did so too. The bean
soup was heavy in their hungry stomachs, the heat from the burning logs
glowed on their faces, the ale was stronger than that they usually drank.
Idleness and warmth, both so rare, and rarer still in combination, induced
a delicious drowsiness. An important ceremony – Mass followed by dinner
at the Hall, so familiar, so vital to their survival – completed, what should
they do but doze in a rare sense of satisfaction?

Tom gave the fire logs a careful shove and Marion opened her eyes and
watched him. Tom was a broad strong man with curly dark hair and a
short curly beard and between them a pleasant expression. He had a way of
narrowing his eyes when he smiled which always reminded her of Simon.
She wondered at this, not realizing that everyone was related to everyone
else in the village, and though everyone knew their siblings, uncles and
aunts, and some were aware of first cousins, more distant relationships were

mostly ignored. Tom had lived all his life at the Hall. Years and years before he had married a village girl, and it was said they were very much in love. She had died when their son was born and Tom had always been devoted to his child, bringing him up single-handed in the Hall and so constantly addressing him as Ed-me-boy that the child was known by this name by all the village. Ed-me-boy was a thin tall youth, helpful to everyone, bullied by Magda, guarded over by Tom, who did not like to let the boy out of his sight.

When Ed-me-boy was still a baby, Sir Hugh had arranged a marriage between Tom and Joan, also a servant in the Hall, but Tom had objected. 'I couldn't do it, sir,' he had said, 'really I couldn't. There's my Lucy waiting in Heaven as faithful as ever she was, and I must go to her the same way, saints willing. Don't ask me to do it, sir, I'm sure it is not God's way,' so when Sir Hugh, who had jurisdiction (by law or custom) over his servants in matters of marriage, said he would allow Tom his widowerhood until after harvest and then he and Joan should marry, Tom's eyes had filled with tears and he had been seen that very day in the graveyard putting daisies on Lucy's grave. All this had been reported to Dame Margaret, who must have had a word with Sir Hugh in private for the subject of Tom's remarriage had not been mentioned again.

Throughout no one thought to ask Joan her opinion on the matter. She had also lived and worked at the Hall all her life. She was older than Tom, and it was widely known that she was the bastard daughter of Sir Hugh's father, and was therefore half-sister to Sir Hugh and Rollo, but being a bastard, and the child of old Mavis, another domestic servant who was still shuffling about half alive, Joan was allowed no taint of social superiority, rather the contrary: utter servility was to be her lot in life. She was everyone's drudge and Magda always disdained her particularly. No one blamed Tom for not marrying her.

The villagers tolerated Joan, but it was Milly, her companion in servitude, that they all disliked, and no one had ever tried to get Milly married. She was a short, bandy-legged woman, a little younger than Marion, with lank hair greyed by the amount of wood ash which had settled in it over the years, round black eyes too close together, reddened nostrils, a grumpy mouth and a heavy jaw, a woman without any grace, but with a wiry strength that had got her through her onerous life. She grumbled, she complained, she deceived, she remembered all slights, she exaggerated evil gossip (when she had not invented it in the first place), she was never to be trusted as

a witness – it was no wonder that the villagers disliked her. As the years
passed and the dislike grew, so did her malice, which was expressed in her
thin down-drawn mouth.

These were the Hall's proper servants, people tied for life to the Manor,
with no land or possessions and no prospect of freedom. None of them
ever questioned, even to him- or herself, this servitude. Hard as it was, they
had their sure places, and their sure places were beds in the straw under the
benches in the Hall and shares of whatever food was going.

In addition to them was Loppy Lambert, who was usually around in
the Hall or in the sheds round the yard. He was the son of Old Lambert
who lived up at Rockwell. Loppy was perhaps thirty years old but had the
mind of a child and a body neither of a child nor a man. His grating voice
was largely incomprehensible, his manual skills nil. He was of no use up at
Rockwell where everything was so orderly and shipshape, so Old Lambert
had given him to Sir Hugh to make whatever use of him he could. That
was not much. Loppy needed constant watching. He could not be entrusted
with the simplest jobs and no one forgot the time when he had been told to
keep an eye on some goslings on the Common and had been found hours
later swinging on a low bough of a hawthorn with a baby fox in his arms
and no goslings in sight.

Dame Margaret woke everyone in the Hall by calling out, 'Tom! Close
the shutters, I feel the night air coming in.'

Tom at once pulled the ropes which closed them, and so darkened the
Hall even more. Only the wide glow and occasional flicker from the fire
lit the room. The villagers knew this was the signal to depart, to leave the
warm shelter for their own cold damp cottages.

'Must get home before dark', 'Still got my cow to milk', 'Don't like the
night air on my chest', 'You're lucky to have a cow in milk' – with such
remarks they collected their children, surreptitiously pocketed bits of bread,
rewrapped their cloaks round them, pulled up their hoods and shuffled out
into the misty pinkish dusk of a March evening.

Marion and Peter were leaving together, following Dick and Hilda, who
carried the younger of their little girls. At the Hall door Tom waylaid them.

'Oh Peter, while I think of it, I need a new spigot for the small barrel
in the brew house. The one in it is rotten and it dribbles.'

'But I'm busy,' said Peter. 'I've got who knows how many jobs for Rollo.

A spigot's a fiddly job – you needn't think making a small thing takes a small bit of time . . . but all right, I'll see. Remind me next week. Ash is best for that job.'

'Thanks. Good night, all,' and Tom shut himself behind the Hall door and Peter joined the others on the bridge. Meanwhile Dick Shepherd had paused on the path, received a bag of food from Hilda, wrapped her cloak around her and the sleeping child, embraced both, and the other child standing by Hilda, and had gone off across the Green. As he went Marion saw a fuzz of orange hair catch the last of the light, his head and body a dark silhouette against it.

'Dick gone off?' asked Peter.

'Up to the pastures,' said Hilda. 'He can't leave the ewes and the new lambs at this time of year. He left Ned up there with them and just came down for Mass and food himself. Hold the rail, Meg. No jumping now.'

Their neighbour, Molly, came up behind them.

'Glad of your company on the way home,' she said. 'Woops – the bridge is slippery, frost's come down early this evening. Your little one asleep, Marion?'

It was quickly becoming dark. They stumped off in single file along the path across the Common to the little collection of cottages always referred to as 'Down the Common'. They parted with Molly at her garden gate.

'You're lucky,' Marion said to her. 'Your mother and aunt'll have the fire going for you. We'll be lucky if there's any fire at home.'

'You send Peterkin round for a bit of hot embers if you need 'em. You too, Hilda.'

More good nights followed. They parted from Hilda at her cottage and watched her stoop as she went in through the door with Meg following her.

At the cottage Peter at once felt under the shelf for the bellows and puffed away till a red glow appeared. Peterkin emerged from the gloom and crouched down beside it. Marion sank down on the curved log and Alice immediately woke up.

'Want bread an' milk,' she announced cheerfully.

'She's better,' said Peter, curtly.

'No, it's bed time,' said weary Marion. 'Straight into the cradle with you.' Alice protested with a wail. 'You be quiet,' said Marion, slapping her. She put her firmly in the cradle and covered her up tight with the sheepskin, then sat down on the log again. Peterkin had shut the door, both top and bottom halves and so the only light in the cottage came from the fire. It was too dark to spin, too dark to make spigots, too dark to do anything but sit by the fire as close as possible and try to keep warm.

'Might as well go to bed,' said Peter, as he did almost every night. 'Come, boy, out for a last pee.'

When they returned Marion had banked up the fire and was already lying down on the bed. Peter felt about as he gingerly climbed over her.

'Did you rehook up the door?' she asked.

'Yes, of course,' he said.

She knew they were both rather ill-tempered. She knew she was better from her illness, and was hungry having had almost nothing to eat for twenty-four hours. A night, as she knew well, was always extra long when one was hungry. This night was bitterly cold too. An hour later, still lying awake in the dark and with her feet like blocks of ice, she felt the cold creeping up her legs to the knees, and envied and marvelled at the ease with which Peter and her children fell asleep. For her, the dark hours dragged on.

APRIL

On the warm bed thy plain supplys
The young lambs find repose
And mid thy green hills basking lies
Like spots of lingering snows

It was one of the many false starts of spring, and though Marion knew cold, frost and snow might well come back to them before a more certain spring, just for today there seemed to be an easing of winter. The evenings were longer, the birds sang, and a faint sweet smell blew from the Common.

The previous day Peter had at last completed the plough he had been making to Rollo's orders and had adjusted it again and again to Rollo's pernickety standards, and today, as a sort of unofficial holiday, he was at home attending to the garden. Peterkin was with him, to Marion's pleasure, for she knew it sealed a relationship between father and son which she valued as part of Peterkin's training to be an adult. For the past weeks Peterkin had been out before dawn in all weathers, up in the new-sown fields, throwing stones and shouting at the rooks, and had returned home an exhausted wisp of a child, red-faced, red-fingered, red-eared and with a croaking voice.

Today was peaceful and Marion felt content. With the top and bottom halves of the door open, the cottage was light inside. Marion had busied herself with sorting and tidying, stacking up her spools of spun wool, getting in logs, sweeping the ground round the fire clear of bits of straw, grinding some dried beans in the stone quern, always with half an eye on Alice, who sat quietly on the floor sweeping up the dust into little ridges with her fat palms. The sun shone, but the wind, flickering over the new shiny grass, had a chilly edge. Marion went out, pulling up her clothes, and squatted at the edge of the dunghill. She concentrated on excreting for a while, then her attention went to a bluebottle, newly awakened by the warm sun, which had landed on a dead leaf near her foot. She looked at its brilliant iridescent blue body, watched it stroking its front legs together. Then it flew to something vividly green nearby. It was the remains of a mallard drake's head, probably last year's, that had been thrown to Tibtab and which the cat had eventually abandoned. Old though it was, the brilliant green feathers still blazed with that strange unearthly colour in the sunlight. Marion watched the bright blue jewel walking on the bright green feathers – a tiny area of each – but so strange, so unlike any colour in nature. If questioned, Marion would have said that both drakes' heads and bluebottles were part of nature, yet the very strangeness of these colours made her wonder if they were not supernatural, some lost angel's jewels or devil's snares. Just for the moment she wondered at the sudden flood of delight that these rare and glistening colours illuminated in her mind. It was not a thought that she would ever have tried to express. Then, realizing she had finished, she pulled some new-sprouted dock leaves growing by and wiped her bottom, for she had been brought up to be cleanly.

Peter was down at the bottom of the garden digging, and Peterkin was toing and froing with small wheelbarrow-loads of midden muck for his father to dig into the earth. Peterkin was, like all village children, so used to the sight of people defecating that he paid no attention to Marion. He could not hold a wheelbarrow very straight and his lollopy walk did not allow him to wheel it very straight, but boys must help their fathers and Peter wanted to get that patch dug while the weather was dry.

The goat had had her kid recently, a nice little nanny, at present sucking at her mother's teats. Marion filled up the goat shed water butt and pulled some more hay down to the goat's mouth level. She stroked the old nanny but did not touch her baby. Marion had already planned that she would allow the kid all her mother's milk for a few weeks, then when grass was more plentiful, wean her, so that come summer the kid would be a perfect gift to the Hall. A healthy nanny kid would be a valuable present and would free Marion from other obligations to the Hall for some time. As the kid was weaned so Marion would steadily milk the goat and there should be plenty of milk and cheese for many months. The grass before the cottage already looked plentiful – perhaps she would get the goat out of doors next day if Peter could help tether her. It was all very satisfactory.

Above the goat's byre a broad shelf ran along the wall at Marion's shoulder height. Peter had put it up many years ago. It was divided into many small boxes, in which on a little straw the hens came to lay their eggs and where all the poultry lived, fox-free at night. There was a little door in the outside wall at the end of the shelf, and every morning Marion prised it open, its leather hinges often stiff with frost, and propped up the 'hen post' outside. This was a stout pole with small branches off each side, and when the top was at the open door and the base on the ground the hens could hop and flutter up and down to their nests and shelter without troubling anyone. Hens with little chickens were kept in coops on the floor below, which was not very safe as sometimes the little chickens strayed too far and got trodden under by the goat. Just now Marion had two hens in coops with large broods of chickens and there was much cooing and cheeping. Most of the other hens had come down the post and were pecking about and squawking in the garden. Marion heard two or three times the triumphant *chk chk chk chk chk chk cha – a – a – ark* announcing egg-laying so she slid her hand into the nests along the shelf and collected six warm eggs. Two hens, still anticipating laying, sat on their straw and glared at her with round golden eyes.

Marion calculated. She knew she was due that week to take a dozen fresh eggs to the Hall, and she knew that no promise of a nanny kid in June was going to free her completely of her obligations over eggs now. This was the moment of the year she knew, and every one else knew, that hens laid most eggs. But she was loathe to give up these new warm eggs. She had in the basket in the cottage eight eggs collected yesterday. She would take these to the Hall, and perhaps one more, not yet laid, but she and her family would eat these fresh ones now.

She carried them to the cottage. Using her forefinger, she scraped a little bacon fat from a tub into her shallow earthenware bowl, broke six eggs into it and stood it on the flat stone by the fire's edge. She then prised open some flat, rather hard, rolls, smeared some bacon fat into each and put them down by the bowl to warm through. She glanced at Alice who was sitting in the sunlight on the cottage floor, still patting dust into little heaps and talking some nonsense to herself. She was sufficiently far from the fire for Marion not to worry.

Marion looked down the garden, a gentle slope, with Peter and Peterkin digging near the bottom. The hedge on the right was full of silver ash twigs, dotted with black buds, sticking straight up above the bright green grass. Beyond the ditch at the end of the garden the forest sloped up steeply, bare of leaf – tall smooth beeches, roughened oaks, corrugated ashes, standing up on the red-brown leaf-mould earth through which patches of juicy bluebell leaves and dog's mercury were now showing. Dotted about this steep wood were dark yew trees and the occasional wild cherry, misty white with opening blossom. Nearer to, in the undergrowth of elder and honeysuckle, hazel bushes were draped in long yellow catkins, sometimes straining out horizontally in the gusts of wind, then bouncing around as the wind released them. Marion looked to the left, beyond the garden fence and her apple tree, still only in tight bud, to the birch trees on the Common. The green veil that covered them today had hardly been apparent yesterday, and the snowy blackthorn in the hedge had thickened. She picked a primrose from a clump in the grass and sniffed its tiny velvety scent, then she called to Peter and Peterkin to come and eat. She went in herself and gave the primrose to Alice, showing her how to smell it first.

They had finished the baked eggs and almost finished the warm bread when two of the Plowright children appeared. There were many Plowright children, all quiet, thin and bedraggled, and of indeterminate sex. Marion often wondered if they really had names, since those given them over the font appeared to have been forgotten soon after.

'Can we have a bit of bread?' the taller one whispered.

Marion felt exasperated and Peter frowned fiercely.

'Hasn't your mam got any for you?'

'No,' said the child, insinuating a thin bare leg over the threshold.

Marion gave half a loaf, carefully broken in two, to each of the children.

'Now that's *all*, do you understand? Share it with the others, don't come for more.' Her severity, she knew, concealed her pity. She wondered again if the Plowright baby, which had died before Christmas, had not succumbed to plain starvation. The children said, 'Yes,' and departed.

Peter sighed. 'Only yesterday,' he said, 'I saw one of them trying to eat an old cabbage stalk by the rubbish heap. Rotten sort of woman that Small Sarah.'

Yes indeed, the Plowrights were a wretched family. Jack, Marion supposed, was all right, a hard worker on the land, sowing and ploughing and reaping, but he was a surly silent man and too often round at the Hall's brew house, cadging a pint of ale. Small Sarah, his wife, with her twisted mouth, was small in body and in mind, and now after many years of bearing children, living and dead, she could cope no longer. She sat idle in their cottage caring for nothing. One could not talk to her for no one could understand what she said, only a gobbledy noise came from her. Her upper lip had a split almost to her nostrils and she had an oddly flat nose. She was born like that and had never spoken properly. It made people wonder if she were lunatic, and there was little in her manner to make anyone think otherwise. At times Marion or Hilda had gone to her cottage, put things aright as much as they could, given bits of clothes to the children, urged Small Sarah to be up and doing, but in vain. Days after, Marion found the fire out, mice at the cheese, bread mouldy and children wailing. Once or twice Father John, urged by Sir Hugh, had stumped down the Common to give Small Sarah a talk about her duties, but she had just sat there, her purple feet in the ashes, looking at him with vacant bloodshot eyes and making no reply. Marion knew that nothing could really be done for the Plowrights and that no amount of admonishing Small Sarah would ever give her the physical strength and the mental resolution to raise her and her family from this sordid poverty.

I'd be like that myself, Marion thought, if I hadn't my health. And she was thankful that she had not had a dozen or more babies over the last ten years. If only Jack would leave her alone . . . but this thought she barely allowed herself, for it was assumed in the village that men should have their wives whenever they liked except just before or just after a birth.

Peter stood up and rubbed his rather fatty hands down his tunic. 'I'll get that bit of ground ready for the peas by noon,' he announced. Marion knew that was too optimistic.

'You'll mind Alice, won't you?' said Marion. 'I've got to take these eggs to the Hall while they're still fresh, and I've told Hilda that Peterkin will collect a bag of food from her and take it up to Dick and the boys.'

'All right,' said Peter, 'be back as soon as you can. Come on, Alice, out to play with Father. Finished your bread?' He scooped up Alice with one hand, picked up his spade with the other and stumped off down the garden.

Marion put the eight eggs from yesterday in a basket on a little straw, sent Peterkin next door to collect Hilda's bag of food and the two of them set off for the village. She watched Peterkin limping along the path ahead of her, and a pang of sorrow for him struck her, as it often did. His twisted left hand was hooked into the belt of his tunic with the handle of Hilda's bag twisted round its wrist, and with every step he lurched as his twisted left foot touched the ground.

The disaster had occurred when he was two, and it was extraordinary that he had survived after that winter's night. They had a tiny candle and the firelight was bright, and Peterkin – Marion could recall exactly his plump baby's body – was sitting on the floor with his bare legs stuck out towards the fire. Peter at that time had been lying on the bed for days, aching, coughing, unable to eat, sweating and trembling and muttering that he would die. It was because of his illness that the stock of sawn logs was running so low, and Marion, unable to manage the heavy old saw that Peter kept at the cottage, had been dragging long branches in, putting one end in the fireplace and then shoving up the branch as the end burnt. She was aware that she must always remember the unburnt end lying in the semi-darkness on the cottage floor. Margery, a little girl then, was banging beans rather ineffectively in the stone quern, and Nolly, fat and contented, was sitting in the cradle. Then Marion forgot, or tripped, or . . . she could never recall exactly, but her foot knocked the unburnt log on the floor and the other burning end, on which the big iron pot full of hot soup was lodged, tipped down and the iron pot fell off the fire on to Peterkin's left foot, pouring the hot soup over his leg. Screaming, he had pushed the pot off his foot with his left hand and had burnt that too. She had picked him up, dipped the end of her cloak into a water barrel and laid the cold wet on his foot and hand and he screamed and screamed. Margery had leapt up, staring in horror, then seized a stick, put it through the handle of the iron pot and righted it, preserving some of the soup.

'What is it?' Peter mumbled from the bed, with the baby's screams aching through his head.

'Soup's upset on Peterkin's foot,' Marion said, and to Margery, 'Go to Hilda Shepherd and get some of her ointment.'

Margery was terrified of going out in the dark, but recognized an emergency, and felt her way by the familiar stones on the path to the Shepherds' cottage. She was relieved when Hilda, taking a horn from a shelf, hurried back with her to the cottage.

Peterkin was still screaming. Nolly was sitting up in the cradle, frightened and wailing. By the intermittent light of the fire and the one tiny candle flame, Hilda gently spread some of her ointment, an impure lanoline mixed with innocuous herbs, on Peterkin's wounds. He screamed even more. She gave him a spoonful of some other concoction of her making which she said would make him sleep. Marion found it the longest night of her life. Peterkin lay on her lap – such as there was of it, for she was six months pregnant – screaming and writhing and touching his foot with his good hand and hurting himself even more. She could do nothing for him. Peter dragged himself up, groaning and shaking, and put a blanket over her. She told him to go back to bed and to take Margery and Nolly with him and to put out the candle as they might need it more later on. Eventually, hour after ghastly hour later, even Peterkin dozed and lay in Marion's arms whimpering and shaking. When light came she could hardly move she was so cold and stiff. She lifted Peterkin into the cradle and pushed open the top half of the door and the wintry dawn light showed her Peterkin's wounds. She gently pulled aside the wet cloth with which she had been trying to cool his foot and hand all night, and with it the skin of his foot came off like a sock. She covered the wounds again as he lay screaming. Then suddenly a darkness clouded her eyes and she lay down on the floor, fainting.

Extraordinarily, Peterkin had survived. His foot had barely suppurated, and new skin gradually grew over the wounds, but the fabric was damaged and his foot had never since grown straight. He had learnt to get about, and even as he got older to climb trees, but he limped badly and had to hop to keep up with other boys in the village. His left hand had not been so extensively damaged as his foot, but the thumb was immovably pressed against the base of the first two fingers which were themselves almost immobile. It was a hand incapable of holding.

Marion watched him hopping along ahead of her and told herself that he would probably never get any better now. A lame, one-handed boy was a liability, not an asset. How could a boy like that ever handle a plough? Or a scythe? And to follow his father and be a carpenter was impossible. But still — he was sharp-faced, like his mother, with deep-set grey eyes, very clear-sighted, and with his right arm could throw a stone at a pigeon, calculating not only the bird's position, but the trajectory of the stone through the branches, so that he could hit the pigeon without warning it. Short-sighted Peter regarded Peterkin's stone-throwing ability with pride and awe.

Marion and Peterkin parted after crossing the bridge, Peterkin to go through the village sheepfold and then up into the hills, Marion to go up the path to the Hall. She met Dame Margaret by the Hall porch.

'Eggs,' she said. 'Shall I take them down the yard?'

But Dame Margaret was sharp. 'Only eight? Shouldn't you bring a dozen?'

'I just haven't got a dozen at present. I thought you'd like to have these while they're fresh. I'll bring more tomorrow if they lay them.'

'I'll tell Rollo,' said Dame Margaret, and Marion knew she would and that Rollo would remember every detail. 'All right, take them down to Joan in the dairy,' but before Marion could do so there was a sudden shouting and crying out and a wild-looking woman came limping up to the Hall door, her hair down her shoulders, a huge bleeding bruise on her nose, blood pouring from her mouth and tears oozing from the crevices of the swollen purple lid of one eye. Her cloak was half caught up round the infant she was carrying. It lay quiet in her arms while blood from the woman's mouth dripped on to its head. She was howling and roaring for Dame Margaret.

'Angels preserve us, Jill!' Dame Margaret cried. 'What's happened?'

A desperate wail of incoherent complaint followed. He'd been drinking again, chased the children out into the dark, hit her, broken the corn pot, knocked her down, upset the cradle, poor baby on the floor, hit her repeatedly, she'd run out of the cottage but he had caught her and dragged her back – drunk he was, horribly drunk, worse than ever before – she'd pushed him on to the straw and he had banged his head on the post and lay quiet and she had escaped with the baby and wanted sanctuary at the Hall, and mercy, and justice, and sympathy, and protection . . . and all this told with shrieks and howls.

Dame Margaret took Jill in, and sat down with her on the edge of the dais, motioned Marion to sit too, and ordered Milly, who had stood there relishing the drama, to bring a pail of water and a cloth. Dame Margaret was, as Marion long knew, always good at such a crisis, calm and practical. She took the baby from Jill's arms and gave it to Marion.

'See what you can do, Marion,' she said, taking the cloth and wiping Jill's face. 'Get out of the light, Milly, and pull the shutters back. I need all the light I can get. Then tell Tom to go and get Dobbin – better take Rollo too, Dobbin may still be mad drunk – and keep Loppy away.'

Jill was calming down under Dame Margaret's ministrations. The pain of the bruises eased under the cold water, and with a broken tooth removed from her jaw, the flow of blood lessened and Dame Margaret wiped the old blood off her chin and neck. Meanwhile Marion had wiped the silent baby clear of its mother's blood. It did not itself seem to have been wounded, but it seemed stunned. She slid her hand up into its tunic and found its heart beating. She turned the baby over and washed more blood off the other side of its head.

'Baby's alive, M'Dame,' she whispered. 'It's not bleeding, it was its mother's blood running down on to its head.'

Jill heaved herself round to look at her baby and burst out into another wail against her wicked, cruel husband. Dame Margaret ordered Milly to heat up a bowl of ale at the side of the fire and to fetch some of the dried herbs hanging on the wall. In due course the herbs were sprinkled into the ale, Jill had drunk it off and had been put to lie down on the straw on one of the benches with a cold damp cloth over her face. She lay quiet.

Dame Margaret came back to Marion, still sitting with the baby on her knee. She turned it over again. There was fresh blood on its neck, and blood was oozing from one of its ears. Dame Margaret and Marion looked at each other and each saw despair in the other's eyes. Marion felt again for the baby's heartbeat, now slower and fainter. Dame Margaret took the baby back. 'It can't last long,' they whispered together.

Rollo and Tom appeared at the door, and Rollo said, 'We've got Dobbin outside, dragged him here, dead drunk still. We've tied his feet to the oak tree.'

'Leave him,' Dame Margaret said. 'It's no use beating him when he's too stupefied to know why.'

There was more shouting outside and Dame Margaret, still holding the baby, Marion, Rollo and Tom went out to enquire. Annie, the old widow, Dobbin's mother, was struggling to approach her drunken son and Ed-me-boy was preventing her.

Dame Margaret, with all her habitual authority, strode over the grass to the oak, commanding, '*Leave* him, Widow Annie.'

Ed-me-boy stepped back and Annie pulled herself up from kneeling. Her eyes were red and her mouth shook and she could not speak.

'*Leave* him. He has beaten Jill, knocked a tooth out, Heaven knows what he has done to this baby. Where are the other children?'

'At their cottage, M'Dame.'

'Have you seen them today?' Dame Margaret was at her most curt and severe.

'N-no.'

'Go back to their cottage,' ordered Dame Margaret. 'Find the children – all of them – take them into your cottage, warm them, feed them, tell them their mother will come home soon. *Now*. Do you understand?'

Annie started a mumbling prevarication, but Dame Margaret insisted. 'Go – *now*. Find the children and look after them in *your* cottage. *Now*. Go,' and she pointed across the Green to the path down Mill field.

Sir Hugh appeared from the orchard. Annie raised her eyes to him. He was after all the ultimate authority. Marion looked at his long tired face, full of weary sadness.

'Oh, *go*,' he said. 'Do what M'Dame tells you. *Go*.' So Annie hobbled off and the little crowd broke up. Sir Hugh, Rollo and Dame Margaret with the baby went back into the Hall, Tom jerked his head at Ed-me-boy to follow them, then looked at Marion with a query in his face.

'The baby won't live much longer,' she told him. 'I'll have to get home to *my* baby,' and with great weariness she walked slowly home across the

Common with the blackthorn bushes on her left like lace, and the kingcups in clumps along the stream, bright chalices of gold on her right, and the first cuckoo of the year delicately fluting up in the forest. Peace there, tumult and misery among men.

As Marion came round the corner of her cottage a flock of sparrows, chattering madly, flew in and out of the elder bush. She glanced over the half-door to the shed – the goat and her kid were all right. Down the garden she could see Peter's bent back as he dug. Alice must be there with him. It was all very peaceful. Contrary to her resolution she milked a little milk into a small bucket, crumbed some bread into it, cut some lumps of cheese on to more bits of bread, and went down the garden.

'Mam Mam Mam Mam,' said Alice, holding up earthy hands.

'Where have you been all this time?' asked Peter. 'Look, I've done all that patch till here. I'll sow some peas tomorrow.'

'We could still get frosts. I've brought some bread and cheese.' He had taken off his hood and hung it over a branch of the apple tree, and Marion saw how very thin and stringy were his neck and collarbones above the low neck of his tunic.

'Tchees,' said Alice.

'The child learns more words every day,' said Peter. 'Alice, what's this?' He held out the spade.

'Thpade,' said Alice, and looked round for applause.

Marion sat down on a big tussock and took Alice on her knee and started spooning the bread and warm goat's milk into her, taking a munch of her own bread and cheese every now and then. Peter sat on the stump of a pear tree which had once grown, profitlessly, in the hedge, and Marion told him of the drama she had witnessed at the Hall.

'They'll beat Dobbin this evening,' she said, 'if he comes round sober, and if he doesn't he'll be tied to the oak all night.'

'What good's a beating going to do, stupid drunkard like him?'

'If the baby dies he's a murderer.'

'Yes, and not the only one. Don't you reckon that Plowright baby that died around Christmas was murdered? No one talks of beating Jack, but it's more likely it was Small Sarah that let that baby die of starvation. Stupid cow.'

'Isn't throwing the baby against the hearthstone and breaking its skull worse than just not feeding it?'

'Don't really know,' Peter admitted. 'For the poor baby it is the same.'
They were silent, pondering the dilemma.

'They won't let Dobbin free this time – at the Hall they're all so furious.
Of course he's often beaten up Jill before. D'you 'think she asks for it?
Aggravates him?'

'Don't know,' said Peter. 'Struck me as an ordinary sort of woman, bit
silly, not a nagger. Ugly as the Devil.'

'Oh Peter!' Marion was made nervous by Peter's casual references to
the Devil. 'I'll go back to the Hall later and see what's happened. Alice,
what have you got all over your knees?' She had pulled up Alice's rough
dress and found her knees, under their earthy crust, were covered with
scarlet lumps.

'She crawled into those nettles just coming up,' Peter jerked his thumb
towards the hedge, 'got terribly stung and yelled and screamed. Wasted a
lot of time calming her. Still, we found some dock leaves, didn't we, Alice,
and it's all better now.'

'Dock,' said Alice. Despite regarding attending to Alice as wasting his
time, Peter was a kindly father. There came a shout from the cottage and
they saw Peterkin jiggling down the garden to them.

'Anything to eat?' he asked.

'Didn't the shepherds share anything with you?'

'Yes. Not much.'

'You can have this bit of bread and cheese,' said Marion.

'Dick cut my toenails,' announced Peterkin, pulling off his old boot to
show them. 'Did it with the small shears he says he keeps for going round
the sheeps' ears.'

Marion inspected Peterkin's feet. The toes of his right foot were all
straight and Dick had cut the nails close and neatly, but the twisted left foot
was a problem because Peterkin always put its outer side and the little and
fourth toes to the ground, and both these toes were twisted inwards, and
the nails, growing into his foot, were difficult to cut.

'Did it hurt?'

'Yes. He made me sit with my foot in a puddle up there for ages. It was
freezing, but he said it softened the nails and then he could cut them.'

'Wish we could all have shears like that to cut our toenails,' said Peter.

'Why's Alice all yellow on her face?' Peterkin asked, as he put on his
boots again.

Marion, inspecting, found that Alice was eating a dandelion. She removed it, Alice squawked.

'She can't *like* it,' said Peterkin. 'Dandelions are as bitter as bitter. I've tried.' Alice let out a bleat of disgust. Marion bent down and scooped a fingerful of mashed dandelion from Alice's mouth.

'Silly girl,' she said. 'First it's nettles, then it's dandelions. Still, you've got to learn.' Marion knew she had said this many times before to her children and would likely say it many times more to future children. Her life was made of such little repetitions – her mother's and grandmother's lives had been the same – and in twenty years or so Alice herself might be standing in this very spot wiping dandelion petals from the mouth of some infant, and so on and on for ever.

Before sunset, Marion and Peter walked back to the village. Marion left Alice with Hilda, and Hilda's elder child, Meg, a round-faced girl with orange curls, had welcomed Alice 'to play baby with'.

The wind had dropped and the sky had clouded over when they crossed the bridge and saw most of the villagers standing about under the oak tree and round the Hall porch, their movements slow, their speech subdued. Beyond them, up the sloping path towards the church, Marion saw a little procession. Father John went first, followed by Rollo carrying a small bundle, and behind him in an orderly file some dozen children, none over twelve, all carrying little bunches of wilting buttercups, cowslips, closed dandelions, lady's-smocks and stalks of wild cherry blossom. She could see Loppy Lambert, a figure apart, neither child nor adult, lurking by a yew tree, watching intently.

'Look,' whispered Marion to Peter, pointing to this procession. Then she realized it was too far off for him to see. 'It's the children – all with flowers, following Father John to the church, Rollo too, carrying the baby. So it *has* died.'

They paused on the bridge and Marion watched the little procession go into the church. There would be the burial tomorrow. Meanwhile, this ritual of all the children carrying whatever wild flowers were about, to be placed round the corpse in the church, was the habitual ceremony for a dead baby.

Even more leaden-hearted, Marion joined the groups under the oak tree. Dobbin, sobered by terror, was standing against the trunk with Tom holding the rope which still bound his feet. The villagers around were hostile. Rollo returned from the church and was standing with Sir Hugh and Dame Margaret on the path watching, when Widow Annie burst through the crowd, knocking down two children, and lunging towards Dobbin. She was caught and held by Hodge, a labourer from across the Green.

Dame Margaret, as authoritatively as before, stepped forward. 'Go home,' she ordered.

Annie started to whine, and to bluster and struggle to get near Dobbin, whether to protect or attack him no one knew.

'Go home,' Dame Margaret repeated. 'Mind your grandchildren, those that are left.' Widow Annie looked round wildly. The children who had been in the procession were now standing in an uneasy little group. They no longer held their bunches of flowers. Annie knew where they had been, and what the procession had meant and her face showed pain as well as fear.

'Go home,' Dame Margaret shouted more emphatically. Annie looked round with terror at the implacable faces of the villagers.

'Go home,' repeated Hodge's wife, Cecily. 'The baby's dead, and we won't let Dobbin off this time.' To a general hushing, Hodge released Annie and she backed away and disappeared over the Green.

Marion crept up to Dame Margaret and asked how Jill was.

'Sleeping, thanks be. Joan is with her. She doesn't even know the baby's dead.'

Meanwhile, Tom and Rollo had tied ropes round Dobbin's wrists, pulled him to the oak tree, pressing his face against the trunk, pulled his arms half round the trunk and tied the ropes together on the far side. Rollo pulled down Dobbin's hood and with long pliable birch branches they beat him on the head, back and his bare legs.

Dobbin roared. The villagers stood around tensely watching. Marion saw Rollo's face as he beat him, calm, indifferent, passionless, unfeelingly following the letter of the law. And that in itself was a reason to fear him. The group of children, subdued with the ceremony of putting their wilting flowers round the dead baby by the altar, still stood together, watching with open mouths the ceremonious assault on big, strong, frightening Dobbin.

The beating over, Tom and Rollo untied his hands and, each holding an end of rope, marched the moaning Dobbin, his neck and legs bleeding, up to the churchyard. Near the top by the line of yews Rollo left him. The rest of Dobbin's punishment was to dig his baby's grave with his bare hands in the rooty earth. There was no escape; Tom stood over him.

The villagers, with tension relaxing, saw him depart. Sir Hugh called Ed-me-boy and muttered something to him.

'Sir Hugh says,' announced Ed-me-boy in his very husky new voice, 'it's a sad day for all of us and there is ale for all in the brewery now.' Here Sir Hugh muttered again. 'And Sir Hugh says no singing and keep your voices down so as not to wake Jill in the Hall.' More mutters from Sir Hugh. 'And Sir Hugh says this is not a celebration.' This was the first time that Ed-me-boy had publicly deputized for his father. It made him feel very grown-up and he was almost glad that Tom was up in the graveyard with the criminal.

The ale was not particularly rich or satisfying, having been surreptitiously watered by Milly half an hour before, anticipating that the offer of drink would be made and fearing there would not be enough, but it was refreshing enough and after drinking and many low-voiced exchanges of views, the villagers started moving off to their homes.

A steady drizzle set in. Marion glanced up at the sky, westwards towards her home. The dreamy orange colour over the forest was barred with dark grey clouds, and all the rest of the sky was gloomily dark. She looked up the hill, and there in the gloom beyond the church she could see Dobbin sitting on the earth with his feet in the shallow little trough that he had scraped out. The rain, perhaps mixed with tears, was running down his beard on to his bloody knees. Marion was filled with disgust, with pity too perhaps, but disgust overwhelmingly. She took Peter's arm.

'We must collect Alice,' she said, pulling her cloak around her against the rain.

'Do you think they remembered to fasten the church door?' said Peter as they went along the Common path. 'Remember what happened to that Rockwell child when the foxes got in.'

'Tom was there,' said Marion. 'He'd see to it.'

'Glad I got that bit dug before this rain,' Peter said a little later. They were both trying to put the horrid events of the day out of their minds.

'I wonder if M'Dame put my eggs somewhere safe,' said Marion, her mind going back to before the tragedy. 'Wonder if she *did* tell Rollo.'

MAY

Above him in the white thorn bush
That oer the leaning stile bends low
Loaded wi mockery of snow
Mozzld wi many a lushing thread
Of crab tree blossoms delicate red

It was a chilly blustery morning, with bright sunlight and swiftly moving white clouds that combined to give Marion a headache. Peter and Peterkin had left for the village at dawn, the latter with a large basket of spools of spun wool.

'*Make* Rollo count them,' she had said to Peterkin, 'out loud, and you repeat the number after him – there's seventeen spools, all full. And bring the basket back.'

She was anxious. The spun wool was most of last winter's work, and its acknowledged delivery should entitle her to extra blankets or extra tanned leather when needed.

'Don't drop any on the way,' she added, but she guessed she was fussing.

Left alone with Alice, Marion went round the side of the cottage where what remained of the firewood was piled up. Stacked against the wattle all the winter, it had made the wall much more windproof, but now most had been burnt, and she would have to be very economical with what was left. She had burnt up quite a lot yesterday, doing the bread, and she worried about that. She wondered if she should go up to the forest now and pull home any fallen branches. She was not permitted to do so, but perhaps no one would see her. She wished she did not feel so very tired. She worried about that too.

She looked into the oak flour-chest, lifting its heavy lid. Peter had made it when they were married and she knew she was fortunate in having an almost mouse-proof container. There was not much flour in it − a fact she well knew, and was annoyed with herself for probing her anxiety by looking in the depleted chest again. She banged the lid shut. A gust of wind, blowing in through the half-door, whirled the wood ash from the fire about and some of it settled on the milk in a wide wooden bucket. She went to close the half-door, but instead leant her aching head against the doorpost and looked down the garden and up into the steep forest beyond.

Above the hazels and the briars, now in small leaf, the forest floor rose in sheet after sheet of misty bluebells, and with every gust of wind their sweet refreshing scent blew to her nostrils. It was a sight so brief, so immense, so familiar, and yet every year so unbelievable, that she stood there staring at it. She considered that the bluebells were some kind of special blessing visited on Down the Common cottagers − for all the other advantages Rockwell had, there were no bluebells in their woods. A brief easing of anxiety filled her mind.

She wandered down the grassy path of the garden. The apple tree in the hedge by the Common was in rich blossom, fat round flowers, thick along the branches, pure white inside, rich pink outside. In spite of the wind, the bees were plentiful. The ground where Peter had been digging and planting was lined with rows of little green shoots where the peas were coming up. Some, she noticed, were eaten by slugs. She felt suddenly nauseated by the sight.

Perhaps she was tired after the long energetic day she had spent yesterday. She had agreed with Hilda and Molly, both her close neighbours, to clear a path to the old bread oven, light it, and they would each make a fine batch of loaves. They did this once or twice a year.

Near the edge of the Common, a little way from Marion's cottage, stood what they called the Old Barn. It was already derelict when Molly's mother and aunt were young, so no one knew how old it really was. It had mostly been built of oak beams and wattle or board walls, as had the Hall, but the two end walls had been built of blocks of smoothed stone, like the church, and against one stone wall was a small bread oven, now very rarely used. Years and years ago in a legendary storm which had uprooted trees (including those that had revealed the spring at Rockwell), a huge beech tree had crashed down on the barn cracking the ridge beam of the roof in two, demolishing one end wall of stone and breaking most of the rest of the roof. It had long been abandoned as a barn. Over the years the beech tree had been cut and split, and the serviceable beams and rafters had been dragged away to furnish materials for other buildings, and year by year ivy and honeysuckle had grown over the ruin, and nettles and elder had flourished inside. Owls had made nests among the remaining rotting beams and semi-wild cats from Down the Common cottages had bred in the gloomy green hollows. Marion had sometimes gone down there and peered into the dark interior where long pale green tendrils of plants starved of light hung down in thick curtains, and the spongy floor at her feet was sour with owl droppings and stank of cats. It was an eerie place, one to be avoided.

But the bread oven was too rare an asset to reject, and with the company of the other two women, Marion would take advantage of it. They had to slash a path to it with sickles through the cow parsley and docks, and then pull strands of ivy, old convolvulus, goose grass and brambles from the semi-domed roof. Then Hilda, by far the most agile of the three, had climbed up and pulled the creepers from the short chimney. They had cleared it, removed the loose arch-shaped stone which was its door and swept out the inside of the oven. Then Hilda and Marion had gone back to their cottage for wood, kindling and a glowing log, which Marion carried in an old iron pot. They filled the oven with fuel and lit it. Then back to Molly's cottage where she, on a good broad tree stump by the door, was kneading the great lumps of dough made from their three contributions of flour. It was Marion who possessed the newest bucket in which to convey the dough down to the oven. It was very heavy and she and Molly carried it between them with a long stick through the holes near the rim. The oven hot, they had raked out the ashes as best they could and divided the dough into lumps. Those for Marion were marked with a cross, those for Hilda with two parallel lines, Molly's with a triangle. They slid them with the help of a spade into the oven and all three together had lifted the stone door back into place.

The pile of hot ashes at Marion's feet gave her another idea. She had pulled off her outer dress of grey-brown tightly woven wool, stiff with all the oozings of babies, and, wearing only her inner dress of once-white wool more loosely woven, had gone to the stream below the cottages.

Here she had spread her dress in the partly shallow water, and had trodden on it, squeezing the muddy water through the fabric with her bare feet. The water was horribly cold and the wind blew very chilly on her bare arms and down her neck. She had pulled the sodden dress out and laying it on the bank, deep in new grass, wild peppermint and cresses, and trod on it again to squeeze out as much water as possible. Then she had walked back along the ditch and, seeing a low ash twig almost horizontal across her path, had hung her dress over it and wrung out as much water as she had strength to do.

Back at the oven, Hilda and Molly were sitting idly on tufts of grass, warming their feet at the ashes and gossiping peacefully. They told Marion she was mad, but helped her to hang her dress on a branch above the ashes, and later when the oven was opened and the bread pulled out, they helped her to spread her dress over the still warm stones of the oven roof. Now, looking back at yesterday's activities, Marion wondered if she had been foolish to use so much firewood in this baking, and to use up most of her store of flour for this delicious bread that would only last their three households a few days. But the other two women had encouraged her, and each other, and they had all shared a sense of achievement. They knew from years of experience that sometimes in May flour or corn, carefully saved and eked out from the previous harvest, could be found to have gone mouldy and so be wasted.

They had previously discussed whether they should involve Small Sarah in this breadmaking, but Molly had slipped into her filthy cottage on some pretext and looked into her flour-chest and found it half full of damp mouldy flour and mouse droppings. 'It will only spoil our bread to use any of that,' she had said, and they all agreed to ignore the feckless family.

Last night Marion had looked back on the day's activities. She had four large loaves in the mouse-proof chest and her dress had been washed. And, as she had laid in bed, a damp-wool pepperminty smell had wafted up.

If yesterday had yielded achievement, today, alone with Alice, Marion's intermittent uneasiness persisted. As she had stood in the garden, idly registering in her mind that slugs had been eating the newly sprouting peas, she had seen Hilda with a long hooked stick over her shoulder, followed by her two orange-headed little girls, going slowly up an overgrown path into the forest, and she felt this to be a rebuke to herself. *Sensible* Hilda, having used wood for yesterday's bread baking, was going into the woods when no one was likely to see to collect and bring back dead branches to replace her depleted log pile. I should do the same, thought Marion, but idleness seemed heavy in her legs.

Away in the village she heard a sudden hysteria of dogs barking. A common enough noise, it seemed to go on for longer than usual, and this irritated her. She knew she would need water before the day was out, so she picked up a bucket, and Alice in the other arm, and walked down the path to the stream.

The water-fetching place was below Molly's garden. The stream here had an extra deep pool and an old willow stump grew aslant it. Peter had built out the bank with a few large stones and had made a small pulley-wheel spinning on an oak dowel plugged into the top of the willow stump. A rope, running over the wheel, was attached to the handle of a bucket. Kneeling on the stones, you could tip the bucket in the water till it filled and sank, then, rising, you would pull on the rope till the bucket could be eased on to the stones. You could then fill your own bucket from it. Marion had fetched water thus daily for years, except when the stream was frozen. It was almost impossible not to get your feet wet when doing so.

It was just as she reached the willow stump that she heard a call from across the stream, and on the bank opposite saw one of the Fletcher boys who worked with Peter.

'Hoi,' he called. 'Message from Peter. He says Chris Foxcap's come and will you bring over the bag of bent nails hanging under the shelf under the corn pot. There's thirty-seven nails in it.'

She called after him but he was already scampering away. This news changed Marion's plan for the day. Water fetching could wait. At the top of the path she met Molly.

'Chris Foxcap's come,' Marion said.

'Thought so,' said Molly, always wise after information. 'Said so to myself when I heard the dogs. That's no ordinary dog-fight – those dogs sounded wild – '

Marion broke in with, 'I've got to take stuff to Peter at once,' and picking up Alice again she got back to her cottage.

The leather bag, heavy with bent nails, extracted from rotting or burnt beams and carefully preserved, was hanging exactly where Peter had said. She sat down, tipped the nails on to her lap and counted them. There were thirty-seven. It was like Peter to know and to be so exact. She put them back into the leather bag. Alice interrupted her, 'Ugh-Ugh'.

'Go out,' said Marion. 'Feet apart. Hold up your dress. Squat down.' Alice obeyed as she was at an age when a precise routine appealed.

Marion was loathe to waste Chris Foxcap's visit by having nothing to mend, so she pulled down from a hook under the hen's shelf the leaky old iron pot in which she had taken the log to the oven yesterday. It had a crack in the base which, though almost invisible, allowed liquid to seep out, thereby not only wasting the soup but risking putting out the fire as well.

'Come, Alice, into the pot with you. We're going to the village.'

Being swung along in a pot was a novelty which Alice relished though it was an awkward and heavy burden for Marion. As she crossed the bridge she could see many of the village dogs tied up under the oak tree, trembling and snapping at each other, and on the other side of the path most of the village wives were collected in a semi-circle round the drinking trough. In their midst stood Chris Foxcap, his laden donkey drinking and his brindled lurcher bitch with mad yellow eyes and uncertain temper, circling his legs uneasily.

Chris Foxcap was an itinerant tinker who arrived in the village sometimes twice a year, sometimes only once in two years. His approach was always from the steep forests above Rockwell. No one else ever came or went that way – the way to the rest of the world lay down the valley to the known village of Rutherford and thence on and on to the other end of the world. But to come from over the unknown forested hills – that in itself added strangeness to Chris Foxcap. The villagers hardly ever saw anyone who was not born in the village. He was an alien, a stranger, intriguing, frightening, but also an entertainment.

To Marion people were a natural part of the earth. As the deer that lived in the forest, the hares that ran in the fields, the thrush that sang in the ash tree, the spiders that hid in the cottage thatch, so to her thinking were people, a product of the earth, sustained by it while they lived, returned to it when they died. These particular fields and woods around her, had, to her mind, produced these particular people, the villagers whom she knew and saw daily. Beyond, all was chaos and unknown.

It was against these unifying feelings that Chris Foxcap struck. It was almost horrific that he was attached to no land, had no rights to any harvest, owed no man any dues. He was free from all obligations, unprotected by any community, adrift in the world, an orphan of nature, and yet, extraordinarily, he did not mind. He always appeared cheerful and whistled as he worked. Marion could only think of him with an unusual mixture of revulsion, pity and curiosity.

Physically, he was revolting. His peculiar jogging gait, not running, not walking, but suitable for moving easily over rough heath and ferns in the pathless woods, leading his trotting donkey, made him stand out among the slow-trudging villagers, whose gait was geared to the pace of their oxen. His face was blackened, the skin pitted with innumerable scars from flying sparks as he bellowed the charcoal fires. His beard, a wiry brown, was patchily singed the same way. His eyes were dark and quick, his glance over the village audience eager and appraising, so unlike the steady cow-like stares of the villagers. The way he would whirl his cloak around his shoulders covering up the bundles on his back, so deft, so quick, made him strange to the villagers who hunched their shoulders and bowed their heads as they pulled their cloaks around them against the cold.

His speech was strange too. Marion recalled how, many years ago when she was a girl, he had arrived one burning hot harvest day and had said, 'Give me a beever, for the love of God,' in his sing-song intonation, still imitated by some of the Rockwell boys. And when 'beever' was not understood, he had made a gesture of drinking. All agreed it was a funny way of talking. He exuded a strange smell, partly derived from the half-cured foxtails which, twisted together, formed his hat. A human stink was hardly noticed by the villagers but this strange animal odour they found repulsive, and it, together with the yellow-eyed bitch, sent all the dogs in the village into paroxysms of barking.

This alien who arrived over the hills, unattached to their people, could easily have evoked a malaise of hostility, and it was Chris Foxcap's unexpected professed Christianity that cooled any hostility. It had been years ago that he had arrived one Saturday evening and had spent the night in the Hall with his dog at his feet in the straw under one of the benches. In the morning he had started to get out his equipment when it was pointed out to him it was Sunday.

'Sunday, is it?' he had said, 'Well, there's a blessed thing. I'm to go to Mass with you all, am I?' Someone had asked with some surprise if he were a Christian.

'Surely I'm a Christian, born on St Christopher's Day, him that carried the Holy Child over the stream. My father had me at church the day after

I was born, so he said.'

'Where was that?' the priest had asked him.

'I'm telling you what my father told me, but I don't remember it myself. Do you remember where it was you was christened, Father? Babies don't look round and say, "This is Rye," or "This is Pevensey," or "This is . . . Rutherford," do they?'

This wide knowledge of the alien world added envy and horror to the mystified minds. But Chris had gone to Mass that day. He had pulled off his fox cap at the church door and had knelt down and said Amen and crossed himself with all the others, a real Christian they had had to admit. But a certain mystery remained in their uneasy hearts. Later that day one of the village boys had asked him where he had been born.

'Under a hedge.'

'What hedge?'

'Well, boy, one hedge looks much like another, specially when you first open your eyes and have never seen a hedge before. But, so they told me, they took me to church and had me christened. It was the church at Rutherford to my way of thinking because that is St Christopher's church, as yours here is St Paul's church. I think St Paul journeyed here with your stone cross many, many years ago and had your church built, same way St Christopher came to Rutherford and there he met the Holy Child and carried him across the stream. There's a picture of him on the wall in Rutherford church. There he stands as some of you must have seen, a really big man, with his tunic pulled up and his bare legs in the water – swirling about it is, just below his knees, fish or two in it – he has a big face and a woolly beard and he twists round to look at the Child on his shoulder – nice-looking little chap Christ was – and St Christopher holds a big pole with leaves sticking out at the top to steady himself in the water. Well, that's what St Christopher did at Rutherford, so that's why he has his church there.'

This recital had been listened to with some awe by the older men there, some of whom had been to Rutherford church and recognized the description of the wall painting.

'Did St Christopher really carry the Christ Child over our stream at Rutherford?' one of the children had asked.

'Surely, boy, he did,' Chris said. 'Between his bare legs and the pole you can see the river bank behind him and there are willow trees on the bank just like there are in Rutherford, so that's where he carried the Child across. Of course, that was before they built their stone bridge there.'

But today Chris Foxcap was in the village to work. Ingratiating himself with all, master of the situation, he was unloading the willow panniers from his donkey and Tom was helping.

'There we go, easy does it, now this one, wo-oh-steady-Caesar, there we go, there's the water trough, Caesar, so have a good drink, and if you have such a thing, Tom, as a manger of oats and a nice straw bed in your stable? It's a long time since Caesar had a good rest.'

Chris unpacked his long iron pincers, his hammers, his long-handled bellows, his iron brazier and bags of charcoal. Sir Hugh and Dame Margaret appeared, with Magda unwillingly carrying her struggling terrier, and Chris bowed to them in a way they would have laughed at had he not been so self-assured.

'Good day, m'lord, God keep you, m'lady, good day, miss, pots to mend, pots to mend, you know the old song,' (they did not) and when Joan brought out a jar of the best ale and he had drunk it and complimented her on it (compliments were rare in Joan's life), and praised Milly for keeping her iron pots so clean inside (they were not), everyone around had succumbed, unwillingly, to his exotic charm.

Joan brought from the Hall's fire a burning log on a shovel and dropped it into the brazier. Chris's charcoal was heaped on it and with Ed-me-boy bellowing steadily the charcoal became red-hot. One by one the cracked iron pots that the villagers had brought were made to glow on the brazier, lifted in the long tongs to the mounting block stones along side to be hammered, back on the charcoal for reheating and so on for hours, and most of the time Chris kept up a running commentary.

'Keep bellowing, Ed, not quite hot enough – stand back, children, you don't want a face like mine, do you – there we go . . .' much hammering, 'that should do it, keep steady with the bellowing – no, not enough yet . . . keep that dog *away*, Miss Magda, no – can't do anything with *that* pot, good lady, that's not a crack, bottom's nearly through all round, no, sorry, mend I can, not remake. Mind the sparks, get back, m'lord, you don't want your good cloak burnt, whew – any more of that good ale, Dame Joan? Yes, you're Peter Carpenter, aren't you? I remember you – nails all bent? Not a difficult job, hand them over – yes, good lady, I'll do a handle for your pan next . . .' and so on and so on with pauses now and then to concentrate on the work, to drink and to whistle.

After a while Dame Margaret went up the yard with Joan and they came back carrying a board with bread and lumps of cheese on it and a bowl of new milk and there was a pause in the bellowing and hammering while they all sat down round the mounting block and ate. Milly filled up a tall earthenware pot from the bowl and passed it round and all the women and children had drinks of fresh cow's milk. It was a lovely change from the routine drudgery of their lives to sit about like this, chatting among themselves, they and their children entertained by the rare sight of the tinker at work, and having bread and milk brought round to them.

Marion's old cooking pot had been mended, or at least it had been treated, and it remained to be seen whether, when it cooled, the crack in the base had indeed been closed. Alice became restive so with the warm pot in her hand and Alice on the other arm, she told Peter she was going home.

'Yes,' he said, closely watching Chris hammering out one of his nails with short deft strokes. She realized his mind was elsewhere, and she departed.

Pausing on the bridge, she looked back. The crowd of people, heavy brown-clothed people, still stood round the mounting stones. Their conversation had returned to its usual sluggish speed. The dogs, tired of inactivity, had mostly lain down in the oak's shade and were sleeping. Still the sound of Chris's hammer, striking hot iron on stone, rang out, filling the whole valley.

Back at Down the Common Marion met Hilda.

'Chris Foxcap's come,' she said.

'Yes,' said Hilda, 'I heard the hammering. I was up in the woods with the girls. You know that big oak that we saw last year – with the top all dead? A bit beyond the big clearing? Well, lots of the dead top has fallen off. I dragged back as much as I could. I wish the girls were bigger, but if your Peterkin went up he'd get lots more.'

Marion asked if she had any iron for mending.

'No – but I could do with a new knife or two. I don't know if Dick heard the hammering – he didn't come down.'

Marion went into her cottage, leaving Alice outside. She wondered if the fire were out. She put down a hand and could feel a faint warmth in the ashes, but felt too tired to bother with it. She looked up at the sooty beams above the fire and knew she should get a knife and scrape the soot off, letting it fall into . . . what? Some dish, if she had one – and take the soot out to put round the pea plants in the garden. 'I'm too tired,' she said aloud to herself, and sat down on the log which made a seat outside the cottage door under the overhanging eaves, and stared down the garden and up into the forest beyond. The beech trees were now in new leaf and the lower branches shifted their broad plates of foliage one over the other, in and out of the sunshine, as the soft wind moved them.

This is *my* place, she thought, *my* earth making *my* peas grow, *my* apple blossom making apples for *me*; *my* cottage for shelter and sleep; *my* child sitting at my feet scooping up the little mud-free stones that lie in a line under where the eaves drip; *my* child, and all of this is hers too. And in the village is strange Chris Foxcap who has nothing – no place that is his home – nothing. His donkey is old, his bitch hasn't much life left in her – but what are they? He has no place to rest in – ever.

Marion's lassitude persisted. She leant back against the cottage's wattle wall, uncomfortable as it was, contemplating her own unusual weakness and wondered if she were pregnant again, but her thoughts wandered off that subject to more immediate ones. When Peterkin came home she would send him with a rope up to the wood to the old oak and its dead branches left there by Hilda.

Thinking of Hilda quickly took her thoughts to Dick somewhere up on the moors with the sheep. She never forgot that she had once been in love with Dick, perhaps only a little in love but it had been such a new experience. Though that was a long time ago and she was, undoubtedly, a faithful wife to Peter, thinking about Dick was always a private recreation. Bringing to her memory the vision of his broad red face, his sky-coloured eyes and his orange curls was always a consolation on dull hard days. That he had always wanted Hilda for his wife she knew well, and she went over in her mind their strange courtship many years ago.

Childhood marriages were not formally made in the village – the number of infant deaths would have made this a vain practice – but mothers, chatting together, would agree that if little Ned and baby Jilly survived, it would be *nice* if they married, providing always that Sir Hugh agreed. For those who survived until adolescence the question would be discussed again and fathers would concern themselves and talk to other fathers, and as such matters were publicly spoken of, by the time the children reached maturity there was a general understanding of who would marry whom. The young couples grew up knowing what was expected of them, and rarely objected.

They all knew full well what a limited choice there was.

Such an engagement, loose but publicly known, had existed between Hilda and Wilfred from Down Mill field. Wilfred was the elder surviving son of Widow Annie, and the brother of violent Dobbin, a man in possession of good land in the village. He lived with his mother and had reached the age when he should marry. He was a gangly, dark-haired man with a lumpy nose and a wide crooked mouth, surly in manner and uncertain in temper, like his brother. Hilda, then about sixteen, was the only child of Hal, a widower, living on the Green and depending since his wife's death on the services of Hilda. He had always been a quiet man and in widowerhood had become withdrawn and hardly spoke, working ceaselessly in field and garden and in winter making willow baskets of marvellous strength and neatness.

He had acquiesced in a few monosyllables to Dick when Dick had asked him for Hilda as his wife, and had not referred to any agreement with Wilfred. No one in the village knew how or when the romance between Dick and Hilda had begun. Dick was already head shepherd, spending days at a time up on the hills, and Hilda had never been noticed slipping up between the gorse bushes to be with him. However they arranged it, their announcement that they wanted to marry caused a flutter of amazed gossip round the village.

'She can't do it. What's her father up to? She's promised to Wilf, isn't she?'

'That's what happens to a motherless girl. Hal never notices what goes on under his nose.'

'She's a sly quiet one, if ever there was one.'

'Still, Hal and Widow Annie had arranged it – and I suppose Sir Hugh agreed. You can't have young people taking matters into their own hands like this.'

'Where'd we be if we all did just as we like?'

'Wilf looked black as thunder when Annie told him.'

'What did she tell him?'

'Why, how Dick had gone to Sir Hugh and said he wanted to marry Hilda – can't think why with her freckly face. There's better girls coming on at Rockwell if he'd waited a year or two. Of course, Sir Hugh thinks a lot of Dick, been so good with the lambs and all that, though he knew Hilda was promised to Wilf. And Milly, she sneaked off from the loom shed and listened and heard him say he must think it over, as he always does – means he must ask M'Dame – and she, Milly I mean, went and told Annie and Annie runs to the Hall – oho, there was a to-do. She wants to complain to Sir Hugh, but he'd gone away to the forest and she pours it all out to M'Dame, and M'Dame keeps a still face, not a smile, not a sneer, yet you know she never could stand Annie. Just says Sir Hugh's the one to decide, say no more now, I'll talk to Sir Hugh, she says.'

And so the gossip went on, fed by frequent reports from sharp-eared Milly – how Dame Margaret told Sir Hugh what a valuable worker Dick was, how desirable it was to keep him in a good mood and faithful, how obviously he was in love with Hilda who was a decent girl in spite of the freckles, and what an ugly uncouth lout Wilf was. A marriage which was so much against the wish of the wife – and M'Dame knew this because she had already had a talk with Hilda privately in the orchard – was unlikely to produce strong babies and a providently run house. There was no advantage to anyone but Wilf in allowing such a marriage to take place, and plenty of disadvantages, so let the lovers have their way. And Sir Hugh, a little wearied by his wife's eloquence, agreed. As all knew, he was always ready to be persuaded by Dame Margaret. So when Annie bustled along to hear what she called Justice and the Law, she only heard that Sir Hugh had agreed that Dick should marry Hilda.

So they had married, and had settled in the cottage Down the Common next to Marion's. Old Annie had sulked, but not more than usual. A year later there was more drama. Wilf had been cursing and muttering for months and had been lurking about Down the Common when Dick was up in the hills. Marion and Peter had seen him several times and had told him to be off and find a wife among the village girls, but he had only cursed them and swore he would be all square with Dick one day.

Then rumours reached Dick, who came down from the hills one evening and found Wilf hiding by the fence under the big ash tree, and shouted at him, and Wilf swung a big club at Dick but missed. Dick picked him up by the shoulders, pinning his arms to his sides with his great hands, and shook him, like a dog with a rat, and threw him down in a patch of nettles and shouted if he ever came round Hilda again he would break every bone in his body. So Wilf crawled away back to the village, cursing, and Dick chopped the club into firewood that evening.

Then Wilf started more rumours, much assisted by Annie, that the baby Hilda was carrying was *his* baby, let Dick think what he liked. This story was repeated so often that the villagers came to wonder if it were true. Then Meg was born, with her head covered in orange fluffy curls and Wilf was the laughing stock of the whole village, and that did not improve his temper.

These reminiscences had entertained Marion as she sat. She eased her position on the log and lay back against the cottage again. It was so peaceful. How she relished this unusual idleness.

The thought of the orange curls of Dick's daughters and his own brassy mop brought to Marion's mind the long familiar story of how this golden hair had arrived in the village. She had heard the story often in her childhood from her mother, and at times entertained herself with retelling it in her mind or to her children, using her mother's phrases, and with her mother's intonation resonating in her memory. It was the story of Golden-haired Osyth.

It was a long time ago, Marion's mother would begin, before any of us were born, in the time of Sir Hugh's grandfather (or sometimes his great-grandfather or even Sir Hugh's distant forebears), that the Lord of the Manor fell sick. He had two sons and the elder, Crispin, said he would look after the farm, and his mother and care for his father while he lived as all good sons do. But the younger son, Will the Tall – a wild, unsteady boy they all thought him – would go off to seek his fortune in the wide world. (Here in the story there was often a diatribe against impetuous and foolish youth.) One fine spring morning he put on a new pair of boots straight from the tanner, and his mother gave him a loaf of bread and half a cheese, and with scarcely a wave to the old people or his brother, off he went on foot down the path by the stream towards Rutherford. (All journeys from the village went to Rutherford, any alternative was to go into the forests and lose your way before nightfall.)

Well, nothing more was heard of him all that year.

When spring came again his mother mourned him afresh and his father's hair whitened further and his elder brother worked unceasingly in the fields and never complained and no one noticed how thin and worn he was getting. And when the next winter came on the old man could not stand the cold and just before Christmas he died, and was buried in the churchyard, just to the east near the path, and all the village mourned for him.

Now the January that followed was the coldest anyone could remember. The snow came down like daggers of ice, freezing where it landed. Sheep died frozen to the ground in caves of snow, birds' feet were frozen to the branches, and as the wind blew in the willows the lumps of ice along every twig crashed together. You never heard a sound like that before. One morning the Dame, still mourning her husband, saw that Crispin had not returned at noon and the whole village went out searching in the snow and they found him lying across a ditch with his beard frozen to his hood, quite dead. Ah, there was lamenting in the village then.

Then when spring was coming, one sunny morning a jingle of harness was heard along the path by the orchard, and behold, there came two horses with two riders on each, and the first rider jumped down at the door of the Hall and called out, 'Father! Mother! Crispin! Here's Will back at last.' When only his mother came out to greet him and told him of the deaths of the others, he wept.

But not for long. 'See, Mother,' he said. 'I've brought home a lovely wife,' and he lifted her down from the horse – and she *was* lovely, no one could deny that. She was almost as tall as Will and she had a green gown down to the floor of such soft wool no one had seen the like, and she wore a gold ring on her finger that shone in the sunlight, and she had a sweet face like a hedge rose. As she pulled off her hood, her golden hair, all curls, fell below her waist. No one had ever seen the like.

And on the other horse, a small pony, was Will's servant, a nice fresh-faced boy who later proved the best bow and arrow maker we'd ever had, and the young wife's little sister, a girl of twelve or thirteen with the same lovely hair, yellow as gorse.

While all stood round gaping with surprise, Will took the tall lady by the hand saying, 'Mother, this is Osyth, my wife. She and I will look after the Manor and the Hall and care for you all the days of your life, and this small one is Edith, her sister, who will be as a little daughter to you,' and he was right.

And his mother said, 'Where have you been, my son Will, all these two years and where did you find this golden girl?'

So he told her and all the villagers standing round how he had walked down the valley to Rutherford where he helped for a bit in the building of a stone bridge over the river, and then he had walked on southwards, keeping the sunrise on his left over a great country they called the Weald, a country of forests and fields and farms and again farms and fields and forests, and then still to the south he came to a great line of smooth hills with no trees, just a hawthorn or two in the valleys, and covered in short grass and there were sheep everywhere. And the earth, just a hand's breadth down was all hard and white. Well, the villagers didn't believe that, but, he said, sure it was white. And he walked to the top of the hills and on the other side he could see the sea – water – water such as you've never seen, as far as the eye could reach, ending at a straight line where it reached the sky at the end of the world. Well, you can imagine if the villagers didn't believe white earth they wouldn't believe in water reaching to the edge of the world. He had gone down the smooth green hill till he reached the sea and – you know how when the wind is fresh and the millpond is full and it is all ripples and they splash on the edge among the stones and grass? The villagers said they'd seen ripples on the millpond, but, says Will, the ripples on the sea were as big as a cottage and crashed down on the pebbles on the shore with a sound of thunder. They didn't believe that either!

He went on to tell how he had walked along the shore and came to a river estuary where the river ran into the sea and there were houses and boats tied to posts on the river edge, and there was a man on a boat fixing ropes and sails. He got talking to this man and, to cut a long story short, he lodged with this man in his house by the river and worked for him mending his boats and the like and the man's wife treated him well for many months.

Now this man had sailed his boat over the sea, still to the south and he said no, that line was not the end of the world, that over the sea was another land. It had white chalk edges too, and grass and sheep and people growing corn just like everywhere, except they spoke in a funny way, and the sailor wanted Will to go with him across the sea. He was taking a shipload of wool and would bring back barrels of salt fish. But Will was already in love with Osyth, the eldest of the sailor's many daughters, so Will did not want to go. The man sailed off with a local boy or two instead, and Will stayed with his wife and Osyth and the other girls and he ploughed their field and dug their garden and cut their wood and mended their byres and caught fishes, big as . . . (a gesture followed) and all the family liked him. When the sailor and his boat came back at the end of the summer with a load of barrels of salt and salt fish and woven hemp and ropes and some gold rings, Will asked if he could have Osyth as his wife and take her back to his village and his old parents and brother, and Osyth was willing enough, and her father gave her a gold ring. She wanted to take one of her sisters with her as company, but only Edith, the youngest, had the spirit to go, so that's how they came to the village.

The villagers always said she talked a bit strange and so did Edith and the boy, Fletcher, but these last two soòn learnt to talk like ordinary people, but Osyth sounded strange even to the end of her life.

Osyth brought with her, in her arms, an osier cage full of young chickens and they grew up into fat brown hens and two splendid cocks, bigger than the little white hens we'd always had until then, and still do. She could spin the finest thread and she taught the girls weaving such as they'd never done before, and for all she was so slender and pale she was strong and healthy and before long she gave the old Dame her first grandson, a strong pink baby with gold fluff all over its head! Well, the old Dame died soon after but she died happy, for Will looked after the Manor well and the crops increased.

Over the years they had many children of which five boys and three girls grew up and many of those had this golden hair like their mother and were tall big men, and Edith too, later, married a free man in the village and had several children as well, and most of them married in the village and that is why even to this day every now and then some children are born with golden curly hair.

The atmosphere of the story and the memory of her mother's voice faded and Marion realized suddenly the passage of time and her aching back against the wattle wall. Peter had appeared round the corner of the cottage with Alice in his arms.

'I found her down by Molly's,' he said, half accusingly. 'You shouldn't let her go by herself. That old dog of Marge's is none too safe with children.'

Marion accepted both the rebuke and Alice and bestirred herself, bellowed the fire, put more quern-ground beans into the pot on it, and listened to Peter talking of Chris Foxcap's activities, stories and skills as he rehung the bag of straightened nails under the shelf. No one in the village was quite untouched by the arrival of the stranger.

Later that night, after Peterkin had come home and they had had their warm bean soup and the lovely bread made yesterday, they went down the garden to inspect the peas and what the slugs had done to them.

'Scrape some soot down,' Peter had said, 'and put some round each plant – it usually helps.'

They went to bed, and as usual Peter had quickly fallen asleep, even before the blackbird in the ash above the cottage had finished his performance of dusk-song. Marion lay awake long, still with a feeling of unease and lassitude that again made her wonder if she were pregnant. Long after the birds were silent, total darkness crept into the cottage and Marion slept.

She woke suddenly, with a feeling that she had only briefly been asleep. Peter snored slowly by her. Both the children were silent. A sudden twinge in her abdomen, as though small red-hot pincers, a little version of Chris Foxcap's, were pulling at her guts, had awakened her.

At least it means there's no baby coming, she thought, but her thoughts were very secret. She knew people expected her to have another child. Only the previous week, Polly Fletcher, stopping her on the Green to admire Alice, had said, 'And when's the next one coming? You've only got the lame boy now besides this little girl, haven't you?'

Marion, as so often, was aware of a secret dilemma. Every pregnancy meant risking her life at the birth, and thereby risking the welfare of all previous children. Could one really trust a father, or a stepmother, or some briefly conscientious neighbours, with the upbringing of one's children? Should one sacrifice the well nurturing of the many to the one new life? She had once tried to explain this dilemma to Peter, but he had dismissed it as 'women's worryings' and so thence forward the worry was buried in her heart, and doubtless in many other women's hearts too.

So secretly Marion was glad that she was not pregnant. She pulled up a handful of straw between her legs and summoned up her resolution to endure a night of pain.

JUNE

Insects as small as dust are never done
Wi' glittering dance and reeling in the sun
And green wood fly and blossom haunting bee
Are never weary of their melody

It was a beautiful morning for Sheep-shearing Day. The air was still and sweet as Marion went to the open door of the cottage and looked down the garden to the rising forest beyond, now thick with delicate new leaves, dainty green in beeches, subdued green in ashes, bronze-gold in oaks, and now all so thick in their greenness that the dark yews were almost concealed. The bluebells had gone but their rich juicy green leaves still stood in sheets up the hillside under the smooth beeches.

Closer to, in the garden the rows of peas and broad beans, neat orderly rows because Peter had planted them, had mostly come up, defeating the slugs, and were growing fast, and small cabbage plants for next year's eating were daily increasing in size. The apple tree was now in full leaf, the blossom gone.

Marion anticipated the day with pleasure. Sheep-shearing was a festival, and cold or wet weather could, and often had spoilt everyone's pleasure. It was a holiday, so everyone said, traditionally, though no holiday ever seemed to lessen work for Marion nor, in this case, for Peter.

He had been up before dawn, pulled Peterkin off the bed and the two of them had gone to the village to put up all the hurdles on the Green into which the sheep would be herded during the day. As usual there never seemed to be enough hurdles and for the past two weeks Peter had been making others, sending his boys into the copses to cut ever more ash saplings for the purpose.

Alice was sitting peacefully by the log, pulling at the grass and half singing to herself, so Marion took a bucket and went down to the water-place to fetch a bucketful. Molly's house was quiet. She wondered if Molly and the two old women were already at the Green, but she thought it unlikely that the old ones could walk that far. Even their old, ill-tempered dog was quiet, slowly scratching itself by the gate. Hilda and Dick's cottage was deserted but Marion knew they had been up and about as early as Peter. No sound came from the Plowrights' derelict-looking place.

Marion filled up the hens' drinking butt, an old wooden bucket half-sunk into the earth. She threw down some rough husky meal for them, then fastened her door with a leather thong and collected Alice. They walked past the cottages again, down the slope and out through the little gate on to the Common. The path was hard earth, trodden bare by their passing feet but each side of it was edged with clumps of cow parsley, thistles with little mauve tufts on them and sorrel with reddish spikes. Marion watched Alice, stumping along on her bare feet, out-topped on both sides with the abundant greenery. When they emerged from the area of small birches, the path was edged with tall grass, lush green below, and interlaced with blue vetches and pink convolvulus, and above them the grass flowers, paler and browner, bending a little to the breeze that brushed over them. A few clumps of marguerite daisies and tall buttercups stood amid the grass, and white bladder campions, with their hollow ovals of whitey green, swayed with the grass.

'Er-er,' demanded Alice, pointing to buttercups.

Marion picked one and gave it her saying, 'Buttercup.'

'Buckercuck,' said Alice.

Marion corrected her but Alice's attention was already on carefully destroying the flower. She pulled off each petal with delicate movements of her tiny fingers until there was just the little green spiked Hercules club at the end of the long stalk. Alice, highly pleased with herself, went trotting on ahead. A little further on they met their goat, tethered by a long rope to a tree and in reach of the stream and plentiful browsing. Marion spoke to it and rubbed its shoulder. Now that the kid was weaned the goat was more tame.

As they approached the bridge Marion picked Alice up and carried her up the log steps and across the planks. She paused to look down on the barely moving water below her, again delighting in the mild air and the prospect of the festivities. She remembered also that she would meet the Rockwell families again and that she had not seen much of them, except briefly after Sunday Mass, for some time, not since her niece Lisa, from the Mill, had married Martin Rockwell the previous year. She knew that both families would walk down through the fields from Rockwell Farm, Wat the Tall and Nancy, his wife, Martin of course with Lisa, and the other son whom Marion hoped would marry her next niece, Ellen, and all their other children, mostly strong, good-looking young people. And then the other family: Edward, Wat's younger brother and his wife, Red Mary, who was Dick's sister – she would not have missed a shearing for anything – and all their small children, and possibly they might bring Old Lambert, Loppy Lambert's father, if they could get a cart down the path for him. She hoped so, as her father and Old Lambert always liked a good natter together.

Anticipating great activity in food preparation once she had joined the crowd at the Hall, Marion continued to pause on the bridge, looking down at the still water the other side of it, and thought of the Rockwells. She had heard stories of the origins of the farm at Rockwell all her life, and mused over them now.

The stories always started with the Great Storm. That storm had occurred since the arrival of Golden-haired Osyth, so its myth had not the same depth and potency as Osyth's story. Besides, a storm, great and damaging as it might be, was still just a storm, whereas the story of Osyth with all its strange background had a rare romance that a tale of wind could never evoke. Still, it *was* a storm, the violence of which had never been seen since. The greatest effect of the storm was not in the village but elsewhere, up in the forests and in the fields. Now, if you walked through the village keeping the Hall and then the church and graveyard on your left, and kept on till you passed the Great Barn (itself part built from an oak uprooted on the Green) and left the haystacks and the open sheds on your right, you came out into the open land with Hall fields left and Mill fields right. All the way the land sloped gently up hill, and the path went on and on up through Great Field. In those days the Great Field was not so great, only part of it was ploughed and as it got steeper it was a rougher pasture with hawthorns and broom and wild roses among the grass, and the ploughs never reached there. Then suddenly a point of very steep land came down into this rough pasture and this point was covered in big forest trees, oaks and ashes and beeches, and no one bothered about it for it was far too steep ever to be brought under a plough or to provide pasture. But soon after the Great Storm one of Osyth's tall young sons was walking up there and found that one of the huge oaks growing on this steep point had been blown over and lay across the slope among the hawthorns and hazels, but – and this was the unusual sight – when the boy examined the huge vertical disc of roots at the end of the fallen trunk, he found that they had exposed a wall of smooth rock, higher than his head, wider than it was high. From all the cracks in this rock wall, from which some torn tree roots still projected, a clear water bubbled out and soaked into the moist ferny ground under the fallen trunk. After such a storm and the days and nights of deluging rain, there is water everywhere, but when a month or so later, and a *dry* month at that, the sweet clear water still ran from the cracks in the rock, the boy got his brothers along to show them. They all realized what it meant: where water flowed, men and animals could live.

Of course, back at the Hall, Will the Tall, by then an old man, had been wondering what to do with all his sons. Hubert, the eldest, would stay and manage the Manor, as he already was mostly doing, but the other four, all big strong young men, went up the fields and started to work. They spent a year cutting up the fallen tree and clearing the ground and all the time watching the running water. It never failed them. It ran quicker after heavy rain, but even in a July drought it still ran sweet. So they built a barn, using the main trunk of the fallen oak for its roof ridge, and some cottages for themselves, and one of their sisters joined them, and they mostly married and settled there. The new cottages were built just above the rock face and under other huge oak trees. One of the boys took an iron spike and a mallet and dug out a stone trough at the foot of the rock face to catch the trickles. It was made at an easy height for the animals to drink from and had a wide smooth ledge at one side so that the women could stand their buckets there when they went down for water. They all said it was much easier than having a well or a stream that you had to drag the water up from. Their water was always clean and fresh, running cool into their buckets. No one knew who first called it Rockwell, but the name stuck and the farm there was always known as Rockwell.

It was a special place, of prestige and riches. How and when its legal status arose no one knew or bothered about, but by Marion's time it was an established tradition that the men born at Rockwell were free men – were they not descendants of the Lords of the Manor? – who owed no labour to the Hall. All they owed were a dozen fat hogs every winter, and that was no problem to the Rockwell men as the remaining oaks, wide-spreading mature trees, rained down bushels of ripe acorns into the pigsties every September. Everyone in the village recognized Rockwell bacon as specially rich and tender. The other service Rockwell rendered to the village – and this in Marion's eyes was of such long-standing as to be unquestioned – was that Rockwell always kept a bull, a stallion, a billy goat or two and a few boars (rams were the charge of the Hall's shepherd) so that the Hall farm and the villagers could eat or castrate their male animals at will, knowing that up at Rockwell their female animals could be served for the price of a basket or two of eggs or a tub of butter.

Yes, Rockwell was a special place, far away enough from the Hall to feel a certain freedom and independence, near enough for all the support of the village craftsmen. Life was thought to be easier at Rockwell, and most of the village girls hoped that they would marry a Rockwell boy. Not many could, of course, and several times had the oldest Rockwell man sent his sons off to establish themselves in the village. As was frequently said, 'There's enough water in Rockwell's trough for so many people and animals and if you drink it dry in winter you'd wait two or three days till it's full again, but you drink it dry in summer you may wait two or three *weeks* before it's full again, and are the women and animals to walk a mile there and a mile back to the stream for every mouthful of water?'

So Rockwell remained the barn and the few cottages, and the families, always, so it seemed, people of greater strength and better health than in the village. Their children wandered up into the steep forest behind the cottages and found other rocks, including a couple like tall pillars, one of which had a huge stone ball, four or five feet across, balanced on top of it. All said the Devil must have put it there, for how else could such a huge stone be raised that high? So the Rockwell mothers advised their children to keep away from a place where the Devil obviously kept his playthings.

As the years went by the ploughs in the Great Field went a little further every season up the slope towards Rockwell, and the hawthorns and wild roses vanished, and the pasture and cornfields increased to each side of the sharp rocky point. Now the ploughed land almost reached the foot of the steep slope where the water still trickled down into the stone trough.

Marion looked at the village, her familiar village, before her. The Hall, that great dark building with the licheny shutters thrown open from the high windows, the bleached thatch roof, the row of sheds just visible beyond – it was all too ordinary a sight to take her eye. But to the right stood the huge spreading oak on the Green with its tiny bronze leaves now greening – that was a pleasure to look at. And the flock of grey geese nosing in the grass before her with gawky fluffy goslings waddling about gave her a feeling of anticipation of richness to come.

Beyond the Hall and church the Hall field sloped gently up, divided into its accustomed strips, thin lines of lush grass with the ploughed earth in between them, now scummed over with newly growing wheat. To the right, beyond the Green and the semicircle of cottages lay the slope of Mill field, now fallow, to be cut for hay later. The grass was deep with buttercups and tall daisies, lady's-smocks and plantains, campions and borage. Marion knew that if she knelt down and parted the grasses with her hands she would see little speedwells and stitchworts and potentillas. Away to the right and half hidden by rising ground and twists in the stream, by hedges of hawthorns thickened by strips of white blossom along every twig and elder bushes dark green with pools of white lace, was just visible the Mill's roof – the place where she was born and where her brother, Simon, and his family lived. Beyond the Mill and beyond the marshy area which part-drained into the millpond, was the wilder land of poor earth, stones and thin grass, of heather, gorse, wild roses and brambles, with every now and then a windblown beech, thickly branched, and a bent hawthorn. Here and there in little dells of soft richer grass were the little turf shelters where the shepherds lived, sharing these low hovels with sheep and newborn lambs.

As a girl at the Mill Marion had sometimes wandered up on to these pastures, pretending to look for a lost goat but really to have a look at Dick. As to all the girls of her age, to Marion Dick Shepherd with his golden curls and blue eyes had been a cynosure. She had not known it at the time but Dick's eyes were already set on that small thin dark freckled Hilda, younger than Marion, and something of a mystery to the rest of the village. Marion had loved Dick very secretly, and then later, her father had encouraged Peter the Carpenter to court her and had told Marion she couldn't do better than marry a sensible hard-working kindly man like Peter – Peter had at that time just completed a great repair and alteration to the Mill's workings – so she had married him and never much regretted it, and had forgotten Dick, or so she had told herself. Only sometimes did she look at him and wish he had loved her.

Marion sighed, partly with regret for what might have been and partly to enjoy the sweet smells of summer. 'Come along, Alice,' she said, and they went up the path to the Hall.

Tom and Ed-me-boy must have been up before cockcrow, for by this time the logs were burning hot below the bread oven and Joan, standing with her back to it under the shelter was kneading dough on the table. She waved a floury hand at Marion and pushed her cap back from her red sweating face, leaving a splodge of flour on her forehead.

'Just the first lot,' she said smiling, and twisting and plaiting a lump of dough till it resembled the plaited tail of a horse. 'Real yeast in it, and the next lot is rising there.' She pointed with her elbow to a wide earthenware basin which stood near the oven. 'Ed-me-boy's getting the long tables out.'

Ed-me-boy came out backwards from under the porch carrying the end of one of the long planks which made up half of one of the Hall's tables. Loppy Lambert emerged at length carrying the other end, walking with dragging feet and holding the plank in his lumpy red hands which were covered with smears of blood where the scrofulous skin had broken, but his always open mouth was smiling.

'Put it down,' ordered Ed-me-boy, patience in his voice. 'Now come on, we must get the other plank.' He pushed Loppy back into the porch and they soon came out with the second plank.

'Come *on* now,' said Ed-me-boy. 'The trestles, Loppy.' They finally got both tripodal trestles out, and with much cajoling, Loppy performed his part in getting the planks placed across them. Putting stones under the trestle's feet so they stood level was beyond Loppy and Ed-me-boy had to do it, jiggling the planks between each adjustment until Joan pronounced it firm.

'You can't knead on a wobbly board, nor cut loaves,' Joan announced. 'It takes your confidence away.'

Milly came round the corner from the yard, holding her head high and with a look of self-importance which mitigated her usual scowl. The spirit of approaching festivities had even touched her.

She put the bucket she was carrying down on the trestle table, saying, 'That's the sour. M'Dame's in the dairy now, getting the cream off yesterday's. I'm afraid a bit of muck fell off the handle,' and she scooped a bit of farmyard straw off the top of the sour milk – lumps of curd floating in greenish whey, 'but it adds to the taste, ha ha.' This jocular remark was Milly's contribution to the festivities.

Having seen that the table was secure and the sour milk ready, Marion went down the yard and past the weaving shed. An unfinished blanket hung there with the shuttle stuck into the bare warp. Dame Margaret met her at the dairy door. She had a clean white cap on, her hair was smoothed back neatly under it, and she had two extra pink dog roses stuck into it, one over each ear. Marion said, 'Good morning, M'Dame,' and complimented her on her appearance.

Dame Margaret's usual tense expression relaxed. She smiled and asked if the tables were up, and if so, whether the flour had been brought, and where was Tom, and did Marion think the weather would last, and Marion must find a flower for her cap, and as Marion would be busy with the baking, she would instruct Magda to bring Marion a bloom. 'You take the cream,' she ended. 'I'll tell Tom to bring you out the flour. Is Hilda on her way?'

Marion took the cream, which lay like thick folded blankets in the bowl, and went back to the trestle table. It had been moved to the shade of the oak and Sir Hugh was there instructing them to see that it stood firm.

'Stood firm enough before he came interfering,' muttered Ed-me-boy, as Marion put down the cream.

'In an hour's time it will be far too hot to work in the sun,' Sir Hugh announced, justifying his action. Tom arrived carrying a sack of flour over his shoulder like a baby being winded, even patting it from time to time with his free hand.

'What now?' he asked, as he lowered the sack on to the table. 'Oh, Magda's forgotten the basins,' and he moved off to the porch and met Magda at the door with flowers in her hands. Marion watched their altercation but could hear no words. Magda approached Marion with some honeysuckle and buttercups.

'Mother said I was to bring you these,' she said, justifying herself for having forgotten the basins. 'All right, Father, don't fuss. I'm just going for the basins,' she said as Sir Hugh approached, but added in a low voice, 'Why can't Milly bring them, the slut?'

No one but Magda would have dared to speak to Sir Hugh as she did, but many were uneasily grateful to the child for so doing.

'It's honeysuckle,' she said to Marion, 'because you're going to make honey-bread and buttercups because we are going to have butter,' and she ran off back to the Hall before her father could rebuke her for her forgetfulness.

Marion pulled a thread out from the bottom of her skirt, wound it round the flowers' stalks and tied the ends round a pinch of her cap. It flopped and the buttercups were already wilting, but she would not disappoint Magda.

She started making the scones, scooping up flour from the sack with a big wooden scoop, made by Peter, and mixing it with sour milk in a big basin, patting out the dough on the floury table and then cutting it into fat rounds with the holly-wood cutter that she had brought in her pocket. It had been made specially for her by Peter years ago, and his skill and years of usage had polished it very smooth.

The villagers were slowly arriving from across the Green, standing around the fencing hurdles that Peter had put up in recent days, talking and laughing, giving sudden shouts to their dogs and their children and all feeling the air of festivity and the sweet summer morning. Peter was pushing the crowd away from the hurdles and shouting, 'Leave it alone,' to the boys who were investigating how firmly they had been attached to the ground.

Marion went on with the scones. She cut them out and arranged them on a large iron grid beside her. Hilda appeared with her two little girls, Meg and Mary. Both children had small caps on and their carroty curls swelled out under them, decorated with daisy chains. Peterkin was approaching too, with Alice in his arms. Magda had hung a daisy and buttercup chain round Alice's neck.

'What you doing?' Meg asked.

'Making scones for the feast,' said Marion, looking down.

'Wanta see,' squeaked Mary, whose head was below the table top. Meg picked her up round the stomach and gave her a brief glimpse of scone-making. Hilda shooed them both aside and, taking the other bowl, started scone-making herself. Peterkin slid Alice down at Marion's feet, then skipped off in his lop-sided fashion to join the other boys round the hurdles. Ed-me-boy came to see if the grid was full, and carried it away with a message to enquire about honey, almost tripping over Magda's dog Trover, who was nosing about round Joan's table for scraps.

Marion and Hilda went on with their scone-making. A lovely smell of hot bread spread to the crowd on the Green. Joan's first batch of small loaves was cooling along the edge of the table and she was kneading the third batch with muscular fingers. Now and then a breath from the waving grass on the Common, mixed with the smell of fresh leaves on the oak, cooled Joan's red face and refreshed Marion. A pigeon high in the oak complained, the dogs snapped occasionally, a cuckoo called, sometimes stammering its usual call, the sparrows round the yard cheeped incessantly and over all these sounds the slow voices and laughter of the villagers came in waves as they stood around the hurdles in unusual idleness and expectation.

'Sheep,' said Meg, in a penetrating squeak, and as the human voices died away everyone could hear the distant baaing, anxious and melancholy. The villagers called their dogs to them, tying ropes round their necks. In the general movement Sir Hugh was striding around, clearing people away from the hurdles and shouting to Magda to tie up Trover. Simon and his wife Betsy were on the far side of the Green chatting to Peter, and they waved to Marion.

From where she stood she could see across the Green and down the path that passed near Nick and Martha's cottage, and it was along this path and through the small sheep field that the procession of the flock arrived.

The villagers gave a cheer as the first sheep appeared and then shouted at their children to keep the path clear. Janty was trotting, high-headed, beside the first sheep, and the boy Ned with his crook over his shoulder was marching along on the other side of the flock as they jostled forward, a grey woolly mass dotted with whiter lambs who ran with awkward jerks. Through the sounds of baaing and barking and cheering came the high penetrating whistle of Dick and Jo's pipes. Then they came round the corner at the back of the flock with True trotting last of all.

Peterkin, officiously, because *his* father had put up the hurdles, opened the entrance and with Ned standing by the gap, the sheep started to pour into the compound. By the time Dick had reached the Green all the sheep were safely confined there, and Dick, followed by Jo, neither of whom had stopped playing their pipes for an instant, started marching in a circle round the compound with their two dogs following. Dick's hood had been pushed back, and his orange hair and beard radiated from his red face so that he looked like a caricature of the sun. It was *his* day, he was a natural showman and he knew his sheep were worth showing. The sleeves of his short tunic were rolled up, his legs bare, his feet in sheepskin boots, his stride easy, strong, confident. Jo, following, a thin boy with a wide brown face and an almost skipping walk, was playing on his little pipe with a skilful abandon which never missed the rhythm of the song. Both shepherds had bunches of broom of blazing yellow at their necks. As they passed the carpenter's shop where Peter was standing with Simon and Betsy, Marion heard Betsy's light high voice joining in the song, and others picked up the tune and joined in as Dick marched round. It was a melody they all knew well, the sheep-shearing song, and Marion put down the scone cutter and lifted Alice up so she could see Dick, and she made Alice wave her arms about in time with the tune.

She looked at Hilda, whom she knew had no voice and never attempted singing. She was standing gazing at her husband, who without seeming to miss a note, smiled as he passed her, and freed one hand from the pipe to wave to his children. Hilda just gazed with shining eyes and smiling mouth.

Just by the oak tree where Marion and Hilda were standing, Dick came to the final verse of his song, finishing opposite Sir Hugh and Dame Margaret. He took the pipe from his mouth and with a broad gesture said, 'Your sheep, sir.'

Everyone laughed. They saw Dick, kinglike in his size, confidence and golden hair, the obvious hero of the day, acting the part of the servant that he really was, to the shy diffident Sir Hugh. It tickled their fancy – and their laughter, though Sir Hugh joined in it, made him feel even shyer.

Dick was the villagers' hero. He had been Shepherd for some ten years and during that time the flock had much increased. The sheep were healthy, the lambs rarely died. Everyone recognized his instinct for nurturing them. Sheep were vital to the village. Though they all belonged to Sir Hugh, they provided the village with its only saleable riches, the only means by which those few materials that could not be produced in the village might be exchanged for wool: salt, iron, hemp and pottery. So the villagers rejoiced in the increase of sheep, half connecting such joy with the anticipated satisfaction of a plentiful supply of those four alien materials so vital to their lives.

Dick and Sir Hugh started walking slowly round the compound, Dick pointing out particular sheep with the end of his crook. He found it strange that Sir Hugh could not recognize one sheep from another. He spoke of them in a quiet authoritative tone to Sir Hugh, the knowledgeable manager speaking with polite tolerance to the more ignorant owner. Ned and Jo, with self-conscious smiles, stood ready to open or shut the entrance to the compound. Janty and True lay down, paws crossed, eyes alert and watching, their panting mouths almost smiling too. Magda approached Janty, and Dick, the circumambulation nearly completed, raised his voice and bellowed at his master's daughter, 'Leave my dog alone.'

'I was only going to fix his flowers,' said Magda. 'They were slipping.' She was rather awed by the way a mere shepherd had bawled at her in her father's presence as if she were only a village slut, but seeing Janty's raised lip and long eyetooth, she retired quickly, making a face at Dick. Her father made no attempt to defend her.

The official inspection over, the crowd began to move around to inspect the sheep themselves, to talk with Ned and Jo and mix with each other. Marion went on with her second batch of scones. Ed-me-boy brought a wide willow-woven tray and she arranged them on it, took the hen's tail feather from behind her ear, dipped it in the cream and brushed it over the raw scones.

She was so occupied when Ellen bounced up. She was Marion's niece, the daughter of her brother, Simon the miller, and Betsy. She was a wholesome-looking pink girl with light ginger hair straggling from under her cap, and a cheerful expression. She had a sprig of intense blue-purple vetch stuck into a thread-hole of her bodice, which she had laced up with what she knew Father John considered 'lewd tightness'.

'Is it true we're going to have cream, Aunt?'

'Cream?' Marion said. 'There's to be butter in the scones.'

'Magda said M'Dame was having butter *and* cream.'

'Magda says a lot of things *are* just to pretend she knows everything. There's just a brushing of cream,' said Marion, and made a little smiling sneer at Ellen. Ed-me-boy arrived to take the willow tray to the oven.

'M'Dame says,' he said, 'that if you've done the scones you're to go into the Hall to help her.'

'Pee,' announced Alice, grabbing at Marion's skirt.

Marion replaced the feather over her ear and lugged Alice round the corner of the Hall, and held up her dress. 'Feet apart,' she said, 'wider.' Alice peed and was brought back to where Meg and Mary sat under Hilda's part of the table. They were instructed to mind Alice. Seeing Alice peeing had reminded Marion of her own need so she went into the yard and into that smelly corner of the cow shed where was the hole that the women could use in comparative privacy.

In spite of the shutters being open on both sides it was dark in the Hall after the bright sun outside. It seemed roomy without the trestle tables. Dame Margaret was at the high table on the platform with the first batch of little loaves, now almost cool, and a little bucket of butter before her. She was slicing the loaves one after another.

'Oh Marion, yes, you must help or we'll never be ready by noon. That lot's cut, here's a baton, smear some butter on each slice.'

The butter smelt lovely, so did the warm bread – both were treats.

'Milly and I have been saving the butter for this for days. I think it is still good in spite of the weather,' said Dame Margaret with much satisfaction. 'There should be a good piece for everyone and some over.' They worked on. Magda's head came round the porch door, Meg and Mary beside her.

'Mother,' said her accusing voice, 'is it true *every*one's going to have butter, not just us?'

'Yes,' said her mother, slicing away, 'butter for the feast for everyone.'

'*There*,' said Meg, very scornfully to Magda and the three girls' heads vanished. Marion wondered how Alice was faring. Dame Margaret sighed and muttered, 'Those *girls*.'

Tom brought in another basket of little loaves.

'It's the second ovenful, M'Dame,' he said. 'Fairly cool now.'

'I don't want the butter to melt and run out and be wasted,' Dame Margaret said, her hand sliding from loaf to loaf. She sliced one. 'It's cool enough,' she said and handed it to Marion.

'First batch of scones is ready,' Tom said. 'They look a treat, *are* a treat. Joan's just putting the next lot on the grid.'

'Don't forget Hilda's square ones,' Marion said, as she went on buttering. A crust fell off, she buttered it and ate it. Jix, Sir Hugh's small white dog, tied up to a hook on a post, whined. Tom threw him a little crust that had been stuck in the crevices of the basket he was carrying away.

Sir Hugh came in to enquire how they were getting on, but perhaps really to escape from the publicity of the crowd.

'All right,' said his wife, slicing away even more diligently. 'We should be ready by noon. Can't be far off by the shadows. See that Tom has the ale. *Quiet*, Jix. Have they started the shearing yet?'

'Poor Jix, missing all the fun,' said Sir Hugh, patting him. 'If you'd only learn to leave sheep alone and stop barking at them, you could have been out there with the others.' Marion had often observed that Sir Hugh was more ready to talk to his dog than to his wife.

'You should be outside,' Dame Margaret said to Sir Hugh. 'You should be on the mounting block, as you usually are, watching over it all. Go on out, we'll bring the food soon.'

He went reluctantly, and stepped up on to the mounting block next to the drinking trough at the entrance to the yard. The two were made from three large blocks of stone. They had been cut and dragged from the stone cliff-face across the stream when stone was being brought from there for building the church – that is, before anyone in the village could remember. Stone from Rockwell could have been used – Rockwell was no further and, being all downhill, the journey would have been easier, but no one, least of all the Rockwell families, would have agreed to chopping a chunk out of the rock-face from where their pure water flowed. This was partly for fear of diverting the secret water courses, partly for fear of disobliging the gods that had sent them this life-preserving water source. And no one dared touch the other lumps of rock further up the forested hill behind Rockwell farm. The idea that they belonged to the Devil had been strengthened by the tale of how one dusky evening years ago, the Rockwell children, returning home with bundles of firewood, had seen the Devil flying in the air and alighting on top of the balancing rock and had fled home screaming. Only Martin, who was eight at the time, had stood his ground and watched and told them it was only an owl – a huge owl he admitted, and he had seen it against the sky giving a dead mouse or something to a little owl also on the rock. This hardly consoled the frightened children, and the suspicion that owls and devils were somehow in league was fortified in the minds of the villagers.

When Marion came out of the Hall the sun was covered by one of the skyful of shining clouds which had been gathering in the last hour. She turned back to the oak tree, recognizing Alice's yells. She was in Meg's tiny arms and Mary was reaching up to pat her back.

'She fell over,' Meg excused herself for misminding her charge. There was a bump on Alice's forehead and one of her squashy little hands was grazed.

'There, there,' said Marion, taking Alice and jiggling her a little. 'There, there, you're better now. Look your belt's untied, you tripped over that.' She set Alice down, retied the leather strip round her stomach and then hitched up the dress in it. The dress was much longer than Alice, but Marion would not have dreamt of cutting it shorter, knowing how soon Alice would grow to fit it.

Marion picked her up and went to a seat under the oak where Hilda was, and sat down to rest. Alice, to her relief, dozed off in her arms. Meg and Mary sat quietly on the ground at Hilda's feet. She also sat in silence, her eyes following Dick as he moved about in the compound with Ned, pointing with his crook at various sheep, instructing him. Then he went to the mounting stone where he had left his hone, and started carefully to sharpen his shears.

One of the gates of the compound had been placed close to the mounting block, and Jo, standing inside the compound, let out the sheep one by one as Dick called. Out bounced a sheep, nervous, alert. Dick grabbed it and pulled it towards him, it struggled and bleated, but as he propped it up on its tail, leaning its back against his legs, it suddenly relaxed and he slid the shears into its wool and down its unprotesting sides. Dick's fingers squeezed the shears rhythmically, his hand moved up and down caressingly, smoothly, and the thick curtains of wool, so white inside, so grey outside, fell in folds on the grass. While he turned the sheep, pivoting it on its buttocks, it remained in a trancelike state, its thin forelegs crossed as in supplication before it. The wool off, he returned it to its feet, the spell he had had over it broke, and, thin in its ridged white underwear, it jerked off with more bleating to be caught by Ned and guided to another part of the compound.

Dick pushed away the fleece with his foot as if this harvest of his year's work were nothing, and called for the next sheep. When some six or seven fleeces were heaped up round the mounting block he called for them to be removed. Tom, pulling a large willow basket towards the fleeces, instructed Loppy Lambert.

'Here, Loppy. You pick up this wool and put it in the basket like this.' Tom demonstrated, and Loppy made his curious throaty noises and started slowly to fill the basket with wool.

After a time Rollo, lounging nearby, glanced at the sun's place in the sky and signalled to Tom.

'Ready for the ale now.'

'Right, sir,' said Tom, and with Ed-me-boy went down to the brew house, soon emerging with a barrel on a low wheelbarrow which Ed-me-boy was pushing while Tom steadied it. They brought it to Sir Hugh.

'Up to the church, Ed,' Sir Hugh said, 'and sound the bell.'

As the *tang-tang-tang* rang out, the villagers broke off their chattering and moved towards the oak, the children running ahead. Dame Margaret was at the long trestle tables handing out richly buttered scones with shiny golden tops, one each for the children, who were then sent away. Then she gave thick slices of fresh bread, still warm with the butter softly soaking into the crumb to each woman, and an extra piece to each woman who had old or decrepit folk at home.

'Give an extra slice to a *man* for his old mother,' said Dame Margaret, 'and he's eaten it before you can say knife. Give it to a daughter and you know the old ones will be looked after.' Some people looked a bit sheepish as she said this, but no one would dare contradict Dame Margaret. Milly standing by her, her peevish heavy face glistening with melting butter, was replenishing the table from her wide basket of scones. Marion heard Dame Margaret's crisp commentary as she worked.

'You're Nick's boy, aren't you? Here you are, no, one each. Tell your sisters to come and get theirs. Magda, take that empty mug from Hal – give it to Tom to refill. Where's Cecily? I've not seen her this morning. Milly, give Loppy a *proper* piece, do you hear? I won't have him palmed off with a burnt crust – there, take it away, Loppy. Ah, Polly – yes, I'll give you something for your old folks. How is Old Fletcher now? Ed-me-boy, take this basket to Father John, under the tree somewhere with Old Sarah and old what's her name Hodge, see they all get enough – where are all the Rockwells? Milly, do some more scones, the Rockwells are coming over.

Magda, keep Jix tied up, I told you before . . . ' and so on, all amiable, no hint of dues unpaid, of labour days evaded, of leverets taken by night from the Hall's lands, of missing Mass, of being found drunk at the side of the fields. On this day of festivities, business would not be discussed.

Tom was dipping a tall jug into the barrel and filling from it the three green glazed pots that the Hall possessed. They were passed round among the villagers with Milly following each pot's progress and nagging at those she felt were drinking too long. Joan brought along a basket of fresh buttered scones, many with sprigs of watercress or peppermint picked on the stream's edge and pressed into the butter.

Marion saw her brother, Simon, and his family approaching the oak tree from near Peter's workshop, and the Rockwell families slowly crossing the Green towards them. The sun was bright and hot on their pink or sunburnt faces, and Marion looked at them all with a sure sense of contentment. Simon, her elder by many years, a stocky man with dark hair and beard, always dusty white from working at the Mill, waved to her, his eyes narrowing with his smile as they always did. Betsy, his wife, waved too – enviable Betsy, always strong and in good health. Marion remembered how she was when she was first married, a plump girl with pale coppery hair falling about round her pink and white apple-blossom face, always with a laugh in her voice and a bounce in her walk. Now, after bringing up five children, the coppery hair was dusty and the face had florid purplish patches, the body had solidified and the bounce had become a lurch, but the laugh was still as ready and the air of health and strength undiminished. She had been a Rockwell girl and her handsome wellbeing was, Marion considered, the result of having been born there. Two of their children were with them – Gib, their second son, a gawky fair-haired sunburnt boy in a very short tunic, and Kate, the youngest. Marion thought how suddenly a fifteen-year-old girl grows up. A lanky thin girl had replaced the dark shy child that Kate had been as recently as last Christmas. Marion observed how her eyes narrowed like Simon's as she spoke, and that she had a look of much tenderness when she smiled. Her dark hair was tied back with a length of white wool and she wore a necklace of pink clover.

'Roger's coming slowly with the Old Man in a wheelbarrow,' Simon announced. 'We three lifted him in, father says every bump shakes up his joints.'

Marion asked how her father was.

'Not bad, I s'pose,' Betsy replied. 'He complains a lot, his feet and legs, knees specially, are very swollen and he says his hands hurt. They are pretty twisted. He often says things three times, forgets in between, but he eats well and sleeps well.'

The Rockwell families joined them then and there was much greeting and talking. The Rockwells, young or old, always walked erect, even in the harshest weather when the other villagers were silent, enduring and cowed. They still had energy to spare, still were masters of their own lives. Perhaps that was where the difference lay, Marion mused: they *were* their own masters, and their fields were their *own*. The yoke of slavery, even so light a yoke as Simon Miller or Dick Shepherd bore, was, for all their irreplaceable skills, still a yoke. The Hall ultimately owned them. None of the members of the Rockwell families, not even the women, *looked* as if he or she knew servitude. Marion was glad that Simon's eldest girl, Lisa, had married Martin Rockwell and, looking at Stephen Rockwell, she hoped again that he would marry Ellen. Surely, she thought, Ellen is the best girl of his age in the village.

Wat the Tall of Rockwell was speaking to Simon.

'Your father here? Oh, coming in a wheelbarrow, is he? Ha, couldn't make Old Lambert come in a wheelbarrow – come in a cart or on a donkey perhaps – no, he can't ride any more. He doesn't like travelling at all. He'll just sit in the sun and if we bring him back some good buttered bread, he'll be content.'

Meanwhile, Dick was shearing steadily, and the two shepherd boys were kept busy bringing him sheep and guiding away the shorn ones. Hilda came to Dick with some fresh buttery bread and a new pot of ale. He released his last shorn sheep, sat down on the grass with her and they shared the bread and ale. Marion too sat down on the patchy grass, rough with ancient acorn cups, under the oak with Peter beside her leaning against the trunk, and they ate their lovely bread and Marion fed small bits of it to Alice. The green glazed pot came their way from Milly's hand and they drank copiously. Peterkin was somewhere on the Green, running about with the other boys in the hot sun, all energetic with full stomachs.

The Hodge family was near and Marion called out to Cecily, 'Where's your Hoddy? I've seen all the rest of you.'

'Oh he's about,' Cecily answered. 'I'm not speaking to him. Polly Fletcher caught him throwing stones at her goslings on the Green this morning, and walloped him and brought him round to me, and I walloped him again.'

'Well, he's got to learn,' said Marion, the standard phrase.

'He *knows* well enough the difference between goslings and rooks – he just likes throwing stones. *Boys*.' Cecily's attention was distracted by one other of her boys requiring disciplining and she moved away.

From where she was sitting Marion could see across the strip of sunny grass to the bare earth in front of the Hall and to the mounting block and trough and the heap of woolly waves, grey, lined with white, lying where they had fallen from Dick's shears. Sir Hugh and his family and Father John were sitting at the trestle tables. Everyone was quiet, concerned with eating. The air was full of the baaing of the sheep.

At the table, Molly, capable and sensible and always very serious, was collecting buttery bread in a pile between her hands and taking it very slowly to a log near the Hall porch where Old Agnes and Old Marge were sitting. Marion had not realized they were capable of walking so far from Down the Common. I don't expect they've ever missed a Shearing Feast, she thought, and they don't want to now. She watched Joan guiding her mother, Old Mavis, who was almost blind, to a seat near them. Her other near neighbour, Jack Plowright, was at the trestle table with several children by him.

Those children never seem to grow, thought Marion. You never know if they're boys or girls, just small wizened faces with straggling hair falling about, open mouths, crooked teeth, any old rag or nothing round their shoulders, stick-like legs, purple and filthy, toenails curling this way and that – and you'd never get a word out of any of them except to beg. Maybe they can't talk, maybe they are all as stupid as Small Sarah. After all, she would never be able to teach a child to talk, gabbling the way she does – and Jack couldn't be bothered.

She watched them shuffling round their father, close together, as if closeness was their only protection, accepting scones in their filthy hands, silent and apathetic. Small Sarah was not with them.

It's the healthy children who tire you out, Marion decided. They are the difficult ones, those with so much energy. These starving children cause no trouble, but will never be any use to anyone.

She sat back to enjoy the peace and the rare contentment. How restful it was to be warm, warm all over, to relish the fresh breeze which occasionally stirred the oak leaves above her. How very comfortable it was to be *dry*, not to have damp shoulders where a child had puked, not to have a wet front where a breast had leaked, not to have wet knees where a baby had pissed, not to have wet thighs where, uncontrollably, blood trickled down. She looked at Alice contentedly scratching in the dry acorny earth with a stick, and felt so glad that Alice was almost a dry child now, and thought how short and how rare in a woman's life were these dry days.

There was more to make for Marion's contentment that day. The piles of wool which had slid from the sheep over Dick's shears, and the further piles which would slide off during the rest of the day, represented so much future wealth for them all. Much work was to be done on the wool, and most of it women's work: washing the fleeces, sorting out the different kinds of wool, carding and spinning, and then, for the yarn that was to be retained in the village, the weaving. The prospect of much work stretched before her, but for the moment it was leisure, warmth, plentiful good bread, dryness, Peter at peace beside her, Alice a thriving little girl at her feet, her familiar neighbours around, and all this enclosed in the dear, dear circle of wooded hills, her home, her existence, reality itself.

She and Peter probably dozed a bit and were awakened by sudden dog-barking and Sir Hugh shouting at Magda to keep Trover from the lambs and she protesting that Jix was there too. This disturbance revived the villagers and they began shifting and sauntering back to their cottages and their gardens, many intending to do a bit of gardening, while most of the wives stood around gossiping and waiting to see if there were to be any hand-outs of the extra buttered bread.

Peter heaved himself up, muttering about getting on with his work, and stumped off to his workshop.

Dame Margaret's voice could be heard summoning the girls to gather up the fleeces and take them down to the stream. Jo, still guiding the sheep to and from Dick at his shearing, suddenly roared out, 'My pipe!' and bent down, pushing a shorn sheep aside to pick up his crushed pipe from under its hooves. He looked aghast at the shreds of dried hemlock stalk that he held in his hand, and showed it to Dick.

'It must have fallen off. It was tied round my neck.' He examined the broken thong still dangling at his chest. 'Oh my pipe,' he moaned.

'You can make another,' said Magda.

'I'd spent *days* making that. You've got to get the holes just right – right size, right place – and fix the little half-plug in at the top end so it don't fall out. Oh my *pipe*! I'd got it just right. It played – ' he was momentarily at a loss for words – 'it played like a bird!'

'Don't mind so, boy,' Dick tried to console him. 'It lasted till today – this was our great day. You can make another when we are up in the hills. Peter Carpenter will lend you a knife and find you a neat bit of holly for the plug.' But Jo kept twisting the bit of thong in his fingers and mourned for his crushed pipe until Dick recalled him to work by ordering another sheep.

Marion went to pick up her bundle of sour-smelling wool – so familiar a smell – as much as her arms could encompass, and slowly followed Ellen and Kate across the Green. Ellen was carrying Alice on one arm and her burden of wool in the other.

Young Simkin and his new wife, Joyce, were at the gate of their cottage talking with Hodge and Cecily, and surrounded by their children, solemn-faced, tow-haired children, all with greasy chins from the unusual buttery scones. Hoddy, a pink-faced four-year-old, was swinging round and round, holding his mother's skirt. She was repeating in her anxious whine the story of the ill-luck that Jo, her eldest, had suffered by losing his pipe, and occasionally swiping at Hoddy's head and telling him to stop, which he did not.

Marion and her nieces waved to them and went on, taking the path that led to a few cottages and further on to the Mill. Every stone in the path, every tussock of grass, so it seemed, had been familiar to Marion all her life. But close to the cottages the path dipped down the bank on to the wide grassy strip along the stream's edge, and so took them to the place where the stream widened out, was shallow with the chippings from the stones for the church.

Strewn out over these stones in the shallow water were some of the fleeces, and a dozen or so of the village girls were spreading out more. With their dresses hitched up above their knees, they were walking to and fro over the wool, squeezing it into the water, calling out to each other, laughing and giggling. Ellen and Kate joined them, Ellen pulling out the cord that laced the front of her dress to use as a belt to hitch her skirt up with. The grey stones were covered with lumps of white wool, the afternoon sun sparkled on the water as the girls' pink feet trod the wool under. This was, traditionally, girls' unskilled work, and Marion felt no obligation to help. She sat down on the bank and watched, amused, as the girls stepped up and down, wobbling, talking and laughing. It all was, as usual, more of an entertainment for the girls than real work. One of the girls was sitting hunched up on the bank.

'Aren't you treading wool?' Marion asked her.

'Got a terrible pain,' the girl said. 'Don't tell M'Dame. I just *can't*.'

'I won't tell her, dear,' said Marion. 'Cold water's bad for girls at such times.'

Alice, becoming adventurous, had toddled down to the stream and was standing in two inches of water, splashing with pleasure. Marion went down to her, pulled her dress off over her head and encouraged her to sit on a flat stone in the stream and splash with her feet. Marion watched her from the bank, easy-minded, amused at Alice's podgy pink body that she so rarely saw naked, and her pale yellow hair falling over her eyes and down her shoulders. She still wore round her neck the daisy and buttercup chain that Magda had made for her. She patted mounds of wet sandy mud and flecks of grey spattered her skin. After a while, Peter came along the path and descended to where Marion sat. She pointed out Alice to him and he went down to the water's edge and called to her. Alice looked up from splashing with a chortle of delight, she had never played with water like this before.

'Buttercup,' she told him, pulling at the necklace. Marion saw a slow smile stir in his beard as he bent down to pick her up. It pleased Marion. It was always thought in the village that loving relationships between father and child were made by a good wife and mother, and that quarrels between fathers and children were regarded as proof of a mother's failure. She took Peter's pleasure in his baby daughter as a compliment to herself. It did not occur to her that Alice, naked, wet, with muddy hands, smelt sweet to him for the first time in her little life.

'Her bum's like ice,' he said, and Marion took her from his arms and rewrapped her in her smelly dress.

'Come *on*,' said Peter to dawdling Alice as they walked back home along the Common. 'We'll never get home at this rate.'

'She's tired,' said Marion, 'been trotting around all day.'

'I'll carry you,' he said, and scooped her up under one arm, his other being burdened with a bag of tools. Alice yelled. 'Now you shut up,' he said in her ear.

'Want pickypack!' screamed Alice.

'*Can't*, got my bag to carry.'

'Want pickypack!' roared Alice. The parents took no notice. Alice continued to roar.

'She'll get tired of that soon,' said Marion as they walked on.

'Not before we're driven raving mad,' he said, but he laughed in Alice's furious face, and she stopped screaming and laughed back.

As they went through the gate and up the incline by Molly's cottage they heard angry female voices, and round the side of the cottage they came upon Old Agnes and Old Marge, both leaning on the doorposts looking exhausted, and Molly fiercely berating Small Sarah who stood before her, bedraggled and dirty as ever but cowed and furtive as well. Molly saw Marion and Peter and directed her berating at them.

'What d'you think? We just got home to find this slut down in *our* garden, by the hen shed, and I says to her, what you doing here? I says, and I grab her arm and she's got half a dozen eggs under her cloak, *stolen*, from *my* nests, and she drops them all on our dung heap and all are broken. Aunt goes into our cottage and finds two loaves gone and a bucket of new milk upset all over the floor and comes out screaming to tell me. All that milk wasted, she says, and we only yesterday gave your brats some bread and cheese, she says – an' what have you got to say to *that*, Sarah? And where's our two loaves?' And so the angry monologue went on, and Small Sarah stood there, open-mouthed as always, with nothing to say.

Molly calmed down a bit, and said to Marion, 'You'd better see if she's been at your place. She could have been stealing everything, sly bitch – us being away all day. She's been at the Shepherds' too, I expect.' Here Sarah protested that she had not.

'Oh, you haven't?' Molly went on. ''Spect that bitch of theirs with her pups scared you away. All the more likely, Marion, she's been rooting through – '

Marion did not wait to hear more but she and Peter went quickly over the mound to their cottage. Tibtab was asleep on the log under the eaves and slowly stretched himself as they came. Several hens were having a dust bath nearby. The cottage door was still closed. Marion opened the upper half. All seemed peaceful inside.

'I don't think she's been here,' she told Peter. 'I'll just check the eggs.' She went into the goat shed and felt along the straw in the laying nests. She counted eight eggs and went for a basket to collect them.

'I'll talk to Jack when I see him,' Peter said, putting Alice down, 'but what really can be done? That's a nice basket of eggs. Will you give some to Molly and the old girls for their supper?'

'I'll take them some now,' said Marion, though she had not thought of so doing. 'After their loss it will be a bit of something.'

'Do you think Molly *does* give the Plowright brats some food, like she said?' he asked.

'I've often seen her give them bits – and I have too – only two days ago, half a loaf and a drink of milk each. I'd more milk than I had buckets for – I could do with a new bucket when you have time. It's only that slut I don't want to help.'

'She's not really right in her mind,' said Peter. 'Probably hasn't got a mind at all. I'll talk to Jack, but what can he do? She'd be just as bad again if he beat her. He shouldn't have married her. Everyone knew she wasn't up to much and she's only got worse over all those children. He'd have done better to marry Molly, she's no worse looking than Small Sarah was, and a lot more sensible.'

He sighed heavily and rubbed his beard with his hand. 'It's cooling down now,' he said, looking at the sky. 'I'll do a bit of digging down the garden. If Peterkin comes back send him down to help me.'

Marion turned indoors and took Alice with her. She gave the child a drink of milk and put her into the cradle. As she did so she saw that Alice's feet were up against the end board even when her head was touching the top board. 'She may have to sleep in the bed with the rest of us by next winter, she thought. Alice's protests at being put to bed were ritual but brief, for as Marion guessed, the child was tired.

'Want rocking,' said Alice. Marion sat on the edge of the bed with one foot on the cradle's rocker and pressed it rhythmically.

'Sing 'bout the rabbit,' said Alice, so Marion began in the vaguely intoned sing-song considered appropriate to babies:

> 'Down by the river in the sand in the sun
> Lived an old mother rabbit and her little rabbit one.
> "Hop," said the mother. "We hop," said the one.
> So they hopped and were glad in the sand in the sun.'

'More,' said Alice, so Marion continued, her mind elsewhere.

> 'Down by the river in the sand in the sun
> Lived an old mother duck and her little duckling one.
> "Hop," said the moth – '

'Thwim,' said Alice.

"Swim," said the mother. "We swim," said the one.
So they swam and were glad in the sand in the sun.'

It should be water, not sand, thought Marion for the first time after
many hundred repetitions of the verses – can't swim in sand. But Alice
did not question it, she was already asleep. Marion sat on beside her, still
and quiet.

Peter came up from the garden, dragging the spade.

'Remember that, Marion?' he said, showing her a little carved wooden
cow. She picked it up from his earthy palm and sad recollections flooded
in. 'I found it digging in the muck heap,' he said. 'Remember? I carved it
for Nolly one Sunday evening. A bit of soft willow it was, it's a wonder
it's lasted . . .' They looked at the little cow, and then straight into each
other's eyes and Peter's voice faded away.

'Funny,' he went on, after a pause, 'I was just thinking of Nolly before
I picked it up.'

Marion felt an unexpected bond with Peter. 'Do you often think of him?'
she asked, twisting the muddy toy in her fingers.

'Now and then,' he said. 'Can't help it. Do you?'

'Not more than once or twice a day,' she said, wondering if he realized
the unusual intimacy that her words revealed.

He looked into her eyes again. 'Yes, Marry,' he said slowly. 'Our Nolly,
the best of all children,' and then even more unusually he put his arms
round her and kissed her face. She looked up at him and saw his kindly
eyes and felt she was fortunate among women. Peter straightened his back
and hitched the spade up in his hand as if preparing to continue digging.

'Can't you have a bit of a rest?' Marion asked him. 'You've been working
all day since dawn, hours and hours on end.'

'I know I have, but it's summer. I must do what I can in the light,' and
he stumped off down the garden again and Marion stood leaning against
the doorpost watching him.

That was what midsummer was – long, long hours of work. Whether
your work was sitting spinning or sawing logs, the hours of daylight
must not be wasted. These long days had to be worked when food was
often short, when sacks of last year's corn were counted, when the flour
remaining in the chests was prudently estimated, when rarely were there
any peas or beans left from last year and the new crops were not ripe for

picking and cabbages were still little stripling plants. It was traditional to say that midsummer was the best time of year but Marion associated it with exhaustion. Autumn, when shorter days sent everyone home to their cottages at sunset, and when the recent harvest, visible in bags of provender and meat sides smoking above the fire, gave a surety of future sustenance, was surely a richer time. Then anxiety could give way before a sense of achievement.

She sat on the log seat under the eaves, looking down the garden. The sky had become golden now. The sunlight gilded only the tops of the trees on the hill before her. She looked to the right down the valley into a deep gloom where the dark trees grew close to the stream on both sides, and the marshy area, just below the Shepherds' garden was dense with dark rushes and the broad leaves of the wild iris. To her left she could not now see very far because the birch trees grew thick on that end of the Common and were now in full leaf, their white black-flecked trunks awash in the waves of pale grass. The sky was becoming a violet blue, a blue of immense depth, of eternal distance. Suddenly she saw a single star, bright and still, which seemed to nail infinity back against the vaults of heaven. Between it and Marion's eyes the swifts, very high and small, were darting and wheeling, chasing each other, slipping sideways in flight. Then, with a flick of wing, soaring up again, and all the while screaming faintly.

Perhaps it was the stillness of the luminous air, and the tiny birds swooping about so high and so far away, giving vastness to the intangible dome above, that made Marion's thoughts turn from the immediate and practical, where they usually dwelt, to the eternal and unknown. This is my life, she thought, my only life. This is all there is for me. Why was it me that my mother bore, not another? Soon – it could be any time – I will be dead and cold in the churchyard and I will know nothing any more and soon I will be as forgotten as . . . but how could her thoughts supply the names of the forgotten? She knew the story of how one day God would come and judge the world and the graveyard tombs would open and their inhabitants would stumble out, confused in the unusual light. But this was a story and Marion had heard many stories in her life, and though they had given her areas for thought to indulge in, they were not real, not as getting water or bringing in logs were real. History, the stories of what had happened; prediction, stories of what might happen; descriptions of places outside the village – all were stories, and only stories to Marion. Neither time nor place outside her life and outside the village had any reality. She looked up to the brightening star and the swallows and swifts still screaming high above her. They will still be there, she thought, whizzing about, after I no longer see or hear. Days and nights, unknown to me will follow, and will be *forever* unknown.

Peter came trudging up the path again and sat down beside her.

'Where's Peterkin got to?' he asked, but at that moment Peterkin appeared round the corner of the cottage. He was carrying a flat basket. 'Look what Joan's given me,' he said, displaying a number of buttered scones with shiny tops and crumbling edges. 'It's the overs. She said Dick told her to give them to me because I'd helped with the shearing.'

'Don't think you did much,' said Peter.

'Yes, I did, she said I'd helped with all the hurdles and I must take the basket back in the morning.'

'Well, let's have it before it gets any staler,' said Peter.

'Did you come back with the Shepherds?' Marion asked through a mouthful of crumbs.

'No, they're still at the Hall, sitting outside, with Sir Hugh and all, eating the overs, like this.' Peterkin took another scone. 'I hung about to see if they'd give me a bit, and Dick saw me, and told Joan, like I said, and they were talking about sheep – nothing but sheep – all day.'

So the three of them sat there in the bronzing dusk and finished off the remains of the feast.

JULY

Beneath the pastures willow shade
Whose foliage shines so cool and grey
Amid the sultry hues of day
As if the mornings misty veil
Yet lingered in their shadows pale

Marion was woken as if by a thud of grief falling on her heart, and instantly attendant anxieties fluttered round the grief. Her sleepy mind likened the feeling to the thud of a new log falling beneath the saw, and dust and shavings flying up in the air where it landed. The image persisted and her dreaming thoughts struggled to separate log from grief and shavings from anxiety. Lying still, eyes shut, body relaxed, she realized that she was fully awake, that a dream was a dream, but the grief was real and terrible – for Dick Shepherd was dead.

His death had caused in Marion and in everyone else in the village, an unusual state of shock. They, so well used to death – deaths of so many of their babies, deaths after brief illnesses of so many of their children, the expected deaths in winter of the old, the not infrequent deaths of young women in childbirth – had nevertheless been shocked and frightened by the death of Dick. He had been a man in his prime, a man with kinglike strength, their father figure, although he was only Sir Hugh's servant. Marion, in numbed surprise, had been trying to get used to this terrifying deprivation. She remembered, more sharply, that she once had been a bit in love with him.

She went over in her mind the events of his death. It had been soon after the sheep-shearing was finished. The sheep had not returned to the hills but were pastured in Sir Hugh's orchard, when it was decided that the grass in the largest pasture field was almost ready for cutting, and the weather as propitious as could be hoped for. Sir Hugh dithered, Rollo advised waiting a week, Sir Hugh dithered again until Dame Margaret told him to take Simon Miller's opinion – which he did, and issued a general order for hay-cutting. This meant almost every able-bodied man in the village must present himself, scythe in hand, at the Hall. The weather had remained dry all that week, not hot and often cloudy, but the rain held off and with every scythe in the village working, after three days of unceasing effort the greater part of the hay-making was completed. Only men scythed; women and children raked and tossed. It was a sight familiar to Marion from her childhood, the row of men, mostly with misshapen straw hats on, many wearing only their loin cloths, but with boots as well, as the hay stubble was prickly even to hardened feet, swaying slowly from side to side as they swung their scythes, and intoning in unison the sing-song repetitions of

> *Dobbin* and *Robin* and Buck and Jo
> Went *up* to the *mea*dow to *mow, to mow*
> Went *up* to the *mea*dow to *mow.*
> *Where we* now *reap* there *once* we did *sow*
> *Up* in the *mea*dow we *mow,* we *mow*
> *Up* in the *mea*dow we *mow.*

Only now and then a mower would pause, pull up the whetstone hanging at his waist on a cord, and the harsh whistle of whetting a scythe blade broke into the rhythm of the song. Then picking up the rhythm and the words, he rejoined the others in swaying and singing.

There followed some more days of raking and tossing, piling up the hay into tall cocks. The weather held, in fact became hot and muggy, and by the fifth day most of the big Mill field and three-quarters of the Common had been cut, dried and stacked on the stubble when the accident occurred. So tiny an accident it was that no one regarded it.

Dick had been one of the party with Marion and Peter and a few others raking in the far corner of the big field. They had stopped work and were resting in the shade of an oak, lying under it on the short grass which was not long enough to be worth scything. Hilda had brought a bucket of thin ale and had kept it all the morning in the cool grass in a ditch beyond the oak. Marion had brought two loaves and a bit of hard cheese, and she had watched Peter holding the loaf against his chest and slicing it by drawing the knife towards his own throat. She had seen him do this all her married life and had never seen the knife slip – but she still wished he would not. Hilda dipped her small horn cup into the bucket and passed it round and the thirsty rakers poured the cool ale down their throats and ate the hard bread hungrily. They pulled the crusts from their teeth, they stuffed the cheese into already full mouths and called on Hilda for another hornful. Marion recalled the scene in detail: Hilda sitting cross-legged by her bucket, her cap off, her dark hair tied back at the neck, her sleeves rolled up showing her thin freckled arms, her body twisting round as she dipped the horn in the bucket and twisting back again to pass it into some red-pricked, thick-fingered hand that reached out for it; Dick lying flat on his back, his orange hair flowing over the hat that he had scrunched up to rest his head on, his eyes gazing up at the branches of the oak, his beard, sprinkled with breadcrumbs, sticking out below his chin and just showing the ridgy redness of his Adam's apple. The grasshoppers whirred, occasionally a pigeon complained in the nearby forest, or a jay screeched. No one spoke for they had nothing much to say. After so many hours of hard work all were glad to lie in the cool undazzling shade and eat and quench their thirst.

Marion had Peterkin and Alice with her. Peterkin worked, raking and tossing, and Alice was minded by the Shepherds' little girls. They had all more or less finished eating when Peterkin said, 'Father, who's Buck?'

'What Buck?'

'In the song. No one's called "Buck".'

'Don't know,' said Peter. 'It's just in the song, always was.'

'Maybe there was once a person called Buck lived in the village,' Dick muttered, still gazing up into the branches.

'Buckercuck,' said Alice, and collapsed into giggles at her own wit. Marion looked at the squirming little girl and thought how different Alice was from other children. No other village child – or certainly none of Marion's children not even Nolly – had ever made themselves laugh. I suppose most mothers think their children are different from others at some time – but she's not my Nolly, thought Marion.

Peter, always conscientious, was the first to rouse himself, start relacing his boots, and then one by one they all rose up stiffly, finding their hats, stepping behind the tree to urinate and arguing whose rake was whose. Someone had left Dick's rake lying on the stubble athwart a depression in the ground. Someone must have stepped on it and partly split the handle, which, when the pressure was removed, straightened out so that the split was concealed. Dick took it up, seeing nothing wrong, but when he ran his right hand up the shaft, a long sharp sliver of wood, lying close to the shaft and barely visible as separate, pierced the ball of his thumb deeply. He yelped, jerking his hand away and the sliver broke off leaving an inch of wood sticking out of his hand. Hilda was by him in a flash as he gripped the sharp inch of wood and pulled it out with, 'Eeeh,' his mouth tense.

'It's nothing,' he said, putting his hand to his mouth and sucking the wound. 'It's out. Give me a bit of something to wrap round it, Hilda. Look, it's not even bleeding.'

Marion saw that the sliver he had pulled out was over two inches long, so that it must have penetrated deep into his hand. What neither she nor anyone else knew then was that the point of the sliver, quite a long bit, had been broken off *in* the wound. He made light of it, bound his thumb round with a bit of cloth that Hilda tore from the cover of the bucket, honed the handle of his rake smooth and went back to the field with the others. Once or twice during the afternoon Marion saw him using his left hand only on the rake and guessed it hurt more than he liked to admit.

They worked long, hour after hour. Marion met Ellen, who was with the party scything the middle of the field, when their raking lines met, and they paused to rest and chat about the weather and Marion mentioned Dick's mishap. They worked on.

The sky was still clear and blue when they all began to feel real exhaustion. Three more long lines of hay on the ground must be tossed and tossed and reraked, but Hilda said she must now take her children home, and would take Alice too and give her some milk. As soon as she had disappeared down the field, carrying Alice in the now empty bucket, followed by the little girls begging for a similar ride, Dick told Peter that he had to go to look at two of the sheep in the orchard that he suspected were ill, and he took himself off. Marion well knew how he and everyone else looked for excuses to leave the hayfield. The pricking feet, the aching backs, the weary shoulders could be endured only so long – and the July days were longer than endurance. 'You go off and rest on the Green,' Peter told her, and gladly she too wandered down the path at the edge of the field on her way back to the village.

She was rather startled when, near the end of the path, she came upon Dick seated on a fallen ash trunk with his head bowed on his left arm and his right arm cradled in it. He had not heard her coming.

'Dick! Are you bad? Thought you were going to the orchard?'

He raised an embarrassed face. 'Must have dozed off,' he said. He smiled, but she saw how gingerly he moved his right hand and how slowly he straightened the arm. 'Perhaps I'm not used to this work – this sort of work. Sheep are quieter.'

He stood up and they walked the rest of the way to the Green in silence. Then he went round the Hall to the Orchard and she saw him no more that day. He must have gone straight home from the orchard for he was not on the Green when Peter and the rest of the scythers joined Marion. The women, who had gone home earlier to their cottages, came out with baskets of bread and small buckets of milk, and Rollo, obviously reluctant, came from the Hall and ordered Tom to bring a big pitcher of ale. The supper was eaten as the golden sky shone on their sunburnt, silently munching faces, and only a glimmer of dusky light was left by the time Marion and Peter had walked the last quarter-mile back to their cottage, with Peterkin limping behind them, silent with exhaustion. The top half of the door was open, but it was too dark to see anything. She felt for the cradle, slid her hand in and found Alice's warm body. Hilda had fed her and put her in the cradle faithfully. Alice was deeply asleep.

After such physical exertion Marion had slept well. It had grown cold in the early hours and she had pulled up the feather quilt over her and heaved nearer to Peter's warmth. At the first still hint of grey dawn she rose and peered out of the top half of the door. It was patchy cloud as before, cool, no wind, dry. They would go on haymaking.

It was later, when Peter and Peterkin had departed for the fields, and Marion had prepared and was packing the bread into a basket, that Hilda looked in over the half-door.

'Dick's suffering with his hand,' she said. 'He says it's nothing, but he was groaning in the night with it.'

'Have you put anything on it?'

'Yes, the soaked herbs Dame Margaret gave me when Meg stepped on a rusty nail. It healed up quickly then. I've bandaged his hand, but it hurt him awfully. At first he wouldn't let me touch it.'

'Where is he now?'

'Gone to the fields as usual. Are you ready? I'm going as soon as the girls are ready.'

'We are ready,' said little voices from below the half-door. So they all went up to the fields and tossed the hay and looked at the clouds and felt anxiety in the thundery air. Dick was working away. Marion saw him some distance down a line of hay, and though he was raking, she noticed he held his rake in one hand while the other rested in the opening of his tunic. When they stopped and relaxed under the oak tree, Marion noticed he ate very little, and when one of his little girls bounced down beside his prone body and pulled his right arm he gave a screech of pain that startled them all, and the child, blank-faced, hid behind her mother.

When they picked themselves up to resume work, Dick muttered, 'I'll rest a bit longer – I feel a bit queer.' He lay there with his head on an oak root, for a long time.

In mid-afternoon Hilda came to Marion to ask for help, her lips trembled as she spoke. 'I think he can't walk much. Will Peter and Hodge help him home?'

In the end Peter and Hodge half led and half carried Dick down the path and through the village. By the bridge he collapsed, semiconscious. They fetched a hurdle and lifted him on to it and with great difficulty carried him home over the Common with Hilda and the two frightened children following. Meanwhile up in the fields Marion finished her day's haymaking as soon as she could, humped Alice on her back and set off for home. At the ash tree she paused for a moment, then turned aside from her own cottage and went to Hilda's. The door, west facing, was fully open, so it was light inside. Hilda sat on a log close to the bed. Dick was lying there, eyes shut, breathing unevenly. Hilda glanced up at once as Marion's form took the light from the interior. 'Look,' she whispered, all in horror.

Marion went in. Dick's right arm lay beside him, naked, unbandaged, so hugely swollen that it no longer resembled an arm, purple and red in patches with a greenish yellow area round the ball of the thumb.

'He screamed when they lifted him off the hurdle,' Hilda said, her voice grating as much as his breathing. 'He hasn't moved since; he can't speak,' and she stopped as if to bank down her rising hysteria.

'It's poisoned,' said Marion. 'All that yellow is the poison.' She spoke firmly as she looked at Hilda. 'There's no one here and no time to lose – we'll have to do it ourselves. We must cut the wound and get the poison out. Where's the sharpest knife you've got? And where's the herb potion?'

Marion had sharpened the knife on the stone threshold. She did not dare wait for any other help as the light was beginning to go. Hilda was to hold his arm still with all her strength and Marion would cut round the hole made by the sliver. Of course, at the touch of Hilda's hands Dick roared and wrenched it away, but Hilda held firm and Marion made two large cuts in the thumb, enlarging the wound so a great deal of the yellow pus came out. They tried again but could not hold him, and Hilda's tears were blinding her in this act of torturing her lover. They had to give up. They hoped most of the poison had come out, but doubted it, the whole arm was so swollen. All they could do now was to drip the herb potion on to the wound.

He lay semiconscious, the two women watching him. The little girls sat in the growing dusk, watching too, not daring to speak or move, holding the sleeping Alice between them. It was almost quite dark when Marion picked up Alice, told Hilda to send for her in the night if she was needed and went back to her own cottage.

Peter and Peterkin had just arrived, having had bread and ale at the Hall as before. She told them what had happened. Before sleeping they had stood at their cottage door looking across to Dick's. No sound came from it.

'Perhaps he's sleeping now,' Marion said. 'Perhaps I did get most of the poison out . . . ' Perhaps – perhaps – all might still be well.

Peter looked at the sky. 'Thunder clouds gone – sky's clear now. We could still get the hay in in the dry.'

At dawn Marion woke because she heard steps outside. She opened her eyes and in the square of light from the half-door, open all night, Hilda's dark silhouette of head and shoulders appeared.

'I think he's dead,' she whispered. Even in whispers her voice was not recognizable. Marion had immediately gone to Hilda's cottage with her. It was too dark to see anything inside but Marion recalled Hilda's trembling hand on her wrist urging her forward, pulling her down to the bed, guiding her hand to the corpse. She remembered with horrid vividness touching the taut skin of the swollen arm by mistake before her hand was guided to his body. The tunic had been pulled open and she could feel under the curly hair on his chest the damp and unresponding skin. She could feel no movement of breath or heart.

'Have you a candle?'

'I've no fire.'

As Marion knew, there had been no fires in their cottages these last few days when everyone had been in the hay fields. 'Open your shutter then,' she said.

The little shutter was pushed open and a faint glimmer from the eastern sky made the rafters of the cottage just visible, and anything of pale tone – the sheepskin hood hanging on a nail, the milk in a scrubbed wooden bucket, the two half-grown chickens huddled together on a log – slowly became apparent to Marion's eyes, but in the shadow of the bed she could see nothing.

'Did he cry out?' she asked.

'No. He groaned and gasped most of the night since you left. He didn't speak, didn't seem able to speak.' Hilda's whispered words took away Marion's own powers of speech. After a moment she went on even more quietly, 'I don't think he knew anything – just lay there with his breathing between groans getting rougher and rougher – and then it – just – stopped.'

Marion had gone back to her cottage, woken Peter and Peterkin, and sent the latter off to the Hall to fetch Sir Hugh and Father John. She failed to persuade Hilda to leave her dead husband but collected the two terrified little girls, who had dozed all night under a shelf with Janty between them, and had taken them home and given them bread and milk.

Peterkin returned with Sir Hugh and Dame Margaret all out of breath and anxious, and Father John followed them with some candles, in a very ill humour at having been wakened so early. When he reached the Shepherd's cottage he had to send Peterkin back to the village for a red-hot log in an old iron pot, having forgotten that there would be no fire at Down the Common to light the candles. It was therefore full daylight before two candles were lit at the head and foot of the bed, carelessly pushed into knot holes in the woodwork so that Marion feared one might tip out and set fire to the straw on which Dick lay. She had put a little salt on an ivy leaf, (having no dish to spare) and placed it on Dick's chest. They had all knelt while Father John recited the Latin words, incomprehensible to them all, that he always said over a death bed, then they had all left, leaving Hilda and Father John sitting on logs beside the corpse.

Outside Sir Hugh said he must get back at once to see Tom about the grave. Dame Margaret wanted to linger and talk over the affair with Marion, but Marion did not want her in her cottage, knowing that the old feather quilt was lying about and there might be questions about where so many feathers had come from, even though they had been accumulated over many years. But tiresome Dame Margaret hung about until at last Marion asked her to come and sit down on the log seat under the eaves and said she would get her a bit of breakfast. She stepped quickly into the cottage, picked up the damp, hardly wakened Alice from the cradle and dumped her on Dame Margaret's lap, thinking, that will keep her quiet for a minute. She whisked the big feather quilt and the cradle's quilt under the bed-straw, caught Peter's eye and they both smiled their only smile of the day, and then made a bowl of bread and milk for Dame Margaret. When it was eaten and Marion had finished relaying Hilda's description of the death, Peter walked to the village with Dame Margaret and was persuaded by her to assist Tom in digging the grave.

Peter told Marion later how the villagers, sleepy but horrified by the news, had been standing about on the Green when he got there and had been angrily ordered up to the hayfields by Sir Hugh. Anxiety made this normally morose man very ill-tempered. He also ordered Rollo, who avoided manual work whenever he could, to go to the hayfield too.

'We've lost at least one pair of hands there,' he said, 'and the dry weather won't last much longer.'

Sir Hugh then went with Tom and Peter to select a site for the grave. He ignored Tom's advice and chose a place much too near a yew tree, and all day they struggled with the summer-dry earth and the iron-hard roots of the yew. By sunset they had only just made the grave deep enough and had broken a spade in the process.

Marion had gone over to Hilda's cottage again, saw her and Father John still sitting in silence. She had asked if she could do anything for them but was told no, so she went home, collected the three girls and half a loaf and went off to help in the hayfield. Sometime later, on returning, she had asked Hilda if Father John had comforted her at all.

'Comfort?' she asked in a faint voice. 'How could he?'

'Did he speak of Dick's soul in heaven? Nothing?'

'N-no – nothing. He yawned sometimes, and searched for fleas in his cloak. Just sat. I didn't want him to say things to me.' Hilda was quite calm, very pale, her eyes only on the distance. She did not weep, she barely spoke, she seemed to have forgotten her children who were still in Marion's care.

Dick was buried next day. Ned, Tom and Ed-me-boy arrived early, laid down the hurdle on which Dick had been brought home and which had been left leaning against the cottage wall, and had carried the body to it, for it was too wide to get in through the door. The candles had burnt to nothing. The men complained in mutters of the more than awful stench of the corpse, and flicked at the flies on the oozing swollen hand. Peter joined them and with one at each corner of the hurdle they carried the corpse across the Common. When they reached the bridge they stopped and carefully, all bending together, put down the hurdle and stretched their shoulders and eased their hands. Hilda bent down and rearranged the blanket which covered the body. All were silent. Marion remembered that moment in sharp detail. It was a cloudy morning, windless, heavy. The path on which the hurdle lay was trodden bare of grass – only a few flat plantains remained on the stony earth. The path's edges were dry grass mixed with camomile fronds, also trodden flat, and beyond that taller grass, pale with darker seed-heads, all interspersed with points of dock and blue-green thistles with their mauve flowers breaking into fluff. By the stones that made the approach to the bridge a small convolvulus struggled, decorating the dry grass with its pink cones.

Communicating with each other with a few grunts and gestures, Peter took the head of the hurdle and Tom the foot, and they carefully lifted it and carried it over the bridge. The two planks did not allow two to walk abreast across it. On the other side Ned and Ed-me-boy took up their places again and with some shifting of hands, the procession continued to the Green.

The importance of the hay harvest competed with the need to respect the dead. This resulted in all the village women and their small children and some of the men standing about on the Green, subdued and anxious. They gathered and followed the procession, which somewhere Janty and True had joined, and stood silently round the grave, while, as ceremoniously as it is possible to do such a thing, the hurdle was tipped so that Dick's body rolled into the rooty slot. Father John said his strange words again and rearranged his four rather nervous boy helpers behind him and waved his red freckled hand at them in encouragement. Their four frightened thin voices joined his intoning dirge in a brief funeral song, tune and words, albeit incomprehensible words, familiar to all but the youngest.

The rain had begun while they sang but the yew trees had kept most of it off them. The song ended, a blessing was pronounced, and the crowd broke up. Tom neatly folded the blanket which had covered Dick and handed it to Marion without a word. Ned carried the hurdle away, the two dogs following him uneasily, their hind legs not running in alignment with their front legs, as lost dogs always run. Peter and Tom, taking up the spades which they had left behind a yew, started shovelling in the earth. Hilda stood there, with the little girls each side of her, the drizzle sparkling on their orange curls, and watched the spades in silence. Dame Margaret approached her and took her arm.

'Well, my dear, we all know how you feel. You'll be better when you've had a good cry. It doesn't do to be too calm you know, but don't worry, we'll look after your little ones and we'll fix you up. I'll talk it over with Sir Hugh.'

Hilda did not move – she did not seem to hear.

The consolation went on even more briskly. 'He was such a good worker, your Dick was, and Sir Hugh's not one to forget that. We'll look after you so you've nothing to worry about. Now Marion'll go home with you, so have a good cry and we'll see what's best to do about you.'

Hilda said, 'Thank you,' in a faint voice, and then turning to Marion in a whisper of desperation: 'Let me be *alone*.' Marion and the villagers had watched her wander off, down past the Green to the bridge, then on to the Common till she was lost to sight behind the birches and the alders.

'Well, one can't do more for her at present,' said Dame Margaret with some relief in her voice. 'Come, children, Magda will look after you today,' and she whisked them off to the Hall.

A dog fight broke out on the Green, and the villagers, glad to relieve their own tension, threw clods at the dogs with unnecessary vigour. The drizzle thickened and the villagers congratulated each other on having got the main crop of hay in safely, as they departed to their separate cottages.

Tom and Peter joined Marion under the oak. She saw Tom wipe his nose on his sleeve. 'The stinkiest corpse I've ever had to bury,' he muttered. He

caught Peter's eye and jerked his head towards the brew house in the Hall's
yard, in an obvious invitation to a secret drink, but he paused, seeing Ned
returning without the hurdle. Marion saw Ned's face was aghast and that
tears were running out of his eyes and into the pale 'fluff on his cheeks.

'Dick's *dead*,' he said, in a voice as if from a cave, and as if he had not
believed it before. Tom gave him a quick glance. 'Who's going to look
after the sheep *now*?' Ned sobbed.

Tom took him by the arm and said firmly, 'You will, boy, who else?'

'Eh, *I* can't,' Ned moaned, weeping uncontrollably now.

'Yes, boy, you can. You can because you must. Why do you think you're
shepherd boy here? Because Dick picked you out as the best and asked
Sir Hugh if he could have you. That's why you can do it, and why you
must.' He patted Ned's heaving shoulder. 'Look, tie up your dogs and come
down the yard and have a good swig with me and Peter.' They blundered
down the yard, Ned's head bent down.

Marion, watching them, thought: Tom does his best, his *real* best, but
what he's doing is what Sir Hugh ought to be doing – or what Rollo should
do. Why do they leave so many important jobs to Tom? Then a tiny second
thought occurred, that Sir Hugh would never think that talking sympathy
to a shepherd boy was important.

The drizzle was of a very wetting sort, and Marion unfolded the blanket
that had covered Dick and put it round her shoulders.

Marion's mind was brought back to the present by the sudden chattering
of a blackbird just outside. She opened her eyes again. It was getting light.
Peter lay unstirring, his face to the wall, just a mountain of bare shoulder
half covered with the quilt. Peterkin, curled up in the straw, his hair over
his face, slept on. There was no sound from the cradle.

Marion eased the position of her head on the straw. The grief was still
heavy on her heart, but she now rationalized the fluttering anxieties into
two. The first she shared with all the villagers: who could take Dick's place
as their chief shepherd? All knew that young Ned was the only candidate,
but he had been shepherd boy for only a few years and was still very young.
Jo, even younger, they dismissed. All he wanted to do was to play his silly
whistle, they said. *Could* Ned learn, *had* he learnt how to guard and protect
the flocks in winter, how to increase them as Dick had done? Dick had
been their hero because of his success. During recent years under Dick's

care there had been no pestilence among the sheep, hardly a lamb lost to a fox, almost all those born were reared. He had found out the best pastures on the hill and had built the turf and gorse shelters in little ravines in which the sheep had survived on the food he had brought them even if the January snows had drifted over. For weeks at a time he was on the hills, Ned or Jo coming down to the village for food and to report on the births of the lambs. Wool was the source of their wealth. It was no wonder that they looked anxiously at immature Ned and worried that this source would dwindle.

The other anxiety had not been spoken of in the village, perhaps for fear that by voicing it, they would make the anxiety more real. It was concern about the supply of salt. As long as the oldest villager could remember, in late May or early June a party of men from Rutherford arrived with their horses or donkeys laden with salt, pottery and iron. The path through the forest, though overgrown with leaves, was usually at its driest and the days were long enough to do the journey from Rutherford in daylight. Last year Peterkin had been the first to see them. He had been on the Common and happened to look up across the stream, and there, between the willows, just coming out of the forest along the path that followed the far side of the stream, he saw the group of four laden horses and three tired men slowly walking towards the village. It had been near dusk and it was not until the following morning that the baskets were unpacked and the sacks of salt crystals set upon the Hall bench, and the brown jugs and dishes ranged out on Sir Hugh's table awaiting distribution. The following morning Marion, standing at the water-place with her buckets, watched the Rutherford men going silently into the engulfing forest again, with the baskets, now packed tight with spools of spun wool, some of it of Marion's spinning, swaying about each side of the horses' backs.

This regular summer visit was the villagers' one link with the outside world. But well into July, no one had arrived from Rutherford this year. Ought someone to take the Hall's horses and go to Rutherford to find out the reason? Should they load up all the spun wool and take it? Had the party set out from Rutherford and been attacked by robbers and all the iron stolen and the pots broken? Had some pestilence in Rutherford prevented men from coming? Or would it be better to wait? Harvest was probably still a month away – when harvest started everyone was busy and no one, and no horses, could be spared for days to journey to Rutherford. After harvest, there was the threshing, the sieving, the killing of oxen and pigs for winter . . . Here Marion's thoughts were overtaken by fierce anxiety: were there sacks enough in the village to put the threshed corn in? Was there salt enough at the Hall to preserve any ox meat in?

'Stop worrying,' Marion told herself. 'It is not for you to decide,' but one cannot always take one's own good advice.

The grey daylight was coming, and though the air still felt damp and heavy, there was a dawn coolness which was refreshing. In spite of death and fear, life must go on and it was usually a woman's job to see that it did. She prodded Peterkin with her foot and woke Peter more ceremoniously by putting her arm over him. He groaned and heaved and sat up. She saw with some surprise that much of the hair on his chest was sprinkled with white though that on his head and beard was still evenly brown. He rubbed his beard with his broad rough hands and gave her a smile. She looked with pleasure at his solid shoulders and muscular arms. She wanted to kiss his bare shoulder, but did not.

After their quick breakfast, Peterkin carrying a bag of bread and soft cheese and a small bucket to fill in the stream on the way, Peter carrying his long leather bag with the biggest saw's handles sticking out, the two stumped off down the Common. They were to meet by the bridge with several other men: Matt, the Hall's ploughman and his son; Steve Hunter; Andrew Fletcher, and Simkin, who always seemed untirable. Roger from the Mill would join them on the path. They were to go miles up into the forest opposite the Mill to fell, dismember and bring down a particularly large oak tree whose height and girth would in due time provide durable posts and beams for future barns. Rollo had marked the tree and had taken Peter to it the week before to get his confirmation of its good points. Peterkin, too young and weak to chop or saw, would be employed, probably with some younger Fletcher boys, in going up and down to the stream fetching buckets of water for the thirsty sweating sawers.

So Marion was left alone and the grief and anxiety came flooding back. She sat on the log seat under the cottage eaves looking down the garden, leant her head against the wattle wall of the cottage and wept.

It was some time later that Alice's urgent, 'Out, Mam, *out*,' roused Marion, and as she attended to Alice, she resolved to go to see her brother, Simon, and his family. The strength, industry, contentment that seemed always to be the lot of the Millers, would restore her spirits. She had a real

excuse to go. From last year's harvest she still had one complete sack of
wheat unground, and though she knew Simon could do no grinding while
the water level was so low, if she took him this sack it could be ground as
soon as rain permitted the Mill to work.

Her last corn sack was on a shelf above the goat's stall. She could only
just reach it. It was Peter's job to inspect the corn stocks every so often to
ensure that mice or rats had not been eating them. It was through mice-
bitten holes in sacks that so much corn could be lost. That and a possible
leaking roof, allowing sacks to get damp and the corn to moulder or sprout,
were their constant anxieties.

It was very heavy and she could only just get it down, standing on the
goat's up-turned manger, but she managed it. It's wonderful what one can
do, she thought, when one has time and when there is no one around to
say you are silly. She heaved the sack into the wheelbarrow, and found a
late marguerite daisy and some camomile daisies and twisted them round
the sack's neck. 'Alice,' she called, 'we're going to the Mill to see Auntie
Betsy. You ride in the wheelbarrow. Pee first.'

'Don't *want* pee.'

'You must.' Marion was not going to risk Alice peeing on the corn sack
on the way. Marion picked her up, pulling up her dress and held her with
her legs apart.

'Don't *want* pee,' Alice repeated.

'Come on now,' said Marion giving her a little shake. Alice peed. 'There
now, into the wheelbarrow. Sit on the sack, yes, legs each side, now don't
wobble about.'

The wheelbarrow was heavy even when empty, and with Alice and the
corn in it, it was almost as much as Marion could manage. The solid wheel,
moving stiffly on its short iron axle, and the rough paths did not help, but
down the slope they went, through the gate and out on to the Common,
with Alice waving her arms about with pleasure.

It was a hot muggy day, the lavender-grey clouds were unmoving. There
was a lassitude about the village, not uncommon at this time of year. Round
the cottage the sparrows had cheaped and fluttered since dawn, but here in
the middle of the Common there was little sound of life. The birds in the
woods were quiet except for the moanings of pigeons, and the cows, now
gathered under a big oak tree, made no sound except from the constant
swishing of their tails.

The lassitude, perhaps exaggerated by the shock of Dick's death, had spread to the villagers and many of the men had an easy time at this moment of high summer. The shearing was over and the sheep and their half-grown lambs had now returned to the hills with Ned and Jo. The hay harvest – or anyway the main crop – was all cut and dried, carried and stacked. The corn harvest was still a few weeks away, the corn standing silvery green in the field strips. The peas and beans all over the village gardens were still growing, nothing ready to pick. Cows, still in milk, grazed peacefully with the calves round them.

Most of the men were therefore waiting on nature. At this pause in the year they knew they should be inspecting fences, mending roofs, clearing ditches, adjusting ploughs, cutting logs against next winter, and a thousand other jobs for which there was little time in the busier seasons of harvest and little inclination in the bitter short days of winter. Those particularly prudent or energetic attended to these affairs even when not goaded by Rollo, but most relaxed, breathed the warm air easily, stretched out stiff feet on the clovery edges to paths, threw off stuffy hoods, looked at the sky with pleasure and sang slow songs as they sat under the oak tree on the Green spinning out a pot of ale in the long summer evenings, easing their over-burdened shoulders and gnarled hands. It was a behaviour which always made Peter grumble.

'Person like me's always working, no seasons in a carpenter's life. Those people,' a jerk of his head towards the murmuring group under the oak, 'spend their time waiting for their crops to grow or ripen. They can be idle weeks at a time, but for me, it's work, work, and always more work.'

And so it is for me, and all other women thought Marion.

Marion had got as far down the Common as the bridge and here she paused and let go of the wheelbarrow to ease her arms. The stream banks were clothed in deep fronds of plants overhanging the water and hiding the contours of the ground. Tall grass mingled with stitchwort and ragged robin; brambles and dog roses arched over the still pools of water which were now all that was left of the stream. A sudden desire to savour the cool water came over Marion. She put a stone against the wheelbarrow's wheel to steady it and slid through the deep verdure on the bank, supporting herself with one hand on the understructure of the bridge. Her feet felt the cold water as they pushed the long grass under, silver bubbles adhering to the stems below the surface. Her feet sank into the soft mud and a line of cold crept up her legs. She hitched up her dress with her free hand and lay back into the deep grass. The stirred water released its muddy smell and this mixed with the scent of the peppermint leaves crushed under her legs. Apart from the grasshoppers it was very quiet. She would have hated to have been seen to be so self-indulgent by any of her neighbours, but no one came that way and the cool solitude was a sweet balm. Her hardened burning feet were cooled and softened.

'Ma-a-a-m,' said Alice, suddenly bored. Marion twisted her head, pushed aside some loosestrife and looked up at her. 'Ma-a-a-m,' said Alice again, and stuck out an arm.

The gesture and perhaps some sibling likeness in shape of head reminded Marion poignantly of Nolly, and her breath stopped for a moment. She wondered why Nolly, now several years dead, had this quality of darlingness about him that none of her other children had. She remembered in sharp detail his round brown head, his round brown eyes, his wide smile of welcome. Was it his responsiveness to her that distinguished him among her babies? Perhaps. Peterkin had mostly seemed self-contained, Alice was lively, Margery had always been too wispily alive to make any impression. Marion did not know what quality Nolly had had, but she realized that no other child ever had or ever would so grip her heart, nor leave so large a scar when he or she died. 'Ah, my poor Nolly,' she said aloud, as if saying his name would make him real again.

Marion rose, picked a bit of loosestrife and gave it to Alice, scooped her up, carried her over the bridge and dumped her down in the short clover the other side.

'Sit still, Alice,' she said, 'while I get the wheelbarrow.' She found that she had to carry the corn sack across too as she could not pull the wheelbarrow up the steps without risking tipping its contents into the stream. These three trips up and down the harsh log steps were hard on her softened feet. On the far side, as she was reassembling Alice and the corn sack, Marion saw that in the open shed against the end wall of the Hall, Hilda stood alone kneading dough on the counter. Marion would have preferred to avoid her, but telling herself that that would be too unkind, she left the wheelbarrow half under the oak and went to ask Hilda how she was.

'I'm here,' said Hilda. 'That is, I suppose I'm here, living in the Hall, with the children, an ordinary servant, making bread. I just feel I'm in a deep dream.'

'I understand,' said Marion, using the usual words of consolation. 'You'll come through that and feel more yourself. It's the shock, you know.'

'I'll never feel better, I don't want to,' said Hilda, very calmly as though she spoke of someone else, and Marion noticed how very thin her fingers were that clutched the dough.

'Oh yes, you will,' said Marion, following the conventional hearty advice, though she had little confidence in it as she spoke. 'You must look to the future, and your children. You'll get used to being by yourself after a bit,' though as she said it she wondered if 'by yourself' really described living in the Hall.

'I'll never get used to being parted from Dick,' said Hilda in the same tone, almost speaking to the dough.

Marion hesitated. Hilda's voice held full measure of hopelessness.

'You were parted from him often before,' Marion went on. 'He was up in the hills for days – even weeks – at a time.'

'Yes, he was,' Hilda's eyes were on the hills now, 'days and nights there in his little gorse hut, or out in the starry wind, and my thoughts flew to him – up there in the hills, up there in the dark – a thousand times in the night, or in the day.' Her shoulders hunched and her head bent down. In an undercurrent of thought, Marion saw the dough was being oversqueezed with Hilda's emotion. Hilda lifted her head again and looked straight at Marion.

'But now,' she said intensely, 'my thoughts dash out of me, up the hills, away, away, over the forests and on and on for ever, till I stagger for there's no resting place for them. My thoughts unwind from me like a thread from a spool, pulled out further and further for ever. I stagger with giving out – giving out – there's no end to it, *no end*, Marion,' and a slight tremor in her voice made her clamp her mouth shut and continue to knead with taut fingers.

Marion was perplexed and silent. It was not only contrary to village custom to describe one's feelings, it was beyond most people's ability. The villagers would only have used a few phrases so well worn that all personal flavour had long been rubbed off. 'It's a hard sorrow,' would be said at the death of a young husband or wife; 'It's a cruel day for her,' at the death of a baby or little child; 'Ah well, it has to come,' at the death of an old person. Marion felt a mixture of compassion and rebuke, overlaid with a strange sense of experiencing new intensities of feeling. The conventional phrases did not fit Hilda, as indeed conventional attitudes had never fitted Dick. Marion wondered for the first time whether Hilda's strange thoughts and unusual words had been what had so attracted Dick to her – for no one ever had thought freckled Hilda pretty – and Marion had a glimpse of unknown bonds made of thoughts and words that could perhaps bind two people together even more tightly than could sexual passion and its resulting children.

Hilda lifted her tearless face, again looking into Marion's eyes. 'You'll think I should not talk like this – perhaps I should not. I just say how my thoughts go. I think *you* know how thoughts really go when you find yourself torn apart. Saying things like, "cheer up now" doesn't mean anything at all – or "your children will comfort you." They say that to me – Joan does. The girls are good children, but how is a little girl to comfort for a dead lover? You know that, Marion – don't you?'

Marion nodded slowly. 'Yes, I do know,' she said. 'There is no curing such grief, no telling others much about it,' and her thoughts went to Nolly.

Hilda clenched the dough, and her voice was tense as she said, 'I can't talk ever, here. M'Dame is all right, stiff but treats me well, and cuts down on blaming *me* for anything not to her liking just to be kind to me. Joan is just a chatterer. Tom's kind, really kind, but he's always busy. Milly's always looking for something to grumble about – I'm quite alone.'

Marion stood silent. Then she put a hand on Hilda's as it squeezed the dough. Her thoughts collected, she dared an unusual expression.

'Hilda, keep your memories. Go over them again and again in your mind. Remember everything you and Dick ever did, ever said. It will be bitter tears for you but it is richer than forgetting.' It was with great emotion that Marion delivered herself of these irreligious opinions, and Hilda looked up again into Marion's eyes.

'Yes, it is,' she whispered.

Marion pressed her hand again. 'You're not doing the bread any good, squeezing it like that,' she said to break the emotional spell.

Hilda, half smiling, collected up the bits of dough, and Marion stepped back to the wheelbarrow where Alice had been quietly lounging, waving the stick of purple loosestrife to and fro. The heavy clouds were breaking and the sun came out as Marion trundled the wheelbarrow out from under the gloom of the oak on to the Green. She saw Milly coming up from the stream with a yoke on her shoulders with two buckets of water hanging from it. Much as she would have liked to, there was no way that Marion could avoid her. Milly bent down, releasing the yoke and standing the buckets on the path.

'Saw you talking to our Black Cloud,' she said with a short guffaw as Marion approached.

'Is she really a black cloud?' Marion asked, hating these conflicting views in her heart but in no mood for argument. 'She's still shocked, can't believe it yet. It takes time you know. He's not been dead a month.'

'It's like having a black cloud come over the sun,' sniffed Milly. 'Always makes you feel in the wrong when you've done nothing, with that moody freckly face around. You hardly get a civil word.'

'She seems to work hard enough,' said Marion, trying to steer Milly to a brighter view. Milly conceded this with more sniffs. 'How are the children?' Marion asked.

'They're no trouble,' Milly admitted, then searching for a cause for complaint, added, 'except it's all extra mouths to feed. Magda keeps them under her thumb and that keeps Magda out of *my* way,' Milly guffawed at her own wit. 'I never liked that red hair – hardly natural. Your little 'un walking yet?'

Marion said she had been walking for almost a year.

'Time he hardened his feet,' Milly grumbled. 'Still, the more he trots about the more trouble he'll get into.'

Marion said it was a girl but Milly did not bother with such details.

'Going to the mill?' she asked. 'Well, I must get back to old Black Misery. Try the patience of an angel, she would, with her silence and dreary ways. Real nasty it is, takes your spirit away to have that gloom around all the time. Want a drink?' Milly waved at the buckets. 'Take it while it's offered.'

Marion scooped up a palmful of water and drank it. It was marvellously cold. She scooped up another and dextrously poured it into Alice's mouth. Alice coughed and said, 'More.'

'Go on,' said Milly, 'give him another, hot day now,' and Alice had another gulp.

Marion succeeded in not spilling any on the corn sack. She picked up the wheelbarrow handles and Milly heaved the yoke up to her shoulders, splashing her feet as the buckets shook.

'Alice, wave goodbye to Milly,' Marion said.

'No,' said Alice, and Milly made a face expressing even greater disgust, if that were possible, and they parted.

How distasteful was Milly's peevish conversation. Marion recalled how she always had to summon her courage and to arrange her cheerfulness to combat Milly's dreariness. Milly *made* misery around her and today Marion had not the spirit to ward off Milly's contagion. Marion walked slowly over the Green, the weight of the wheelbarrow handles pulling on her arms, and the weight of Hilda's grief and Milly's poison weighing down her heart.

She trudged on along the stream's edge, until, round a curve in the stream, the path forked. The left fork went up to the level of the millpond and the top doorway of the Mill, and the right fork went down over the broad cart-bridge above the lower sluice into the Mill yard.

Just by the bridge Marion put down the wheelbarrow handles again to ease her shoulders. At her feet, half embedded in the path was a kidney-shaped stone, whitish with yellow flecks, still there, as it had been all her childhood. She paused to relish the awareness of how she had changed and the stone was unchanged. She crossed the bridge and went into the Mill yard, passing a row of apple trees on her left along the lower sluice, with several grey geese and their goslings pecking about in the bright grass. There was the neat garden on her right, the Mill and the house before her, all so familiar that she could hardly see them as they were. But today, perhaps because of the shock of Dick's death, all her sensations had a great poignancy. She realized how solid, tall and substantial were the buildings before her. The beams of which the Mill was constructed were twice the girth of those of her own house, thicker even than the great posts and rafters of the Hall. Even the Hall had only one room, whereas the Mill had three rooms, one above the other, strong floors in between them with ladders going up through square holes in the corners of the ceilings, and the Mill's door was like a barn door, wide and high enough for a laden cart to be backed in. The house, which abutted on to the Mill, and where Marion had been born, was equally strongly built, and, though not as tall as the Mill itself, was high enough to have a half-loft inside approached by a ladder, where the family slept. Both buildings were covered with solid horizontal planks of wood pegged on to the close-set uprights – almost windproof.

The ground in the yard was all dried ruts from wheels, sunken crescents from horses' hooves, all hard and uneven and very nasty to walk on or to push a wheelbarrow over. No one was about in the yard. Some hens wandered in and out of the Mill, idly pecking at the pale ground, and by the wood pile against the house, a tabby cat lay sleeping in the sun.

She pushed the wheelbarrow in through the big door, and as she stood, looking round, the dusty corny smell from her childhood filled her nose. It was all as it had ever been: the three huge oak posts slanting from the floor to meet together at the ceiling, on whose combined tripartite strength the millstones above were supported; the massive shelves along two walls, now carrying only some piles of neatly folded sacks, a row of shallow sieves of woven osiers, and a row of cylindrical measuring pots hanging on their wooden handles from pegs on the edge of the shelves; the long wooden shovels and scoops leaning against the wall beneath them and the pale dusty floor. Marion looked at the ladder in the corner. Each rung was worn into two slight dips by the millers' feet treading up and down for decades. The bottom rung had a knot in it, towards the left side, which being harder, had not been worn away but stood up as a smooth shiny lump. Marion remembered when this lump had been level with her face and she had sucked its hard smoothness. How near to the ground it now was! Yet she knew exactly the feel of the knot in her mouth and the slightly bitter dusty taste.

The meal bin, a solid wooden box built into one corner, had been emptied and swept out and its lid, hinged with two thick leather straps, was propped open. On the floor and on the shelves above it were rows of fat sacks, each identified by a sprig of hawthorn, a wreath of goosegrass or a lump of wilting vetch. Each villager had his own identifying plant.

She could hear shuffling on the floors above, but otherwise the building was quiet, none of the creaking and groaning that the structure emitted when water poured on to the water wheel outside and the millstones rumbled and crunched and sighed with the effort of heavy work as if they were human beings.

'Simon,' Marion called up the ladder.

'Oho!' came Simon's voice above.

'It's Marion. I'm coming up.' She felt the lumpy knot, cool, smooth and bruising under her instep as she went up. She emerged through the ladder hole into the gloom of the stone room, as it was called, where the grinding stones and the wooden mechanism were. Only a small window, its shutter almost closed, let in a shaft of light, laying a bright finger across the thick wooden wheels. Motes of dust strayed around in the beam and as Marion approached, the motes thickened and whirled in the light. It was quiet, not a drip of water from the great wheel outside, only the shuffling feet above.

It was a long time since Marion had been up here in the mechanics of the mill, and it gave her renewed pleasure to see in the warm gloom each side of the sunbeam, the heavy wooden wheels and the cog-plates of thick applewood set at so precise an angle, all satin-smooth with years of rubbing. She recalled again the sight of the water-shaft that came in through the wall from the water wheel, beginning to turn as the sluice gate outside was opened and the connecting wheel, the wallover, which changed the direction of the power from horizontal to vertical turning, being dropped by two men into place with a loud 'chlock', and the upper millstone, thus engaged, starting to turn slowly, the cog-plates coming together like the palms of two hands, then slowly releasing each other, and at the same time the magic of the great upper stone smoothly sailing round. The sounds were vivid in her memory, the creaks and groans of the wooden machinery, the rush of grain pouring down the hopper and the crunch of the corn between the stones. It was a triumph and a wonder, an enormous saving of back-breaking effort and a promise of food combined, and an aesthetic pleasure as intense as any she knew. She remembered how, after a day's milling, the wooden wheels were warm with friction and she would be sent up the ladder in the dark with folded blankets hanging over her shoulders to spread over the warm wheels, and oh how comfortable it was, having fetched them later, to be wrapped up in a warm blanket for sleeping. But all was still now except for the motes in the sunbeam, and all was silent. Marion went up the ladder in the corner to the top room.

The heat under the rafters and thatch hit her as her head came level with the floor. It was bright up here, for the wide window with the pulley wheel outside it was open, and so was the door to the plank bridge over the water wheel opposite. She observed Simon's stringy legs, the black hairs on them whitened with the flour and meal which pervaded the whole building. He helped her up the last steps.

'Not wanting grinding, are you?' he said.

'I brought my last sack of corn,' said Marion. 'It's in the wheelbarrow with Alice downstairs.'

'No hope,' he said. 'You saw all the other sacks down there? You'll have to take your turn. Rollo will expect to be first once the pond's full. Come and look at it.'

'I'm not out of flour,' she said, 'and I can do a bit in the old quern if needed.'

'You women and your old querns, do me out of my livelihood,' but this stock grumble was given with a smile. They went out of the little door to the plank bridge which went over the sluice to higher ground beyond. The sluice, lined with thick elm planks was bone dry, and the broad water wheel below them, with all its elaborately made scoops, rested motionless, with a few strands of dried waterweed hanging from the edges of the scoops.

'Look at that,' said Simon, pointing to the millpond on his right. It was an oval dent in the hillside with alders and willows on the far bank. Marion was used to it brimming with water, rippling up against the sluice gate at their feet. Now there was only a patch of stagnant water in the middle, surrounded by a wide area of shelving cracked mud.

'Never remember it as low as that,' Simon went on. 'I can't do a thing. Roger and me got this new sluice post in last week – old one was rotten – and we've mended two buckets of the water wheel. By the way, tell Peter to look out a good trunk of hard applewood for me. We've replaced two blades on the wallover, but come winter I'll need to replace another two or three.'

Marion felt a deep satisfaction in the easy and trusting relationship between her brother and her husband. She knew the two men respected each other's skills. With her gladness, some of the burden of Dick's death was lifted.

'Is your corn cleaned?' Simon went on. 'Properly? I sent the Fletchers away last week to get what they brought me properly sieved. It was full of chaff and grit. We'd better go down and see what Betsy's got for us.'

Marion heard squeals of laughter below and saw that the pulley ropes outside the window were jerking. Alice had been tied round in a sack and was being pulled up and down on the pulley rope by Gib, and Betsy was there watching, all full of laughter.

'I came to call Simon to eat,' Betsy called up, 'and I found this poor little girl all alone in a wheelbarrow in the Mill. Not so high, Gib. There you go, Alice, come to Auntie now. Come down, Marion.'

'How's the Old Man?' Marion asked Simon as they went backwards down the ladder.

'Very up and down. Some days he doesn't know who I am, and calls Betsy "Elinor". Then he says, "Is the sluice shut? The wind's westerly and there'll be rain." He repeats this whatever the weather is like — it's just something to say, means nothing, but he thinks he's sensible as ever. Can't walk more than a step or two and his mind is always on the past. Betsy gives him mush and eggs and when we have a chicken he gets the liver, which is all he can manage. We think another winter'll finish him off.'

They had reached the ground floor and Simon lifted the sack of corn out of the wheelbarrow. 'Might as well take my bit now, same as I always do.'

He took a wooden measure from the shelf, Marion undid the sack, he plunged the measure into it, levelled off the corn with his palm and showed it to her.

'All right?'

'All right,' she agreed and tied up the sack again with the camomile daisies at its neck. Simon emptied his measure into an elm chest and closed the lid. This was a ritual that Marion had seen performed by her father, and now by Simon, all her life, the miller taking his measure of corn from each sackful brought, as wages for grinding. The villagers knew he was meticulous about this, but the reputation of all millers as dishonest thieving men died hard. At best, grudgingly admitting Simon's honesty, they muttered the other traditional phrase: 'millers' children don't go hungry.'

Marion and Simon went round the corner of the house, past the wood pile, to where the family was assembled to eat, and Marion again thought, millers' children don't go hungry, as she looked at her strong handsome relatives.

Near the end of the house stood a close-planted group of tall pendulous holly trees whose hanging branches, intertwined, made a thick semicircular curtain, the branches on one side having been cut off to make an aperture. This was called, for as long as Marion could remember, 'the holly cave', and it made an almost completely dry shelter for hens and geese. Over its lower interior branches clothes and sacks were often hung for drying. Marion remembered it much more overgrown and wild, and the ground thick with dead prickles, horrid to the feet, but now the branches had been trimmed back and the ground swept clean and smooth and broad logs had been placed for the family to sit on.

Marion's father, the Old Man, or Grandpa to the children, had been carried out there to his special chair, a chunk of solid elm wood with a plaited wattle backing, and there he sat in the holly shade, his pink bald head bowed, his sagging features losing themselves in his straggling beard, which itself became lost in the grey-brown blanket which covered him. His hands, with swollen red knuckles and contorted fingers, lay in a muddle on the blanket, and his purple-blotched legs, covered in a network of ill-knotted veins, were part hidden in voluminous sheepskin boots. Even to Marion's unfussy nostrils, he stank.

'Father,' she said, touching his hand, 'are you awake? It's Marion come to see you with Alice.'

The Old Man made vague sounds, half opened an eye and closed it again.

'He's asleep again,' said Betsy, 'best leave him,' and Marion thought that one time soon, he would look the same, and they would try to waken him and would find he would never wake again.

Betsy plumped herself down on a log, picked up the loaf and started slicing it, holding it against her body. Marion sat down too, took Alice on her knee and looked round at her nieces and nephew. Gib, the second son, a gangly boy in a sacking loin cloth, sat with his long sunburnt legs bent up under him, and his long sunburnt freckly arms flung out. On his bony shoulders patches of freckled skin had peeled off leaving blobs like squashed raspberries on the points of bone. His pale hair had been cut off round his ears and his more gingery beard split wide every time he put a huge slice of bread into his mouth. Ellen had just come up the grassy path from the stream with a bucket of water. She was, Marion thought, so like what her mother had been when Betsy too was seventeen. Lisa, the eldest child, recently married to Martin Rockwell, was the same type – plump and pink with gingery hair and blue eyes, wide laughing mouth, and, where not freckled or sunburnt, with the very white skin that was so much admired. Kate, the youngest, a girl of about fifteen, was different, slighter and dark-haired, with a brownish skin and deep-set dark eyes under straight brows and a thin arched nose – like Simon, thought Marion. She had always been surprised that villagers had commented on how alike Kate and Marion were, but Marion could be no judge of that as she had no real knowledge of her appearance – nothing more than the dim silhouette in a puddle or in a full bucket of water.

Betsy was chattering away as she sliced bread and spread it with butter from a little tub, and bits of meat from a trencher by her.

'We've a real treat for you, Marion, for all we didn't know you were coming – cold sucking pig. Not much of it, we roasted it yesterday, made a fire in the yard – '

'Was lovely,' Kate broke in.

'It was only a little one. It drowned. Roger found it by a deep bit of the stream between the alders and went to get it out, but it escaped and fell into a still deeper bit and by the time he got to it, it was dead – so now we've only five piglets left. There's not much to eat on a piglet, but it's juicy meat, so here are little scraps on your bread.'

Only five, Marion thought, taking her slice. I've not got one.

'Could you make children's shoes from the skin?' Ellen asked.

'Not tough enough. I made cuts in the skin as it was roasting and the fat ran out on to the bits of bread on the stones. That was what you ate last night.'

Ellen had poured water from her bucket into an earthenware pitcher, which being porous was sweating on the outside and cooling the water inside. She passed the pitcher round and they drank in turn, even Alice. The rich food eaten in cool leisure in these so familiar surroundings, in the easy company of her brother's family – this was the blessing on her grieving heart that Marion had come looking for.

'How's your cherry crop doing?' she asked, nodding towards the large cherry tree at the corner of the house yard, after a long silence while they all concentrated on such rare succulent food.

'Not ripe yet, but there seem to be a lot of them, that is if we can keep the birds off,' said Betsy. 'Simon, have you seen Gib's scarer? Get it, Gib. The sooner you can put it up the better. When Roger's home tonight you and he'd better get the long ladder and tie it up in the tree.'

Gib went round to the yard and returned with a wide board with a bit of rope trailing behind.

'See, Father,' he said, 'Roger and me'll tie it up on the main branch, there, above the top fork, with this rope hanging down. Whenever you pull the rope, the arms go up and then fall with a bang.' He demonstrated. 'I drew Milly's face at the top of the board. I reckoned that'd frighten the birds as much as the banging!' The board which was roughly whitened with lime had at the top a caricature in broad charcoal lines of Milly's face, the eyes two round blobs, too close together, two long vertical lines for her nose, a thin horizontal line dipping at each end for her surly mouth, a broad U-shaped line imitating her heavy jaw and black marks round the top imitating her dark wispy hair and low forehead. The likeness was marked. The family roared with laughter and amazement. Marion felt surprise and intense unease. So obvious a portrayal of Milly was, she felt, an invitation to some evil emanation of Milly's spirit to revenge itself on Gib and all the family.

'Ooh – you shouldn't,' she gasped. 'What if Milly saw?' but this was not her real objection.

'Why not?' said Simon, who was obviously much entertained by it. '*She* won't see it, and if the birds are scared off that's all that matters.'

'And,' Gib went on, smiling at his work, 'when any of us passes the cherry tree we just give the rope a pull and the arms will fly up and bang down and off go the birds. I tried to do hands at the ends of the arm boards but I couldn't get the fingers right so I rubbed them off.'

'Beats me how you got Milly so well,' said Betsy, still gasping with laughter and very much enjoying her son's skill. Marion was a little reassured by the family's easy acceptance of the caricature and wondered at her own fear of it.

'Seen her often enough – too often,' said Gib. 'I can't help remembering what her face is like.'

'Is the sluice gate shut *properly*?' the Old Man asked loudly, suddenly waking up and looking round.

'Yes, Father,' said Simon, 'tight shut, but the water level's so low it couldn't matter.'

'Low, is it? Well, that won't last. We'll have rain before night. I feel it. Help me up, son.' Simon helped him up and supported his feeble body a few steps outside the holly cave and held him while he peed jerkily into the dry grass.

'What you got there, Alice?' asked Ellen, sitting down beside Alice on the ground. Alice held out the stick of purple loosestrife.

'That's a long purple, Alice,' said Ellen, taking Alice on her knee.

'We used to call them dead men's fingers when I was a girl,' said Betsy.

'Ooh, how horrid,' Kate remarked.

Gib joined in, 'I've heard the shepherds call them – '

'Now you shut up, Gib. She's only a little girl still, no need to tell her all that. There's a good girl, Alice. Want another drink of water? Come to Auntie Betsy then.'

The Old Man was eased back to his chair, and Ellen, picking up the trencher, fed him with little bits of the crumb of the bread and tiny pieces of pork. His toothless mouth mumbled over the food and the dropped crumbs bounced in his beard as he ate.

'Water, Grandpa?' said Ellen, holding the pitcher to his mouth. He gurgled and blew drops of water about, then lay back tired and pleased. Marion took his hand again.

'Ah, Elinor,' he said, stroking her hand, 'how's the baby now? We must get a bigger cradle. The sluice gate must be shut before sunset . . . I've told Simon that already – oh, it's Marion . . . haven't seen you for ages . . . Marion, how's the baby . . . ?' But his voice was getting slower and he relapsed again into sleep.

Betsy left them and went back into the house yard and returned with a small wooden tub in her hands.

'Here's something for a good little girl,' she said, sitting down by Ellen and Alice, 'a lump of honey on bread?' She tried with the bread knife to cut into the hard crystalline brown honey in the tub. 'It's all that's left of last year's,' she grunted, struggling, 'hard as a rock now, but I must finish it as next month we'll be getting the new lot from the hives. Apples were in flower late and beans followed quickly so the bees had plenty. Since the beans there's been the heather up on the hills, so I'm hoping for a lot of full combs. We've five hives now, Marion; here, Alice, try a bit of honey.' She gave Alice a flake, who dutifully put it into her mouth and then smiled broadly.

'Give the tub to me,' Gib said, and he hacked at the remaining honey with more strength.

'Here, Gib, here's more bread. Put lumps on to it and Marion can take it back to poor old Peterkin – he doesn't get much in the way of little treats.'

'The Old Man's off to sleep again,' said Simon in a lowered voice. 'Well, this won't get the work done.' He stood up, stretched his arms, thick muscular arms projecting from slits in his sleeveless tunic. 'Back to the sluice. Gib, bring the new planks up, the ones I left by the cow shed. I'll get the saw and hammer.' He moved off and Gib gave the honey tub back to his mother but put a lump of honey into his mouth on the way with a sly wink at Marion, and followed his father.

'Now, Ellen,' said Betsy, 'I need all six buckets scrubbed out, they're by the door. You can't take them all at once so don't try, and when you've done them bring them up to the yard to drain – but leave one down by the stream as you'll need it for milking Parsley this evening, and turn the blanket over on the drying hedge while you're down there. Kate, get the yard fire going and put all these piglet bones on to stew. Get an onion or two and put them in too, and some sage. It'll make a good soup and Roger'll need something when he gets back.'

Marion got up and picked up Alice from Betsy's knee.

'Bring Marion's wheelbarrow first, Kate,' said Betsy. 'You needn't go round by the village with that wheelbarrow, Marion. Go down the garden and cross the stream there and you can go all the way along the Common. The marsh is all dried up and the ground's hard as rock, and now the hay's cut you can push the barrow along the edge of the stream all the way.'

They said goodbye in a perfunctory manner as was the habit of busy people. Marion dumped Alice in the wheelbarrow with slices of honey-bread between dock leaves on her lap, and wheeled it down the garden, past the beans, darkening as they ripened, past the peas, palening as they ripened, past the neat rows of onions and cabbages. A strong wattle fence ran along the edge of the stream to keep the cows from the garden, with a gate giving on to the plank bridge. Marion wheeled Alice on to the plank, carefully closed and hooked the gate behind her. Ellen was already at the water-place a little way up stream, kneeling on the edge plunging the thick wooden buckets into the water, pulling them up and scouring the insides with birch twigs.

Marion looked round and wondered again at the rich orderliness that surrounded the Mill. Parsley, the Millers' red cow, was lying in the shade of a clump of willows, chewing slowly, her half-grown calf grazing nearby. The grass here, close to the stream, was already growing soft and green again after the hay harvest, and further up the field and towards the woods, some haycocks still stood in ordered rows in the sunlight. She thought of the rich meal they had all had, the plentiful bread, new butter with droplets of water in it, scooped up with a broad wooden blade and spread on the bread so thick that you could see your teethmark in it, the cold meat, so juicy and tender to bite off the little ribs, the cool water to drink, the lavish long drink of fresh cow's milk that Alice had had, the honey-bread – all taken as a matter of course. Marion thought of the neat productive garden, the swept yard, the orderly wood pile, the *six* buckets all to be scrubbed and filled, the cool of the holly cave with the logs ready for sitting on. She looked at peaceful Parsley, she thought of the geese plucking grass under the apple trees, the sow and her five piglets fed on sweepings from the Mill, and the bees droning away round the straw skeps in the orchard. It all bespoke a wealth that brought ease with it.

It had not always been thus, she realized. In her own youth when the Old Man was Miller and her mother, Elinor, ran the house, a certain cheerful slapdash attitude had prevailed. Elinor was not orderly. Houses were not swept, straw blew about the yard, vegetables grew, sometimes. If a fox got the goslings – well, what could you expect? Marion remembered how Simon and her other brother, Hughie, who had died young, used to grumble to each other about their feckless mother and their father, who, though careful and skilful in the mill, tolerantly left all domestic matters to Elinor. But Simon had married Betsy the year after Elinor died, and Marion knew that the comfortable orderly life at the Mill was mostly Betsy's doing. Betsy had strength and to spare, she had a love of routine, she foresaw what would be needed, she organized her family – she did all this, as Dame Margaret did, but Betsy did it with a laugh, with a generous enjoyment of whatever went right, and when disasters came, such as the cow breaking a fence and trampling beans, or when storms caused the millpond to overflow and drown the hens, Betsy coped. She mended the fence, she cleared the sluices, she had other stores to replace the lost beans. She did not wail, she did what was necessary and she ruled her five children, making them work for the benefit of all. She also saw to it that Simon, however he might have criticized his more self-indulgent father in his youth, now attended to the Old Man with exemplary tenderness.

'It's Betsy's hard work,' said Marion to herself, as she pushed the wheelbarrow through the rough grass, but she knew it was more than hard work. It was the harmony in which Simon and Betsy lived, and that harmony spread to their healthy self-sufficient children. Marion had found the solace which she had set out to seek that morning.

The way along the edge of the stream was hard going with a wheelbarrow, for it was a little-used path. The marsh, where a stream from the wooded hills sometimes oozed into the main stream was, as Betsy had said, quite dried out, with patches of rushes and thistles standing among the tussocks of grass. There were hard deep hoof prints from the cows, which hurt Marion's feet. She pushed on, past the steps to the main village bridge, on through the more familiar pasture of the Common, past where her own goat and the half-grown kid were sitting under an alder tree.

A certain envy kept Marion's thoughts going back again and again to Simon's family. There were the three girls: Lisa, already married and perhaps pregnant up at Rockwell; Ellen and Kate, already skilled cooks, dairymaids, spinners and gardeners; the boys too, Roger and Gib, strong and capable, being taught partly by showing, partly by exhorting and partly by the long familiarity that went with the grinding of corn and the maintenance of the Mill. It's not only that they are *told* what to do, she thought. 'They *see* their parents doing it, and carefully. It's not only that they are told to work hard. They see their parents doing little else.

She compared these children with her own: poor Margery's twelve years of half-life, half-death; Nolly, the child of such promise, dead at three; the two babies dead almost before they breathed and another smothered by a cat when a few weeks old; Peterkin, maimed for life when he was two, and Alice. She watched Alice, who was tired of being banged about in the wheelbarrow, stumping ahead of her up the slope to their cottage, a stocky cheerful little girl with the belt of her dress trailing behind her. That was all Marion had to show for so many years of ceaseless toil and endurance.

It was very peaceful when she reached home. She took the dock leaves from a reluctant Alice. Some of the honey had melted and run out of the bread. She gave Alice the leaves to lick. She sat down on the log under the eaves, stretched out her tired legs and aching feet into the soft clover, and sighed heavily.

AUGUST

When the sun stoops to meet the western sky
And noons hot hours have wandered weary bye
They seek an awthorn bush or willow tree
Or stouk or shock where coolest shadows be
Where baskets heapd and unbroachd bottles lye
Which dogs in absence watchd with wary eye
To catch their breath awhile and share the boon
Which beavering time alows their toil at noon

Without opening her eyes, Marion rolled over and stretched. Her foot encountered Peterkin's back, but he did not move. Automatically her right hand swung out to the cradle and felt Alice's warm sleeping body. Her left hand, equally automatically stretched out to touch Peter, but it encountered nothing but cool crumbling straw. This woke her properly and she opened her eyes. The grey gloomy dawn of this late August day was visible over the half-door and it dimly lit the interior of the cottage. The familiar lump which was Peter, was not there and she remembered with a pang the events of two days ago. Peter had been chosen to be one of the small group of people to go with Sir Hugh to Rutherford to enquire about, and if possible, to bring back, *salt*.

The unease that had slowly been building up in the village since June over the nonappearance of the men from Rutherford with sacks and jars of salt to be exchanged for spun wool had come to an audible climax at the Harvest Supper. Not that the harvest was really complete – there was much gleaning to be done everywhere, some strips of corn were still to be cut and carried, and all the threshing was yet to do, but the bulk of the corn harvest was over, and as the weather had mainly been satisfactory, the villagers had by and large a feeling of achievement and less anxiety of a meagre winter diet. But at the Harvest Supper, held this year in the Hall as the weather looked too threatening to have it on the Green, Tom had started the salt discussion.

Sir Hugh, by long tradition, had provided a young bullock for the feast, and Tom had dismembered it and prepared a good fire in the Hall. The large joints had been roasted, with Joan and Ed-me-boy taking turns with the longest wooden ladle to pour the running fat over the meat.

When Milly had brought in the ale and Hilda had gone round the tables with her basket of small loaves, and all the villagers, exhausted by the long toil of harvest, were silently eating the thick slices of roast veal that Tom had smacked down on their bread, then Tom had said loudly, 'It's fresh meat today, men, and it will be fresh meat next week if we kill the other bullock, but after that there will be no meat from the farm all the long winter through if we have no salt.'

Marion suspected this raising of the subject had been rehearsed. An uneasy murmur resulted, mixed with sounds of mastication.

Then Rollo spoke. 'The salt men from Rutherford have never been so late – after harvest now – in all my memory.' This too sounded rehearsed.

'Between hay-cutting and corn-cutting's their time,' added Tom.

This studied introduction, coinciding with the first satiation of appetites, was followed by a general release of talk among the villagers, all expressing their previously concealed anxiety about the nonarrival of the salt men. Rollo, sitting at the end of the table on the dais, looked towards Sir Hugh and told him he should consider sending a party of men to Rutherford to investigate and bring back salt.

Tom, serving more slices of hot veal to Dame Margaret on the end of his long knife, said, 'Yes, sir, the horses are all ready, I've got all the harness mended, and there are pannier baskets, with straps, for all the horses.'

The conversation had then been taken up by Dame Margaret and Sir Hugh in lower tones, with Rollo only occasionally raising his voice with advice and encouragement. Everyone knew that Sir Hugh was a ditherer, a procrastinator of decisions whenever possible, and that it usually needed the combined voices of Rollo and Dame Margaret, with Tom making judicious additions at intervals, to bring Sir Hugh's mind to a firm decision. Their deliberations were interrupted by the wild barking of Jix as he scrabbled with his forepaws at the earth just below the dais.

'He must have seen a rat there. Go on, Jix – get him.'

This was Magda's contribution. She was bored with the discussion of a journey to Rutherford which she knew *she* would never be allowed to make.

'That dais,' muttered Tom to Peter, 'just perfect for rats, all those planks put down across logs – too low for a dog or cat to get in. Rats can play Old Harry with us all. Stupid dais. Better live on the true earth, like we all do.'

'Magda!' shouted Sir Hugh suddenly. 'Keep that dog quiet. He can't dig up the whole Hall just to get at a rat. Tom, send someone to Rockwell tomorrow and get them to bring down a couple of ferrets. They'll do for the rats for a bit.'

Then Sir Hugh raised his eyebrows and jerked his head, and Rollo and Father John, the priest bemused and silent from too much ale, moved close at the table and literally put their heads together. The villagers eyed them between mouthfuls. Dame Margaret moved to the table end and made someone take Jix outside, and then supervised more bread and ale distribution. Rollo straightened his back and beckoned to Tom and Peter to join them, and they all muttered together. Seeing Peter summoned to this conference caused a sudden tightening of Marion's breathing and made her realize how anxious she was. The anxiety was two-fold: first that salt must be procured, and second that Peter was to be selected as one of the fetchers.

Before the supper was considered to be over, Sir Hugh stood up and with his melancholy voice suiting his melancholy expression, announced that he had decided that in two days' time, unless it rained very heavily, he himself, with the four horses, their panniers filled with spun wool, with Peter Carpenter and Ed-me-boy, would journey down the valley to Rutherford and with God's grace (here Father John nodded emphatically), they would be back in a few days with as much salt as they could carry. He went on to instruct the women who still had spools of spun wool at home to bring them to the weaving shed tomorrow and hand them over to Joan. Ed-me-boy looked round-eyed at his father, and as Tom nodded to him, smiled a wide smile of amazement. Tom and Peter rejoined Marion at her place at the table. Peter seemed rather sheepish in his pleasure at having been selected.

'It will only be a few days, Marion,' he said, 'a day's journey there and a day's journey, or a bit longer if we are much laden, back, and a day or two there to count out the wool and load up the salt – that is, of course, if they have got any for us. We don't know what we will find there, that's what Sir Hugh kept saying.'

'He didn't want *me* to go,' said Tom, half proud, half resentful. 'Said I was needed here – least Rollo said I was – and he, Sir Hugh, had noticed how Ed had grown recently and was strong and how good he was with managing the horses. There he's right, Ed's got a way with all the horses, and you need steady horses specially on the way back with all the loads of salt – '

'If there *is* any salt,' Peter said.

'– and we may find the forest path very overgrown. It'll be an adventure for the lad . . . ' But Tom's voice trailed off and his eyes followed Ed-me-boy down the Hall, and Marion knew how very reluctant he was to have his boy go off into the almost unknown world outside the village.

She too was reluctant, not that anyone would ever ask how she had felt to have Peter go off into the strange unknown. Familiarity of *place* was security; not even being able to imagine where Peter would be was insecurity.

She had passed the next day in collecting and sorting out the spools of spun wool which she still had in the cottage. Most of her year's work had long since been taken down to Joan's weaving shed and duly notched on her stick by Rollo. Then by filling her holly-wood needle with a length of wool and carefully darning the tear on the shoulder of Peter's tunic and finding a new leather thong to tie his boot, she had filled her anxious day.

'You fuss too much,' Peter said, but he looked pleased, and she knew she took extra trouble over these little services for him to allay her fears.

The departure had been before dawn, a grey heavy dawn with a hint of mist over the Common. Peter had left the cottage with Peterkin to help carry the leather bag with bread and cheese in it. Marion had gone down to the water-place and waited there with the bucket beside her and Alice heavily asleep on her shoulder until she saw the little procession on the far side of the stream.

Sir Hugh rode in front on his dark brown horse, Heart-of-Oak, its tail and mane newly clipped by Tom. Tethered to it followed the young gelding, with two willow-woven panniers each side. Then came Peter, leading the third horse, a bright chestnut with a white line down its nose, also with panniers each side, and last Ed-me-boy, taller and lankier than ever, walking along with a springing step, a long willow wand in his left hand and the bridle of the last horse in the other. He did not know that Tom had followed him some fifty yards behind in order to get a last look at his son before the procession disappeared into the forest.

The panniers had all been packed the night before with tightly pressed in spools of wool, covered with half-skins of leather firmly tied down to the wattle. As they came opposite Marion at the top of the bank above the stream, they all three waved to her and she waved back. They called out messages, nothing that had not already been said. She woke Alice up and made her wave too and Peter called, 'Goodbye, Alice. Be a good girl,' and then the path entered the thick forest and they were hidden from sight.

Marion resolutely put Alice down, filled her bucket with water and laboured back up the path with it, with Alice slowly following. As she approached her garden, Alice came running up behind her.

'Alice found a *fairy's* poppy,' she announced.

'Don't you go touching the fairies' things,' said Marion, automatically using the common phrase, her mind on Peter.

'*Look*, Mam.' Alice held up a scarlet pimpernel flower, no bigger than her little finger nail. There was no tradition in the village that this was a fairy's flower, so Marion could only smile and wonder at her child's invention.

Back at her cottage she put down the bucket and sat on the log seat under the eaves to rest and to summon up her spirits to deal with her solitariness. She knew she was not really alone, for Molly and the two old women, Agnes and Marge, were at home. Marion had seen Molly in her garden as she was coming up from the water-place. The cottage where Dick and Hilda had lived, now that Hilda was settled in the Hall with her two little girls, had been taken over by Lisa and Martin Rockwell, and she knew Lisa was busy tidying up and cleaning out the cottage after it had been left empty for the ritual weeks following Dick's death there. She sat, resting, looking down the garden. Peterkin would be at the Hall all day. Rollo had engaged him the evening before to work in the Hall's pea fields, picking the ripe pods, and, no doubt, One-eyed Wat, Dobbin's son, would be working with him. This was considered to be unskilled work, suitable for boys with some disability. Wat had, as a baby, fallen on to the boot-drying stand in his cottage and put out one of his eyes, and was now a scar-faced skinny boy of twelve. His inability to judge distances did not prevent him from picking peapods – so Rollo reasoned.

Perhaps Marion should start harvesting some of her own garden pea crop. She would go down the garden and look at the plants, although crops grown in the more open sunny areas ripened sooner than in her garden.

Her speculations were suddenly arrested by the realization that Alice was not with her. She jumped up and called her. There was no answer. She ran round the corner of the cottage, under the ash tree and on to the rough grass, the highest point of the hamlet and called again. No answer. She went left to what she still thought of as the Shepherds' cottage. She could see Lisa down the garden and called to her, but Lisa had not seen Alice. She went down the slope to the Plowrights'. A group of lousy children were leaning against the wall of the cottage doing nothing, but they, as far as anyone could understand what they said, had not seen Alice. She went to Molly's cottage and saw Molly coming up from the pig shed. Molly had seen the procession go along the path the other side of the stream and had waved, and had seen Marion and Alice at the water-place waving, but then she had gone into the pig shed and had not seen them again.

'She was following me – I know she was,' said Marion desperately. 'As I was coming up with my bucket full, I heard her humming to herself behind me, and she spoke to me, and I didn't turn round again to check on her after that. She could have gone back to the stream. You know how children like stirring water.'

Molly accompanied her down to the water-place but Alice was not there.

'Not so deep that she couldn't climb out even if she had fallen in,' said Molly, poking about in the mud with a stick, but Marion well knew a child could drown in a few inches of water. They called again, and started along the path towards the village, and then suddenly Alice appeared from between birch trees ahead of them, trotting about unconcerned.

Marion ran ahead and picked her up, angry. 'Where have you *been*, running off like that, you naughty girl? Where have you *been*?'

But Alice's vocabulary was not up to an explanation. She wailed at Marion's angry tone. She had been perfectly calm when lost, but quickly picked up fear from her mother's agitated voice and began to cry, which at once softened Marion's heart.

Marion carried her back to her cottage, leaving Molly on the way who said, 'Well, it's all ended happily this time,' as if deprived of the thrill of a disaster.

Holding Alice in her arms and saying, 'There, there, shush, shush,' Marion vividly remembered her own terror at being lost as a child.

She had been older than Alice, probably about seven, and had gone out with a group of children, mostly a bit older than her, with sacks to collect beechnuts in the forest. Memory did not supply details of the outward walk, nor of the finding and collection of beech mast, which was probably some hours of work, but started on the intended journey home. She had found an oak apple with a small oak apple, still soft, attached to it, and with three short twigs projecting from one side on which it could be made to stand. Ever toyless, she had pretended it was a cow and managed to stick two little curved bits of twig into the small oak apple for horns. She was talking to herself as solitary children often do, and started making a little cow shed for it. She pushed four sticks upright into the moss at the foot of a tree and scratched out other bits of moss to lay against the sticks for walls and roof. It was absorbing. Then she delicately balanced her 'cow' in the doorway of the shed and looked round for an audience. No one was there. She suddenly heard the silence of the forest. Incredulity struck her and she shouted. As her cry faded the silence returned. Panic arrived. Which way could they all have gone? She had no idea; there was no particular path. She shouted again. No answer.

She remembered her father standing her by the Mill sluice some years before and pointing out to her how all round the village the hills sloped down, sometimes gently as with the fields to Rockwell, sometimes steeply as with the woods above the Common. 'If you're ever lost, Marion,' he had said, 'lost in the forest, if you go *down* hill you will come to the village.' He had also said something about the sun but she had forgotten what. Anyway it was a grim overcast October afternoon with no glimmer of sun even if she could have seen the sky above the thick canopy of trees. But *down* hill? On her left the ground did slope down but only into a little leaf-filled dip and rose again the other side. Great beech trees were everywhere with an undergrowth of bushes making it impossible to see far. With no hope in her heart she had rushed down into the dip and clambered up the rooty slope the other side. It seemed here that the forest extended level on all sides as far as she could see, which was not very far. She shrieked again, and on hearing the panic in her own voice, her terror increased. She ran ahead as fast as she could, then gasping for breath she paused, and suddenly the sweet, sweet smell of wood smoke came to her nose, the smell of the village, of home, the smell familiar to her from infancy. She stood trying to scent what direction it came from, and looking round saw that to her right the trees were thinning and the sky visible between their upper trunks. She ran on, fearing she might be approaching one of the many small clearings in the forest, but the smell persisted, giving her hope. She noticed as she ran that she was running down hill, even as she twisted this way and that between bushes. Then the beeches gave way to hazels and the hazels to an open view, and there far below her was the Mill, and further still the big oak on the Green partly hiding the Hall, and far away down the edge of the stubble field was the line of the other children slowly ambling towards the village. At the head of the line two boys walked one behind the other with a long branch over their left shoulders on which was slung the sack of beech mast, and all the other children followed, dragging dead branches behind them. It was a rule: never return from the forest without as much dry firewood as you can carry.

Marion shouted again and the last two in the line looked round and waved casually but did not pause. Marion realized she had not even been missed. She realized too she had been crying. She gulped and calmed herself. She saw she could follow the line of children a short distance and then branch off to go home to the Mill by herself, while the others went on to deliver their beech mast to the Hall. Her legs were trembling. She caught a foot in the unravelling edge of her skirt, tearing it more as she fell in the tussocky grass. She was not hurt and went on more soberly to the Mill. Her mother, tall and gaunt, was sitting on the ground near the door with a sieve half full of corn and chaff between her knees and a sack with dust and bits between her feet. She stirred the contents of the sieve in an absent-minded way.

'Hullo,' she said calmly. 'What are you huffing and puffing about? Did you get a load of beechnuts?'

'Yes,' said Marion, 'a whole sackful.'

'That's not much with seven or eight collecting. What have you done to your skirt?'

'I caught my foot in it and fell in the grass.' Her mother examined the skirt in a desultory manner.

'You'd better sew it up before dark this evening, it'll only get worse if you leave it. Didn't you bring any firewood?'

'The others found firewood. They're taking it all to the Hall with the sack.'

'You might have found some too, you'd nothing else to carry,' her mother grumbled, calmly, and the very ordinariness of her voice and sentiments dispersed further the terror in Marion's mind. She resolved not to tell of her panic, and from that day she had never mentioned it.

Marion comforted Alice with hugs and a drink of goat's milk, set her down by the cottage and herself dropped on to the log seat under the eaves. She wondered why she felt so particularly exhausted. Perhaps it was her hardly admitted anxiety; perhaps it was the thundery weather. The air was heavy with impending rain, yet none fell. It was very still. She looked down the weedy garden and the grassy path running between the beds. Some pods among the tangle of pea plants and their supports were ripe for picking, but not many, so it was no use tidying up that area until picking was complete. Then there would be a great pile of haulms to be taken to Molly's pig shed for the autumn fattening of their jointly owned pig. But now the pea bed was sprinkled with groundsel, little yellow tassles and tiny beige tufts and clocks, stalks of feathery yarrow with their white discs of flowers stained pink in places, a few late poppies, and, upon the worn grass on the path, flat rosettes of plantain leaves, silvery potentillas and white clover, now browned and trampled.

The apple tree by the fence was, Marion noticed, bearing a good crop of apples, for as the growing apples paled, they became distinguishable among all the greener leaves. Thistles grew against the fence too, and as Marion sat there she watched, every now and then, a starry sphere float from the thistles across the garden.

Her thoughts were of the recent past – of Dick, of death, of change, of the feeble transiency of life. When she had gone that morning to the Shepherds' cottage in her search for Alice, she had passed the open door, glanced in and, not seeing Lisa there, had gone down the garden and called to Lisa about Alice. She had been too anxious about Alice to register any feeling about the cottage, but now, sitting idly before the very familiar view of her own garden and the woods beyond, she recalled precisely the interior of the cottage which had been Dick and Hilda's home.

It's the same place, she thought, but all different. I will never again see his crook leaning against the wall by the door. The row of shears that he kept hanging along the edge of the shelf inside will never be there again.

She had seen a row of small tubs on this shelf and two tall earthenware jars, one of which had belonged to her mother at the mill once, and on the bed the straw was covered with one of those very large brown and white

striped blankets which were often made at Rockwell. The high beams of
the barn there enabled these extra large blankets to be woven.

It's not as it was when Dick was alive. It's the same place but it doesn't
look the same, Marion's thoughts went on. It will never be the same again.
Dick is dead. Things can change so much in a few weeks – how much
more will they change as time goes on and on . . . and on . . .? Marion's
ideas hovered around Eternity and then backed away in fear. It now seems
almost as if he were never here, she thought, that all the past years were
a dream, a story, yet his presence *is* still here. He might come round the
corner, under the ash tree, as he so often did, any moment, his deep voice
enquiring for some post or tool of Peter's to mend a hurdle.

'He will never come again,' said Marion aloud to herself, 'never, never,
and Hilda'll stay at the Hall and I will never see them again of an evening,
walking down their garden with their sunburnt arms round each other's
waists. What *is* a person that one can be rubbed away so quickly?' Marion's
unseeing eyes were surveying the spears of pink willowherb by the fence,
but her mind repeated, 'Never, never,' in a kind of incredulous despair.

Unnoticed by her, the weather was changing. The clouds had lifted and
thinned and though no sun was apparent, a dazzling light pervaded the
garden. It hurt her eyes and she was aware of a sharp headache. Endurance
being by now second nature to her, she prepared to endure it, when she
realized that she had eaten nothing all that day. She went in and found
some rather hard bread, several days old, and almost the last bit of mature
cheese. She crumbled some of each on to a scooped board, poured a bit of
milk on it for Alice.

Alice, who had been sitting on the floor by the open door, pulled herself
up by holding the doorpost and let out a piercing wail. She held up her
small open palms to Marion. There were several little splinters of wood
in them. The doorpost, low down, was rough from Tibtab scratching his
claws there. Marion recalled, with sharp pain, the sight of Dick pulling the
rake's splinter from his hand, and in a surge of fear she bent down and took
Alice on her knee and very carefully with her long rough fingernails pulled
out every bit of wood from Alice's palms.

'There now, all better. Don't touch the doorpost again, that's Tibtab's
scratching post.'

'Is Tibtab naughty?' Alice asked, who had been watching the treatment
of her hands with interest.

'No – he's only a cat,' said Marion with sudden weariness. She pushed Alice from her knee, rose and got the food and fed Alice and herself. Then they both dozed.

When Marion woke she was aware that her headache had gone but that her buttocks were numb from sitting with Alice on her lap on the hard log under the eaves, with its rough bark. The weather had altered again and the air was fresher. The sky seemed to have lifted and extended. It was full of bright white clouds, puffy and lumpy on top and straight underneath. The sky between them was a deep intense blue overhead, paling to turquoise behind the forest trees. One bit of ragged grey cloud floated on a massive white one, like a cygnet enfolded in a swan's raised wings. A gust of warm wind, scented with heather, blew a thick patch of floating thistledown across the garden.

'Let's get some blackberries,' Marion said to Alice, and they walked together down the garden to the hedge at the bottom, Marion carrying a wide willow basket.

It was when they were coming up the garden again, Marion carrying the basket which she had lined with dock leaves and which was now heaped with blackberries, that they heard the shout from the other side of the stream. Plonking down the basket, Marion dashed round the corner of the cottage and up the slope of rough grass, and there, emerging from the trees on the far side of the stream, was the procession – four laden horses with three men walking, Peter in front. He saw her and waved and a sudden rush of relief and of happiness flooded her mind. The procession did not stop but was moving slowly to the pace of tired men.

'Come to the Hall,' Peter shouted. 'Bring a basket. Tell the others.' Excited, Marion ran to the Shepherds' cottage but neither Lisa nor Martin was there. She approached the Plowrights', seeing a small group of derelicts by the door.

'Tell your parents Sir Hugh's back,' she said and left them.

Back in her cottage she surveyed the basket brimming with blackberries. It was the only basket she had, but Peter had ordered her to bring it. She tipped the blackberries, or most of them, out on to the shelf and barricaded them there by rearranging two jars and a tub. It was not very safe, but the best she could do. Then, picking up Alice, she ran back up the slope.

Molly was sitting on her threshold, putting on her boots.

'Nothing to tell *me*,' she called out with a wide ugly smile. 'I saw them too. I'm coming at once. We can take turns with carrying your little one.'

They hurried along the Common path, watching the little procession on the other side of the stream as the men and horses appeared and disappeared between the alders and willows. Alice delayed them a little by the bridge by deciding she must be put down to pee, and though the delay irritated Marion she was also glad that Alice was becoming sufficiently trained to ask.

When they got to the Green the procession had already arrived at the door of the Hall and Dame Margaret and Magda were welcoming Sir Hugh, and Tom was smiling to split his face and clapping Ed-me-boy on the shoulder a hundred times. Villagers were running across the Green from their cottages, Father John came stumping down from his cottage, and all the dogs in the village barked in wild excitement. Peter at once came up to Marion and put his hand on her arm.

'All well?' he asked looking her closely in the eye.

'Yes. All well,' she said, amazing herself at her fervent tone.

'All well, Alice?' he asked, stroking her cheek with a finger.

'Alice's hands better. Tibtab's post,' she said, holding out her starry palms, but of course Peter did not know what she meant. Peterkin appeared from the crowd.

'Father, did you see the bridge made of stones?' he asked. 'Did you really? Is it true they can take a cartload of hay over it?' He got no answer as Tom, with a large leather jug of ale in his hand, gave Peter a drink.

'You can finish it,' Tom said. 'Sir Hugh and Ed have had a good swig each.' Tom did not mention that contrary to custom, Ed-me-boy had had first drink from his father's jug.

Marion looked at Sir Hugh with curiosity for he was really smiling, which was rare, and though he was obviously tired, he had a physical ease, which was even rarer. She imagined that after his long delay about deciding to go to Rutherford and his deep anxiety about making the journey, now, having returned in safety and presumably with lavish provisions, he was almost euphoric in his reactions. He was busy supervising the unloading of the horses.

Dame Margaret had during the last two days seen to it that there was a good supply of ale, and while Milly and Joan were fetching more jugs, the villagers crowded round the pile of eight pannier baskets heaped together on the grass before the Hall door.

Sir Hugh was saying, partly to Rollo and Dame Margaret, but loud enough for all to hear, 'We walked back all the way. Your brother lent me two extra panniers so we loaded up all four horses, as much as they could carry. Somehow, in spite of this, the journey home was easier than we expected. Probably we were sure of the way then. Your brother sends his greetings to you, Margaret, and his wife too. You'd be surprised how she's aged. I've so much to tell – '

'Did you bring *salt*?' Dame Margaret's sharp voice broke in, expressing everyone's urgent question.

'Indeed we did. Rest easy on that account.'

Marion noticed how often he said 'we' and she imagined that in this adventure the three men had been bound together with a bond of friendship which the hierarchy of the village could not comprehend.

'Fetch M'Dame a stool, Matt,' Sir Hugh ordered, and when it was brought he placed it near the panniers and led Dame Margaret to it. Magda hovered around, bursting with curiosity.

'Now, Magda, don't touch. Leave it alone.' He took from the nearest pannier a large bundle and unrolled from the sacking covering a fat earthenware jar. Holding its rough rotundity to his chest, he pulled something white from its neck which he pushed up his sleeve, then placed the jar carefully on Dame Margaret's lap.

'That's a gift from your brother and sister-in-law,' he said. 'Look inside.' She slid her hand into the neck of the jar and then showed everyone some black shrivelled pellets. She looked questioningly at Sir Hugh. He smiled, enjoying everyone's wonder.

'Is it seeds?' she asked. 'Do I plant them?'

'Looks like baby rabbits' shit,' said a boy.

'No, no,' said Sir Hugh, frowning at the boy, 'it's fruit. You eat them.' There was a grunt, half disgust, half incredulity.

'Can I try one?' asked Magda, bouncing up, and they all watched while she picked one off her mother's palm and put it into her mouth.

'Little show-off,' muttered Milly, but no one noticed her.

'Mm – it's nice,' said Magda. 'Can I have some more?'

'Can I try?' one of the Fletcher boys said, working his way to the front of the crowd, but Marion noticed he did not dare take more than one black pellet. A wide smile spread over his face almost at once.

'It's sweet,' he said, 'not like fruit, and not like honey but *sweet*. Is the whole jar full of them?'

'Where do they come from?' asked Dame Margaret, still holding out her hand with several on it.

'Your brother had a big barrel of them – said they came from a traveller, from over the sea.' This at once gave them an aura, part fabulous, part suspicious. 'They mix them into the dough before baking the bread.'

'Won't catch *me* spoiling good bread with that muck,' said Milly, audibly this time, and to general agreement.

''S like putting flies in bread on purpose,' said another female voice.

'It's not.' Peter's voice was full of authority. 'It's good. They swell up juicy in the baking – real nice to eat.'

'Did *you* eat some, Father?' Peterkin asked with respect and awe.

'Yes, everyone had it at supper in the Hall at Rutherford, big slices of bread, all spotted with these black things, and smeared with butter. No one any the worse for it, either.'

'I'll try one,' said Peterkin. 'If I may,' he added, with a glance at Marion. Dame Margaret held out her hand to him and everyone watched as he picked up one and put it into his mouth, chewed, and smiled.

Magda took some more from her mother's hand and said, 'You try one, Mother. Did Uncle only send that jarful? It won't make many spotty loaves.'

'*One* would be too much for me,' said Milly.

'Meg, you try one, Mary too,' said Magda, offering a few on her hand to the little girls, but they shook their orange curls and Mary hid her face in Hilda's skirt.

All this was felt to be light relief. The men and the serious housewives now looked to Sir Hugh for more important matter to be unpacked. Sir Hugh lifted another earthenware pot from a pannier, unrolling it from its hemp-sack covering, and pulled a coil of fine cord from its neck, handed it casually to Joan, and then peered into the jar. He enjoyed the close attention that all the villagers gave him.

'More dried flies?' asked Milly, but she was ignored again.

'Iron nails,' he said, clinking them in the jar. 'That's all for your keeping, Peter. Take the lot now, but bring me back the jar in the morning.' Then to the villagers in general he added, 'If I'd let Peter have his way, we'd have brought back nothing but nails.' Though Peter protested he took the jar and smiled.

Another large pot was produced, its top covered with a circle of fine leather tied down with a thong. Sir Hugh opened it and put his hand inside.

'Salt,' he said, and a sigh of relief went up. 'Tom, you and Rob go and get two or three dry tubs, big ones but quite dry. We'll empty the salt into them at once and divide it up in the morning. I don't want to have salt spoiling the inside of these pots a moment longer than necessary. Did anyone tell the Rockwells we were back? They'll have to have some salt.'

Sir Hugh stood up and stretched and patted Heart-of-Oak's neck. He started speaking in a low voice to Rollo, but Marion was near enough to overhear – 'and I'm glad I took Peter Carpenter . . . Yes, I know *you* told me to take him, but he was really very helpful. I doubt if my brother-in-law would have parted with so much stuff if it had not been for Peter speaking up. He spoke well – so everyone there could understand how it was with us . . . ' Marion breathed easily with pleasure. Peter had not overheard it – he was talking to Simon and Betsy – but she would tell him later and she anticipated this telling with delight.

Tom and Rob appeared from the yard with some new large buckets and barrels, and pot after pot was taken from the panniers and the white crystals emptied into them. The villagers watched every movement of Tom and Rob's hands, and gave grunts of satisfaction at the sight of so much salt pouring from jars to buckets. The empty jars were picked up one by one by Milly and arranged in a row along the kneading table under the shelter. Joan collected the sacks that the jars were wrapped in, shook each of them upside down and carefully folded them and piled them up by Dame Margaret's seat. In the last pannier was a bundle of iron rods, the raw material for bolts, for hinges, for hooks, for harness bits, for hammering out into knives and sickles, for shaping into arrowheads, for blades for spades, for saws, for chisels. It was not interesting to look at, but it was as a breath of life to the villagers. Then, last, so they thought, there were three fat, round, iron cooking pots, with rings at the brims to hang them by and with three short feet each to stand them among hot embers.

'Who's the lucky family getting one of those?' asked Margery Hunter in her deep voice. Marion knew she was hinting at her own family because she always produced more spun wool than other women.

'They will be handed out tomorrow,' said Sir Hugh severely. 'You know M'Dame always remembers who had iron pots previous years,' and everyone knew this was true. Sir Hugh pushed his hand into the last pannier and pulled out a sack of something soft and heavy.

'What's that?' said Magda, pushing forward again.

'Not for you,' said her father, unfolding the sack and showing a roll of woollen cloth of a rich dark red colour. An 'Oooh' escaped the mouths of women as he passed it to Dame Margaret.

'Your brother and his wife sent this, to make you a new gown.'

Dame Margaret took the roll on her knee and unwound a bit. 'So thick and soft,' she exclaimed, impressed. 'Where did it come from?'

Other women peered at it and commented, 'How did they get that colour? Is it from sloes? Or elderberries? What a loom they must have to make anything that long. There must be *yards* in that roll.'

'Your brother didn't know where it came from,' said Sir Hugh. 'It wasn't made in Rutherford, that's for sure. He said some men travelling north from the seacoast came to Rutherford, same men as brought the currants – '

'Currants?'

'Those little black sweet things – in the jar. They also brought this great roll of woollen stuff. There was more of it, but your sister-in-law made a gown of it for herself and she's a big woman, and for her daughter too, and this bit was over. She said it ought to be enough for a gown for you with sleeves. And this is really the last thing.'

He pulled from his sleeve the little white bundle he had secreted there at the beginning, and gave it to his wife. She looked at him with wonder. 'Unroll it,' he said. She gently unrolled a length of smooth white fabric over the crimson wool on her knees. She had never seen anything like it before.

'It's another present from your sister-in-law,' Sir Hugh went on, happy to still be the centre for all eyes. 'It's for the new baby. It's what they call linen. It came from over the sea too, I think. Your sister-in-law has a cap made of the stuff, wears it all the summer, light and cool, she says.'

This confirmed what Marion had suspected by now – that Dame Margaret was pregnant.

'Make a nice cap,' said Dame Margaret, running the fabric through her fingers, 'and more than one cap,' she added glancing at Magda.

'She said it was for wrapping the new baby in,' repeated Sir Hugh.

'Pity to let a baby mess up that lovely stuff,' said Milly, putting coarse fingers on it.

Having delivered up all he had been charged to do, and having given all the family messages, as he thought, appropriately, Sir Hugh said to Tom,

'We've not eaten since early this morning. Let's go in and see what Joan has for us. Your boy Ed must be in need of something solid, he's worked and walked enough.' Sir Hugh made a sweeping gesture to the group of villagers. 'Tomorrow, all you wives come along with your tubs and things and Dame Margaret will give out some of this salt – can do no more this evening. Matt, see that all these baskets and sacks are under cover tonight – we could have rain. Marion, I hope you've got some hearty supper for Peter, he'll be in need of it too.'

So with a general sense of relief and achievement the villagers went off their separate ways. Peter gave Peterkin his jar of nails and told him to put it down carefully on the shelf at the back of his workshop and then follow them home. Marion picked up Alice, who had been pottering about quietly unconcerned, and they went down to the bridge, Marion still carrying her empty basket. Down the log steps at the other side of the bridge, Peter paused and opened his big leather bag swinging at his waist. He pulled out two small earthenware jars with leather tied over their necks.

'This is for us,' he said. 'Their man, Steve something – a steward, keeps the stores and stuff down there – gave me these. That one has got goose

meat in it, cooked and solid, under a layer of fat, and this smaller one is full of apple that's been boiled with honey and what he called cloves, spicy stuff. Now – oh, Peterkin, there you are – don't go telling anyone about this. It is just for us and Sir Hugh and Ed-me-boy don't know about it.' It was almost too dark to see Peterkin's eyes, bright with expectation.

'Got currants in it?' he asked.

'Don't think so. Could have. Got some good bread, Marion?'

'Yes – some,' said Marion, wishing that the bits of hard bread she had had that morning had been fresher and more plentiful.

'We'll have this goose pot for our supper,' said Peter. 'Yes, a bit for you too, Alice. We must finish it; once you scratch off the grease it won't keep.'

'Can we keep the pots?' asked Marion.

'Yes, of course, no one else knows about them. They're only small, don't hold much.'

'Any pots are useful. Why did you tell me to bring a basket?' Marion thought of all those blackberries tipped out on the shelf unnecessarily.

'I thought Sir Hugh'd start dividing up salt at once.'

In the dusk, as they walked along the Common path, they could see Lisa and Martin, also returning, some hundred yards ahead of them. Marion remarked to Peter on their presence.

'I could see something,' he said, 'but I couldn't see who it was. I did think when I was in Rutherford that perhaps I saw more than I used to see. Perhaps their air is clearer than ours. Still, it does seem strange it's not Dick and Hilda there.'

Yes, indeed, strange, and terrible. Marion had temporarily forgotten, in her happiness at Peter's successful journey, the misery that Hilda must still be in, somewhere in the crowded indifference of life in the Hall. Marion felt that now she regarded Dick in a different way to how she had while he lived. He had, she now felt, deceived them all with his appearance of strength when all the time he had carried death concealed in him. Her rationality told her that they all equally carried death with them but – suddenly her heart exulted – *she* was still alive, *Peter* was still alive, and he had been returned to her from that fearful hostile world of Rutherford. Then, again suddenly, Marion remembered Dick's dying face, eyes shut, mouth open and tortured, his orange hair and beard matted, and that huge swollen purple and yellow arm lying across his body and her memory rebuked her exultation.

They sat on the log under the eaves in the August dusk and ate the goose meat paste on slices of bread with relish and amazement. Alice dozed and Marion carried her indoors and put her into the cradle. On her way out, she scooped up a lot of blackberries in her two hands and they all three ate mouthfuls of the sweet fruit.

Nearly all the time, Peter was talking. He spoke of the huge size of the Hall at Rutherford, of the special chamber built on at the back of the dais where Sir William, M'Dame's brother, and his wife slept and sometimes took meals, of the large brew house and dairy attached, the numerous cows, of the stone bridge wide enough to take a haycart – 'But why doesn't it fall down, Father?' Peterkin kept asking.

'There are keystones. When it's light tomorrow I'll show you, with marks on the floor, how it's made with *arches* of stones. They have the same in their church. It is all stone, up to the roof, and there's St Christopher standing in the water like Chris Foxcap said, and Wat and his two boys – they are carpenters there, I saw what huge saws they have – they were making a big cart for two oxen. Great wheels, they showed me, all oak. Last a few hundred years they said – till the end of the world . . . '

Peterkin dozed off and was stirred by Peter shaking his arm.

'You sleepy already? Did you have a lot of that new ale Joan was handing out?' Peterkin protested he was not sleepy but admitted Joan had given him a swig.

'And you and one of the other Fletcher boys went round to the brew house and helped yourselves to more from the jugs standing there?' Peter was more amused than cross. 'And then you filled up the jugs from the water butt so no one would see?' Peterkin protested, but feebly. 'Oh, go along with you,' said Peter, 'I know how boys carry on. You go round to the midden *now* and pee and then to bed. I don't want you to fall asleep here, you're too big to carry now.'

'And don't wake Alice,' Marion added.

Though Peterkin again protested, he went, and soon they heard the rustle of the straw as he lay down on the bed.

'Why didn't the Rutherford people bring us the salt in June like always?' asked Marion, getting the question in in a gap in the monologue.

'Ah, yes,' said Peter, glad to have been reminded of an interesting bit of his story. 'It seems that the usual train of packhorses, about twenty, I think, coming up from the sea to Rutherford over the Weald . . . '

The Weald, thought Marion. How strange, how far away that sounded. She was faintly aware of confusing 'weald' with 'world'.

'And at some point on the journey they had to cross a ford and – of course, this is all hearsay – the water was deeper than they thought. Two horses stumbled and fell in deeper water and pulled some others after them – all of them with panniers of salt and stuff, so of course all the salt got wet and just melted away into the river. In the end only about five horses arrived at Rutherford with any dry usable salt at all, so they hadn't enough for themselves, let alone any to spare for us. They said the merchants took the horses away again, back to the shore, and they only returned with more salt in the middle of harvest. They wanted double quantity of wool for double journeys but the Rutherford people said they'd give wool for *salt* not for journeys made with no salt at the end. Don't know what was settled between them, but I do know Sir William only let us take what salt we did against a promise that we'd return his two panniers this *autumn* with more wool in them. It was bad luck those horses falling and wasting all that salt but is wasn't *our* fault, and I don't see we should be called on to give them extra wool for less salt.'

Marion agreed with him out loud, but had a secret sympathy with the strangers who had made two journeys and had lost so much salt on the way.

'Let's go to bed,' he said, but neither felt like moving.

'Supposing,' said Marion, 'them at Rutherford had had no salt themselves, and you and Sir Hugh'd come back empty-handed, what'd we all have done?'

'There'd have been no meat preserved for winter when what's in the tubs was eaten – and that's not much, Ed-me-boy said. That would've been that.'

'There's geese, of course,' said Marion.

'Not much to eat on a goose, enough for four or five people only. There's the fat, of course. There'd be some old sheep too, usually is.'

'And a bullock,' said Marion. 'Once killed there's hearty meals for the whole village for a day or two, but you have to finish it up quickly while it is still good.'

'We could get extra deer, not just the Michaelmas and the Christmas ones. I know the law only allows us those two, but Rollo might get Father John to change the law.'

'Does Father John make the laws? About deer?' Marion was amazed. 'I thought he only did Church laws.'

'A priest's always about when they make laws,' said Peter, rather uncertainly. 'After all, God wouldn't want us all to go without meat with all them deer running about in the woods.'

'Wouldn't He? He made all the corn go mouldy when Father was a boy – so he often told us.'

'Don't really know,' Peter admitted. 'It's certainly law about us having two deer from the forest each year, but whether it's God's law or priest's law or Sir Hugh's I don't know. I'd get a deer, if I could, if we were hungry, same as I'd get a pigeon, only I'd try to keep quiet about it.' He sounded unconcerned. Marion wondered whether the forest deer were God's, to be doled out to hungry people as He decreed – but pigeons were wild and fed on one's peas and belonged to no one . . . just as foxes and crows were wild . . . only they were no good to eat.

I wonder and wonder about such things, thought Marion. Peter doesn't. He just thinks whatever is simplest to think, even if it's something he can't ever know. Then he never bothers his head about it again.

'Come,' he said, rousing himself, 'bed. I'll tell you more in the morning.'

They went round to the midden together, then felt their way into the cottage to bed. Neither Alice nor Peterkin stirred and it seemed almost at once that Peter's breathing became slower and heavier and Marion knew that he too slept. She lay awake a long time, open-eyed. Through the open upper half of the door she could see the changing pallor of the sky as clouds thinned and thickened as they drifted over the half-moon. Peter gave a sudden sniff and she was aware that he had woken. His hands felt for her, pulling up her dress, and she was glad to take him. The straw on the bed was at its oldest, last year's straw, now no more than lifeless shreds with no resilience in them. The boards under this dusty covering felt very hard below Marion's back as she accepted Peter's heaving weight. She was glad that in spite of his recent absence in the unknown world of Rutherford, he still smelt the same.

Then she suddenly remembered she had forgotten to tell him what Sir Hugh had said to Rollo about him. It would have to wait for the morning for Peter was already asleep again.

SEPTEMBER

Where autumns shadows idly muse
And tinge the trees with many hues
Amid whose scenes I'm feign to dwell
And sing of what I love so well
But hollow winds and tumbling floods
And humming showers and moaning woods
All startle into sudden strife

After many dark hours of dull wakefulness, Marion had, before dawn, fallen into a deep sleep and was dreaming a muddled dream of Dame Margaret questioning her about new wooden buckets, and Tom chipping in with well-intentioned but pointless remarks about how all the prepared staves had been used at Rollo's orders for making steps for a new ladder. All ordinary, and plausible, but *not* true. She was awakened from the dream (she was by then wondering if Peter had been consulted about the ladder) by Alice crawling over her and patting her face. Alice could easily climb on to the bed now by herself.

Having woken her mother, Alice now sat, upright and tubby, on the straw and observed, 'Father's gone to Rockwell.' Peter had been working for the last three days at the main house at Rockwell, fitting new horizontal planks all round the lower part of the walls. The previous autumn a big beech tree had been felled close by and the main trunk had been sawn into long thick planks with enormous physical effort by Peter and his boys and two of the Rockwell lads. These planks had lain one above the other, separated by short blocks of wood, for drying out ever since. The time had now come for cutting and fitting them to the walls and Peter would be using some of his cherished Rutherford nails in this work.

Though Marion had been without Peter for several days, she was this time quite calm about his absence, for this was quite different from when he had been in the unknown world of Rutherford the previous month. She felt annoyed that she had overslept for she had plenty of plans for the day, so she rose at once and woke Peterkin. She had previously arranged that Peterkin should go off to the woods every day from now with a length of rope and the company of two of Nick and Martha's boys, to collect as much loose dry firewood as they could before the masses of sodden autumn leaves covered up any fallen branches and made them too wet for burning. So Peterkin departed, with a hunk of bread in a bag and a length of rope round his waist, to collect the other boys in the village.

Marion had instructed him firmly: 'Now *work*. Don't play around, you're not a child any longer, and if there are bits that you can't all three drag, try to prop them up against a tree and remember *where*, and tell Nick when you get back.'

Peterkin said, 'Yes, yes,' impatient to be off for a whole unsupervised day with his mates.

Marion wished to spend as much of her time as possible during Peter's absence in spinning. For reasons of economics beyond Marion's comprehension, the two panniers that belonged to Sir William in Rutherford were to be returned there as soon as possible, filled with more spun wool, to pay, so it was said, for salt already supplied. Sir Hugh had been party to this bargain and had assured Marion, and anyone else who would listen, that it was only his outspoken pleading that had persuaded the Rutherford people to let him take as much salt as he had done.

Up at the Hall Ed-me-boy was raring to go down to Rutherford again with a horse with the two panniers full of spun wool, and Tom was anxiously trying to prevent or to postpone this journey. Marion saw well how it was. She knew Tom's every thought was of his son and how he lived by the boy's presence and he had suddenly realized that Ed-me-boy was almost grown up and might wish to separate himself from his possessive father. The exciting adventure of a journey to Rutherford lured Ed-me-boy, and Tom was fearful. However, the panniers must be returned and the journey should be made before winter set in, but it was no good making the journey until enough wool had been spun to fill the panniers. Marion had a private hope that if it were known that she had supplied most of the spun wool, more even than Margery Hunter, some extra bonus such as a new earthenware milk bowl might be brought back for her particularly. The more she could spin the better.

But first there were the ordinary jobs to be done. She must go down to the water-place with her smaller bucket, the larger one being full of goat's milk souring for cheese. She brought up the water, tipped some of it into the Rutherford pot, now empty of goose meat, for the day's drinking and then filled up the hens' drinking butt in the garden. This was an old leaky rather shallow tub which she had half sunk into the earth, and there was a broad bit of wood leaning up against it for the hens to walk up to reach the water. Then, having told Alice to be a good girl, Marion took up the now empty bucket and went to milk her goat.

The half-grown kid had been handed over to the Hall with some careful bargaining with Rollo. He had said that whoever lived in her cottage must pay rent to the Hall in the autumn in the form of a dozen young laying hens, but that summer most of the chickens hatched at the Hall turned out to be hens, and as Marion did not have a dozen fowls of either sex to give or to keep, to substitute a female kid would benefit the Hall very much more. Even Rollo, who always wanted the laws to be obeyed exactly, even if it were in no one's interest that they were, had realized that a healthy nanny kid was a bargain that he had better accept. But Marion's parent goat was

still in milk and if she could be fed adequately might still be giving milk throughout the winter, so Marion was determined to cosset the animal.

However, when she got to the top of the incline of rough grass the hawthorn stump to which the goat had been tethered showed only a few feet of plaited leather with a frayed end tied round the trunk and no goat in sight. The gate in the wattle fence that protected the cottages from the Common was open, and Marion cursed careless Peterkin for leaving it unhooked. She went down and fastened the gate, looking anxiously round and down to the water-place, but she could see no goat. Then she heard a commotion in Molly's garden and Old Agnes hobbled up waving a stick and shouting at the goat, which was eating Molly's cabbages. The goat bounded away and Marion caught her by the remains of the leather strap that dangled from her neck. She apologized to Agnes, who admitted after examining a cabbage that the goat had not done much damage and could not have been there long, but it took some time, a good deal of pushing and cajoling, and a dish of bran and oats to entice the goat back to the hawthorn stump and for Marion to tie the frayed leather strips together. She knew the goat would have to calm down before she could be milked so Marion returned home leaving the empty bucket by the goat.

Alice was peacefully sitting on the dry earth under the eaves making little piles of dust and patting them down with her fat palms and talking to herself. Marion went into the goat shed and felt along the shelves in the hens' boxes. They had almost stopped laying now, so she was pleased to find three eggs. But, leaving the shed, she tripped on a bit of wood and in saving herself dropped two of the eggs which smashed against the doorpost. Marion cursed her ill luck – only one egg left now.

She put the one egg carefully on the shelf in the cottage and thought she might as well see what ripe dry peas there were while she was waiting for the goat to calm down, so she picked up her wide basket and went down the garden. Three hens and the cock were scratching about in the dying bean haulms. Marion concentrated on searching for peas. A sudden loud squawk and agitated poultry noises interrupted her and another hen flew up on to the fence from the far side. Marion ran to the fence and saw a young fox savaging another of her hens. She picked up a stone and with an aim she thought worthy of Peterkin, hit the fox on the shoulder. It dropped the hen and fled into the undergrowth. Marion dashed up the garden (glancing at Alice who was still peacefully playing), round the cottage, up the hill, and through the gate on to the Common, but by the time she reached her wounded hen it was dead – just a mess of blood and feathers. It was only a small pullet, nothing worth saving. She cursed the brazen fox, coming in broad daylight, and she cursed herself for not clipping the pullets' wings so that they could not fly over the fence – but what could she have clipped them *with*, now that Dick Shepherd's row of shears no longer hung in the next cottage? Having abandoned the remains of the hen to the bluebottles and the beetles, she went to the hawthorn to look at the goat. She was now peacefully grazing so Marion took up the abandoned bucket and sat down on the grass and milked, hoping that this rhythmical occupation would calm her annoyance.

Leaving the goat contented, she carried the bucket of milk back to the cottage and put it down carefully. Alice was down the garden and was wailing, 'Mam – Mam – *Mam*!' Marion went to her. There were lots of tangled threads round Alice's ankles and round the stubble of a thistle plant, and Alice, in attempts to free herself had pricked her hands. Marion crouched down and with soothing remarks tried to free Alice's legs.

A ghastly thought struck her – all this knotted twisted tangled stuff was her own spun wool! With a shout of anger at Alice, she traced back up the garden the tangled threads, sometimes mixed up with pea sticks, sometimes in coils on the grass, to the almost empty spool lying on the ground near the cottage. It was horribly apparent that Alice had got hold of Marion's spindle and a fat spool of spun wool, both of which Marion had left on the log under the eaves the night before, and had played with the spool, unwound it, tangled it, thereby wasting hours and hours of work. Marion sat down on the log with her head in her hands to contemplate this further disaster. To her bitterness she added the recollection of her thought the evening before that she had left her work well out of Alice's reach. A few months ago it *would* have been out of Alice's reach, but the child had grown a lot this summer, and Marion had not reckoned on this.

The first spinning of wool, a single strand, or *one* ply, must be wound tightly and firmly on a bobbin or spool as it is made. If it is not held in this tension, it twists back on itself in a spiral fashion making itself into bits of *two* ply. This is what had happened to the wool as Alice had cheerfully unwound it from the spool. Then it had got round one of her feet, then she had trotted down the garden, unwinding yet more as she went, then the twisting threads had caught in the pea sticks, then Alice, trotting to and fro, had muddled up more and more of it round her legs, round thistles, round more pea sticks until she had found herself bound to some prickly sticks and had roared to her mother for help.

Marion sat on the log with the almost empty spool in her hands, and the tangled mess going from her feet down the garden to where Alice was still standing roaring. In her fury and despair Marion strode down to her and picked her up roughly, shouting abuse at her and pulling at the wasted wool round her legs. Alice roared loudly in fear and bewilderment. She had no idea what her crime was, she only knew her mother was furiously angry. Having extricated Alice's struggling legs, Marion tried to salvage what bits of wool she could. There were several short lengths which, having twisted themselves together, would lie inert and be strong, and these could be used for tying things up, for lacing clothes together, or tying bits of fabric on to one's legs in winter. A lifetime of training to waste *nothing* made her start collecting what short lengths of this she could, pulling them from pea sticks, gathering them up from grassy tufts and unwinding what she could from the thistle stalks. Engrossing herself in this fiddly work somewhat calmed her anger. She left Alice to wail and moan by herself.

Suddenly, from the village came a ringing *tang-tang-tang-tang-tang*. The old cooking pot hanging by the church door was being banged with the signal that induced a sense of urgency into everyone who heard it. It meant something in the village was dangerously on fire, and Marion must present herself, with a bucket, at the scene of the fire as soon as possible. All thoughts of tangled wool pushed aside, she ran round the cottage and up the hill, from where she could see, above the Big Oak on the Green, a pillar of ascending smoke.

One of the stream cottages, she thought. *Not* the church, *not* the Hall, which she could see to the left of the oak was safe, and, though the smoke was in the direction of the Millers', *not* the Mill, her precious birthplace. Molly appeared at her garden gate, bucket in one hand, the other hand trying to stuff her loose hair under her cap. She looked elated.

'Bring your little girl to my mother,' she said, and started off running down to the Common.

'Must just get a bucket,' shouted Marion, and ran back home. At the door of her cottage she paused. She possessed only two buckets. The larger one stood on the cottage floor full to the brim with rich milk souring to be turned into cheese. The smaller, which she had just milked the goat into, now also brimmed with fresh rich milk. She had nothing to empty either into. The earthenware jar that the Rutherford goose meat came in, now full of water, would not anyway have held a quarter of the contents of the smaller bucket. Her spirit revolted against wasting all that good hard-won food by pouring it away, just to assist some careless neighbour who had let her cottage get ablaze.

She remembered the hens' drinking tub. She seized a spade leaning up against the wall, and knocking aside the hens' plank, started prising up the old tub. The earth round it was slimy and sour with hen droppings and she splashed a lot of water over her feet as she dug, but she got it up, leaving a round hole with a smooth earthy base on which pink worms curled. She tipped out the remaining water, and then realized it had of course no handle. She looked round, the continuing *tang-tang-tang-tang* increasing her desperation all the while. She found a couple of sticks in the wood pile. The first was too short, the second too thick to go through one of the holes in the taller staves. She looked round again. A broom was by the door. She tried it – yes, it went through the holes. It would just do, if she could break off the end with all the birch twigs tied to it. She tried and failed. It was too strong so she realized she must take it as it was, twigs and all. The long-sodden bucket was very heavy and its width made it very difficult to carry. No matter, it's the best I can do, she thought.

She picked up yelling Alice under her other arm and rushed up to Molly's cottage. The two old women had come out to their garden gate, and accepted Alice as a matter of course. Alice's yelling became wilder. Poor Alice, she had been shouted at by her mother for some unknown crime and was being punished by being abandoned with these old ladies while her mother rushed away without a word, without a caress, but Marion, lolloping away down the path to the Common was unconcerned.

The wide bucket was even more awkward to carry than Marion had guessed. She had to hold her arm out sideways to prevent it hitting her legs as she ran. Reaching the bridge, she paused for breath after the supreme effort of lugging the bucket up the steps. The burning cottage was half hidden by the branches of the Big Oak, but she could see that it was Hodge and Cecily's cottage, the last one along the top of the bank before you reached the sheepfold.

As she paused she saw Matt come running from the Hall yard carrying one end of the longest ladder, followed by Rob, his son, with the other end.

They ran under the Big Oak, shouting to Marion, 'It's Hodge's! Get there at once!' and ran on.

Marion picked up the bucket again and ran on. There was a crowd round Hodge's. This cottage stood close to the top of the stream bank, which there fell steeply down some seven or eight feet to the stream. A tall alder tree grew on the water's edge, its twisted roots making a little platform overhanging a deep pool. In what was midstream in winter was now a low muddy slip thick with grass and reeds, and here two men, Simkin and one of the Fletcher boys, stood astride, one foot on the rooty platform, the other among the reeds. The emptied buckets were being rolled down the bank to the Fletcher boy who plunged them in the pool, pushing them to Simkin who lifted them out and with great swings got them halfway up the bank to Gib. Gib stood mid-bank with one bare foot bent under his body pressing on a wobbling tuft of grass, the other stretched out below, sliding about on the wet earthy slope. He kept his position by his left hand grasping a forked bramble root half pulled from the bank. With a tremendous effort of arm and shoulders he took a full bucket from Simkin and swung it up to where some other boy, kneeling at the top of the bank, could take it and pass it to the chain of six women who themselves passed it to Ed-me-boy up the ladder. At each heave of Gib's arms the bramble root was pulled a little further from the soft earth. The ladder on which Ed-me-boy stood, was propped against the lowest beams of the cottage. Half the thatch was burnt away, some still smoking thickly but it seemed that by the time Marion arrived, most of the flames were out. While Ed-me-boy paused in his bucket emptying, the long ladder had arrived at the other side of the cottage and Rollo was there ordering the female chain of bucket-carriers round to the other side. This much Marion saw and took in in a second. The whole place was crowded. Everyone was shouting and dogs were barking and frightened children stood in groups. Cecily, who had been helping in the Hall's dairy all that afternoon, was running up and down, screaming hysterically.

'I *think* that's done it,' shouted Ed-me-boy, with authority in his new bass voice. 'Father, get some rakes. We'll have to get the rest of this thatch off and stamp it out on the ground. It might still flare up. Rob!' as the tall ladder and the boy's head appeared over the roof from the far side, 'Get rakes, get the thatch off! A bit of wind could blaze it up again. Ooh! There go the rats – must have been a nest in the roof. Ah, the dogs have got them.' There was a yell from the bank as the bramble root finally ripped apart and Gib, waving one earthy end in the air, slithered down the bank and all but pushed Simkin into the water.

'Keep the water coming,' shouted Sir Hugh. No one had seen him arrive. Nor had Marion seen Peter arrive, but there he was, with a short sharpened stake, pulled from a sheep hurdle, in one hand and his elm mallet in the other. Finding a foothold somewhere, he drove the stake into the soft earth where the bramble had been with deft powerful thumps. Gib was still on the water's edge, bent double and gasping with exhaustion. Peter took his place on the bank, holding the new stake, and the flow of full buckets recommenced.

Meanwhile, up ladders and with rakes, three or four men were pulling at the thatch. There was another flare up of flames, quickly subdued by the dexterous arms of Ed-me-boy directing the flung water. Through the hissing steam, thatch was being pulled off leaving blackened beams. Smoke and horrible smells filled the air, and all the while there were shouts of instructions, warnings, advice and curses.

'May yet save most of the beams.'

'Some this side are gone. Could be replaced.'

'Lucky the cow was out on the Common.'

'Ridge beam looks sound enough.'

'Can't tell yet. Could be charred through.'

'Who sent word to Hodge?'

'He's at Rockwell – but Peter's here now.'

'Hodge was up in the woods above Rockwell.' That was Peter's voice.

'They sent a boy up to tell him. By the Devil's toys.'

'Hope he can get that silly woman to shut up screaming.'

'She's lost everything.'

'Needn't scream like that. We all lose things.'

'*No*, Ed, don't go in, bits on fire could drop on you – '

'It's out, father – ooh, another rat!'

'*Don't* go in.' It was Tom's agonized voice.

But Ed-me-boy stepped in through the door and came out with a blanket in his arms.

'All the bed's burnt,' he said. 'Bits of burning thatch must have fallen on it. Hellish smelly mess in there.' He held up the blanket which was full of holes, each hole edged with crisp black-burnt wool and large tawny scorched patches, the remains stinking horribly.

Cecily saw it and let out a huger wail. 'My blanket, my new blanket, what'll I do now? And my three big cheeses, new pressed – where are they?'

'No, Cecily.' It was Sir Hugh's authority which temporarily calmed her. '*Don't* go in. Nothing can be saved now. That blanket's ruined, you can see, not a square foot of unburnt stuff in it. How did it happen?'

As the great effort ceased and the men scrambled up the bank to look at the ruin and to get their breaths, and as the women broke up their lines with the buckets, all were looking at the smoking, steaming ruin and asking how the fire had started.

Hodge, huffing and puffing from his run down the fields from Rockwell, burst in among them, shouting, 'My *house*! Are the boys safe? Oh, my *house*! How did it happen? Cecily – how?'

'Don't know,' wailed Cecily. 'I've been in the Hall dairy all day.'

'Yes, she has,' said Dame Margaret, also appearing suddenly. 'Where have your boys been all day?'

Overcoming her hysteria, Cecily explained. She had been summoned to the Hall that morning by Joan. They had been straining curds, pressing cheeses, saving whey all day. She had left her three boys – the eldest was eight so he was responsible enough to look after the others – at home. There was a pile of washed fleeces they had to sort out – mostly goat's hair, all the long hairs to be kept straight . . .

Sir Hugh broke in, realizing she was going off the point. 'Yes, yes, you left your boys at home all day?'

'But, sir, I left them some bread, and they had lots of work to do, and the logs were only just alight, warm embers, nothing dangerous, and I've always told them never to touch the fire and to sweep up bits of straw that might blow into it. Now if I'd have had a girl or two they'd have looked after it, but boys . . . ' Her voice rose again into incoherence and hysteria.

Sir Hugh turned aside. 'Get the three boys here,' he said. The three younger Hodge boys, Harry, the eight-year-old, Edwin about six, and four-year-old Hoddy had been standing together fearfully all this while, watching the destruction of their home.

Sir Hugh addressed Harry. 'How did the fire start?'

'Don't know – sir.' Harry was terrified and furtive.

'You were in the cottage when it started. Joyce says she saw you all run out shouting, and flames in the thatch, and she ran and told me, and I got Tom to ring the bell. How did it start?'

'Don't know, sir,' said Harry, his knees visibly shaking.

'Edwin, you were there, weren't you?'

'Yes, sir.' Edwin's normal shout was now greatly reduced in volume.

'How did it start?'

'Don't know.'

'What were you doing?'

'Sorting wool,' said Harry.

'All day? All three of you?'

'Er – yes, sir.'

'Did you touch the fire?'

'No.'

'So how did it start?'

'Don't know.'

Marion, overhearing this inquisition, knew that Sir Hugh was frightening the already fearful children and that he would get nothing intelligible from them. As she was thinking this, Dame Margaret pushed forward and brushed Sir Hugh aside in a manner that astounded the villagers. She sat down on the grass and pulled Hoddy to her. She smiled at Hoddy.

'You've been working all day indoors, have you?' she asked him in a conversational tone.

'Yeth,' said Hoddy.

'You and your brothers?'

'Yeth.'

'What were you doing?'

Hoddy looked at Harry for advice and was given a gesture. 'Thorting wool,' he said, still looking at Harry.

'Sorting wool all day?'

'We had our bread too.'

'It's dull sorting wool all day, isn't it?' said Dame Margaret. Sir Hugh and all the villages were standing close and listening to this enquiry. Hoddy could not answer this, but Dame Margaret went on, 'It's more exciting to make the fire blaze, isn't it?'

Hoddy looked at his brothers for an answer, but their faces were blank in anxiety.

'You could put a stick in the fire and stir it round and watch the flames come.'

'Yeth – yeth – ' Hoddy was enthusiastic and bounced about.

'A stick with dead leaves on it makes lovely flames.'

Hoddy remembered his delight and a wide smile spread over his round red face. 'Oh yeth. Harry got a thtick with d'yed leaveth and puthed it into the fire and it wath all flameth – '

Harry lunged forward to assault his little brother, but Rollo had him by the hair.

'And waved it about?' Dame Margaret went on.

'Yeth, an' it wath all thparkth,' said Hoddy, gesticulating suitably and ecstatic at the recollection of so much fun.

Harry roared at him.

'Well, Harry,' said Sir Hugh, 'is that what you did?'

Harry was silent.

'Edwin, is that what happened? *Answer* me.'

'Don't know,' said Edwin, sobbing hopelessly, and the urine ran down his legs as he spoke.

Hodge, who had overheard this interrogation, turned to vent his anger on Cecily. They were parted by Tom, and Hodge sank down on the lowest rung of the ladder and buried his face in his hands. 'What have I done to have such villains for sons,' he moaned.

'Beat them, Rollo,' said Sir Hugh, and while Simkin pulled up their tunics and held them with their arms over their heads, Rollo took off his rope belt and beat the two older boys on their bare buttocks. The boys screamed with fear and pain. It was a long beating.

'Hoddy too?' Rollo asked Sir Hugh.

'Yes, Hoddy too,' said Sir Hugh. 'He can't learn too young.'

Released from his beating and yelling loudly, Hoddy rushed to his mother for protection. She was sitting on the grass weeping over her stinking burnt blanket, and roughly pushed him away.

'You'll have to come to the Hall,' Dame Margaret said to her, 'and stay there until we can get this place mended. But you must keep an eye on those boys of yours.'

Next day, Tom meeting Peter at his workshop, described how when he had been pulling out the benches in the Hall and arranging the straw for the night, he had come upon Hoddy still shaking and sobbing under one of the benches curled up with Magda's dog, Trover.

When Marion and Peter were walking home over the Common, Peter complained of the weight of the empty bucket and queried its broom handle. Marion explained, and it seemed the right moment to remind him that she needed another bucket. 'I've nothing even to fetch the water in tomorrow morning,' she said. He agreed she needed another, but he spoke absent-mindedly and she could see his thoughts were elsewhere.

After a while he said, 'What did M'Dame think she was doing, barging in like that, questioning the littlest chap when Sir Hugh'd been talking to the others?'

'She questioned better than he did.'

'Nonsense. That's not women's work. They should keep out of it.'

'But she got the truth. He didn't.'

'It's not right.'

'What do you mean, "right"? We wanted to know how the fire started, she got the truth from Hoddy. The way Sir Hugh was going on at the elder boys was getting nowhere. He just frightened them.'

'So he should. Those boys are criminals. You saw the wastage.'

'Yes, they are, but frightened people don't tell the truth, and it was the truth we wanted. She got it out of Hoddy because he's too young to see where his answers were leading.'

'It doesn't seem right,' repeated Peter, not really following Marion's train of thought. 'It was Sir Hugh's job, or Rollo's.'

'Rollo would have been just the same, blundering in and frightening and confusing. He'd have been further from the truth at the end – and wouldn't even know he was.'

'You always like the last word,' said Peter, affectionate and tired, and added, 'Is there anything to eat? I've had very little all day.'

His remark brought her thoughts back to domesticity and the awful recollection of the wasted wool. She told Peter what had happened and this reminded her of the broken eggs and the fox killing one of the pullets.

'Well – all that's lost,' he said calmly.

When they reached Molly's cottage, Old Agnes was standing by the garden gate holding Alice.

'We saw you coming across the Common,' said Agnes, 'didn't we, Alice?'

Alice's eyes were red and she was trembling and gasping. 'Mam – Mam,' she cried, holding out her arms to Marion, who took her.

'She's been roaring and crying all the time, poor little button,' Agnes said calmly. 'Don't know what's the matter with her. Couldn't get her to have anything, not even a bit of honey on bread. Is the fire out? It was Hodge's, wasn't it?'

Marion briefly explained Alice's crime in unwinding the wool and her own fury at her.

Agnes ignored the loss of the wool and just patted Alice's head saying, 'There, there, you'll be a good girl now Mam's come home.'

Back in their cottage Alice sat on Marion's lap and was fed with sticks of bread dipped into the fresh milk in the smaller bucket, and almost as soon as the last mouthful was swallowed, she fell heavily asleep on Marion's knee.

'Poor little brat,' Peter commented. 'Probably thought you'd given her away and gone off yourself and would never come back. Put her in the cradle and let's have something ourselves.'

Marion, kneeling down, put Alice in the cradle and covered her and remained there, watching her little sleeping face. How *quiet*, how ordinarily quiet and peaceful it was in the cottage. Tibtab, a hump of speckled fur, lay curled on the shelf by the jars, the end of the log seat was at Marion's left hand with the star-shaped pattern of cracks across its sawn end, the hood of the cradle before her, smoothed and darkened by the pressure of so many greasy hands spread on it while their owners stood up after laying down babies. The rocker at the other end was worn smooth by her foot, rocking this Alice child, and all her previous babies, and probably her mother's foot rocking Marion herself, perhaps by her grandmother's foot too. The origin of such pieces of family furniture, so necessary, made to outlast generations, was not known now. Marion wondered who had made the cradle and when. Any object older than the oldest living memory in the village took eternity to itself quite easily. Next time she went to the mill she would ask the Old Man when it was made, but even he might not know, or remember.

As her eyes wandered round her gloomy cottage, she recalled the shocking interior of Cecily's burnt home. With the thatch burnt or pulled off, the interior was displayed in an unusual light and with unfamiliar clarity, the half-burnt straw on the bed, the two charred bacon joints on the ground – the thongs that had tied them to the beam above had burnt through – and by them, bits of an earthenware basin, which might have been full of milk, broken by the falling bacon. Spilt from somewhere, spreading over the edge of the bed, was a great pool of white cheese, melted by the heat, burnt all along one side by the flames, spattered with ash and burnt straw –

a patch of stinking wastage. But most of all Marion remembered the smell, the awful terrifying smell of burnt bacon, burnt cheese, burnt thatch and burnt, wet wool.

Marion felt a sudden flood of gratitude to the chance that had preserved her cottage while destroying another's. She managed to express this thankfulness by saying to Peter, as she pressed her hand on the cradle's hood and stood up, 'Poor Cecily. It must be terrible for her, all that work for nothing,' and then she busied herself with getting them some supper. As she did so she saw the near-empty spool and she remembered Alice and her tangled wool and repeated to herself, 'All that work for nothing.'

They had finished eating when a sound of dragging preceded the appearance of Peterkin round the corner of the cottage. The rope that he had left with now bound a large bundle of dead branches, some almost small trees which he had dragged along.

'Look at all that,' he said proudly, pulling up the bundle in front of his parents. 'We got lots. We found an oak that had lots of dead branches, some on the ground broken off and some at the top we couldn't get, but lots in the middle, and I put a stone into my bread bag – that was after we'd eaten our food – and tied it with one end of the rope and I threw it over the dead branch and when it fell down the other side we all pulled on the ends, swung on them, and the branch cracked off and Kit fell down on his back . . . ' Much laughter here interrupted the triumphant tale. 'Then we found another tree with dead on it and did the same – and a yew tree, but we couldn't break off any of those branches, not with all three of us pulling. Can I have something to eat?'

'Did you divide the wood up properly?' Peter asked, handing him some bread.

'Yes, when we got down to the Common we spread it all out and we each took it in turns to pull out the best bits for ourselves like you told me before.' Peterkin was munching away smiling at his achievement and his virtue.

'But that was dividing it into *three*,' said Peter. 'You were collecting for *two* families, us and the Nick's, not for *yourselves*.'

Peterkin stopped smiling and looked blank.

'But, Father, you said that people must divide everything out fairly and we did. We took proper turns each of us to pull out the best bits till there were only some twiggy bits left and we didn't bother about them.'

'What I said was about dividing things between *people*. You ought to have divided it between *fires*, one in this cottage, ours, and one in Nick and Martha's. Don't you *understand?*'

Peterkin was much downcast; his father's view had not occurred to him.

Peter went on, hammering his point: 'What it means is that Nick's family have twice as much wood as our family. It should have been evenly divided. When you come back tomorrow, you see you divide it evenly.'

Peterkin agreed nervously, but he already knew he would not be able to explain to Steve and Kit this new division of their spoils, specially as it would be disadvantageous to them. Marion thought what a strict steward Peter would have been had he been born different, just as strict as Rollo was, and remembering all the details just as Rollo did.

'Well, it can't be helped now,' she said. 'Pull it round to the side and untie the rope. You'll all have to go out for more tomorrow while the dry weather lasts.' But she realized that explaining the new division of their spoils to the other boys was going to be difficult and she would not know what to say when Peterkin questioned her – all that, of course, after Peter was out of the house.

Oh dear, she thought. There's a trouble which we need not have had. Well, it is tomorrow's trouble, not today's.

She was very tired. But Peter had not finished his day.

'I must be up at Rockwell at dawn tomorrow,' he said. 'Put me up some food in my bag. That stupid fire interfered with our proper work. There's another wall and a half to do still.' So before Marion could drop down on the bed she had to find enough bread and some cheese to fill Peter's leather bag.

It'll be Michaelmas soon, she thought, to comfort herself, and a great roast deer in the Hall, and everyone having to eat as much hot meat as they can. Ah, that'll be a change.

OCTOBER

The flying clouds urged on in swiftest pace
Like living things as if they runned a race
The winds that oer each coming tempest broods
Waking like spirits in their startling moods
Fluttering the sear leaves on the blasting lea
That litters under every fading tree
And pausing oft as falls the pattering rain
Then gathering strength and twirling them again

It had *rained*. It had rained day and night for three days, steady, windless rain, now heavier, now lighter, falling from an evenly dark grey sky. Their clothes were wet. Their boots, stuck upside down on the boot-rack, remained sodden. The blanket on the bed was heavy and stiff with moisture. The two rather bent rafters in the roof above the door had bent even more with the weight of the sodden thatch over them, sodden because in the depression in the roof the rain did not run off at that point. In the summer Peter had put on more thatch to level off this depression, but it had not really worked and there was now the additional weight of extra thatch, as wet as the old. There was a puddle on the floor just inside the door and all day and night Marion had listened to the regular *pit pat pitty pit – pit pat patty pit* as the drops fell into the puddle.

Before the steady rain had started there had been gales. The wind blew up the valley and lashed all its westerly violence, Marion felt, on the cottages of Down the Common. She had listened to it all one night, roaring in the thinning leaves of the ash tree and rattling the ivy round its trunk. Lisa and

Martin's cottage would perhaps suffer more than hers, but for hour after hour she heard her cottage walls groaning and squeaking in the buffeting wind, and in the morning she found that most of the dried moss which had been so laboriously stuffed into the wattle to make it as windproof as possible, had been blown in and lay about in dark tufts on the blanket.

On top of this damp misery, Marion had had a cold for several days. The worst of it was over, but she knew she would have to summon up her habitual courage over the coming days. Lying in bed, disturbed by the constant dripping in the corner, she moved her head to ease her aching neck, and pulled the heavy blanket over her head. Even in the dark her eyes smarted, and one nostril felt as if it were filled with flame, yet it dripped a cold fluid which ran down her cheek on to her supporting hand. Her lips were dry and stiff, yet her mouth seemed to pour saliva, and every swallow made her aware of the prickly lump, like a small teasel, in her throat. She lay there suffering.

She knew she should pull out, from under the bed, the loose woollen shift that she had worn last winter and which Peter had scorned so. It had come about when one of the Rockwell girls, come to help Joan in the Hall's weaving shed, had told them how at Rockwell they had made a cloth with loose-spun wool, just twisted enough to take the loom weights, and had spaced the warp much wider than usual, and then they had run the shuttle backwards and forwards but never pressing the weft together so that they made a sort of net fabric. Then they had brushed both sides with teasels so it was all a soft fluffy light mass, the tangled fluff holding the threads in place. Marion and Joan had experimented, and Marion had made herself a shift with the resulting fabric. It only reached down as far as her knees and it had no sleeves but she had been amazed how warm and, when she had got used to the tickles, how comfortable it was. She had shown it to Peter, taking off her outer gown and demonstrating the quality of the new.

'But there's no *wool* in it – or hardly any,' he said, fingering it. 'It's all holes. That won't keep you warm.'

'But it does.'

'It can't. Look, wool keeps you warm, doesn't it? So *more* wool'd keep you warmer, wouldn't it?'

Marion had to agree, reluctantly.

'So it follows that *less* wool'd keep you *less* warm. Stands to reason, woman.' He usually addressed her as 'woman' when he thought she was silly.

'But I do feel warmer, much warmer, with this loose one,' Marion protested. 'You should try it, Peter, you'd feel the difference.'

'Of course it couldn't,' he said, but when he took her to him that night he had to agree she felt unusually warm. But, he said to himself, no doubt women's bodies were as irrational as everyone knew their minds were – it was, after all, natural that irrationality should overflow from the mind to the body. Peter continued to wear his own tightly woven thick woollen shift, which was damp, and to shiver.

But now, on this wet October night, Marion shivered and snorted before eventually dozing off, in spite of the pitty pat drips. Then a gnawing sound woke her. Marion was at war with mice and rats. They wanted her family's food, and it was the life of her family against the lives of the vermin. It was a perpetual war. She leant out a hand to the ground and felt around for a stone and threw it to where the noise came from. Her family stirred but slept on. Then she heard the soft plop of Tibtab jumping down from the shelf where he slept. He gave a quiet interested mew and she could hear him creeping about. Soon she heard his mews of triumph. He wanted to show her what he had done. She guessed he had the still living mouse in his jaws. How he managed to mew like that through a mouthful of mouse, she never knew. He was quite likely to let it go again, into the bed, where it could shelter in the tangled straw till morning and then quietly depart through some slit in the wattle walls. Marion put out her hand again. 'Good Tibtab, clever puss,' she whispered. He had come close and was arching his back under her hand. She pushed him away, always fearful he might jump into the cradle to sleep on warm Alice and smother her. She would never forget how one of her babies had died thus.

'Go and eat it,' she hissed, and a few minutes later she heard his neat jaws crunching it up, and then the plop as he returned to his patch of hay on the shelf. Marion slept again.

It was grey morning when she dragged herself up. Pushing open the top half of the door, she looked down the garden. It had stopped raining. The ground outside the hut was thick with pale fallen leaves from the ash tree, though when she looked up at its branches they seemed still as thickly leafed as in summer. She slid her arms into a sheepskin jacket, but it was too damp and chilly. I must get a fire going, she thought, woke a reluctant Peterkin, and sent him round to Molly's with the little earthenware pot from Rutherford and with a request for a lump of glowing charcoal.

Peter left, grumbling about his wet cold boots, but Marion knew he was off to the Mill to do some repair work for Simon and she was sure Betsy would have a fire going and there would be a pot of warm ale with sprigs of sweet cicely in it for Peter as soon as he arrived. Peterkin came back with a bit of incandescent log and emptied it out on to the hearthstone.

The evening before, Peter had spent some time carefully instructing his son in the job of pollarding the two willows near the water-place.

'I've told one of the Hunter boys to come over and help, and he'll bring his knife. Now I'm going to lend you this knife. It's on a long thong and you must keep it round your neck all the time – do you understand? I've had that knife since I was a boy, and this knobbly wooden handle – it's a briar root, smooth as an apple, just fits into my palm. I've sharpened the blade, but take the little whetstone in your pocket in case. Get the Hunter boy to give you a leg up into the tree – he's tall enough to get up himself – and cut *all* the saplings off. Cut them off right at the bottom. Don't leave bits sticking out so each tree looks like a rolled-up hedgehog. If you do that it will be hurting your feet like murder *next* year when you go cutting – anyway, you've seen men pollarding year after year before now. And *keep* the thong round your neck, and when you've done both trees lay the withies out, cut ends together neatly, in three piles, long, medium and short. Now is that all clear?' Peterkin had said it was.

Marion wondered how Peterkin, with his twisted foot and damaged hand, would really manage. She sometimes thought that Peter ignored or forgot his son's disability in his eagerness to have jobs done properly. Now Peterkin's over eight, she thought, we'll really have to find out what he *can* do, and train him for the possible jobs. There's so much he'll never be able to do.

However, this morning it was not raining, thank the saints, and Peterkin hung the little curved knife round his neck, pushed a little worn whetstone into his tunic pocket and ran off to meet the Hunter boy at the edge of the stream.

With husband and son departed, Marion went over in her mind the various jobs for the day. She made a fire, then sat down on the log, exhausted. Her throat was very painful, her nose congested, her forehead aching. Autumn was always a time of unceasing work. Even after the actual corn-cutting, at which everyone helped in the fields, there was the stacking and carrying of the sheaves, the cutting of the ears, the threshing and winnowing

in the wide barn behind the church, and then the seemingly endless sieving
of the corn, collecting the chaff, the sweepings to be saved for the hens
and pigs.

Then there was her own garden: digging the leeks and onions, picking
the ripe beans and peas as they hardened, podding them and storing them
in sacks, hanging up the sacks from rafters to keep them from mice, saving
the apples as they ripened on the tree by the fence – there was no end to
the heavy back-breaking jobs. And as well as all this, she must find food
for her family every day. In spite of fatigue she *must* go on. It had always
been thus, and the consequences of an alternative way of life, idleness, were
always before her eyes in the Plowright family: silly, morbid Small Sarah,
who sat all day with her feet in the ashes of her fire, sometimes weeping,
always idle and feckless and with her group of idle, feckless and starving
children around her.

Hearing the fire making encouraging little noises, Marion knew she must
stir herself and take back to the Hall one of the panniers belonging to the
Rutherford people which had had its lining torn and which Marion had
been mending with some strips of leather. She must go over that last heap of
pea haulms, piled on the log seat under the eaves, and if still really dry, save
all the pods and take the haulms down to Molly's, to their jointly shared pig
at the end of the garden. The pig was being fattened for the winter killing.

Alice, who sat on the floor with her fat legs spread out near the
hearthstone, was quiet and unusually still – so much so that Marion
wondered if she were going to catch the cold. As Marion went over the
pea plants and collected a lapful of hard pods she had to keep turning her
head and hunching up a shoulder to wipe her dripping nose on the harsh
leather shoulder of the jacket. It was very painful, for her nostrils and upper
lip were red and rough. She tried sniffing but this barely helped. The teasel
in her throat felt larger and made her want to swallow more frequently,
which hurt more sharply.

She stuffed all the old pea haulms into the newly mended pannier, dragged
unwilling Alice from the fire and took her to her cousin Lisa to be minded,
and Marion herself went on to Molly's. On her way there she saw one of
the wretched Plowright children, half clothed, unkempt, standing on its
bare, stick-like legs, attempting to eat a cabbage stalk. The sight troubled
Marion's conscience yet again. She knew she should always do more for
those miserable desolate children – but not just now. The rest of us, she said

to herself, us, Lisa and Martin, and Molly and the old women, *we* save our cabbage stalks for the pig, and then when it's killed we have our shares – but those Plowrights – I don't think they ever give anything to feed the pig, but they still expect their quarter at the killing.

No one was about at Molly's, so Marion went down the garden, getting her dress even wetter in the long grass, and threw the pea plants over the wall of the pigsty. The pig walked out from under its shelter to investigate. It was fattening nicely.

The wet ground was very cold and there were frequent puddles on the Common path, and Marion reached the Hall with her bare feet pink and purple with the cold. She was glad to see that the bread oven against the end of the Hall wall was alight, and Milly was in the bread shed kneading dough. Marion put down the pannier and joined her, sitting on a bench with her feet on the warm stones at the oven's base.

'We're in trouble here,' said Milly, sniffing, but relishing trouble. 'M'Dame's screeching blame on us all.'

'What's happened?' Marion asked, shifting a foot to a warmer spot.

'A side o' bacon fell down from the beam.'

'Into the fire?'

'No. No one heard it fall, or saw it. Must have fallen on some straw and the dogs got it. M'Dame found that bitch of hers and her pups at it. Mangled it was, not much left. Dogs were sick after too, but she'd turned them out of the Hall before that.'

Marion groaned at the loss and asked how it had happened.

'Don't know. A bit of rope was still round the foreleg, could've been a spark on the rope burnt through slowly. Leather would've burnt too. Ed-me-boy's been sent down to the orchard to get the long ladder to go up and see if all the other sides are hanging firm.'

'Iron chain's the only safe thing,' said Marion.

'Iron chains? How'd we get enough iron chains for all that load of meat? It's a terrible loss and all that work that went into the making of it, and all the salt too – it was one of the biggest sides. Still, when it's gone, it's gone. No need to blame me and Joan that it fell down, screeching like that, and it's *her* hellhounds that ate it . . . '

Milly's voice faded away as Dame Margaret and Tom came out of the Hall towards them. Marion noticed how Dame Margaret's gown, still the old grey one – she had not yet made up the rich red fabric from Rutherford

– hung out in front. Poor woman, she thought, with all those previous dead babies to think of.

Having greeted Dame Margaret politely, as village habit demanded, Marion turned to Tom and pointed to the mended pannier.

'So there's nothing now to stop your Ed taking the two back to Rutherford,' she said. 'I've got a bit of spun wool to go, but not much – been so busy.'

'Would be as well to wait till we've collected a lot,' said Tom, looking at Dame Margaret, hoping for agreement, but Marion knew he was trying anything to postpone Ed-me-boy's journey there. Dame Margaret was no help.

'No, Tom,' she said, 'the sooner the better, before winter comes. He can take what wool is ready. They've had more than enough already for the salt they let us have, and we won't get more salt this year however much wool we send. Ed can load up the baskets and lead Heart-of-Oak all the way there, and ride him back next day. I'll ask Sir Hugh when he can best spare the horse.' She went back indoors and Tom had to face another absence of Ed-me-boy, and, even worse, this time Ed-me-boy would do the journeys on his own.

Tom could not understand why Ed-me-boy was so eager to do this long journey again. Tom himself had always been content to stay in the village. What Ed had not told his father was that when he was in Rutherford in August, he had seen and talked with Annie, the nearby miller's daughter, who had a face like a hedge rose and eyes the like of which Ed had never even imagined, and now, to Ed, all eyes else were as dull as dead embers.

Milly pushed Marion away from her warm seat in order to get at the wide bucket of dough, rising under a bit of old cloth.

'Your voice sounds funny,' she said. 'Got a cold?'

'Yes, had it many days.'

'You ought to get some comfrey or camomile from M'Dame. She's got all sorts of stuff hanging up drying, back of the Hall. That Hilda does it with her. Says Hilda knows a lot about such plants. Hilda's down the yard now, weaving shed, I believe, with Joan.' Marion did not want to go down the dirty muddy yard. She could see a huge puddle round the drinking trough, churned up by the feet of the horses and cows. Nor did she want to be confronted with more of Hilda's strange misery. She had enough to cope with by herself, she thought.

Dame Margaret came out of the Hall again carrying a pile of folded sacks and followed by the orange-haired Mary and Meg, who looked subdued compared with their bouncing laughing selves that Marion had always seen when the children were her neighbours. A number of children had been gathering outside the Hall, one of them leading a donkey which was harnessed to a sledge. Dame Margaret organized them.

'Now, Andy Fletcher, you are in charge. There are ten sacks here and I want them all filled – beechnuts – just beechnuts, and no sacks full of old moss and leaves and a handful of beechnuts on top – are you listening, Harry? Yes, I mean you – you're off to work, not play. Go through the orchard and up into the woods there, it's mostly beech trees. Take Loppy with you and watch him – Yes, take Hoddy too and keep him out of mischief – No, no other young children. They only get in the way. This is work, not baby-caring – you can shelter under a yew if it comes on to rain hard – Izzy Fletcher, have you got the bag of bread safe? Well, don't come back until the sacks are full. They're only little sacks – you'll easily carry them when full. So off you go.'

The group of children moved off, following Andy with his hand on the donkey's bridle and the sledge bumping over the rough ground – quiet, subdued children in their damp heavy tunics, peering out of their damp heavy hoods, their muddy bare legs dragging through the rain-sodden grass, their dirty red hands every now and then steadying the pile of sacks on the wobbling sledge. It was not a pitiful sight to Marion, it was too usual. Every autumn children had to gather acorns and beechnuts for the pigs. It was unskilled work – what else could the children do?

Dame Margaret was about to re-enter the Hall when Marion asked her for a remedy for her cold. She was taken in and up on to the dais where on the back wall between the two great leather-curtained beds were hanging neat rows of dried herbs.

'Hilda's arranged all this,' Dame Margaret said. 'She knows a lot. She's put the bunches in order, so she and I know what's where – oh dear, that one looks mouldy. This damp stone wall doesn't help. I'll have to show it to her – but here, this is comfrey. Take some leaves and stew them in hot water. Have you got a fire yet Down the Common? – Good, and drink it as hot as you can, and put a bit of honey in if you have some.' Marion thanked her and put the leaves in her pocket. She glanced again at the wall of dried medicinal plants, in far greater variety and more precisely arranged than they had been when Dame Margaret alone had been responsible. Perhaps the village as a whole would benefit from Hilda's presence at the Hall.

'And please, M'Dame,' she said, 'I need more fleece for spinning. My little girl unwound and wasted some of what I had spun.'

Dame Margaret frowned and tutted, but went to a large chest against the wall. Marion had to help her lift its thick heavy lid, revealing piles of soft inside wool from many sheep.

'It's all washed and sorted out,' M'Dame said. 'Take a good bundle. It's short staple wool for loose-spinning for a weft. I've got some of the old women on the long staple making warps, they always spin very tight and strong, those old women. You ought to wear boots with a cold like that. Still, wet boots are not much comfort – don't keep your feet warm. Difficult to keep anything dry in this weather. Try the comfrey when you get home.'

Some nine foot of horizontal ladder came in at the door, then Ed-me-boy, carrying it with the back nine feet balanced behind him.

'Ah, Ed-me-boy,' said Dame Margaret, 'get the ladder up there, against the beam – that's right – now go up and look at the ropes on all the sides of bacon. I don't want another accident. There will be more to hang up there when the next hogs are killed.' Dame Margaret's attention was on her next job and she barely noticed Marion's departure with a fat bundle of wool under her arm.

On her way home, as she came along the path on the Common, she looked down at the stream to where Peterkin and Paulo Hunter were cutting the willows. There were two willows, both leaning over the water – thick, old trunks with great heads of sprouting withies, trees that had been

pollarded every autumn for decades for basket-making. She could see Paulo, a lanky twelve-year-old, on top of the half-shorn larger tree, and Peterkin crouching and cutting away but surrounded still with a maze of withies on the smaller. She could see, as they cut, that lots were falling into the water, which, after the recent rain, was flowing much more swiftly than before.

The boy will come home soaked, she thought, by the time he's collected all that from the water. He's not really up to such work. That agile Paulo has done much more in the time.

The boys, gratifyingly intent on their work, did not see her and she passed on and up the slope and through the gate. As she approached her cottage she was glad to see a thin line of smoke going up from the hole in the Plowrights' roof. If there was a fire there, there would be some warmth, and if Small Sarah had any sense, which Marion doubted, there would be bread of some sort baking, or a pot of some sort of stewing beans simmering. How these feeble-minded neighbours nagged at Marion's mind, but she knew in her secret heart that Small Sarah had long since given up trying – and there, but for my better health, go I, she thought.

At what she still thought of as the Shepherds' cottage, she turned in and looked over the half-door. The fire was smoking away comfortably and Lisa was crouching beside it grinding barley in the round stone quern with Alice at her knees playing with some fir cones. The floor, bone-dry even in this weather, was neatly swept of all straw and bits of twig and the feather broom was leaning against the wall under a shelf of pots and small buckets. It was all as orderly as was the Mill house. Lisa was certainly her mother's daughter, and Marion felt proud of her niece.

'Alice has been as good as gold, but she seems to sniff a lot and her nose is running,' said Lisa, putting down the stick with which she had been turning the upper grinding stone in the quern, and picking Alice up.

'I hope you're not getting a cold too, lovey,' said Marion, taking an indifferent Alice from Lisa's arms. 'Come along, we'll get home and see to our fire.'

'Your voice sounds rough, Aunt. Would you like some honey? Mother gave me a little tub of her new honey last week.'

'M'Dame gave me some comfrey for my cold,' said Marion, glad to pause in the warmth of the cottage.

'I've got some warm water here. Give me the leaves and I'll put some honey in, and you drink it here and now.'

It was a luxury to be cosseted. Marion put Alice down, and sat on a little stool while Lisa busied herself. She gave Marion a pot of sweet, scented, hot drink – how comforting was a *hot* drink – and she drank every mouthful gratefully. She thanked Lisa, enquired after Martin, picked up Alice again and went home.

The three green logs that she had put on the hearth that morning were now alight. Stuffing a new bit of hollow cow parsley stick into the neck of the bellows, she gently worked the lungs and got a little blaze going. She lifted her three-footed iron pot, already half full of soaked beans, on to the fire. She fetched some new-dug leeks from a pile outside the door, roughly cut off the roots and the muddied part of the tops, and dropped them into the pot as well. *There*, there was sufficient food for when the others returned.

Marion sank down on the log by the fire. Her head felt very hot and heavy and her nostrils and upper lip very sore. The comfort of the hot drink had worn off, though she told herself that the medicine must soon make her better. She had not rested long when Peterkin's head appeared over the half-door and his twisted hand, very muddy, slid over the top and unhooked it, and he came in dripping and shivering. She could see at once that something was wrong. She asked him what was the matter.

'I dropped Father's knife,' he said, almost crying.

'Oh Peterkin – where?'

'When I was up the tree, it dropped.'

'But it was tied round your neck.'

Peterkin looked guilty and sheepish and desperate all at once.

'It couldn't have dropped unless the thong broke – or you took it off.' Marion was emphatic in her accusation. '*Which*?'

'I had to take it off,' Peterkin complained. 'The thong was too short, it wouldn't reach. Then it got tangled in some of the withies, and I had to unwind it, and the thong slid out of the knife handle – out of the hole through it – and it fell.'

'Into the water or on to the bank?'

'Into the water. I heard it plop.'

'Well, there's a terrible thing. What'll your father say?'

'Don't know. Paulo and me felt around in the mud under the water there for ages but we couldn't find it. He had a pointed knife and he stuck it into the bark when he wasn't cutting. We did search for it, truly, Mam, we did, and it was awfully cold. He'd finished cutting his tree, and I'd almost finished cutting mine, so he got up into mine and finished cutting – and we laid all the withies out like father said in three piles on the bank, and then we searched again. I thought that the water might have cleared and we could've seen the knife, but the water's hardly moving and we couldn't and the mud's very soft and very deep – up to here on me – and Paulo tried walking about to try and feel the knife with his bare feet, but he couldn't – ' Peterkin burst into crying.

'Well, it's no use crying over spilt milk,' said Marion, a thing she had frequently seen done when a frisky cow had kicked a bucket over. 'I don't know what your father'll say.' But she knew very well what Peter would say and when he came home soon and was told the fate of his knife, he said it all exactly as Marion had anticipated.

'Stupid, careless, disobedient boy. I *told* you to keep it tied round your neck – nonsense, it was quite long enough, you'd be crouching down on top of the tree anyway. I hope you cut what you did close to the bark. Why didn't you do as I told you? I've had that knife since I was a lad and *I* never lost it. That fat handle, smooth, round, just fitted into the palm of my hand – I had it all these years and you had it hardly half a day and you lose it. It's all very well to say you'll go and look for it again and you know where it fell, the stream mud is deep and soft and I expect Paulo walking about in it stirred it all up. My knife might be anywhere now – No, feckless, thoughtless, wasteful boy – '

Peter was standing up against Marion as she sat on the log and she felt his body tightening for striking the boy. Only the faintest glimmer of sunset dusk came in over the half-door. She stood up instantly and put her arms round Peter, holding his arms down. His struggle was perfunctory. She knew, as indeed everyone knew, having had it hammered home to them from childhood, of the dangers of a fight in a cramped cottage; how easily a misdirected blow could hit a precious hanging sack of beans, break the string and spill them into the straw; how easily a struggling child could kick a log which would spew out sparks on to combustible bedding, how easily a pot of precious milk could be tipped over and the children's food wasted in the rubble on the floor.

'No hitting indoors,' she said, as firmly as her croaking voice would allow, 'specially not in the dark,' and as she spoke she felt his body relax, but he went on with his angry speech.

'Thoughtless, disobedient, stupid boy. There's no hope of finding it. What will become of the village if all the boys grow up as careless and foolish as you – throwing away everything your fathers have made and looked after all these years . . . ' And so the angry lecture went on and on and Peterkin snivelled and wiped his eyes with his muddy hands as he sat crouched on the floor by the fire with his twisted foot curled up against his other straight, muddy shin.

Marion agreed with everything Peter had said. He was expressing something almost too fundamental to be spoken of. Deep in her mind was the belief that whatever happened to individuals, like Dick, the village *must* continue, and that it was every generation's sole duty to see that it did. The eternal life of their own souls, whatever Father John might ramble on about, was of piffling importance compared with the eternal life of their village. Men must build halls and mills and bridges for future generations to use, and must scratch and scrape crops from the surface of the earth year by year to feed those presently living, and women must turn this hard-won corn frugally, regularly and constantly into food and give birth to as many strong healthy babies as they could. This was the unspoken be-all and end-all of their lives. But what if the new generation never came to understand this?

Peter had still not finished though he had calmed down.

'Did you pile up the withies like I told you to,' he asked, 'in three lots?'

'Yes.'

'Where are they?'

'Left them on the bank, by the water-place.'

'Well, in the morning you are to take that bit of rope by the wood pile and tie up the *long* withies in a bundle – tie it in three places, tight, so none drops out – and hump it on your back and take it up to Rockwell. Don't go through the village. Get across the shallow bit of the stream down by the Shepherds' cottage and go up the edge of the fields keeping close to the forest. No one'll see you then.'

'But that's *much* further than through the village, and it's a big bundle,' objected Marion.

'Yes, of course it is, but I don't want Rollo or anyone to see him with that bundle and wanting to know what he's up to. This is a private arrangement that I made with Edward Rockwell when I was doing his walls. I said I'd let him have a bundle of big withies, fresh cut, for mending his cow-byre – nothing to do with Rollo or the Hall. They seem to think, or he does, any rate, that they own everything in the village that anybody makes. I know Rollo sent me up there to board their walls up and I'd bet Rockwell had to send some mighty cheeses to the Hall for my days' work – that's the law maybe, but the extras I did there – new trestles for Nancy, and a new side to a corn chest where the rats had got at it – for that they gave me that side of bacon, and I promised them these withies. It's our affair and we don't want Rollo or Sir Hugh to go poking their noses in.'

'But why must I go all the way round by the forest path with the withies? You brought that side of bacon home through the village quite open.'

'*Wasn't* open, boy. I'd got my long saw-bag with me, and other tools and it fitted into that and no one any wiser. It was heavy but everyone expects a tool bag to be heavy. No, you do exactly as I say, *exactly* this time, mind, and don't you mention this to *anyone*, do you hear? And hang around a bit in Edward's place and if Red Mary gives you a bit of something, a hock or half a cheese – not that that was in the bargain, but she might – you bring it back here *at once*. Don't go through the village, come back round the fields and give it to your mother, and no word to anyone.'

'Yes, Father.'

'And see you bring the rope back. Untie the withies when you get there. I promised them withies, not rope too.'

'Why can't they cut their own withies at Rockwell?' Peterkin asked, sensing that paternal anger was fading.

'Willows grow by water, stupid, not up on the hill at Rockwell. Are those beans ready yet?'

Marion too felt that Peter's anger had subsided but she knew him of old, and how his sense of the seriousness of the loss of his knife would return to his mind and reinflame his anger.

She pushed a twig into the fire and when it lit, she put it to the rush in the little candle that stood on the shelf. By this glimmer she peered into the pot, scooped out a bean with the handle of the ladle and tried it. It was about soft enough to eat. She pulled the wooden bowls towards her from the shelf and ladled the beans and leeks into them. There were only two spoons and usually she waited while her husband and son ate, and then she fed herself, and Alice, with whichever spoon was finished with first. Now, as an indication to Peterkin that he was still in disgrace, she made him wait. She realized that she had forgotten Alice, who had been dozing beside her on the floor, leaning her head sideways against the log. By the feeble light

Marion saw that her mouth was open and two glistening streams of mucus with crusty edges descended from her tiny nostrils.

'Want some soup, pet?' Marion asked. Alice moved her head and opened her mouth more while Marion spooned some in. 'More?' But Alice turned her head away with a faint wail and lay back.

A pang of fear struck Marion. There was no doubt that now she had Marion's cold, and Marion knew from her own heart-rending experience how quickly a child, even a strong child, could wilt, fade and die in a few days. She got up and, leaning over the partition to the goat shed, pulled a bit of hay out and put it in the cradle on top of the damp straw and made a little mound under the cradle's hood. Peter had picked Alice up and was attempting to feed her from his own bowl. Alice took a few spoonfuls and then coughed and turned her face away.

'Poor little button,' he said, suddenly tender. 'She's all in a mess with that cold. Pop her in the cradle and cover her up, she won't take any more soup – then you can give me some more.'

As she refilled her own bowl for Peterkin, her hand encountered his skinny knee, damp and very cold. He shivered. 'Eat that quickly,' she said, 'then pull off your tunic and roll yourself in your blanket tight and get on the bed. Don't want you to have a cold too.' How white and ghostly his thin body appeared in the faint light as he stripped off his tunic. Had he the strength, she wondered, to carry the bundle all the way up to Rockwell? But she said nothing.

She pulled the half-empty pot on to the hearthstone and knocked the glowing logs together for safety. She had had enough of the day. She dragged herself to the door and stepped out. The sky westwards over the trees still had a faint light about it, between the horizontal slabs of brownish clouds. The air was cold and the wet ground at once chilled her feet again. She relieved herself, not stepping out as far as the midden, and returned as quickly as she could. The little flame had gone out, the cottage was dark except for the reddish glow from the fire. She sat down again, scooping up a little extra straw to soften her seat, leant back against the log and tried to rewarm her feet on the hearthstone.

Oh she was weary. Every breath scraped laboriously over her aching throat; a burning nostril now dripped a hot liquid on to her cracked lips; her eyes, open or shut, ached in her heavy head and a strange pressure thumped in her ears. Every sense seemed to have its centre in her painfully congested head. The tiredness seemed to lie in lumps down her legs. I can do no more, she thought. I hope they've finished quarrelling, but even if it starts up again, I can do no more.

Some time later, perhaps hours, perhaps only minutes, she was aware of Peter's hand on her shoulder. 'Aren't you coming to bed?' he whispered.

With a huge effort she managed to whisper back, 'Warmer here,' and drifted back into her uneasy sleep.

I must remember to ask him what to do with the other two bundles of withies, she thought as she woke stiff-necked and miserable in the dark silent night. She crawled over the small intervening space between log and bed, and hitching herself as close to sleeping Peter as she could, she pulled up the damp blanket and tried to sleep again.

NOVEMBER

The village sleeps in mist from morn till noon
And if the sun wades thro tis wi a face
Beamless and pale and round as if the moon
When done the journey of its nightly race
Had found him sleeping and supplyd his place

Marion woke with a rare and delicious sensation of having slept long and deeply and to have woken, not by children's cries, or by Peter requiring breakfast, but because her need of sleep had been appeased. The bed was marvellously comfortable. The straw was all new, dry, thick and fresh from the harvest, each hollow stalk resilient, so that she almost lay on air. She had also just received, in her due turn, a large new blanket from Joan's weaving shed and Marion had carefully sewn it all round on to her old blanket and put in between them all the feathers, hens', cockerels' and pigeons', that she had been collecting for the last two years. (The wing and tail feathers, too stiff to be used for bedding, she had tied in bundles to sticks to make domestic brooms.) The resulting bed quilt was much thicker and warmer than the one they had had before. With it and with her loose-woven shift, Marion had spent warm nights even when frost was in the air.

She was in better health. Her cold had quite gone; so had Alice's. Supper the evening before had been lavish: a cockerel stewed up with leeks and beans – a rich, hot, juicy meal. Warmth, comfort and good food had all induced this restoring sleep.

As she lay awake, with satisfaction she went over in her mind the stocks of food which she now had in the cottage. The pig had been killed and quartered. Marion's quarter this year was a shoulder and half one side of the back. Lisa had the other shoulder and half-back, Molly had a ham and some back, and the Plowrights (though it was probably a waste of good meat) had the other ham and some back. After the careful division, all four families had feasted on the less preservable bits, the head, the feet, the liver, and Molly had made sausages from the blood and all the remaining scraps. The skin had been stretched out against the wall of Molly's house where the wind and sun would dry it, and then she would rub it with sheep fat and beeswax till it was supple and waterproof. It should be enough to make a pair of boots for an adult and, with care, a little pair for a child too. They had not yet discussed who were the most worthy recipients of boots. Marion knew a possible argument was impending.

Marion's forequarter of pig, duly salted, now hung from a beam over her fire where the smoke was slowly drying it. She must be sure to keep the smoke-hatch shut when it rained, for rain on half-cured bacon rotted it quickly. Halfway down the plaited leather thongs on which it hung was a large thin wooden disc with a hole in it through which the thongs went. This prevented mice running down the thong and eating the bacon, for as they ran on to the disc it tipped and dropped the mouse off into the fire below. Yes, the bacon was there, the product of many months' nurturing, a promise of many tasty salty meals in the coming wintry days, and there were two more cockerels in the coop being fattened – but she must not waste much corn on them, they must be eaten soon. There were also several large cheeses made from her goat's milk on the shelf by the corn jar. It was a pleasure to think of all this.

The October rains had filled the millpond and Simon had ground half the sack of corn she had brought him in July, so now the oak chest in the cottage was full of flour. On the shelves over the goat's stall were several other sacks of the new harvest's wheat and barley, and between the sacks, on some hay, lay dozens of sweet rough-skinned apples. Other sacks, swinging on cords from the beams, all with anti-mouse discs above them, were filled with dried beans and peas, and outside under the eaves hung many bunches of orange-brown onions. Under them, piled high against the house wall were stacked the cut logs, and round the corner of the cottage was an even higher stack, piled almost to the thatch, adding strength and wind shelter to this more exposed side of their home. With Peterkin's help, Marion had replaced most of the moss that the wind had blown from the crevices in the wattle.

Peter had begged Sir Hugh for a couple of days off to mend his own cottage, and, picking a short spell of dry weather and with Ned Fletcher's help, he had pulled off all the sodden thatch above his door, prised out the two bent rotting rafters (which were now drying out under the eaves for firewood) and put in two new straight rafters. 'You don't have to be too accurate, Ned,' Marion had heard him say. 'As long as it is all quite rigid it doesn't matter if these rafters are closer together than in the old work.' They had then rethatched it with their new straw, and there had been plenty of straw over for the bed, and for the goat's stall for the coming winter.

It was all as satisfactory as possible – food, warmth and fuel for the coming winter. How that phrase 'the coming winter' kept filtering into all Marion's thoughts. She was aware that every autumn, she had felt a sense of achievement and satisfaction, and while indulging in it, had forgotten the true horrors of winter. It was like forgetting the agony of one childbirth when preparing for the next. But surely *this* winter she would be better prepared, better equipped, more sensible, more enduring than in previous winters? And she had, she reminded herself, now only two children to feed and care for. 'Yes,' she said to herself, 'you've felt like this, all pleased, every autumn, and yet every winter, come February, you've felt as though you'd reached the end of your endurance.' But this self-knowledge did not weaken her present optimism.

They had all got up and had something to eat. Marion had attended to the fire and put her split earthenware jar on the hearth to heat. She swept the floor round it carefully with a new feather broom, Alice following her with a tiny feather broom she had made for her. While doing so, Marion instructed Alice on the importance of keeping straws away from the fire as so easily a little flame could run along a lying straw and set light to the wattle walls – and so easily could a house burn down. Alice paid no attention; sweeping with her little broom was more interesting.

The interior darkened slightly and Marion looked up to see Lisa standing at the half-door. She had no cap on her coppery hair and Marion thought how pretty she looked. So few village girls ever looked pretty. The frequency of bad teeth, dirty skins, untreated sores, greasy hair overlaid with the dust of wood ash kept the bloom of youth away even from the healthy.

'I was over at the mill yesterday, Aunt,' she said, 'and Mother gave me this tub of honey for you. The boys took the hives last week, and didn't get stung neither, though I suppose most of the bees were dead or sleepy. Anyway, here it is, and can she have the tub back when you've eaten it?' She handed over the small wooden jar with a bit of old sack tied over the top.

'But can they spare it? And what of yourself and Martin?'

'Mother gave me and Martin another tub. She said the hives had a lot in them this year – she thinks the bees went up to the heather over the sheep pastures in September when it was those hot days, as well as in all the apple blossom we had earlier. Yes, Alice petty, brought you some lovely honey – you'll like that, won't you? Martin's mother gave him some too from Rockwell, but it's paler stuff and runnier, and we both think Mill honey's nicer but don't say so at Rockwell. Mother's making a barrel of mead. Father likes that, and she says it helps Grandpa to sleep winter nights.' So after a few enquiries about Simon and her father, Marion accepted the honey and Lisa departed.

Peter's dark woollen hood had a rent in it where he had caught it on a twig, and he had asked Marion to mend it. She picked it up from the log seat and examined the tear. On the shelf was a twisted pile, like an old bird's nest, of bits of spun wool that Alice had spoiled – the saved bits which might be of use for mending. Marion selected a dark strand, and picked up the smooth holly wood needle which she kept stuck in a little hole in the shelf. It always had a blue-speckled jay's feather in its eye to identify it and distinguish it from a thousand other smooth little twigs which littered the cottage. She gazed at the feather, feasting her eyes on the brilliant colour. Nowhere else did she see such colour, not even in the tiny forget-me-nots which grew by the stream's bank in April. She sat down on the log, keeping her feet warm by the hearthstones and sewed up the rent. Then she very carefully replaced the feather in the needle's eye and went outside to give Peter his hood.

He and Peterkin were, as she expected, kneeling on the ground half under the eaves with bundles of the smaller withies round them. Peter had announced earlier that as he could be at home that day too, and out of Rollo's sight, he would teach Peterkin to make a basket. Marion was rather uneasy about it, for she doubted Peter's patience lasting very long with a boy who had only a hand and a half to do anything with.

'Remember,' she had warned him while Peterkin was round at the midden, 'that he's no thumb on his left hand, or not one that can act as a thumb.' Marion well knew the digital dexterity needed in basket-weaving.

'Yes, yes, I know,' Peter had said, but she believed he had forgotten. She had never thought he was any good at imagining what things were like for other people.

Father and son were engrossed. Peter was instructing.

'Yes, now take the long one over – now under, yes, now the next. We'll make a flattish base first about the size of a small cheese and then start curving upwards – not over *that* strut, over the next – there, you see how the pattern's coming? Now, tap it down in place, hold it firm – no – I'd better tap it.'

'Your hood,' said Marion.

'Put it on the log. Now, boy, push another withy in there. Line it up with the others – no, no, hold the others down with your thumb – well, try it with your knuckles – no, that's too loose, try again, that would come undone with the slightest weight, press harder – let me come . . . ' and so it went on.

Marion could see that Peterkin was subdued, for though he was trying he knew that he had not the fingers to imitate what his father was doing. A wobbly lopsided basket was emerging.

Marion left them to it and went in. She scooped up some flour from the chest on to the flat top of the log seat, skimmed off some fat from the iron pot in which yesterday's cockerel had been cooked, and adding a little sour milk made a stiff dough. The old earthenware jar – it was cracked and had almost a third of its walls missing – had by this time got very hot in the embers. She put her lump of dough down on the flat ashy hearthstone and placed the hot jar upside down over it with the broken side towards the flames. This hot jar became a little oven and cooked the dough in a fairly even heat. She wiped her hands down her dress, an unconscious action indicating a job done. Alice stumped in and out of the cottage, talking to herself. Marion thought that really Alice was a good little girl.

The basket-making seemed to be going more smoothly because Marion heard Peter and Peterkin talking as they worked.

'Father, are owls the Devil's birds?'

'What nonsense you children talk. Who told you that? 'Course they're not. *Think*, boy, what do owls eat?'

'Mice and rats.'

'Yes, and what do mice and rats eat?'

'Corn.'

'Whose corn? Press it in harder.'

'Ours?'

'Yes, of course, *ours*. So rats and mice are our enemies and owls are our friends because they catch and eat our enemies. No, that one's too short. *Think* who eats what.' Peter paused for this lesson to sink in, then he went on. 'What else is our enemy?'

Peterkin had a ready answer. 'Rooks,' he said.

'Why? Pull it towards you – bit more – yes.'

''Cause they eat the corn while we're sowing it.'

'*Our* corn,' Peter emphasized, 'yes, and what else?'

'Don't know,' said Peterkin after looking round for inspiration.

'What do foxes eat?' asked Peter.

'Rabbits?'

'Yes, and . . . ?'

'Chickens.'

'*Our* chickens, that's why foxes are our enemies. Think always that those who eat our enemies are our friends. We struggle hard enough for our food and don't want it wasted or stolen by our enemies – push it down harder – nor by the Devil sending us evil spirits disguised as our enemies – turn it round a bit more – '

We are *all* struggling for our food, thought Marion, us and the mice and the owls and the foxes – but such thoughts she never voiced.

Peter went on after a pause, 'Why did I leave that hole in the top of the wall in the big barn? So that the owls would fly in and out and make their nests in there and catch all the mice for their young ones and so save our corn. Now hold it down firm while I tap them down harder – ah, clumsy boy – *hold* it, that's better.'

Marion was still busy in the cottage. Wrapping a bit of old cloth round the handle of the broken jar, she lifted it off, turned the half-cooked loaf round and replaced the jar. She collected a number of ripe apples and one of the round goat cheeses and put them in her wide basket with a bit of hay for packing. The cheese would be her last contribution to the Hall's stocks this year, and would have to be officially accepted by Rollo. The apples were for Hilda and her little girls. They had always enjoyed these russets when they lived next door.

The cottage darkened as Peter filled the doorway. He was cross.

'It's no good,' he said to Marion, 'he can't do it. It's all over the place – no shape at all.'

'He's never done it before,' Marion pleaded. 'He's got to learn how it all goes.'

'Oh, he's quick enough in his learning,' Peter said, 'he knows how it's done. After all, he's seen baskets made all his life, but he just can't hold it steady.'

Peterkin appeared behind his father with the misshapen basket sprouting withies in all directions. He looked very disconsolate.

'I *could* do it, Mam, if I had someone to help me.'

This she thought was true, but she knew Peter would not agree.

'What's the point of that? I could make a basket myself, and so could anyone, in half the time I'd be helping you make one. Besides, there isn't enough room for two people at one basket, not with keeping on turning it round. What's the point of *knowing* a thing and not being able to *do* it? No, boy, see what you can do with yourself today. Pile up all that small kindling for a start – I'm fed up.'

At that moment Alice appeared, her face pink and shiny and with a wide smile.

'Look,' she said, holding a scarlet pear-tree leaf to the top of her head with one muddy hand, and another under her chin with the other, 'Alice is a cock,' and she gave an accurate rendering of a cock crowing. They all laughed, and the laughter was a relief. Alice was pleased with her success. Again Marion felt what an unusual child Alice was. None of her other children had played in this inventive way, none had ever sought to amuse *themselves*. Alice did seem special, but Marion never had a moment's regret that any future life that Alice might live to would be one of unceasing domestic toil and childbearing – for that was all life offered. It *was* life.

'You'd better both have another try and finish that basket since you've begun it,' she addressed her husband and son, 'and mind Alice, and take the jar off the loaf on the hearth soon, and put the loaf on the shelf. I'm off to the Hall with their last cheese,' and she picked up the wide basket and left them. Alice was too busy patting coloured leaves on to the earth to notice her mother was leaving her.

It was quite a good day for mid-November, chilly but not icy, the wind fitful, the sky blue in between plentiful white and grey clouds. Marion looked up into the wooded hills where the steep slope of the ground, thickly covered in dead leaves, was visible now that the undergrowth of hazel and hornbeam was bare. The pale smooth trunks of the beech trees stood out, and here and there was a dark furry mass of a yew tree. The oaks, further up the hill still held their thick ochre foliage and far away the distant trees were a tangle of purplish branches against the slow moving clouds.

She stumped down the Common, the path bare from their constant tramping. The grass on each side, where it had been grazed for most of the summer, was now resprouting a rich vivid green, and several of the villagers' cows, which they hoped to keep alive through the winter, were languidly grazing. The hawthorns against Molly's hedge were dark and bare of leaves now, but still decorated with lumps of crimson berries, and among them grew ash saplings, smooth and silver-grey, with black buds, all round their bases a tangle of old nettles, rusty docks, collapsed thistles and fluffy willowherb, all rotting away, the whole held together with skeins of old man's beard, a grey scum over the dark twigs.

Seeing no one in the open baking shed, Marion went straight into the Hall. Dame Margaret was there with a group of girls to whom she was allocating work.

'All right, Nellie,' she was saying, 'if you've promised your mother you'd better go, but another time tell her to ask *me* first. And you, Sal Fletcher, go down the yard and help Milly with the new bacon.'

'Oh I can't, M'Dame,' said Sal with a triumphant giggle. 'I'm bleeding.'

'Nonsense,' said Dame Margaret, 'you always pretend to be bleeding at bacon time.'

'Really, I am, M'Dame.' Sal looked round to see if Ed-me-boy was watching, stepped into a more prominent patch of light and lifted her skirt to reveal a smear of blood down the inside of her thigh.

Dame Margaret clicked her tongue with annoyance and said crossly, 'All right, Sal, go to the weaving shed and sort out wools with Joan – or whatever she tells you to do.' Sal was about to think up a protest when Dame Margaret hustled her off.

Tom, with a fat log under each arm, approached Marion from the gloom and greeted her. He jerked his head towards departing Sal.

'Little cheat,' he muttered. 'Don't believe she's bleeding. Comes too pat. Rob was killing cockerels this morning, and it's my belief she just smeared some of that blood on her legs.'

Sir Hugh came into the Hall at that moment, his long split gown hitched up, indicating that he had just dismounted from his horse. Rollo followed him.

'Tom,' Sir Hugh said, 'help me off with my boots, and bring me my other pair.' He briefly acknowledged Marion's presence as Tom put down the logs and obeyed. Marion wondered at the delightful luxury of having two pairs of boots, of being able to take off the wet, muddy, smelly pair, sit by a fire and put on a warm, dry and probably soft pair. How she would love a new pair herself – but she had business with Rollo and turned to him.

'I've brought the big goat cheese, sir,' she said, 'like you said I should last week.' He looked at her with his dark eyes peering through his thick over-hanging eyebrows, with, as usual, no expression on his long face.

'Come to the wall,' was all he said.

Against the wall, near the dais, hung a number of sticks, one for each household. Rollo knew exactly whose was whose. Notches of various widths were cut in them representing the receipt of bushels of corn, pigs, poultry, eggs, cheese, days of labour and so on, that by a tradition too old for anyone to query, the villagers were obliged to give to the Hall.

Rollo took the cheese from her, pressed his thumb on it here and there, tested its weight in his hands and said gruffly, 'Take it while I make the mark.' She watched him take up the knife that hung from his belt and cut a neat notch in her stick just below the notch he had made a month ago when she had brought the previous cheese. He took it back from her.

'So that's all I have to bring this year?' she asked, needing his confirmation for her peace of mind. He ran a finger over the notches before hanging up the stick, and said, 'Yes.' Grumpy, dull, sour in speech as always, but all agreed that he was mainly honest, and that was something to be thankful for. Marion sometimes wondered if it were Tom's ever-present sharp eyes, retentive memory and passion for justice that kept sour Rollo from cheating the poorer of the villagers. No one *liked* Rollo.

Marion went out of the Hall and round into the yard. It was all very messy after the rain the previous month. All the heavy carts, toing and froing with grain and straw from barn to mill, from mill to yard had churned up the ground and it was now a sea of mud mixed with horse and cow dung, spilt straw and dead leaves. Marion crept round the edge as near to the Hall wall as she could to avoid the wettest parts till she reached the weaving shed and looked in. A wide warp was hanging from the beam and Hilda was crouching on the ground under it, carefully tying the pierced stone weights to the ends. Marion realized that Hilda had not heard her coming and she continued to work, her thin freckled fingers sorting, pulling, knotting with deft movements.

Marion was surprised that she had to summon up her courage to speak – and yet they were such ordinary words.

'I've brought you some apples, Hilda, just a few. You and your girls,' she could not bring herself to add Dick's name, 'always liked our apples at this time of year.'

Hilda stood up and came towards Marion, looked at the apples and thanked her in a rather faint voice. Marion thought her narrow freckled face looked even thinner than usual. She asked how she was.

'I live,' said Hilda, with a small brief smile. 'I don't like it. The girls are kept at work by Magda; I'm not allowed to play with them. Play is not thought seemly for the poor or the fatherless.'

As so often with Hilda's speeches, this disturbed Marion.

'Are they good to you?' she asked. She knew how readily some people would grind down in slavery the poor and their widows.

'Good – in a way. The other day Sir Hugh and Father John had me to see them – here in the weaving shed. They sent Joan off on some errand and told me I should marry again and that Tom would be a suitable husband and I should think about it.'

'And have you?'

'There's nothing to think about. Apart from Tom not wanting to marry again after his wife died, and that's sixteen or more years ago, I couldn't marry anyone, not with *all* my thoughts with Dick day and night. They don't understand at *all*. Sir Hugh said it was my duty. To whom? Not to Dick, not to anyone in the village – and what sort of a wife would I be to anyone when I was forever mourning for Dick?'

'The time *might* come,' Marion ventured, 'when you'd mourned enough for Dick – it does happen – and perhaps Sir Hugh and Father John thought that time had come.'

'Well, it hasn't, and whatever they say, or anybody says, I know it never will. I wish they'd leave me alone. Thank you for the apples,' and Hilda turned away and knelt down again, and Marion, after an embarrassed pause, departed, meeting a reluctant Sal on the threshold.

When she reached home she found Peter and Peterkin at peace with a lopsided, rather bendy basket emerging from their three and a half hands. She asked if anything had happened and was told that both the children had wanted to drink, so that although he was a man, Peter had taken the bucket and emptied it of the last of the russet apples, and gone down to the water-place and brought up a bucket of water.

This was an implied rebuke to Marion that she should have done this herself before leaving, but when he added, 'Does seem we need another bucket. I'd better see to it,' she was glad he had been reminded.

'I saw Father John on the Common,' Peter went on, 'and he was going along our hedge, picking things. *He* had a nice new basket.'

'Getting sloes to make his red wine for the church,' said Marion. 'Rather him than me drinking that stuff, sour enough to curl your teeth,' an expression which made Peterkin giggle. But Marion suddenly realized what Peter had said. She turned to him. 'Peter, how could you see who it was?'

'I could see that rusty brown hood with a white bobble on top that Joan made him – that he always wears.'

'And how could you see it was a new basket? He can't have been very near, unless you followed him along our hedge.'

'Well, I did see him, recognized him, saw the basket.'

'Once upon a time you couldn't have seen all that.' They stared at each other in mutual surprise.

'No, once I couldn't,' he admitted.

'Do you think your sight's better?'

'Perhaps it is. Hadn't noticed it specially, but now you say it I *can* see things further. I can see across the Hall now and, if the shutter's open, can see quite clearly who's where the other side of the Hall.'

'Supposing you'd be able to plough now?'

'Not likely in my old age, never having learnt it as a boy. Who'd trust his ox to *me*?'

Marion was astounded. She had never thought that Peter's short-sightedness would improve.

He had been born short-sighted. It had been noticed by his mother when he was a tiny boy and finally accepted by his father, who while putting up a fence had told his five-year-old son to hold up the next post, some six feet away, in line and to mark the spot where it should be driven into the earth. The child Peter had said, 'What post?' and had had to be taken to it. 'That? I can't see anything that far off.' The parents had shaken their heads and wondered what was to become of the boy – their only surviving child. Peter had also been born with an inherited right to strips of land but the impossibility of his ever being able to cope with the most ordinary agriculture was generally recognized. His father being dead, the rights to the strips were taken from Peter and the land was used by the Hall and Peter was apprenticed to the village carpenter with the understanding that he should work for the Hall as carpenter, doing whatever was needed, and that in exchange the Hall would work his land and supply him with so many sacks of corn from his old strips. The arrangement extended into the future in that should Peter have a son who would be capable of ploughing, the strips of land and its produce would revert to that son. It had all been discussed with Sir Hugh and Rollo, with the priest as witness, many years ago and no one forgot any detail of what was agreed.

So this was how Peter had lived ever since he had married Marion, and lucky he was to have got the miller's only daughter, everyone had said. The arrangement had worked. They had had their annual supply of corn, perhaps more regularly than if they had had to produce it themselves, and they had all the usual rights of pasture on the Common and share of the hay loads every summer, and Peter had worked, and had been respected, as a skilled and reliable carpenter in the workshop near the Hall. Everyone could see him at work there daily and knew he was no idler and no botcher.

Over recent years Marion had looked at Peterkin's limping walk and at his twisted hand and had realized that the rights of the strips could never revert to him. Nolly's early death and Alice being a girl had been other reasons for abandoning any idea of the family being more than servants at the Hall. Finding Peter's sight suddenly so much improved made her wonder for a moment if he could not return to the more respected position of a land-worker, having his own rights, but the vision soon faded. He was now too old ever to be any other than the village carpenter, and, if he could see further and clearer, so much to the good. She *might* have another son, who might grow up straight and strong – but again she might not. And Peterkin? Poor lopsided Peterkin, with his floppy lopsided basket – what sort of future would there be for him?

It was sad how early dusk came. Marion had been round to the midden and paused on her way back to look at the sky, for weather foretelling was of importance to all. Now, over the Common and the village it was all a clear blue-grey, but westwards, down the valley, it was a clean aquamarine colour with bands of woolly grey clouds lying across it. The air was very still, raw and damp. The trees, now bare twigs, that rose up the hill behind the Plowrights' cottage, were sharp black against the pale sky, and to Marion's surprise, low down between the black branches the moon was rising, a huge warm orange disc.

Moon's very big tonight, she thought, but could not remember what this was supposed to presage.

After the knifey air how welcome was the little glowing fire in the cottage and the hot chicken soup simmering in the iron pot.

It was when they were in bed that evening that Peter reverted to the subject of Peterkin's disabilities. Marion knew that when Peter reverted to subjects of conversation it was a sure sign that he had been worrying and turning over the matter in his mind. They spoke in whispers for their heads were close and they did not want to waken Alice or be overheard by Peterkin if he were awake.

'You know, Marry,' Peter whispered, 'seeing Peterkin with the withies – he really can't manage it, and apart from his hand, his left arm is weak from never using the hand. I really don't think he'll ever be able to hold a plough.'

She was amazed that Peter had ever thought it possible. She said, 'I've always known he wouldn't be able to. He can't hold things, not firmly, with his left hand. Didn't you know?'

'I've always hoped it would get better as he grew bigger, that he'd be able to open his hand as he got older. Now I'm afraid there's no chance of that. I despair, don't you?'

'I don't despair any more. I never had any hope. His thumb has just grown pressed tight against his palm. I don't think there's skin between them, I think the flesh is joined.'

'He'll never be able to plough, nor do lots of things,' Peter repeated as if trying to convince himself.

Marion thought how strange Peter was to have lived with the sight of Peterkin's deformed hand and foot for about six years and only now was he realizing what it implied for the boy's future. It was almost as if he never speculated about the future, just did what was obvious, what was before his eyes, at that particular moment. As she lay on the comfy straw thinking of his strange limited character, she heard his breathing rhythm alter, then slow down, and she knew from his long drawn, rather trembling breaths that he was asleep.

The boy's future can't be troubling him very much at present, she thought. It must be strange to be so little aware of what goes on round him.

She would soon be asleep herself, in this delicious straw and with these warm covers, smelling slightly of hens, over her. Her left hand slid out and caressed Alice's cold-nosed face in the cradle. An owl hooted, close to, perhaps in the ash, and another answered from further away. Catching our enemies, Marion thought, smiling at the recollection of the lesson Peter had given Peterkin that day. The owl hooted again and the thin sound in the chilly moonlit air made her bed all the more secure and cosy.

DECEMBER

Hung wi the ivys veining bough
The ash trees round the cottage farm
Are often stript of branches now
The cotters christmass hearth to warm
He swings and twists his hazel band
And lops them off wi sharpened hook
And oft brings ivy in his hand
To decorate the chimney nook

The nights were very long and very cold. It was often too cold to sleep in spite of the feathered quilt, and too dark to get up and do anything. All her life this is what December nights had been to Marion, lying long hours in the cold dark. Her nieces, Lisa, Ellen and Kate, had once told her that as girls in the Mill, they had all three lain close together and had passed the dark hours whispering to each other stories of fairies and dragons and witches that roamed in the forest, the basic folklore, much embellished by their imaginations, so half amusing and half frightening themselves, but succeeding in making the hours pass. But Marion had had no sisters to tell such stories to, and both her brothers, so much older than herself, would have scorned telling such tales to a little girl. So Marion was inured to boredom. She opened her eyes at intervals, but still unbroken darkness surrounded her. Occasionally there was a little click on the hearth, a charred log flaking perhaps, but enough to tell her that the fire was not quite out. She moved closer to Peter to share his warmth, but her feet remained icy blocks, and their cold was creeping up her legs to mid-calf. An owl moaned somewhere over the forest and was answered by another much nearer, then silence again. The long hours crept on and on. She sighed. She endured.

Later, needing to urinate, she pushed aside the cover and with hunched shoulders crept out. The sky was lined with grey clouds. All was deadly quiet. The grass outside the door was greyed over with a film of frost which crunched as she pulled up her shift. She went quickly back to bed and lay with her body pressed up against Peter's.

Eventually she dozed again. When she woke the blanket before her mouth was stiff with her frozen breath. This is *real* winter, she thought, colder than snow. How gladly she remembered that today was the day of the great Christmas feast in the Hall, one of the yearly celebrations, almost competing with the sheep-shearing feast – though that, of course, being held in summer, went on much longer.

That morning Peter left early for his workshop. She had wanted him to wait and to help her to the Hall with Alice, who was being peevish, but Peter had said he was making a low stool for M'Dame and he must finish it for her before the feast.

Alice had been horrible these last days, wailing at the least thing, satisfied with nothing, co-operating never. Marion had realized the cause was constipation, and no wonder, for Alice decided she was too old to be 'held out' by Marion, and would squat like other people, but the thick frost on the grass and dead leaves was so painful to her little feet that she with yells refused to go out. Marion had no baby shoes. She contemplated putting Alice's feet into a pair of boots that Margery had had, but they were much too large for Alice, and Marion knew that if she put them on the child, Alice would mess them up when excreting. Marion had complained about all this to Lisa, and she, having had to go to the Hall anyway, came back with some costmary leaves from Hilda, to be made into a purging infusion. It had worked more quickly than Marion had expected and she found Alice squatting in a corner by the door. Her relief at the speed of the cure prevented her from rebuking Alice for doing it indoors.

'I done lots,' said Alice, standing up and looking round with satisfaction. She had indeed, and Marion had had to clear it up, but from then on Alice was cheerful and active again.

What an awful lot of motherhood is concerned with the child excreting, thought Marion. She, being the youngest of a family, had not grown up with a baby or two always around, and had not realized until she had had Margery, what a constant concern a child's bowels were to the mother.

Feast day it might be – a day which all men, except Peter with the stool, felt was a rest day – but Marion had many ordinary jobs to be done, feast or no feast. Water must be fetched and in this she was lucky in that someone, probably Lisa, had already been down to the water-place and broken the ice. Then the goat must be fed, and some corn given to the few chickens which she was hoping to keep alive through the winter to provide eggs next spring.

They all at Down the Common had arranged to go to the Hall together – Marion with her two children, Lisa and Martin and Molly. Contact with the Plowrights was so rare that it was assumed they would make their own way there as they liked. Molly would have to leave her old mother and aunt behind. Martin had offered to take one of them along in a wheelbarrow and so Peter had offered to take the other, but when the old women realized that at the bridge they would have to get out and climb up the frosty steps and cross the slippery plank, they both said they could not face it. Molly must bring them back something, M'Dame was usually very good at seeing that the old and the sick had a share in the feast food. Marion knew that her old father – even more crippled than Agnes and Marge, would be brought in a wheelbarrow by Roger or Gib – but then if they left the mill at the top floor and crossed the sluice bridge, they could wheel Grandpa all the way on the north side of the stream – a rough path certainly, but with no steps on it.

After Marion and her party had crossed the plank, which was very slippery, she sent Peterkin on to the Hall with Alice, while she herself stepped aside to collect Peter, hoping he had completed the stool. As she approached his work-shed, she saw him standing outside, back towards her, looking down at Paulo Hunter, who was crouching among the shavings and chips of wood on the stony earth in front of the sawing bench. Peter was talking with anger and exasperation in his voice.

'There were seventeen nails in that bowl. I *told* you not to put it so near the edge. Now, you find them *all*. How many have you got there?'

Paulo held up his cupped palms with some nails in them.

'How many?' Peter asked again.

'Just these.'

'*How many?*' Paulo looked blank. 'Count them, into my hand.'

'One, two, three, four, six – '

'*Five*,' said Peter.

'Four, six, five, seven,' Paulo went on, piling confusion on innumeracy.

'Stupid boy. Start again.'

'One, two, three, four, six, five, seven, eight, ten . . . '

Peter sighed violently. 'Listen, you fool. One, two, three, four, five, six, seven, eight, nine, ten, eleven, twelve, thirteen, fourteen, . . . is that all?' Paulo's hands were empty. 'How many more must you find? There were seventeen.' Paulo still looked blank. 'Saints in heaven, can't you even count? What do these mothers do all day – not even teach the children to count?'

Marion resented this accusation of maternal idleness, but it was ever so. It was easy to blame women for any failings in children.

'There should be three more nails somewhere,' Peter went on. 'Look for them, feel about. Or have you hammered any into that joint so far?'

'Yes. One, there.'

'Then you have two more to find. You're to stay here till you have. Oh hallo, Marion – what is it?'

'We are all going into the Hall now,' she said. 'Did you finish the stool for M'Dame?'

'Yes, Paulo took it round, then he was just finishing *that*, and the silly boy upset all the nails on the ground.'

'I found them, sir.' That Paulo called Peter 'sir' was a mark of his contrition. Still kneeling he held up the two nails to Peter.

'Yes, that's them, all right, put them in the bowl with the others, then put the tools away, *all* of them, and on the proper hooks, before you come over to the feast. Come, Marion.'

It was amazingly, marvellously hot in the Hall. In these wintry days the shutters to the windows were rarely opened and today they had been closed most of the time. Only the dim December daylight from the great open door, some tiny candle flames on the high table and a glow from the fire in the centre lit the hall. The fire was at present two huge incandescent but flameless logs, kept in that state by Rob with the long-handled bellows. On the iron struts over the fire, large pieces of a calf were roasting, and every now and then Rob dropped the bellows, picked up a five-foot ladle and poured some fat, from the long earthenware trough on the hearthstone, over the meat.

Sir Hugh had described how at Rutherford they had roasted a calf whole, but Tom had resisted this. Such a big fire was too dangerous and, anyway, the outside got burnt and the inside remained raw and tough, he had said to Sir Hugh, and M'Dame had supported this view. So the calf had been cut up into joints which were roasted separately. Every now and then a flame from a drop of fat shot up from the fire, briefly illuminating the scene.

The Hall was already full of people, or so it seemed, for they were crowded round the fire. All the trestle tables had been put out along each side of the Hall, and one across it, just below the dais. This did not allow much space except round the fire, and its fierce heat did not permit anyone to stand close to it. On the dais the high table was in place and Magda stood by it with the two little Shepherd girls. Before them were two large wooden bowls of red apples. Magda was teaching the children to spit on the apples and rub them on the hems of their dresses so that they shone with reflections from the candle flames. Magda was not using her own dress for this polishing as she was wearing a loose over-dress made of the wonderful deep red cloth that Sir Hugh had brought from Rutherford in August. The little candle flames shone on the red apples and made the rich red of Magda's dress glow and lit the bouncing orange curls of the children as they solemnly spat and rubbed. In all the darkness of the Hall this warm red scene took Marion's attention with its strangeness. In her long experience everything indoors, whether her own cottage or the Hall or any shed, was brown or grey or black or speckled mixtures of all three. She liked looking at these various reds and the little shaking flames. The good smell of the roasting veal pervaded the air and associated itself in her mind with the rich colours.

'Look at those little girls' heads,' said Milly, suddenly appearing at Marion's elbow. 'Hair that colour you'd think as good as a fire, you could warm your hands at it.' She guffawed. 'Not that it seems natural.'

'Dick had hair like that,' said Marion, thinking with great sorrow of Dick at last year's feast.

'What have you got burning there, Tom?' Peter asked, indicating the fire.

Tom gave him a sly look, and said, 'It's that old apple tree, was by the corner in the orchard – not born fruit for years.'

'Apple? They could have used that down at the Mill.'

'Your Peter,' Tom said to Marion, 'he'd always have a use, other than burning it, for every bit of wood in the village. We've got to burn something, Peter you old misery. You'd be the first to complain of raw cold food.' This banter between Tom and Peter as to the uses of wood was a regular pastime, and each man respected the other. There were not many suitable subjects for jokes in their lives.

The feast was formal. It was the only formal meal, sitting at a table with food before them and ale being brought round, that the villagers enjoyed in the year. At the Michaelmas feast, everyone stood around in the Hall and cut bits off the huge joints of deer meat and took them to their families on the points of their knives, and at the pre-Lent feast the food was more ordinary and everyone ate knowing how low the general food stocks in the village were, so it was not an occasion for rejoicing but for eating while they could. But this Christmas feast was a ceremony and one that they could all enjoy, and it was mainly due to Dame Margaret that it was orderly, warm, and as lavish as possible. She also saw to it that portions of meat and bread and whatever luxuries there were, were sent to the old and the infirm who could not be present.

The Hall darkened as the great door was shut to keep out the cold. It became even more crowded as newcomers arrived, shuffling up to the fire and standing as close to it as they could. The steam from their cloaks rose with a smell of damp wool and long-unwashed bodies. Then with burning faces and hoods thrown back, they retreated a little and a new wave of dark hooded villagers sidled up.

Marion, standing on the far side of the fire, behind the back of bellowing, basting, sweating Rob, looked across the glow to the red-lit faces of the villagers beyond. Dobbin was there with Jill, both looking sullen and subdued, for since the death of his baby no villagers had spoken to Dobbin although he had been working with them as usual. With them was One-eyed Wat, his dark hair carefully pulled over his scarred eye socket, his good eye constantly swivelling around in anxiety, and with him stood several more silent children, also from Dobbin's first marriage.

In contrast the Hunter family moved into view, each wrapped up in a thick cloak. They came in red-faced, smiling, blowing, stamping their frozen feet, greeting Sir Hugh and Dame Margaret, then Peter and Marion with a gesture and their three broad-faced adolescent children stood with hoods pushed back and the firelight shining on their faces. Paulo, their youngest, having put away Peter's tools, sneaked up to them and warmed himself partly under his mother's cloak. He was still uneasy at having shown himself to Peter Carpenter as being bad at counting. They did not talk, they were gasping with the effort of getting there through the bitter air, and bemused and silenced by the strangeness of warmth and crowds and the high darkness in the beams over their heads.

Then a group from Rockwell arrived: Old Wat, his enormous beard, black and grizzled, flowing down on his chest as he pulled off his hood; Nancy, his wife, who was Molly's sister, and who sought her out and they disappeared into some dark corner to chat; Stephen, whom Marion persistently hoped would marry Ellen, and several other teenage children. The other Rockwell family joined them: Edward, his wife, Red Mary, their son Tim, with eyes like speedwells even in the gloom, and who helped at Mass every Sunday, and several more children, and with them, more bent and gaunt and haggard than ever, Old Lambert. The Rockwells, who had had by far the longest walk to the Hall, down through the fields, still appeared to be the most animated, and their talk and laughter enlivened the rest of the party. Old Lambert, on the arm of a nephew, was eased round the Hall to where his son Loppy was standing, leaning back against the wall, his head back, a faint smile on his long bristly face and a red fire-glow on his lumpy nose. Old Lambert greeted him with pats on the shoulder, but Loppy showed no recognition and continued to smile vaguely.

Sir Hugh, in a rare positive mood, was busying himself and giving orders. This was his social manner, put on for the occasion.

'No, all dogs out, I said so before. No dogs in the Hall tonight. Tie him up to the oak tree – they'll all keep themselves warm there, well – let them fight out there. You should have left them at home. I've enough trouble with my own family dogs. Ah, Wat – and Nancy! God's Christmas blessing – how are matters up at Rockwell? Water frozen? You – Stephen – you'll have to mind your head on the beams if you go on at this rate – mind your head on the hams, at any rate. It's often said a tall man's head smells of bacon, still, there's worse things – little girls well? Father John, you know where your place is at the high table. Magda is there I think. Sarah, come and warm yourself – Dobbin, make room. How's the meat getting on? Where's Dame Margaret? Oh in the bread shed still. *Magda*, keep that dog of yours quiet . . . ' and so on and on, in an unusually expansive mood as if all anxieties were suddenly lifted.

Meanwhile Ed-me-boy, having despaired of Loppy's help, was still moving the low benches about in lines by the tables. He was busy as usual but his mouth was tight and he did not speak. He had been silent like this since the disastrous autumn days when he had disappeared. He had been sent out with a sickle to clear the weeds from round the Hall's beehives, which stood under a shelter against the back wall of the cow sheds. When he did not reappear at supper, Tom became anxious and called and called, and then Rob went round to the beehives and found all the weeds neatly cut down and piled up and the sickle across the top of a skep, but no Ed-me-boy. For three days there was a search and Tom had been distracted. Had the boy drowned in a ditch? All ditches were searched. Had he got lost in the forest? But why should he have gone into the forest? Had he gone up to Rockwell for some reason? But no one at Rockwell had seen him. Then on the third evening through the pouring rain he staggered into the Hall, banging the great door, soaked to the skin, crying and exhausted. Tom, like the Prodigal Son's father, would have killed a fatted calf had he owned one. As it was he made Ed-me-boy a bed of clean straw by the fire, stripped off his soaked tunic and boots, wrapped him in his own cloak and fed him with warm soup from Joan's pot, and fended off all enquiries of, 'Where have you been?'

It came out later, and bit by bit, that he had decided he *must* go and see Annie, the rose-faced miller's daughter in Rutherford, and having finished the beehive clearing, had run away through the orchard and taken the now familiar path to Rutherford, where he arrived during the night. It was a disastrous visit. What had gone on between him and Annie on the occasion of his taking back the empty panniers, no one ever knew, but this time his hopes of any further relationship were at once dashed. He had presented himself at Rutherford mill, Annie was sent up into the loft and the miller told Ed-me-boy very clearly to go home, that he would not dream of giving his pretty daughter to the seventeen-year-old son of a hall servant somewhere up the valley – *so he said* – and that anyway Annie had long been promised to a proper steady young man with a field of his own and prospects of a team of oxen, and Annie was brought down and made to confirm in her father's presence that this was so – and, yes, perhaps she should have told Ed-me-boy this when he last came, but somehow she had not, and perhaps he did not give her time to speak, but Ed-me-boy saw tears in her exquisite eyes as she repudiated him. So he had walked all the way home in the rain with his heart broken, and it had not mended since, and the brazen advances of that slut Sal Fletcher just sickened him.

The great door of the Hall opened again, letting in a blast of icy air and some dim December dusk and a hoarse male crowing sound. Marion, shading her vision from the firelight, saw her father slumped in a wheelbarrow, his flour-white boot soles sticking up, being wheeled in by Roger, with Simon and the rest of the family following. He at any rate was in a jovial mood.

'Not going to miss the feast, not me,' he announced to the Hall at large. 'Get me up, boys – here, here, go easy.'

'Take him under his *knees*, Gib, not feet,' Simon ordered. 'There you are, Old Man. Ah, Marion, got a seat ready for Father? Oh, Tom's put out the real chair – there's a treat for you, Father,' and with much reassuring chat, the old man was lifted into a chair with a woven willow back, similar to those on the dais on which Sir Hugh and his family sat. The chair was eased up to the end of one of the tables near the dais, and Marion, with Alice on her knee, sat down on the bench beside him. She could see him smiling with pleasure and achievement, but she also noticed in the flickering candle light the bluish veins standing out on his temples and the transparency of the surrounding skin.

Dame Margaret, who had not been seen before, arrived through the gloom with a wide basket of small loaves between her extended arms.

'Grandpa Miller! So you got here after all?' she said.

'That's what I got grandsons for, M'Dame,' he said, still laughing. 'They brought me all the way in the wheelbarrow. They took the wheelbarrow over the sluice plank – didn't like that – but I had to get up to top of the mill first. They put me in a sack and pulled me all the way up like I was a sack of corn! And the boys kept shouting, "Don't laugh so, Grandpa – or you'll have the rope off the pulley!"' He chortled with excitement over this adventure. 'Got something good for me to eat, M'Dame, after coming all this way?'

'*He* came easy,' said Gib, appearing in the gloom and rubbing his long red hands. 'It's me and Roger need that something good. I thought my hands had got frozen to the wheelbarrow.'

'No touching yet,' said Dame Margaret, jerking the basket away from their hands. 'Here, Grandpa, here's a treat for you.' She balanced the edge of the basket on the back of his chair and picked a small flat loaf from it, the top of which was spread with baked honey and hazelnuts. 'You eat this now and we'll all have ours after the meat.'

Magda bounced up, all inquisitive. 'Oh, Mother, you shouldn't. Every-one will want theirs too now. You know, Grandpa Miller, Mother's saved the liver. It's been stewing by the fire. It's for you and some for Sarah, and Molly's to take some to her mother and aunt. They've not got grandsons – '

'It's the bridge steps that stop them,' Marion said. 'Peter and Martin would have brought them.'

The old man only half raised his eyes from his honey-bread – the nuts were too hard but he licked the honey happily. The glance showed him Alice's face peeping out from the cloak round Marion's shoulders.

'Ah, my little Allikin, my fat little Allikin, come and sit on Grandpa's knee.' Alice hid her face in Marion's cloak again.

'She's a bit shy still, Father,' said Marion. 'She'll remember you soon. Alice, sit up and say Happy Christmas to Grandpa.'

Alice shook her head without raising it.

'Come and sit on Grandpa's knee and have some honey-bread.'

Alice dug a podgy elbow in Marion's breast to lever herself up, and stared at Grandpa who held out a bit of honey-bread. She took it daintily in fingertip and thumb, then a slow smile swelled her cheeks.

'More,' said Alice, holding out her hand and the old man laughed with delight.

'Not such a big bit, Father, she'll choke.'

'No, no, she's all right,' and he guffawed again, showing his pink gums in which were set a few stumps of teeth like broken wellheads filled with black poison. His breath came sour and bitter over them. 'Come and sit on Grandpa's knee,' he repeated, but though Marion put Alice down on his lap very gently, the child's weight caused him much pain and he became subdued and Alice gladly returned to Marion's embrace.

An extra loud sizzling over the fire was heard, and a flame danced up from one of the legs of veal, and by its brief light Marion saw Molly approach her. She spoke in low confidential tones.

'The Plowrights have come.'

'Well, I thought they would. They never miss a feast.'

'How many children have they?' Molly's voice was conspiratorial.

'Five, I think, including the youngest – and he must be over two now. The littlest died just before last Christmas.'

'That's what I thought,' Molly went on, 'but there's only *four* here and that's counting the baby.'

'Perhaps one of them is ill,' said Marion.

'I asked Small Sarah, but of course I only got the usual gobbledy noise, but she looked troubled – something to hide.'

Marion could not be bothered with this searching for trouble.

'Why not ask Jack? He must know how many children he's got.'

'I did,' Molly was triumphant, 'and he says, "Four, as you well know. Why do you ask?" and he points to the four standing around, all close and silent like always.'

'Well – that's that,' said Marion.

'I *know* they had five, boys or girls I don't know, but five there were. If one was sick at home he could have said, so what I want to know is, where is the lost one? Is it dead and they never told anyone?'

Marion thought it quite likely. One miserable little starved life, flicked out some cold winter's night, and neither parent doing the right thing like getting Father John and having a proper burial. Probably they felt ashamed and hid the body in the midden.

'You'd better tell M'Dame about it if you really think there were five,' she said. But she too had thought there were five.

There was movement. People were finding themselves seats on the benches. Tom and Rob were heaving the roasted meats off the hooks and laying them on the huge wooden bowls. Whetstones rattled along knives. Joan was bustling round dropping thick trenchers of bread on the tables. Sir Hugh and his family and Father John stood in a row behind the high table, Rollo was fussing around with a number of earthenware vessels and a large bucket brimming with ale that stood on the end of the table. Ed-me-boy was going along the trestle tables sticking candles, from a bundle under his arm, into the wooden blocks along the length and lighting them one from another as he went. Many careful eyes watched him. Candles in this profusion were a luxury.

Sir Hugh, in the centre of the high table, banged on it with the handle of his knife, and in the following silence, announced that Father John, Tim Rockwell and three other boys would sing the blessing. Father John, who always conducted Mass in a vague monotonous sing-song, insisted on a sung blessing, such as he had learnt at Rochester as a young man. Musical he had never been, and the intervening decades had weakened what memory he had, but the Christmas ritual must be followed. So, as always before the Christmas feast, the four boys were ranged in a row at the side of the dais, and at Father John's raised hand descending, the boys, not quite in unison, started intoning *Non nobis, Domine, non nobis* without understanding a word.

All were startled when Jo Hodgson, who seemed twice as tall as he had been at the sheep-shearing, said loudly, 'No, that's wrong,' and joined in the singing himself in a newly acquired powerful tenor that surprised everyone. But an interruption could not be tolerated and several voices called out, 'Shut up, Jo,' and, 'It's the priest's song – he knows how it goes,' so the boys started again, in less unison, while Jo sat looking annoyed and preoccupied and the youngest singer collapsed into giggles. Father John was obviously relieved when it was over so that the eating could start.

Tom was serving at the high table, placing slices of roast veal on the bread trenchers, which, because there were gentry at the high table, had been put on wide wooden bowls which collected any fat and gravy that the bread had not absorbed. Joan followed him with a big earthenware jug containing the hot fat and gravy that had poured into the drip-pan. It was flavoured with thyme and sage, and the hot perfume was added to the smells of roast meat, steaming woollen clothes and tallow candles. Matt, the ploughman, bringing with him, as always, a whiff of the stables, was filling pots with ale from the bucket near Rollo and passing them to whoever happened to be sitting at the tables' ends nearest the dais.

Joan, having switched to another big earthenware pot which she held in one hand, brought a wooden bowl and a spoon to Grandpa Miller with the other, and filled the bowl with bits of the calf's liver and breadcrumbs and gravy. Marion stirred it up for him, and with a trembling hand and spilling bits into his beard, he concentrated greedily with many sucking noises, on his great meal of the year.

Marion picked up her portion of hot veal, and gnawed at it, juicy, greasy, rich and satisfying. The pot of ale came her way and she held it to her father's lips and he gulped a lot though how much he actually swallowed she did not know. Then she took a long drink herself of the refreshing, sustaining enlivening stuff. She gave Alice a drink too, and fed her with bits of meat and bread from her own trencher. She looked down the length of the table to where Peterkin was sitting with some of the Fletcher boys – all silent, all serious, all holding long veal ribs to their mouths, the candlelight glistening on their smooth greasy cheeks and in their solemn eyes. Eating such food was an important matter.

The pots of ale went round again and needed more frequent refilling at the bucket. Fresh slices of bread were brought by Joan, and more pieces of meat – though in less neat slices than before – were offered, dangling from the point of Tom's knife. The warmth penetrated, the hot meat satisfied, the ale loosened tongues. Talk increased. The Rockwells' loud voices from the other side of the Hall dominated, and one of them spoke of some shortage of corn. Marion saw her father pick up the phrase, but not the context, and he raised his head.

'Short of corn?' he echoed, the familiar words overcoming his usual deafness. '*Shortage of corn*? You young men don't know what shortage is.' A child giggled at hearing his father addressed as 'young', and so drew the old man's attention to him. 'Yes, you too – given everything you could want from the time you left your mother's breast. *Bread*, every day, all ground by my hands at the Mill.' Marion, to her amazement, saw that her father was standing up so as to get a better view of his audience. 'And good fat bacon all though the winter. *Rabbit*,' he threw out the word as if it were a curse, 'and not a month goes by from September to Christmas and beyond that there is not a feast of one sort at which you stuff yourselves at Sir Hugh's generosity. You boys don't know what it is to go hungry – '

'We do,' interrupted a husky breaking voice. Seemingly the speaker realized he would never have a better opportunity for public speaking. 'We feels hungry every day, us boys all do. It's only because you sit still all day and do nothing that you don't feel hungry.' The old man did not seem to hear and went rambling on, and the boy's concluding remark, 'And you haven't any teeth to eat with if you were hungry,' brought laughter from his companions.

'I remember what it was like to be short of corn – no, not short, what it was like to have *none*.' The old miller steadied himself with one hand like an eagle's claw, his uncut nails curved like talons, clutching Simon's shoulder. '*None*,' he emphasized, looking round at the dim faces of his audience. Marion glanced up to the high table to see how Sir Hugh was taking this outburst, but he sat there quietly, his long face supported on his long hand and his lugubrious eyes on the old man. Marion looked back at her father. The nearby candle flame lit every white bristle on his face and shone on the tear, draped between upper and lower eyelid, which trembled as he spoke but did not drop. '*None*. It was May that year when we first noticed the blight. Corn – wheat it was – had come up well, nice drop of rain in

April, warm and moist in May. Ah, we were all promising ourselves a great harvest, and then old Oz – Osbert I think he was, you wouldn't remember him, sir.' He had turned a little and was addressing himself to Sir Hugh on the dais. 'He found it up in Hall field, near the forest. His wheat heads were dropping and there was some browny stuff, fluff sort of, on each ear and when you touched it all the little seeds fell off. Only a little patch like this, but we was all worried and we all – I was only a boy then – went up Hall field to look at it. They all told Oz you cut it down and burn it and we'll all give you a bit of ours. 'Course, he didn't want to but they made him and it was all cut and burnt, but Devil take it, next week there was lots more of this blacky stuff on the wheat, not just by Oz's strips but up to Rockwell, and old Humph Cartman had it on his land, and it all had to be cut and burnt. Then we found some on your land, sir. That would be in your father's time, sir – '

'*Grand*father's,' came a voice from the dark, but the old man did not hear it and went on, 'And while we was cutting that, old . . . what was her name? she was a young girl then, came running to us to say this dark fluff stuff was all over the wheat down by the Mill. Well, sir, we all tramped off, your father leading. It was terrible – all this fluff stuff, and when you touched it the little withered seeds fell like bits of nothing to the ground. Ah, there was lamenting that evening. No one was safe. We all knew what it meant. I recall your father, sir – '

'Grandfather,' came the voice again, a little louder.

'– standing there in the lower part of Mill field, just looking at us. None of us knew what to say and his face as white as a new-born lamb. We didn't know then he was a sick man. Perhaps it was the same poison in the wheat that had got into his vitals – '

'No, coursh it washn't,' a blurred drunken voice came from the dark, seeking controversy.

'– but we cut and cut and burnt and burnt. He wouldn't let us save nothing to feed cows or pigs with for fear of this brown stuff spreading more, all he said was cut, cut, and burn *carefully* and watch your barley. But barley never had this browny fluff – never has since – but we didn't know that then. There was grim faces everywhere then, and he, your father, sir, he never got back his strength, vomiting and not pissing proper and his face as yellow as a buttercup. I recall well he came to the door of the Hall – yes, right here – to give some orders and he had to keep hold of the doorpost to keep himself up, and his hands as thin as a corpse's, and *yellow*. He was a corpse a few days later, and all this only a few weeks after finding the blight. And him a young man – well barely twenty-four, I reckon – and your mother, sir – '

'Grandmother,' said the voice, more insistent now.

'– a goodly young woman and not long married – came from down the Weald, I believe, and expecting but didn't show it yet.'

The old man paused and took some ale from the pot that Ed-me-boy had been holding out to him unnoticed in the gloom. He wiped his beard with the back of his hand, but the pause in his story had made him forget where he was. His audience was silent. Marion saw their rows of pink faces in the faint candlelight, all intent on her father. Simon was obviously enjoying this reflected attention. Sir Hugh sat with two candles before him, the flames still as high as his face which he leant sideways on one hand, with his bloodhound eyes fixed on the old miller. Dame Margaret, sitting next to him, had untied her cap strings and thrown them back over her shoulders, a mark of how warm the Hall was. She too had her eyes on the old man. Her new crimson dress, though amply cut, was already pulled tight over her belly. Marion observed how thin her neck was, with long taut tendons stretching down from her ears and disappearing into the crimson wool. It was as if her swollen stomach was hung on strings from her neck and her every movement showed the weight of her pregnancy.

The ale had revived the old man and he picked up his story again, but not quite from where he had left off.

'He died soon after – had to – couldn't hold any food, not even a bit of pappy bread, and she fed him like a motherless baby, patience itself, and him sicking up every little while and as yellow – '

'As a dandelion,' came a mocking voice, followed by laughter, but the old miller did not seem to hear.

'But when he was buried – you know his grave, don't you, sir? – the yellow had all gone and he looked as pale as any other corpse. Ah, it was a sad time and him still young and had been strong, and she a widow and barely twenty. Ah, she was a woman a man could be proud of, your mother, sir, no, no, your *grand*mother she'd be.'

'Told you so,' said the voice from the dark.

Alice had fallen asleep on Marion's lap. The heat from the fire was hot on her back, so she pushed off her cloak. She crossed her feet and spread her knees so that Alice slept in a hammock made by her skirt slung between her thighs.

'No pining or moaning from her. When Father Stephen – he that was here before you, Father John, long before – said over the grave it was a punishment for his sins that he died young, she, well she didn't say a thing while we was in holy ground, but when we got back to the Hall – here – for the burial feast, she let fly at Father Stephen. What do you mean, she cried at him, about his sins? He'd lived a decent life and every Sunday to Mass and never stole nor took anything but what was his due in law and wouldn't take from widows what *was* his due, and a good husband and no fornicating youth. What sins are you talking about, taking a man's good name away as soon as he can't answer back? And Old Holy – we used to call Father Stephen Old Holy, least us boys did – he looked really muzzed in his mind. Never been questioned like this before – front of everyone – least of all by a young woman. He said about how God knows all men's hearts and she burst out with God hadn't told *him*, priest though he was, what was in her husband's heart and it was poisonous talk to say about his sins – and he'd had the Last Sacrament and confessed to Old Holy himself and been shriven not three days before . . . And . . . and Old Holy didn't know what to say, just muttered about Eve's daughters and not reverencing him nor Holy Church. But there was good cheese and a cask of old ale for the burial feast and I saw to it, 'cause I was serving boy at the Hall, that was before me two brothers died, that Old Holy only got a mouldy rindy bit and a short drink afore I tipped the pot so he couldn't get no more . . .' The old man's mirth at his boyhood jokes got the better of his speech and he guffawed in self-appreciation. 'She calmed down after that and had a short weep – ah, she was a brave woman – and us boys jostled Old Holy out of the Hall to leave her in peace.'

The whole Hall seemed to get hotter. Great quantities of roast meat, and the strength of the new ale were making many of the villagers drowsy. Marion felt a sudden warmth over her ankles and found that Alice had peed copiously in her sleep. There were sounds of children squabbling at the far end of the Hall, paternal slaps and maternal, 'Be quiet now,' and whispers of, 'He hit me first,' but for the most part the old miller's story held their attention. Many of them had heard stories before of the great famine, but in their fictionless, monotonous lives any story had power to grip their minds. The candles had shortened and no longer lit up the old man's eyes. Only the white bristles, roughly trimmed by Betsy, and his claw-like hand, swaying to and fro with gestures, caught the light. Marion realized that his memories were flooding back, and each remembered detail of his famished boyhood brought a host of other recollections. She knew there was no stopping him, not that anyone wanted to. Drowsy though they might be, the villagers listened to the flow of words and the events they told with solemn attention, so unusual was it in their monosyllabic lives to hear so much spontaneous speech. The old man had collected his thoughts; he found an attentive audience wonderfully stimulating. Joan was doling out small loaves covered with honey and hazelnuts and in a breathy whisper urging people to take one and pass on the basket.

'And all the time through his sickness she said to the men, look at your wheat and if there's this dark stuff, cut and burn, and they did. They cut and cut and carried it all to the waste corner by the nut tree – '

'Nut tree's long since gone,' called out the know-all's voice.

'– and burnt it there so as there'd be no danger of the burning spreading to the standing barley. Barley was all right, the Devil's blight never touched barley, but there was no wheat left, nowhere, and she said burn the stubble as it stands and they did – as much as you can burn green stubble. Oh, it was sad faces all round then, so much work gone to waste, and the little brats looking on and asking why, and all of us wondering . . . wondering . . . ' His voice faded to a mumble as his memories overtook his narrative.

'Tell about the lady,' Simon prompted.

The old miller raised his head again. 'She stood there,' he pointed to where Sir Hugh sat, 'day or two after the burial – it was a day, pouring rain, sky so sodden and dark, not a breath of wind, not a chink in the clouds – you know how you get it in June sometimes. Though it was noon it was dark in the Hall, shutters hardly open,' he gestured up at them, 'the rain dropping in both sides – and she had all the men called to her and I go too though only a boy not ten years old, and she *talked*, oh she talked, clear and sensible, and no one could fault what she said, woman though she was. We're in bad trouble, she said, all of us, there'll be no wheat this coming autumn, not a grain, and that means no bread all the winter, and nothing save our barley, if we harvest that, and our peas and beans, and we've no seed corn for sowing next year unless we can get some from Rutherford. Nick Carter – you don't remember him, sir, long ago dead – says maybe they have the Devil's blight there too and she says maybe they have. We've only got our barley and she says anyone as still got peas and beans it is not too late to sow them now and might get a crop before winter. Better go a bit hungry now and live next year, she said. It seems most people still had some peas and beans, so she says everyone must bring her *all* their stores, flour, corn, peas, beans and if anyone hid any she'd have him, or more likely her, whipped. She says we'll all mostly live if we work together and if we don't we'll certainly all die, she says – for even if one family finds enough to eat this coming year and everyone else in the village is dead, how's that family going to live all by itself? And the men all realize she talks sense and she says barley's what we'll have to eat and food is more important than drink and God sends us water for drinking and there was to be no barley made into ale. She called it wasting the good grain which we all needed. Well, there was much groaning and grumbling at that, but as it turned out she was right and in the end every barley grain was precious, but it was miserable all the men said to come in after all day ploughing and me shouting at the rooks behind a plough all day and in an easty wind and we have a drink of cold water like you was a horse 'stead of a pot of good warming ale to give a bit of heart to your body. And old Mam . . . what was her name? down by the marsh, dead long ago – she'd hidden some barley in her wood pile and she was making a little cask of ale, quietish. But Tom – that's your father, Tom, he was a lad my age or a bit older – caught her at it and tells me and I say you make out you've seen nothing, but the lady's promised a honey cake to any tattlers of this sort. So Tom tells and gets his barley cake, mighty small it was too, but with honey, and he gives me a bit – and she sends down to the marsh and they catch her at it and she was beaten by the big oak with a withy and the cask taken away and when the ale was ready the men all got a little sup of it, all round next Sunday after Mass – not Mam Beattie – ah yes, that was her name, Beattie – ' and he relapsed into a chuckle.

Simon prompted him again.

'Yes, yes,' he went on, 'she held all the corn and all the flour and all the peas and beans not needed for sowing, and she had it all in sacks and barrels here, on a board out of the damp and she measured it all out with a wooden scoop, smallish like, and she counted the people and the days till we thought we'd get another harvest. She was a great reckoner, marvellous how she had it all in her head. Every Sunday after Mass we all came to the Hall, the women with their bags and baskets, and she scooped out so much

barley or beans according to family size. She wouldn't give it to the men.
She said wives were more like to deal it out fair in families and make it go
furthest. It was very little my mother got, I remember, and after our Sukey
died that winter we got even less, but we could all see it was fair. And the
lady, she didn't take no more for herself than she gave us, though we could
see she was getting big-bellied as the autumn went on. The Hall had but
five cows that summer, all with calves and with all the spring rain the grass
was good and there was a good hay crop. The milk was good and she ran
the dairy here, saw to it every day, and more cheese was made from those
cows as ever I saw. The whey she gave to all the women, herself too, as was
with child, to keep the babies steady, she said, and she watched everything
to see it was done proper. If it wasn't for her doing all that I reckon the
village would have starved. You boys – you got everything you could want.
You don't – you don't . . . '

Simon again drew his father's mind off the boys present and back to
the past.

'It was a bad winter, that winter, fog and ice, not much snow, but frost
as never seemed to melt. We had our fires and we had our cheese, and
a chicken now and then, but not much to a chicken that's had no corn.
There was no ale to warm us and many of the old ones died, of course,
more'n usual. The earth got so frozen hard as no graves could be dug, and
the men just put the bodies one on top of another in one grave and put
a board over the top with a stone on it to keep the foxes off and waited
for the next death. Wasn't Christian burying but Old Holy said prayers for
each so we thought it'd be all right.

'We were getting pretty hungry that spring. The lady had her baby and
a good fine little boy it was and that all gave us a bit of hope. How the
mothers had milk for their babies I don't know. Terrible thin, she was. I
remember her scooping up our little bit of beans – that was like the first
day of spring – all warm and sunny and the bees in the orchard buzzing
away, and I saw how thin her arms were, she had been on the plump side,
comely girl like I said, but not then. The brats in the village couldn't do
a thing, sat about weak like and cried to their mams for bread and the
mothers weeping to look at them. Many died, of course. Only some strong
ones lived.'

'Why didn't you go down to Rutherford and get some corn?' a young
male voice called from the dark.

'*Rutherford?*' repeated the old man scornfully. 'D'you think we didn't? Three or four men went down with horses and panniers and the Rutherford men chased them away with sticks, and said all their wheat had the Devil's blight too and they'd not a grain to spare. It was a cruel thing to hear and they came back down at heart to give the rest of us that news, and by summer we were all so weak – I'd see men, young men, going up the Green here holding on to the garden fences to keep themselves up and stopping every four or five steps, heads hanging. As for getting the barley harvest in that August, I just don't know how it was done – and the threshing. It was a good barley harvest from all the fields, but not enough to make up for the lost wheat. So it was stingy allowances for all again that next year and barley makes a poor sort of bread by itself. That year there was more than usual deer in the forest and we'd had our Michaelmas stag as usual and come St Nicholas' Day the lady says to the men, go out and get another deer as we need every scrap of food. Old Holy hears of it, dogs barking excited like, and he comes bustling round.' Here the old man's high voice took on an even higher tone. 'No, no, he says, it's not lawful. Law says one stag at Michaelmas and one at the 'Piphany feast and no taking them at other times. And she says would God have sent us this great flock of deer up by Hall field if it wasn't a sign of his caring for us? After all, we've prayed enough about being in need. And he nattered on about it not being lawful and what would a woman know about law and she says, well, Father, she says, you be careful you don't let a morsel of hot venison pass your lips, and she just nodded to the men who had their dogs on their leads all ready and keen as anything to go and got us a good stag very easy before noon and in frosty weather and it was skinned and cut up and roasted and all come to a good feast like it was Michaelmas again. Old Holy was there and I served him – oo-hoo, he ate hearty, I can say – and I kept saying have another bit, Father, and dangling a juicy slice before his nose, and Tom, my friend, with a big bowl and a spoon says another spoonful of rich gravy, Father? And as he laps it up Tom says now you'll roast in Hell, won't you? 'Tisn't lawful, you know – and everyone roars with laughter. The meat had given them strength. Oh, we were happy and jolly that evening. Eat, drink – though it was only water – and be merry we says and Old Holy looked pretty sheepish but he ate away all the same, and the lady, she'd had the liver saved and cut up small and sent to all the women as was new delivered of their babies and couldn't come to the feast. So we all had a good feast and no evil came of it to any, and the fine skin was cured and she put it up by the bed there,' he pointed to the dark behind Sir Hugh, 'to keep cold air out.'

'It's still there,' Magda's voice called out.

So clearly had the past held the old man's mind, that this call to the present disconnected his thoughts.

'Yes, yes,' he mumbled irritably, 'she was a fine woman, your mother, sir, and – no, no, she was your *grandmother*, sir, your *grand*mother. How time flies . . . ' The old man's voice trailed off. He was exhausted and Simon took his arm and lowered him into his chair.

'He never said how they got seed – corn – wheat, that is, for the next year's sowing,' came another voice from the dark.

The candles were burning low, some of them at their last flicker in the wooden blocks, and the Hall was darkening. The villagers started reluctantly to gather up their cloaks again. Roger, at a signal from Simon, brought the wheelbarrow close to his grandfather's chair and they helped him into it, wrapped his cloak round him closely and pulled his sheepskin hood over his head, tucking his greasy beard in. His mind was now wholly on getting home, and he barely glanced at Marion as the wheelbarrow was turned round and Roger pushed it out of the door into the icy night. Marion watched him go and wondered if she would ever see him alive again.

Tom had put some small logs on the fire and they blazed up, lighting the Hall far more than the candles had, and by this orange flickering, farewells were said. Marion picked up heavily sleeping Alice, Peter wrapped and tied her cloak round both of them, called to Peterkin and the family departed.

They met Molly with her pot of stewed liver and pocket of honey-bread at the bridge. The air was misty, the moon glimmering disfused through the mist, and this faint light made the path and the bridge just discernible. Two figures, no doubt Lisa and Martin, were already across the bridge and down on the Common path.

'It's very slippy,' said Molly, venturing a foot on the glistening plank. 'Hold the rail.'

Peterkin followed her.

'O-ooh, it's ever so slidy,' he said, and attempted to do so.

'Don't be a *fool*,' commanded Peter. 'Hold the rail, don't make it worse for us behind. Go steady, Marion. Wait, I'll give you a hand down the steps.'

The frost was as sharp as ever, the grass crunched under their feet, and the ice over the cows' footprints tinkled as they broke it. As they walked

Marion could feel her wet skirt stiffening as it froze, and at each step it scrunched a little. They said goodnight to Molly at her gate, called similar greetings to Lisa and Martin, fumbling at their cottage door. Whether the Plowrights were already home they knew not, all was silent at their house.

It was pitch-dark in the cottage. Marion pushed open the upper half of the door and the faint reflected moonlight showed her the familiar dark shapes of log, shelf, cradle and fireplace.

'Come and pee, boy, before we go in,' said Peter, and Marion could hear the hissing before they followed her inside.

She put Alice, damp as she was, in the cradle and covered her with the sheepskin. She could hear Peterkin rustling the straw as he settled himself in his corner. She pulled down her skirt, still stiff and crunchy with ice and hung it on a nail in a beam over the fireplace. There was still a faint red glow there.

Peter pulled off his boots and scrambled into the straw, and Marion, in her loose woollen shift, her legs shaking with the cold, spread her cloak over the quilt and joined him. It always amazed her how warm he could be, even on a night like this, as she rolled close to him. He put his rough warm hand on her unusually naked leg and then slid it up under her shift.

Ah no, not now, she thought. It's too cold and we're too tired – but his hand stroked inquisitively. She recalled the village women's saying, 'If you refuse him too often, he'll go to the next best thing – and that could well be your daughter.' Ah well, she thought, there's no grown daughter here, not now – but she knew the wisdom of the saying.

'Marry,' he said in her ear, and his hand slid down again to part her legs and a shiver of unwelcome desire ran over her buttocks.

This was how darling Nolly was made, she thought, realizing that she had not thought of Nolly all day, and for Nolly's sake she pulled Peter towards her.

When he had finished, his last grunt was quickly followed by a trembling snore. He lay very heavy. She desired more but would not wake him. Her feet, touching Peterkin's sleeping back were aching with the cold. A sudden intense sweetness pervaded her mouth. She licked her lips and realized a sticky blob of honey on Peter's beard was against her mouth.

If only my feet could get warm, she thought, rubbing them together slowly. It was long before she slept.

JANUARY

The shepherd too in great coat wrapt
With straw bands round his stockings lapt
Wi plodding dog that sheltering steals
To shun the wind behind his heels
Takes rough and smooth the winter weather
And paces thro the snow together

It was well into January, all nature in abeyance. There was nothing to do but to endure. That was how January had always seemed to Marion.

The mid-winter feasts were over, there were no festivities to look forward to until the pre-Lent shriving. *Survive*, how to survive, was in everyone's mind: eat frugally and remember next week; keep a little fire going and remember next month; nurture your animals and remember next year; wrap your cloak around you and endure, endure, endure. January was always a very hard, hopeless month, and it seemed to go on and on and on.

It was so often so dark in the cottage that day merged into night and neither dawns nor noons were apparent. In Marion's mind the tiny events of one day became muddled with the tiny events in another. She often felt dizzy and was vaguely aware of sitting long hours on the log seat, her aching feet on the hearthstone, in a kind of stupor. Past events came and went through her mind, but none she could place in any chronological order, even if she tried, which she did not. Feel like my mind is frozen solid, she thought in a rare moment of self-awareness. Sometimes she roused herself with the intention of struggling down to the water-place with a bucket, only to realize that she had already done so, for there was the bucket, almost full, standing under the eaves. She sometimes found herself fetching an armful of small logs for the fire only to find that several were already piled up by it, drying out. She knew she was eating little, but felt too lethargic to get herself food. She knew she slept little at night, but so much of the supposed daylight hours they all spent on the bed under the covers, dozing the time away. Alice, usually so active, seemed to sense her mother's stillness and imitated it – or perhaps she too was in the state of half-hibernation which they all called 'getting through the winter'.

There had been snow soon after the Christmas frosts had gone. One day Marion was trudging back across the Common after a brief visit to the Hall for more spinning wool. She had looked in at Peter in his workshop and found him with many bloody scratches on his arms tying and weaving blackthorn twigs to a harrow for use in the coming spring, and he was nagging Paulo, who with red chilblained fingers was trying to hold the hard branches in place.

'Tom says it looks like snow,' she said, 'any time now.'

'Likely,' said Peter, his mind on work.

'If it does snow thick, you'll stay at the Hall?'

'Oh, it won't be that thick, I'll be home before it gets dark. Press it down *harder*, Paulo.'

She had left them, but glancing up at the sky as she paused on the bridge she saw it was an unbroken luminous pale grey, very low, and almost trembling with a burden of unshed snowflakes. The air was still and icily raw, and before she was halfway across the Common the first large flakes were slowly floating about. She collected Alice from Molly and got home as it began to settle on the ground. She called the hens, sacrificing a little corn to entice them in and up to the shelf of nests. She propped their pole up inside so that they could get down to the goat's drinking butt and up again to their nests. She tried to close the trap door over the smoke-hole in the cottage roof, but the leather hinges were frozen stiff and it would neither open nor close properly. She busied herself with the fire and with food, and when she looked out again over the half-door even the garden had vanished into the twirling snowflakes and the nearby ground was all soft white hillocks. Peterkin arrived home through it. He had been on some mission for Rollo at the Hall and Martin had found him snowballing with Kit

Nickson on the Green and had firmly dragged him away and accompanied him back over the Common. Peterkin had come in with his hood and tunic plastered with snow, which was beginning to freeze into the fabric. His good boot was not waterproof, and the other boot, an improvised affair to accommodate his twisted foot, had filled with snow. He was pale and his teeth chattered. Marion pulled off his frozen clothes and put a blanket round him and he sat on the floor by the fire leaning against the log and breathing with long trembling breaths not far from sobbing. She noticed how thin his legs were, almost with waists above his square boy's knees. How perilous were children's lives! She told him, in spite of her concern, that he was a silly boy to go snowballing and should have come straight home, and he had replied he had not thought snow could be *so* cold.

Peter did not come home that night. Marion had guessed he would not be able to. The wind had got up, and the unceasing snow had piled up against the cottage walls, the ash tree and the garden fences. She had looked out the next morning and all was magical. The garden was obliterated under an undulating slope of white with occasionally a bent thistle-stalk projecting. Up in the woods, the tree trunks were all plastered on their western sides with a crust of snow. The black yew trees had splayed open, each branch with its burden of snow, and every little twig in the undergrowth carried a thin vertical wall of white. The air was still now, the sky an unmoving grey. All was utterly silent. Feeling Alice's hands on her skirt, Marion bent and lifted her up so she could see out over the half-door. Alice was astounded.

'Oh,' she said. 'Oh – oh!' Marion put her down again and noticed how the snowy ground reflected a strange chilly light up into the rafters of the cottage.

Later that day, aware that a likely frost would make the ground even more treacherous and turn the stream to ice, she had gone down to the water-place with a bucket. The stream was not frozen over then but was narrowed by the fat domes of snow that overhung the black water, domes supported by lumps of dead grass and reeds bowed down over the water. Marion had supported herself by leaning on the snow-covered willow as she pulled the rope to get up her heavy bucket. Carrying it up the steep path with her feet slipping and the bucket wobbling was very onerous and by the time she got it to her door the bucket was half empty. She shovelled some snow into it, but a terrible lot of snow was needed to fill it up to the brim. Her hands and feet ached with the cold. She put two more logs on the fire and collapsed on to the log seat in a sort of stupor.

The family hibernated. They sat silent hour by silent hour by the little fire, half stupefied by the cold, half by the smoky air. Sometimes a little snow at the cracks round the roof-hatch melted and drops sizzled on the log below. They ate little bowls of warm barley porridge, sometimes a bit of cheese. They went out reluctantly to the midden when they could wait no longer. Tibtab, dropping down from his patch of hay on the shelf, had jumped up over the partition to the goat's area and they heard him scraping in the straw round the goat's feet.

Marion was in constant pain from her feet. She had started a chilblain under one heel on the frosty walk home after the Christmas feast and it had not healed. Every step pressed the raw wound, and now she had found chilblains, red, shiny lumps, on most of her toes. They itched and ached and when she rubbed them the skin split. Her sheepskin boots were soaked through, for one had a crack above the instep and the other a split in the sole. It would be days before they would dry out even on the boot-rack and by the fire, and then they would be so hard and stiff they would hurt her as much to put them on as to go barefoot. And, of course, if she went out in them in the wet they would be soaked through again in two minutes.

By the fifth day the snow seemed to have been reduced. More sticks and more tufts of grass down the garden were visible. A little gust of wind had rattled the ivy on the ash tree, a shower of ice had been flung about and the ivy was green again. The sun came out around noon, the snow on the roof melted a little and all the afternoon there was a steady drip from the thatch which melted the snow below and showed a line of clean-washed pebbles, white and pinkish and toffee-brown. Next morning the drips had become long ribbed icicles, a silver fringe hanging along the edge of the thatch. Peterkin was delighted and broke off some and sucked them. Alice demanded an icicle too and got wet all down her front.

The silence, except for the daytime dripping, persisted, sometimes broken by a blackbird's chatter. That afternoon, Marion, returning from her unwelcome visit to the midden, felt a stirring wind on her face and looking up, saw the tree tops against the sky were slowly waving about and the clouds of a now uneven grey were sliding up the valley from the west. The air was cold and penetratingly raw, but it was not freezing, and after listening all night to the steady dripping and the occasional rush of sliding snow and a thump as it hit the ground, she looked out next day to see large patches of the garden earth exposed and in the patchy ground in front of the cottage dark holes full of water where their feet had passed to and fro to the midden.

The thaw continued all day. By noon the cottage roof was clear and most of the garden was bare earth with lumps of dirty white here and there. She had endured the pain of pulling on her boots and had gone round to Lisa and Martin's cottage. They had survived much as she had, and Lisa gave her some goose grease to rub on her toes. She had skirted the Plowrights' but had observed a little smoke coming from their roof, and she went down to Molly's.

Molly had met her with eyes more red than with just hearth smoke. Weeping, she told Marion of how on the first evening of dense snow her aunt, Old Marge, had gone down to the water-place, fallen there, broken or sprained her ankle, and fainted. How long she had lain in the snow no one knew, and Old Agnes, dozing, and with very little idea of the passage of time, could not help. Molly had eventually heard Marge calling.

'I found her,' Molly said, 'with her foot all twisted and like a bone sticking out of her ankle, and blood on the snow, and more dead than alive. I got her by the shoulders and lugged her up the path in the snow, she crying out with pain. It was almost dark by then. I kept looking out to see your Peter come by to spread the news, but he never came. I got her in and we bound up her foot and Mother got her something warm to drink, but she couldn't get warm and she just lay there faint and quiet and come morning I saw she was dead. Well, one couldn't be surprised, seeing her age. That morning the snow was piled up against our door to the roof – no hope of getting out – so we laid her on the ground by the wall, and now the snow's gone I'm off to the village to tell Father John. D'you think the Common path is clearing?' and Molly's weary face crumpled into fresh grief.

Marion remembered with relief that Sir Hugh had, as always in winter, arranged for several graves to be dug before the ground got too frozen. Marion felt no shock, she expected old people to die of cold, nor really did she feel grief.

Molly must have got to the village, for that evening men from the village had arrived with a hurdle and carried Marge's body off to the graveyard. Father John had given the briefest service he could in the raw air, his voice hoarse as he did so, and his nose dripping. Molly had described it all in detail to Marion.

Peter had got home by then, rather ill-tempered by his intended work timetable being upset, but he had brought in a lot more heavy logs. He had prodded the roof-hatch with a pole and it could now be propped open or could fall shut, at will. Marion could see, amid the sooty rafters, that Peter's action had broken one of its leather hinges, but he could not see this in the murky interior and she forebore to mention it. It served well enough for the time being. He was sympathetic over her chilblained feet, gently rubbed on the goose grease and wrapped them up in bits of cloth, but even his kindly touch was agony. She never understood why he, exposed as he often was, never had chilblains. Neither did Peterkin, even on his twisted foot.

Not only was she enduring the pain in her feet at every step she took, she often felt rather faint. She knew she was not having enough to eat. She had so often experienced this shaking faintness mixed with a darkening of vision during the hungry months of winter. She had kept the feeling at bay by scraping out some honey from a tub Betsy had sent her, but the tub was scraped clean by now, and little chance of a journey to the Mill to beg for more. She daily watched the stores of corn and peas and cheese, and speculated on how long it would be before any replacements could be there. She had looked at Peter and at her two unconcerned children, and ate less herself. It had always been thus in winter.

In the sea of amorphous days that followed the partial thaw, no new snow fell, but the lumps that remained by the fence and in the ditches by the common melted only on the surface by day and refroze every night into hard networks of ice. Peter daily stumped and slithered his way to his workshop in the village, and dragged himself home before dusk. He always arrived with the cloths that were bound to his legs soaked up to his knees and the edges of his tunic and cloak heavy with half-melted snow. It was impossible to dry clothes.

He had arrived with a very stout ash stake over his shoulder. One end had been sharpened and charred to render it more waterproof. He propped it up under the eaves and told Marion it was for mending the Plowrights' door.

'Jack asked me, days ago, about Epiphany,' he had muttered. 'Said their doorpost was rotten and the soffit was adrift, hanging – thought it'd come down on his brats. He was right, it was all crumbling at the bottom. 'Spect his brats had been pissing against it for years – and the dogs – so I'll put this new one in on Sunday after Mass. He'll have to help me then.'

Marion had acquiesced. Doing anything for the Plowrights both alarmed her and eased her conscience. It alarmed her that any contact with them could result in illness to herself, for she believed that the plague was caused by poverty, and her conscience was eased by the effort of doing *anything* for them. But she stifled her conscience with the thought that most of the comforts of her life were produced by her own hard work and that feckless Small Sarah brought all her miseries on herself.

But the following Sunday Peter had gone scrunching over the snowy grass to the Plowrights' with the stake over his shoulder, dragging the spade and a sharp iron spike with the other, and with his largest mallet stuck in his belt, and during the afternoon Marion had heard the thumping of the mallet. He had returned some hours later, very tired.

'Well, we got it done,' he told her. 'Pity there's no other able-bodied man around here. I had to get out the old post and dig a proper hole for the new one while Jack stood there holding up the soffit and all the weight of the rafters and thatch above it. I was as quick as I could be – ground was squelchy luckily – but I was amazed he could stand there so long holding it all up.'

'Pity Martin was off at the mill with Lisa. Couldn't Small Sarah, or any of the brats help?'

'Small Sarah was just sitting indoors on a log. She never tried to help, nor did he say anything to her. Doubt if she could have helped. She's so short the top of her head's not up to his shoulder.'

'And their brats?'

'I don't understand those children. Don't know if they're boys or girls. They never seem to grow up. There was – '

'How *many* did you see?' asked Marion, just remembering the rumour that there were fewer than there had been.

'Couldn't see. It was pretty dark inside, even with the door full open. I saw a heap of old blanket on the floor, with some skinny little legs sticking out, and once a corner was lifted and a small face, just big eyes really, peeped out. I just said hullo sonny, or something, then the face went under the blanket again. It's a sorry state they're all in there, that's certain. Small Sarah does nothing and you can't talk to her as you can't understand what she answers, just gobbling, and Jack's surly enough, works hard though. Anyway, we got the post in and the soffit fixed on top, and I gave him a bundle of willow wands to put round the post and weave into the wall. That should tie the wall in with the new post. I wouldn't be surprised if they just put the wands on the fire and forget to fix the wall. One can't stand over them all the time and do everything for them. The place does stink, too.'

Marion had listened to this all last Sunday, and any pity she had felt for the Plowrights now focused on Peter. She saw he had exhausted himself for them, struggling to dig in the cold wet rooty earth to plant the new post, and they had offered him nothing in return. That they had nothing to offer she was sure, but some token bartering was the custom in the village. She doubted if the Plowrights' lives were any more secure for all the help that had been given them, and then there was the mystery of the vanished child. Perhaps there was no mystery, perhaps everyone had miscounted and there had never been another child, but the idea left uneasiness in Marion's mind. Even if one wretched little life had been rubbed out by the Plowrights' careless indolence how could she — she who had seen two of her children, her well cared for children, die, and three of her helpless tiny babies' lives so quickly ended — how could she feel any real outrage over the disappearance of some anonymous little Plowright?

This particular day, she told herself as she lay huddled on the bed, was Sunday, and she decided again she could not face the walk across the slushy Common to go to Mass. Peter would go by himself. Everyone would understand. This thought made her remember how, many years ago, when the Rutherford men had arrived in the village with the pots and sacks of salt, they had slept the night in the Hall and expressed surprise next morning that no Mass was to be celebrated in the church.

'We have mass on Sunday mornings, always,' Sir Hugh, then a newly married man, had said.

'But this *is* Sunday,' the Rutherford men insisted.

'No, it is Saturday,' said Sir Hugh, and Father John arrived and confirmed this.

'Well,' said the Rutherford men, 'it's Sunday in the rest of the world. You must have miscounted sometime.' So the message got about and work stopped in the fields and Father John said Mass that evening and the next day was Monday however anyone felt. But the incident impressed the villagers with an uneasy doubt about the truths that Father John so often announced, and some maintained it was a purposeful error to get one more day's work out of them.

'*There*,' said Milly, 'I knew it wasn't proper Saturday. I always said we'd had two Thursdays afore sheep-shearing!'

'She never said nothing of the sort, sir,' Tom muttered to Sir Hugh.

Still, today, everyone agreed *was* Sunday, and Mass would be said as usual in the church, but the old and infirm from Rockwell, from the Mill and from Down the Common would not be expected to attend. Later that morning Peter returned home from church, bringing with him Lisa and Martin who had braved the walk. Peter had picked up his measuring stick and replaced it behind his ear (he always removed it for Mass for it signified work), and he and Martin had gone to Martin's cottage to put up another shelf, and Lisa came in and she and Marion sat on the log by the fire and put their feet on the hearthstone, although Marion knew it was not good for her chilblains. It was nice to have a bit of company.

'I saw Mother and Father at Mass,' Lisa said. 'The boys and girls stayed at home to mind Grandpa.'

Marion asked how he was.

'He seems the same. They've kept him well wrapped up during the snow, in his chair, in a feathery quilt – and he doesn't seem to have taken cold or anything. He talks about things long ago, and he doesn't seem to remember the Christmas feast – and that's barely five weeks ago. But if one of us mentions it, he tells about the famine again. It is strange he is so well. Poor old Marge, though, she must have died of cold. It's a wonder Agnes did not miss her sooner. They say in the village that Hal is poorly. They don't think he'll last long and M'Dame allows Hilda to go and be with him. She wasn't at Mass so I suppose she was with her father. M'Dame was there. She must be very near her time by now. Sir Hugh and Rollo were supporting her, one each side, up to the church for fear of her slipping on the slushy snow – and that reminds me . . . ' Lisa pushed her cloak aside, and put her hand into the leather pouch slung round her neck and pulled out a small pair of pointed shears.

'We found these on top of the beam across our cottage,' she said. 'I think Dick must have put them there to be safely out of the children's reach. Well, as you know he was tall and could easily get them, but I suppose when Hilda moved out she forgot or did not know they were there.'

'Or was too miserable with Dick's death to care,' added Marion.

'Yes, I suspect she was. Anyway, Martin rubbed them down and sharpened both blades and points on his finest whetstone, and I was going to give them to Hilda today only she wasn't there, and I didn't want to give them to Joan or Milly – you'd never know what'd happen to them. I think he used these with the pointed ends for castrating the baby rams. The thing is, would you like to use them for your nails and I'll give them to Hilda when I go down to the Hall next? How are your feet now?'

Marion pulled her feet out from the boats of loose wrappings which helped to protect them, and displayed red and swollen toes, some with raw places on them.

'They are healing,' she said, 'but they are still very sore. I think it would help if the nails were cut, but it hurts so when Peter binds them up, I don't know how I could bear it if I cut the nails.'

'I'll try, Aunt,' Lisa said, and she knelt down and very tenderly, and in spite of Marion's yelps of pain, cut all her toenails as short as possible. Alice stumped up and watched with solemn interest. Marion admitted that her feet felt better, so Lisa offered to do her hands as well, and her cracked and broken nails were trimmed. Peterkin rolled out of the straw where he had been idling and Lisa and Marion spent some time on his feet, specially the twisted one with a nail growing into the sole. Peterkin ooh'd and i-i-i'd but also agreed it was more comfortable to walk after.

'Alice too,' said Alice, flumping down and stretching out her short dirty legs. Marion took her on her knee and Lisa carefully snipped her tiny nails, toes and fingers, all as soft as the flakes in an apple core.

Alice's hood had, as usual, fallen back and revealed her pale wispy hair, the ends falling over her face and much of it with dried porridge or milk sticking it together into a smelly mess.

'Cut her hair too, Lisa,' Marion said. 'It's falling into her eyes all the time. Cut it short over her forehead. It can't be good for her sight that she's always looking through it,' and with Marion holding her head Lisa snipped a few inches off all round Alice's baby-piglike face.

'Alice's hair,' she murmured, impressed, watching Marion collect the wisps and throw them on the fire, 'all *burnt*.'

'I must get home, Aunt,' said Lisa, rising and putting the little shears back in the pouch. 'I'll be going down to the Mill in a few days if the thaw keeps up, and I can tell Mother you are all right here.'

'When Peter's finished doing that shelf with Martin,' said Marion, 'cut his toenails if you can persuade him. I don't know when we'll have another chance of doing it, and he scratched Peterkin's arm badly in bed last night.'

Lisa departed, leaving the upper half of the door open, and some pale sunlight crept in.

The little change of company and conversation had cheered Marion up and her cheerfulness reflected on her children. She swept the ground round the hearthstones – always a safety measure, and at once the cottage appeared neater and well cared for. She put another small log on the fire, and by the light of its flames and the faint sunlight outside, she took up her spindle and the basket of carded wool. Her fingers were mostly swollen and all stiff, and this made twirling the spindle jerky and the yarn she made was rather uneven, and her hands hurt. But to spin was an excuse for sitting down on the log, with her rebandaged feet near, but not on the hearthstones. Peterkin had taken the hen-tail broom and had reswept a patch of the floor clear of bits and on its dusty surface was drawing with a bit of stick, Alice watching him closely.

'Whassat?' she asked.

'It's our cottage,' said Peterkin, concentrating, 'and that's the ash tree hanging over it.'

'Where's door?'

'Haven't done it yet.'

'Do smoke in roof,' said Alice. Marion, listening, realized that Alice had acquired many more words recently, though she had not consciously taught her. Peterkin scribbled in some smoke.

'More,' said Alice, 'more smoke all over.'

'Can't, it's mixed up with the ash tree.'

Alice picked up a stick and with almost equal skill drew an oblong house with voluminous smoke pouring from it.

'I like doing smoke,' she said, continuing. Peterkin, slightly jealous of her ability, said, 'Do the ash tree with ivy on it.' Alice scratched in the ash tree, bending over the roof because the drawing area was restricted by the hearthstone. Then she scratched a rough circle above the house with radiating lines.

'What's that?' asked Peterkin.

'Sun,' said Alice, adding more radiating lines.

'Looks like a dandelion,' objected Peterkin, wishing he had thought of doing one.

'Dandelion like sun,' said Alice and was enchanted by her own thought and flopped over in her laughter, thereby spoiling Peterkin's drawing. He objected and there was a squabble and while Marion was separating them, Peter returned.

'Done the shelf?' Marion asked him, returning to her spinning.

'Yes – a good long one. That cottage's very strongly built. We put up a shelf along some six uprights. Lisa's got a lot of jars and pots. Your sister must have set her up well. What's there to eat? I'm as hungry as a horse.'

Marion put down her spindle again and busied herself getting him bread and cheese, from both of which he cut thick slices. She watched her stores anxiously.

A little appeased he looked up at his children and said, 'What's happened to that child's hair? Come here, Alice.'

'Alice hair burnt in fire,' she told him.

'What do you mean?' he asked, running his hand over her head. 'That's cut, not burnt.'

'Alice hair burnt in fire,' she repeated, pointing to the fire. Marion explained about the little shears and the toenail and hair cutting.

'But she's a little *girl*,' Peter objected. 'You don't cut a girl's hair – it looks silly. It ought to hang down her back under a cap. Well, it should when she's older.'

'It was all over her eyes,' Marion said, 'but too short to tie back. Besides, it was all messed up with bits of food. It'll grow again.'

'I don't like my little girl to have short hair,' he grumbled. 'It's not proper for a girl. Pull your hood up, child, and wait till it grows again – and don't put porridge in it, see?' He patted her bottom and sent her off and started to cut himself more thick slices of bread and cheese.

'That bread's supposed to be for tomorrow as well,' Marion said.

He looked up, a bit ashamed. 'I'm famished with hunger,' he said, but he only took one of the slices he had cut. She knew that he was eating so much because he was annoyed with her for having Alice's hair cut. Peterkin came up, eyeing the cut slices, and said, 'Can I have these?'

'Well, I suppose so,' said Marion, giving a slice to each child with a thin bit of cheese, but she herself had nothing. She took up her spindle again.

Peter suddenly clapped his hand to his ear, and said, 'Where's my measuring stick?'

'On the shelf?' said Marion, 'It's Sunday.'

'No, I had it when I went to Martin's, today, to do *his* shelf.' They all searched in the gloom, but it was not on their shelf, nor was it behind Peter's ear. The stick was something so familiar to Marion that she could hardly 'see' it now. It was almost part of Peter's anatomy, for it was always behind his right ear, supported in his stiff beard and curly hair. It was a piece of white holly wood some six inches long, straight and smooth, squarish in section, but not quite square because of long use, and not quite round, so that it should not roll. On each of the four sides were short scratches at regular, but different, intervals, each scratch ingrained with soot and dirt showing clearly on the white wood which was satin-smooth, having been pushed through his greasy hair a dozen times a day for years. He, and perhaps he alone, understood the measurements marked on it. They were all small, fine measurements. For longer ones he always had a cord round his tunic with knots along it at various intervals.

The top half of the door was open and Peter opened the lower half as well and a little more wintry dusk filtered in, and they all searched again in vain.

'Nip round to Martin and ask if I left it there,' he said to Peterkin, and Marion, standing outside under the eaves, watched Peterkin loping round under the ash tree with his lop-sided hopping gait.

More snow had melted during the day, and now only a few crusty remains were piled up against the fence and under the apple tree. The late afternoon dusk – a pale yellow glimmer from behind grey clouds – shone on the bare trunks of the beeches up in the forest beyond the garden, and lit spots of yellow lichen on them. The forest floor was a thick red-brown of sodden leaves with patches of blue-green ivy trailing across it, and the low undergrowth above the ditch was smeared with the dark brown lumps of old man's beard, the grey fluff long since blown away. In the declivities of the ditch patches of speckled snow still remained. The air was cold and Marion shivered as it chilled her damp clothes, but she paused there, shifting from one aching foot to the other, to watch the pale fading light, so clear over this familiar, this astonishingly dear, familiar scene.

Peterkin came lolloping round the corner of the cottage, holding up Peter's measuring stick.

'Lisa'd found it on the new shelf, when she was arranging the pots and things,' he said in triumph.

They went in together and closed the lower half of the door and heard Peter's 'Ah-h – my stick,' as he stuck it back over his ear. Marion picked up her spindle again. She wondered if she had spun as much as one yard of wool all that day. Peter sank down on the log beside her.

'Tired?' she asked.

He grunted, assenting.

'You don't get any rest, not like the men working in the fields. They at least have the seasons.'

'I know. They have days with nothing to do but watch the corn grow – or not grow.' A slow smile twisted in his beard.

'You were working all last Sunday too,' she said, concerned.

It was somehow easier to remember what he did than to remember her own monotonous formless days.

'Well, that's how life goes. I try to put things off. Rollo's often nagging me for this or that, and I have to do, or pretend to do, what he says – seems to think as soon as he's told me to do a job it's done. And other people need things – like Simon and his new applewood spathes – yes, I'm sorry I forgot to ask about honey – and like the Plowrights' doorpost. Bet they've not bothered to weave in those withies I took.' He sighed and rubbed his beard. She had forgotten he had been at the Plowrights' last Sunday. He went on, 'One could work day and night doing things for the Plowrights and I don't think it'd make any difference to their lives. Sluts – the lot. All Small Sarah ever does is to get herself with child every year – and then neglects it when it's born.'

Marion said that if she did keep becoming pregnant it must be Jack's fault.

'Suppose so,' Peter said grudgingly. 'Suppose he can't help himself.'

FEBRUARY

And oft dame stops her burring wheel
To hear the robins note once more
That tutles while he pecks his meal
From sweet briar hips beside the door . . .
Thus nature of the spring will dream
While south winds thaw but soon again
Frost breaths upon the stiffening stream
And numbs it into ice

Since the slow thaw had petered out at the end of January, it had rained. It had rained and rained, frequently, heavily, for days. Then there would be half a day of still clouds and mist over the tops of the trees, then at dusk the wind would stir again and more rain come swirling up the valley.

As in the January snow there was nothing much Marion could do but to maintain existence as much as possible, to stay indoors, to keep a little fire going, to eke out the food, to spin when she could, to keep the animals alive, to endure, to endure, to endure. Endurance wearied them all, and tempers became short among the strong, but most people, specially the women, felt too apathetic for resentment.

In the damp air that pervaded, nothing in Marion's cottage was dry. Their heavy woollen clothes absorbed moisture and retained it. The blankets with the feathery layer lay heavy and chilly on them at night, their boots never dried out. Marion had constant difficulty with the fire because the roof-hatch above it leaked. Since Peter had banged it in the snowy weather and had broken one of the hinges, it had not fitted properly and in the rain storms drips fell on to the logs below, either extinguishing their glow or making them too wet to ignite. She had had to go out and half demolish the wood pile in order to get dry logs from the bottom and from against the cottage wall, bring some in, then pile them up somewhere in the hope of keeping them dry. In doing so she had come across a bit of old woven wattle from a garden fence, brittle, dry and a good but brief kindling. Then she must go out and rebuild the wood pile.

One mercy was that she did not have to go down daily to the water-place. A bucket left out in front of the door was often three-quarters full with soft zestless water by morning. The great earthenware corn pot, which always stood on the shelf, and which Marion had always believed to be damp-proof (perhaps because it *was* proof against her other enemy, mice), she discovered to be damp inside at the bottom. The glaze, which was only on the inside, had cracked and through the porous earthenware the damp had seeped up. Some of the corn at the bottom of the jar was mouldy. The hens ate it after her family had complained of the taste of the bread she had made from it. Marion secretly agreed that this bread was nasty, but she knew it was partly so nasty because it was undercooked before the meagre fire.

All domestic problems seemed to be interrelated, one increasing another. In spite of all her chilblains healing, Marion did not feel well herself, but then feeling well was so rare a state that she did not regard her unease as important. She put her nausea down to eating the last of the quarter of bacon which had hung in the smoke all the winter, gradually lessening in size over many weeks as slices were cut from it. The last few slices had tasted decidedly rancid. No doubt the melting snow, dripping on it through the ill-fitting roof-hatch, had helped to turn it. She had been chatting, in a brief dry spell, to Molly who had told her that she and her mother had had the bellyache after eating the last of their bacon.

'Everything upsets Mother these days,' she told Marion, 'what with missing Marge. No one to argue with all day now. They'd had a lifetime arguing together, mostly about nothing. It wearied me, I can say – bicker, bicker, bicker – and now she complains to *me* all the time instead. The bacon was very reasty in parts, not that there was much left. I put the last bit in the pot with beans and we had it. Not good, but what could we do but eat it? And we both had the bellyache and squits and she was sick all one night, and I had to throw the rest away – waste of beans. Teaches you to eat while things are good, can't save everything,' to all of which Marion agreed, and this confirmed to her the cause of her own sickness.

But there it was, the bacon was finished, and there would now be many months before any meat could be eaten. Some fools killed a pullet or two at this time of year and so deprived themselves of eggs and flocks of little chickens that could have come in spring.

Peter worked hard, and when he got home of an evening he was silent from exhaustion and cold. His cloak, heavy enough when dry, was almost as much as Marion could lift, sodden as it was with rain. One of the Hall's ox carts needed new sides and Peter was sawing thick planks of elm wood and fitting them on to the cart's structure. This meant going backwards and forwards from his workshop to the Hall's cart-shed in the yard, always through pools of muddy stinking water. It had always been thus in February.

On this particular day in late February, Marion had woken early, still in the dark night and not a glimmer of dawn above the top of the door. They had gone to bed the previous evening to the sounds of the wind whooshing in the ash tree and rattling its ivy, and the rain falling heavily outside and the roof dripping. But now, as she lay awake, all was silent – no sound of wind, no dripping, and if it were still raining it would be a soft steady drizzle, the sort that the thatch absorbed.

Her shoulders were stiff and ached. She moved about on the damp straw and under the heavy cover but could not ease herself. The faint nausea persisted. In spite of this, she considered she was better off than Dame Margaret. The previous evening Peter had returned home reporting that Dame Margaret had gone into labour and that Mam Fletcher, who had delivered scores of babies over the last twenty years, was now with her. No one in the village had much hope for a happy and successful birth after M'Dame's labour. Since Magda, their first child, was born, there had been so many – one forgot how many – wretched little babies either born dead or who died soon after. Thinking of babies, Marion's right hand went out to check that Alice slept and it met Alice's cold button nose, but the child slept deeply, and so did Peter, with long slow breaths.

Into the silence dropped a strange distant *kwah kwah kwah* sound, and at the same instant Marion felt a jerk by her feet and intensity in Peterkin's movements. She lay absolutely still, listening to him. The straw rustled as he sat up and got out of bed. There was a pause while she guessed he searched for a cloak or tied his belt on, then she heard furtive movements as he unhooked the lower half of the door. She opened an eye and saw a faint dawn light as he crept out and then gingerly pulled the door to behind him. She smiled a little to herself in the dark and stretched her feet down to where he had left a warmish patch of straw. She lay there long, shoulders hunched up, occasionally shivering violently, awaiting the dawn. The distant *kwah kwah* continued. Marion waited and wondered. Alice whimpered, and Marion sat up and helped her into the big bed. Alice's marvellously warm body snuggled against Marion's stomach, and Alice's icy face pressed on Marion's aching shoulder. They both dozed again.

A much louder and quicker *kwahkwahkwah* sounded, and faded, but the noise had woken Marion finally. She rose, and left Alice asleep close to Peter's heaving back, and tied her belt round her waist and wrapped her now almost warm feet in the strips of damp cloth, pulled on her cap, tied it firmly under her chin, stuffing her loose hair under it, and prepared to start the day. She pushed open both halves of the door and in the dim light, attended to the fire. It took much patience with little bits of twig, as dry as she could find, and much gentle bellowing to get a little flame going and then to balance bits of old woven fence on the twigs. Peter was waking up with many grunts and heaves.

'What you doing here, Allikin?' he muttered, stroking her face. 'Where's your mam, my poppet?'

Alice sat up and pointed, 'Mam doing fire,' she said.

At that moment the light from the open door dimmed and Peterkin appeared.

'*Look*, Mam,' he said, and held up two dead ducks.

'Oh – ' she said, enraptured.

'The place is all underwater,' he explained. 'All over the bottom of Martin and Lisa's garden, and the bottom of our garden, and all the ditch, is full of water – and all the grass by the stream with the trees sticking out. Come and see.'

Peter heaved himself up from the bed and as they followed Peterkin out they saw he was soaked to the waist.

'Don't leave the ducks, take them with you. I don't want Tibtab to get at them,' said Marion.

They went round the cottage, under the ash tree and along the side of Martin and Lisa's garden fence. Here the ground sloped down and they saw to their amazement how the whole of the marshy area between the stream bed and the ditch was one great sheet of water.

'It was all a mass of wild ducks,' Peterkin was saying, dancing about partly to keep warm and partly from excitement, and swinging the dead ducks about by their necks, 'swimming about, hundreds of them – well, anyway, a lot. I got three with four stones, quick, one after another. They were swimming so thick, you'd be bound to hit some. One of the Plowrights came too – '

'Did he hit one?' Peter interrupted.

'No, he threw some stones but missed. Lots had flown off by then – but I – I – ' Peterkin looked furtively at Marion with a sideways glance that was so like Simon – 'I gave the Plowright boy the duck I'd hit and we got the two drakes. I had to wade in to get them when all the others flew off. It's not deep there, you can see bits of rushes sticking up.'

'That's all right,' Marion said, to Peterkin's relief, 'not but they'll probably waste it. Is the water moving?'

Peter walked down to the water's edge, and prodded about with a stick. 'I don't think it is yet. Probably a tree down the valley has blown over and blocked it, and leaves and stuff piled up against it have made a proper dam. I wonder if Molly's pig shed's flooded.'

'The bank there's pretty steep below it. It could be all right; she's only got hens in it at present,' said Marion. They all three hurried up the slope again and across the rough grass to the pig shed beside Molly's garden. Molly, hearing their voices, came out and exclaimed at the expanse of water at the end of her garden. As Marion had said, the pig shed, now occupied by Molly's hens, stood at the top of the bank, and the water was still a few feet below its walls.

'Is it still rising?' Molly asked anxiously. Peter threw his stick in. It landed near the alder tree by what was still the far bank of the stream.

'Watch it,' he said. Very slowly the stick floated down stream.

'Could be a swirl in the current,' said Marion. She threw in a bunch of dead grass. It landed nearer to her feet and it too started to float slowly down stream.

'Looks as though it's going down,' said Peter. 'If the rain keeps off we may be all right. Go and look at the water-place, Peterkin.'

He ran off, and Molly, seeing the ducks in his hands said, 'What it is to have a boy handy with a stone – not that there's ever much to eat on a duck.'

'Wonder how they are at the Mill,' Marion said. 'They must have had the sluice open all night and the water thundering down. I can remember how it was in the flood when I was a girl.'

Peterkin rushed back shouting, 'The water-place is underwater. It's halfway up the tree stump, but it must be going down now as there are bits of grass hanging all wet on the branches over it, about this high over the water,' and he indicated a space of a foot between his good and his twisted hand.

'Nothing we can do,' Peter said, waving a greeting at Martin who joined them, bleary-eyed. 'We're all lucky not to have been washed out of our beds in the night. Come along, Marion, Alice could be up to all sorts of mischief by now.'

When they got back to their cottage Alice was sitting up on the bed with Peter's measuring stick perilously balanced over her tiny ear and in her short hair.

'I'm Father,' she said to him, and he laughed as he took it from her and put it behind his own ear.

Marion attended to the fire again, a job to be postponed always at her peril, and then looked at the two mallard drakes which Peterkin had dropped on the log seat. They were not large birds and she agreed with Molly that there was not much to eat on a mallard, but all that wonderful duck fat, she thought with relish, and the fresh meat stewed up with beans, beans which would absorb some of the fat and be richly satisfying. The next day, when the stew was cold in the pot, she would scrape off a layer of thick soft fat and spread it over slices of bread. How good, how sustaining, how *warming*, a food that was. She stroked the emerald head of one drake, full of admiration for its unearthly colour, while her mind planned rich meals ahead. She tied the necks together and hung them up outside under the eaves. She would see about plucking and drawing them later. She surprised herself with a sudden sick feeling in spite of her pleasurable anticipation of eating the duck and had to go out to the midden to be sick.

That bacon again, she thought. Can't get rid of it, like Molly and her mother.

Peterkin had watched his mother's pleasure at his kill, and a mysterious feeling of pride flooded his mind. He decided to boast about the ducks to his mates in the village. He had not, with his lame foot and his bent hand, previously had anything to boast about to them.

The flood was no immediate threat, nor was there anything to be done about it, so when the excitement it caused and the interest in the two drakes calmed down, Marion had to settle to an ordinary routine. Peter went off to the village, the Common path being nowhere under more than six inches of water. He had plenty of work waiting for him. His measuring stick was safely over his ear.

The stock of flour was getting low, and Marion saw little prospect of getting to the Mill – where Simon had half a sack of her corn newly ground – or of getting the flour home dry. She must watch the weather, but this morning there were still dark grey clouds, looking as though they had been roughly torn apart, slowly sailing up from over the valley. No, she could not risk going to the Mill for her flour. Too many sacks of good flour had been wasted by being rained on in the wheelbarrow.

She went to the fire and turned over one of the flat hearthstones on which a pot often rested or on which scones were baked. On the other side of it was carved out a shallow depression. From under the bed she retrieved a cylindrical stone of a rare flintlike hardness. She filled the depression of the one with a large handful of wheat, and kneeling before it, pressed and pushed and rolled the cylindrical one over the corn. This was the ancient method of grinding corn in a quern, and as it was forbidden by Sir Hugh, because home-grinding deprived the miller of his lawful and paid job of grinding at the water-mill, it was something to be done in secret. Marion, being a miller's daughter, had ambivalent feelings about using her quern, but as she told herself, one must eat and eating is more important than the law. Sometimes Rollo, when in particularly litigious mood, had been known to go round the cottages and catch out women with querns. Marion knew well enough how to conceal hers: turn the quern stone upside down and put a cooking pot on it by the fire, and roll the grinding stone – which looked like any old bit of whetstone when separated from the quern – under the bed. Grinding corn in the quern was hard work. Very great pressure was needed and one's knees hurt after a time. No woman would do it for pleasure, but it was essential sometimes when milled flour was scarce and the children hungry. Most cottages had their secret querns and every one knew about them. Even Rollo had been known to wink at the practice, particularly when a drought prevented the mill from working.

Recently the 'Rockwell' type of quern had come into Marion's life. This was Lisa's circular quern, one flattish circular stone placed on top of another, which Martin had brought from his mother at Rockwell and which Marion had watched Lisa using. She put the corn in the lower, saucer-shaped stone, lifted the heavy, slightly smaller stone on top, pushed a stick vertically into the hole near the circumference and twisted it round. Lisa maintained you could grind more corn that way, but it was not really easier work – at least that was what Marion thought when Lisa let her try. 'You won't tell Father, will you, Aunt?' she had said, but laughed as she spoke.

With either type of quern Marion had found that the rough ungrindable husks and bran made excellent food for the hens, and if too much of this were left in the flour, the resulting bread was apt to upset the human bowel. Having ground it as fine as she could bear, it was simply a matter of sieving it through some coarse sacking and then giving the most gritty bits to the hens. Hens must be properly fed at this time of year for soon they would be laying and getting broody, and everyone knew that well-fed hens laid a lot more eggs, and fertile ones too, than did underfed scrawny hens with their thin drawn-out squawking.

So the corn was ground, the hens were fed, hay was pulled down from the shelf for the goat to eat, its water butt had to be filled up and a bit more straw put down for its bed. Marion patted the goat's sides. She wanted to know if it were in kid or not. So far it showed no sign of it, yet before Christmas Marion had had a long slow walk leading the goat up the path through the fields to Rockwell and loosed her goat into the pen where the billy goat was kept. He had looked with a very disdainful expression at Marion before turning his attention on her goat. Marion had then gone into Nancy's cottage at her invitation and had warmed her feet and had been given a rich drink made of honey. Rockwell honey was reputed to be the best, and this bubbly drink made from it was a Rockwell speciality. Marion found it most sustaining as she sat there talking with Nancy, and then found that she must have dozed off for Nancy was waking her and telling her that surely by this time the billy goat had done and she had better get home. So she had retied the rope round her goat's neck and led her away, but she found the journey home very difficult as she kept wobbling about, and she did not know whether the billy goat had succeeded in getting her goat pregnant.

She had used the last of the rain water on the hens and the goat, and took the empty bucket down to the water-place. She saw that the great triangle of water below Martin's cottage was much reduced and when she got down to the stream the platform below the willow stump was now just clear of the water level. The ground all about squelched at every step, and tufts of old grass, branches and leaves were left in a line on the bank, showing the water's high mark. She filled her bucket with difficulty as the stream was now flowing very fast. The water was very muddy. She guessed that whatever had dammed the flow in the night had now been broken and the water was rushing away on its path to almost mythical Rutherford, and on and on into the greater unknown world.

The clouds of the morning had broken and dispersed, and Marion was surprised to see how intensely blue the sky was, with only wispy pale clouds high up and far away. The wind was light, almost mild. The alder trees on the opposite bank were covered in stiff sharp-green catkins interspersed with dark bobbles like little fir cones, and as Marion looked along the stream bank, she saw a new pallor hanging over the willow trees and the occasional vertical stems of the pussy willows were dotted with silver knobs.

'It could be spring at last,' she said to herself, but she knew that spring often came early, and then degenerated again into icy winds and snowstorms.

She carried the heavy bucket up the slope and met Agnes, who had hobbled as far as her garden gate.

'The water has gone down,' Marion said. 'Tell Molly. You can get to the pulley and the rope, but the ground's very wet.'

'We had some through the roof,' Agnes said. 'Wet came in on the bed, soaked the straw. Can't seem to get warm ... ' She would have gone on and on in similar complainings but Marion did not wait to listen. She had heard so much talk like this from Agnes and Marge, hours of it, year after year.

Back in her cottage Marion berated Peterkin for not attending to the fire, which was very low. He excused himself by saying she had often told him not to touch the fire.

'Of course I said that when you were a child, same as I'd say to Alice now, but now you must learn to look after it properly. You are old enough to do that sort of thing. Go out and get another log or two, dry ones if you can.'

How difficult children could be. Sometimes you thought they were old enough to be sensible and then they behaved like infants, and another time quite a small child would act in a responsible manner such as you would not have believed. They got sensible and then they got silly again, just like the spring – coming one morning and going back into winter the next.

While so thinking she busied herself making thin scones, mixing her roughly sieved flour with water, banging out little balls of the paste flat on to the hearthstone with the palm of her hand, and waiting for them to cook. It was a poor kind of food, this unleavened stuff, but there was no more of the rancid bacon fat to tempt her to add it to the flour. She had to bang the dough out thin or it burnt on the outside while still raw inside. Proper bread, the best, made with ale-froth yeast, was only possible in an oven; flour mixed with sour milk and cooked on the hearthstone under her broken jar was not bad, but today's meagre, hard, thin, saltless, fatless scones were all there was to eat in these cold February days. She thought again of the ducks and the rich treat they promised.

They were eating some of these thin scones when Lisa appeared at the door.

'I've just come from the village,' she said. 'They say that M'Dame's had her baby and it's dead, like the others.'

'God have mercy,' exclaimed Marion, though on whom she did not know. 'Yet another? Was it born dead?'

'They don't know. Joan told me they had fetched Father John along, before it was born, so he could christen it right away – which she said he did – I suppose to be on the safe side, though whether it was alive then I don't expect anyone knows.' Lisa came in and sat down on the log beside Marion.

'How's M'Dame?' asked Marion.

'Joan said she was just lying there crying and crying. That's not like her, usually so stone-faced, but after all those hours in labour she'd have used up all her courage. Terrible disappointment again.' Lisa took Alice, who had been watching her closely on to her knee.

'Wonder what it is that makes her babies die like that,' Marion said, 'or be dead when born. It must be nine or ten she's had since Magda, and Magda was always a healthy baby – and yet all those others . . . ' Her voice trailed away in sorrowful thoughts.

'Joan said the baby was a funny grey sort of colour, not red like proper newborn babies. The others too were this odd grey colour. Joan doesn't think they ever got the others to breathe properly, so they all died at once.'

'Was it a boy or a girl?'

'It must have been a boy because Father John christened it Edmund like all the other dead boys were after Sir Hugh's father.'

'Good thing there were the graves ready dug,' said Marion, 'not that a baby takes up much room. Sir Hugh must be sad, yet another boy gone, yet another hope lost. There can't be much chance of him having a son by M'Dame now.'

'Joan said he couldn't speak. He just sat with his head in his hands by one of the trestle tables. His face looked that drawn as if life had been washed out of it – that's what Joan said, and she looked much the same to me – After all, the baby was her nephew, sort of. One wonders what they've done to have such punishment. They're not wicked people – and all those dead babies.'

'Even good people can have cruel lives,' Marion said, feeling very old and experienced compared with her pretty niece.

Lisa rose and turned round to warm the other side of her skirt at the fire, saying, 'And what's to happen to all of us when Sir Hugh dies and there's no son to follow him?'

'They may get some stranger in to marry Magda, someone from down the Weald.' Marion added this detail in order to impress Lisa with her knowledge of worldly affairs. 'Someone who doesn't know our ways in the village, a younger son from foreign places. After all, no one here could marry Magda, it was always to be a stranger . . . ' Marion's voice again trailed away.

'Then the stranger would be our ruler,' Lisa went on, 'and none of us would like that. There's Rollo – '

'Not for always there isn't. He can't be as much as three years younger than Sir Hugh.' They were both silent, contemplating the dangerous future.

'Rollo's strict, but he's mostly fair,' Marion admitted. 'It would be terrible to have some ignorant wastrel at the Hall, ordering things, just because he was Magda's husband.'

In the silence both women thought of the authority of the Hall, that refuge in disaster, that harbour in trouble, that ruler of their lives, that spindle which spun together all their diverse activities. Neither could imagine a life without the framework of authority manifested in the Hall. Grumble as they did, and as all the villagers had always grumbled, at the compulsory gifts of hens, of goats, of geese, of calves, of days and days of work when they most needed to work their own land, yet no one *really* ever wished the Hall and its family to vanish. Unorganized freedom had too many unknown terrors in it.

Lisa turned back to the fire and Marion looked up at her with pleasure and admiration. She was really prettier than her mother had ever been, and she also had that air of wellbeing, of physical content, of repose and strength that her mother had. 'Light of heart, light of foot,' Marion repeated to herself an old village saying.

Lisa bent down to give Alice a hug, saying as she stood up, 'Pooh – Alice, you do stink.'

'It's probably her clothes,' said Marion complacently. 'She's mostly dry all night now, but she always wants to feed herself and she drops bits down her clothes and slops milk too – awful waste. I suppose when the weather's warmer I'd better wash her, and her clothes.'

After Lisa had departed the day dragged on. The fire had improved and most of the thin scones had been eaten at noon. Marion sharpened her knife on the side of the quern and put it back, upside down by the hearth and then gutted the two ducks. She threw the heads and feet and the guts out on to the rough grass and pushed Tibtab, who disliked going out in the wet, after them. She then hung the ducks up again outside under the eaves and plucked them, carefully stuffing the feathers into the pocket of her dress. Glancing at Tibtab, who sat beside her with his head on one side as he deliberately cracked one green-feathered skull, she could not quite bear to waste all those green feathers, and picked up the second skull and carefully pulled out two or three whose emerald glint most took her eye. It will help to show up a needle, she thought. Not as eye-catching as a jay's blue feather, but bright enough.

She put her iron pot, wiped out with dried grass since the rancid bacon had been cooked in it, on the fire, half filled it with water and dropped in the two ducks, adding some beans and an orange onion or two. Peterkin, watching her, asked, 'Can we have the ducks to eat tonight?' but Marion told him they would have to cook all night and most of tomorrow, and that all they could have for supper that evening were the ducks' two livers, sliced and spiked with sharp sticks and toasted over the red logs. Peterkin was momentarily satisfied when Marion showed him the two large livers protected from Tibtab under the half-broken jar.

As dusk crept up over the Common, Peter arrived home, tired as usual, and with the same sad story of Dame Margaret's baby.

'So you've heard?' he said. 'Does seem very sad and they say it was a well-made boy – just this funny colour, and they never got a whimper out of him. They say Sir Hugh will see him buried tomorrow. What's for supper?'

So they all sat down on the log seat, with Alice standing between Peter's knees and, spiking the slices of ducks' liver on sharp yew twigs, they held them over the fire and then dropped the sizzling lumps on to the thin scones.

'That's not done yet, Peterkin. Hold it closer,' Marion said.

'But my hand's burning, and I like it juicy.'

She felt too weary to argue with him.

Later, before getting into bed, Peterkin had sidled up to her, just as she was banking up the glowing logs with ash, and whispered, 'Mam, will you really do the ducks for tomorrow?'

'They're already in the pot, with onions. Can't you smell them? They'll be in the pot all night.'

'Are you really pleased I got those ducks, Mam?' She was a little surprised and gave him a rare hug.

'Yes,' she said, with emphasis. 'Always get wild ducks when you can, and pigeons – they are good food but smaller – rooks too, but not much to eat on a rook, but the more of them you can kill the better the corn will be. Now, into bed with you.'

But when she got into bed herself she was not comfortable. Her clothes were damp and heavy about her, so was the cover. In spite of this chill, Peter had fallen asleep almost at once. She had seen how exhausted he was when watching his hands trembling as he held his spike with liver on it over the fire. She knew this was not from cold but from hours and hours of heavy sawing of elm boards. Alice had objected to being put into the cradle – she really was getting too long for it – but she too had fallen asleep quickly.

But Marion could not sleep. The death of Dame Margaret's baby preyed on her mind, used as she was to childbirth resulting in a dead baby. She felt very tired, very dispirited and was aware of this contrast with her mood that morning when Peterkin had brought the ducks and when she was planning rich food. Now all seemed wearisome. She wondered if this change of feelings indicated that she was about to bleed, and then realized that she had not had a bleeding period for some time, she couldn't remember for how long. Women often did not when food was very scarce, as it usually was in the spring months, and when food was scarce it was always the women who went without first, and for longest. She knew she had often been hungry since the Christmas feasts were over, and this was probably why she had no bleeding. She remembered years ago – it was after her Margery was born – that there were two years of very poor harvests and every one had gone hungry, and that during that time most of the women had no bleedings.

Then suddenly, with the swiftness of an arrow, the notion came to her that she was pregnant. The sickness of recent mornings may not have been caused by the rancid bacon, but by a baby in her womb. After all, Peter and the two children had eaten the bacon and they had not been affected by it.

Her mind ran on, still staggered at the thought. Another baby – well why not? She was not all that old. It would be born around harvest time, the time of the greatest and heaviest amount of work for everyone. But then during the autumn, when she might be suckling the child if all went well, that was the time of greatest plenty. Then despondency took over from surprise, despondency at the months of increasing effort that would be needed to do all she had to do for her family, despondency over the prospect of more years of watching, suckling, wiping, hushing, rocking, feeding, dressing, minding – it seemed to drag out before her eyes into an endless future. She groaned privately.

Then again her despondency changed, this time to fear: fear of a long and ghastly labour, perhaps in the dark; fear that, as often happened, a few days after a birth, the mother became feverish and died. If this happened would her baby die too? It probably would unless some other woman in the village was newly delivered of a dead child and could, and would, be wet nurse to her baby. But what would happen then to Alice, poor little Alice, barely three years old, such a promising child. Peter was a kind father she knew, but what really could a father do to nurture a little girl?

Alice snuffled a little and was quiet again. Peterkin stirred his feet about and then was still again. Peter's sonorous breathing continued its slow rhythm. None of them was concerned with her problem. She was utterly alone with it. She would not mention the possibility of another baby to Peter until she was much more sure. She would keep her counsel, as indeed she usually did over many matters.

Her mind was now wholly on the possibility of another child, and though she was full of foreboding, she knew that the whole village would approve, and that the unquestioning approval of all her acquaintances was the only strength, the only sustenance that she would have to overlay her fears. She briefly imagined the future of her new child, living and grown tall, hearing the rustling of the ash trees, seeing a mist of bluebells in the forest – season following season, year following year. She could imagine no other life.

It never occurred to her that she should drill her mind to accept her destiny. She had never considered that she had any power or any choice over anything that might happen to her.

In this quiet acceptance of her ordinary impotence, she fell asleep.

58383